More praise for *Dark Justice*

"The wondrously ornate plot climaxes like a fireworks display, with an exciting escape from sure death and multiple surprise revelations. The loose ends are tied up as neatly as in a Shakespearean comedy, though the final twist is far from comic."

—*Ellery Queen Mystery Magazine*

"Tulsa lawyer Ben Kincaid takes on a defense case as hopeless as anything back home. . . . Newcomers to the series will be impressed at how completely Ben can turn a lost case around."

—*Kirkus Reviews*

"The sexiness of Ben's opponent, 'stunning young prosecutor' 'Granny' Adams, raises the courtroom stakes. . . . Bernhardt juices the suspense with chapter-ending teasers."

—*Publishers Weekly*

By William Bernhardt
Published by The Ballantine Publishing Group:

PRIMARY JUSTICE
BLIND JUSTICE
DEADLY JUSTICE
PERFECT JUSTICE
CRUEL JUSTICE
NAKED JUSTICE
EXTREME JUSTICE
DARK JUSTICE

DOUBLE JEOPARDY
THE MIDNIGHT BEFORE CHRISTMAS
THE CODE OF BUDDYHOOD

DARK JUSTICE

William Bernhardt

BALLANTINE BOOKS • NEW YORK

A Ballantine Book
Published by The Ballantine Publishing Group

www.randomhouse.com/BB/

Library of Congress Catalog Card Number: 99-90805

ISBN 0-345-43476-5

Manufactured in the United States of America

First Hardcover Edition: January 1999
First Mass Market Edition: December 1999

10 9 8 7 6 5 4 3 2 1

For Harry and Alice,
my favorite campers

The question is not what you look at, but what you see.

—HENRY DAVID THOREAU,
Journals, November 16, 1830

* *

PROLOGUE

* One Hundred Years Before *

In 1906, a journalist named James MacGillivray struggled to think of something different to fill the pages of the *Oscoda Press*, a small-town northern Michigan newspaper. In those days, papers were more flexible and often used fiction pieces to liven up their pages. Because the town had recently seen an influx of lumberjacks and businessmen in the fledgling logging industry, MacGillivray concocted a tale, based in part on stories he had heard around town, about the Goliath of loggers, a superhuman lumberjack called Paul Bunyan. In "The Round River Drive," the mighty Bunyan fells "about a mile a day" of forestland. "You see," MacGillivray wrote, "back in those days the government didn't care nothin' about the timber and all you had to do was hunt up a good tract on some runnin' stream—cut her and float her down."

The Bunyan story was very popular, and in the years that followed, more appeared by a variety of writers. In 1914, an advertising copywriter working for the Red River Lumber Company produced a booklet collecting and embellishing the Bunyan saga—adding, for instance, Babe the blue ox. The company's advertising circulars gave the "legend" national prominence, popularizing both the logging industry and the stouthearted, manly lifestyle of the lumberjack.

The logging industry boomed. Settlers came from far and wide to be a part of the "taming" of the national wilderness. Ancient forests, silent for centuries, were suddenly noisy as factories, as men and equipment swarmed through cutting down everything in sight. Lumbering, dominated by larger and larger corporations, was an attack operation in which profits depended on the speedy, efficient felling of trees—as many as possible, as quickly as possible. In 1850, more than forty percent of the United States was densely forested; by 1920, less than ten percent was. Entire forests disappeared, and to their surprise, the loggers learned that, even when new trees were planted, the forests did not grow back . . .

* Six Years Before *

Ben Kincaid gripped the podium, a grim expression set on his face.

He was staring across the courtroom at the man in the witness box. Evan Taulbert was his name, and he was the critical witness for the prosecution. He was a lab researcher in a clinical research facility in a small town near Tulsa called Chesterson, and one of only two staffers on the premises the night of what the *Tulsa World* was calling the "Great Chesterson Chimp Raid." As the jury had already learned, the research facility was conducting experiments for a major cosmetics company, using chimps as test subjects. A local animal rights group, the Society for Prevention of Cruelty to Our Other-Than-Human Neighbors, had been protesting outside the facility for months. On the night of the raid, they stopped protesting and took decisive action.

And by the time the raid was over, a man was dead.

Ben was representing the leader of the raid, one George Zakin, a young activist. He claimed that the death of Dr. David Dodd was an accident in which he played no part. Zakin admitted trespassing on the property, but claimed he did so to free the chimps, not to harm anyone. The prosecution, unfortunately, took a different view. They were pushing for Murder One, arguing that Zakin had entered the premises with the express premeditated motive of killing Dr. Dodd. The case was built entirely on circumstantial evidence, but there was plenty of it. Ben had spent the better part of the last three days cross-examining prosecution witnesses, bolstering his client's alibi, proving those witnesses didn't see what they thought they saw.

Except for Evan Taulbert. He resolutely maintained that he saw the defendant race past his office window at 3:05 A.M., just before the time of death—which destroyed Zakin's claim that he had left the premises about an hour before.

Ben felt certain Taulbert was mistaken or lying, but how to prove it? He could only do what he always did in these circumstances—try to get the man talking, on the theory that if Taulbert talked long enough, eventually he would trip up.

"So you were in your office when you claim you saw my client race past your window?" Ben asked.

"I was," Taulbert replied, supremely confident. "When I *did* see him race by."

"Awfully late to be at the office."

"I often stay late. I'm very dedicated to my work."

"Were you planning to sleep there?"

"Indeed. I have a sofa in my office that folds out into a bed."

How cozy. Ben flipped a page in the outline Christina had prepared for him. "I see from the police report that you also had a lab assistant in your office."

"Nothing unusual about that," Taulbert replied, but Ben thought something about the way the man stroked his beard suggested otherwise.

"You know," Ben said, "I don't seem to have the assistant's name. What is it?"

Taulbert coughed into his hand. "That would be Kelly Prescott."

A suitably ambiguous name, Ben thought. "And would Kelly be a man or a woman?"

"A woman."

Out the corner of his eye, Ben saw some of the jurors leaning slightly forward. This cross was already more interesting than they had expected. "You were alone with a female assistant?"

"Male or female—it makes no difference to me," Taulbert

replied, still stroking away at that beard. "I don't discriminate in my hiring."

"And was Ms. Prescott also awake when you saw George Zakin run by the window?"

"She was. But she didn't see him. She was facing the other direction."

"She was facing the other direction." Ben's imagination reeled. "Were the two of you . . . engaged in an experiment at the time?"

The first red blotches began to appear on the man's neck. "No. We had closed down shop for the day."

"So the two of you were just . . . ?"

"Unwinding. Relieving the stress of a difficult workday."

Ben nodded gamely. "And did the two of you employ any special . . . stress-reduction techniques?"

A titter emerged from the jury box. The prosecutor, Jack Bullock, rose to his feet. "Your honor, I object. Relevance."

"I'm exploring the circumstances surrounding the man's identification of my client," Ben explained. "Testing its credibility."

Judge Peters brushed a shock of hair out of his eyes, looking supremely bored. "I'll allow it."

Ben thanked the judge. "Now where were we? Oh yes—stress-reduction techniques."

Taulbert straightened. "I don't know what you're trying to insinuate."

"Well, I was hoping I wouldn't have to insinuate . . ."

"If you're trying to find out if Kelly and I are fond of each other, we are. But it doesn't alter the fact that I saw your man running down the corridor just before my colleague was killed."

Ben frowned, then flipped another page in his outline. It was, of course, always pleasing to take a pompous ass and rake him over the coals a bit. But ultimately Taulbert was right. The fact that he was messing around with his lab assistant didn't prove he was lying about seeing Zakin.

"Mr. Taulbert, do you know what I find most unusual about your testimony?"

"I'm sure I don't know," he answered, folding his arms across his chest.

"What I find most unusual is your behavior."

"My behavior? I was exactly where I was supposed to be. Your man was the one who trespassed and killed—"

Ben cut him off at the pass. "Imagine this situation with me. It's late at night. You and your female assistant are . . . relieving one another's stress. Suddenly a man you don't know races by your office window—and you don't do anything."

"I reported the incident to the police—"

"By phone, yes, about five minutes later, when it was far too late to do Dr. Dodd any good."

"I moved as quickly as I could."

"Five minutes later? Why didn't you chase after the intruder immediately?"

Taulbert's left eye twitched. "What?"

"The man you saw in the window was an intruder, right?"

"Y-yes."

"He wasn't supposed to be there."

"Right."

"You had tons of valuable equipment on the premises."

"That's true."

"You had ongoing experiments that could easily be ruined."

"And they were. Your client—"

"So why didn't you run after him?"

"I—I don't see—"

"Well, if I saw an intruder in my lab late at night, and I knew he could destroy months of work without even trying hard, I'd run after him. I think most people would." Ben was relieved to see several heads in the jury box nodding in agreement. "So why didn't *you*?"

"I—I guess I didn't think of it."

"Didn't think of it?" Ben couldn't have shown much more disbelief if the man had claimed he'd been beamed up to Saturn. "Are you the absentminded professor or the nutty professor?"

Prosecutor Bullock jumped to his feet. "Your honor—"

"I'm sorry," Ben said quickly. "I'll withdraw that. Mr. Taulbert, why didn't you run after this alleged intruder?"

"It—it could have been dangerous."

"So you're saying you were too scared to step out into the hallway?"

Taulbert pressed a hand against his forehead. "All right, to tell you the truth—I couldn't move."

Ben tucked in his chin. "You were paralyzed with fear?"

"No." Taulbert's eyes drifted downward. "I was handcuffed."

Ben closed his eyes with sweet, sweet joy. Some days you get the bear . . .

"Excuse me, sir. Did you say *handcuffed*?"

"Oh, you know perfectly well I did." Taulbert's head twitched, rather like a dead frog receiving electroshock therapy. "There's nothing wrong with it. We're both consenting adults."

Ben spoke slowly, making sure everyone absorbed all the details. "*We* being—you and your assistant. Ms. Prescott."

"That's correct."

"The handcuffs were part of your . . . stress-reduction technique?"

"That's one way of putting it."

"Could you perhaps describe . . ."

"She cuffed my hands behind my back. I couldn't budge."

"And she was facing the opposite direction."

"We were making love, you pious twit, and she was on top. It's not against the law, you know."

"No, of course not."

"But I couldn't move. As soon as I saw your client race down the corridor, I told Kelly to uncuff me, but it took her a while to, um, stop what she was doing and find the key. By the time I was free, your client was gone."

"I see. Thank you for clearing that up." Ben eagerly turned another page in his trial notebook. It was all downhill from here.

Bullock rose to his feet. "Your honor, are we going to continue prying into this man's personal life? This is of no interest whatsoever."

The judge smiled. "If it was of no interest, you wouldn't be trying to shut it down."

"It's all right, your honor," Ben said. "I'm moving on." He returned his attention to the witness. "You know, Mr. Taulbert, there's one detail I haven't been able to clarify. The local Chesterson police received *two* 911 phone calls that night, one around two A.M., the other just after three. Unfortunately, they did not yet have Caller ID trace capability, so the operator did not get an automatic record of the calls' places of origin. The first call was so garbled and incoherent they couldn't understand it. The second was the one that brought them to your lab."

"My call would have been the second."

"I can see where you would want us to think that. The 911 operator reported that the first call was an 'incoherent blast from a man either frightened out of his wits or totally insane who wasn't even able to tell us where he was.' "

"Clearly that wasn't me."

"Ah, but here's the rub, Mr. Taulbert. I think it was. I think you saw my client around two, when he was still there and Dr. Dodd was still very much alive. I think later, when you read the police report, you changed your testimony so your call would be thought to be the one that brought the police to the scene, not the one from the man 'either frightened out of his wits or totally insane.' "

"You don't know what you're talking about."

"I think I do."

"I have never been incoherent in my entire life, much less totally insane."

"Well, sometimes in a difficult situation—"

"I am perfectly capable of handling a difficult situation!"

"Mr. Taulbert, the way I see it, you saw the intruder or intruders and panicked."

"I most certainly did not. You should be careful what you say, young man. There are laws against libel."

"Uh-huh. Against perjury, too."

"I have given you my testimony, and I'm sticking by it."

"But I still think you made the two o'clock call."

"Don't you think I know what time it was when I called?"

"How could you?"

"How could I? I made a note the moment I saw the man in the corridor."

"Made a note of what?"

"Of the time, of course."

"But how? I've seen pictures of your office. There are no clocks."

"I didn't need a clock, you fool. I had a wristwatch."

"You did?"

"Of course I did. Every lab clinician does."

"Where was it?"

"On my wrist, you nincompoop. Hence the name."

"You're sure about this?"

"Absolutely positive."

"And that's how you know when you saw my client."

"Exactly."

"Because you had a watch."

"It was the only timepiece in the room."

"And you checked it?"

"The second I saw the man race down the corridor."

Ben paused, drew a breath. "Mr. Taulbert, would you please explain how you could check your wristwatch when your hands were cuffed behind your back?"

All at once the agitated bobbing of his head ceased. His lips froze as if in mid-thought.

"As I recall, you said you couldn't budge an inch. So how could you possibly look at your watch?"

"Well—uh—"

"Excuse me?"

"I—uh—"

Ben turned toward the jury box and smiled. "Is the word you're searching for by any chance *oops*?"

Ben had almost made it out of the courtroom and into the elevator when Bullock stopped him.

"Well, Kincaid, I guess you're—"

"Stop right there. I know the drill. You complain because I had the audacity to defend the accused and actually win. I say that every man has a right to a zealous defense. You say that doesn't mean I have to put crooks back on the street. I point out that my client was working for a good cause and should never have been charged, since the only real evidence against him was unreliable, as you probably knew from the start.

Eventually we start shouting and calling each other names till the bailiffs drag one or both of us out of the courthouse. Neither of us convinces the other of anything. So why don't we just skip it this time, okay?"

Bullock pursed his lips together. "Think you're pretty smart, don't you?"

Ben rolled his eyes. "Smart enough to avoid this conversation." He stepped around Bullock and punched the Down button for the elevator.

Bullock didn't disappear. "You made a mistake in there today, Kincaid. You set a dangerous man free."

"Dangerous? He's an animal lover, for Pete's sake. He protects chimpanzees! He's harmless."

"You're wrong. I looked deep into the man's eyes. And I didn't like what I saw."

"That's ridiculous."

The bell rang and the elevator doors opened. Ben started to step inside, but Bullock grabbed his arm. "Remember this, Kincaid. If that man kills again—and I think he will—it'll be on your head. It'll be your fault."

Ben brushed Bullock away. "Stop being so damn melodramatic. You're just bitter because you can't stand to lose a case." He entered the elevator. "The truth is, we'll probably never hear from the man again."

The elevator doors closed and Bullock faded, first from Ben's vision, then from his consciousness. Only years later would Ben learn that, of his last two statements, although the first was certainly true, the last was altogether, absolutely, wrong.

* Present Day *

Tess O'Connell pushed the thick foliage out of her path, but her hand snagged on a sharp thorn. She yelped, then let go. A tree branch came crashing back into her face, knocking her onto her backside.

Mumbling unrepeatable obscenities under her breath, Tess brushed the dark, dank loam off her pant legs and pushed herself back to her feet. She hated the Great Outdoors. Hated it with a passion. When she found out who volunteered her for this gig deep in the forests of northwest Washington, miles and miles from civilization as she knew it . . .

She detoured off the path, avoiding the unbreachable thicket of thorns and bramble. She knew there was a clearing somewhere—wasn't there? It was so dark out here at night, even with a flashlight. Fear began to creep into her brain, making her breathing accelerate and her palms sweat. What if she never found the way out? What if something else found her? She had heard that grizzlies liked to roam at night.

She tried to put all those what-ifs out of her head. First things first: she needed to find the clearing. She couldn't see where she was going and she was constantly bumping into things that were dirty, squishy, or alive. Her clothes were a mess, and her hair was a disaster. And she itched almost everywhere there was to itch. She had inadvertently stepped into a nest of seed ticks the day before, and she still hadn't managed to scrape all those tiny black crawling dots off her skin. And trees were everywhere—densely packed huge trees, everywhere she looked. All day long she'd heard the sound of high-powered machinery clear-cutting trees at a breathtaking rate. So why was it she couldn't see anything but trees?

She should've known better than to come out here at night. On a good day, she was—how to say it?—geographically challenged. And this wasn't a good day. And she had no experience with woods or wildlife or whatever it was that kept making that creepy *ooh-ooh* noise. Even as a girl, she had never gone in for Girl Scouts or camp-outs or any of that living-off-the-land rot. So why was she stuck out here, lugging two cameras around the Crescent National Forest, all by herself?

Granted it had been a lousy year for the *National Whisper*. Their circulation figures had been dead last of all supermarket tabloids, and being the lowest of the tabloids was pretty low indeed. Tess had watched the rag sink lower and lower in its increasingly desperate attempts to pump up sales. The paper had gone from covers featuring movie stars and royalty to alien abductions and two-headed babies.

And as the paper goes, so go its reporters. Tess had sunk from stalking celebrities to unearthing freaks, misfits, and mutants.

And then there was Sasquatch. Honestly, did anyone still believe there was some big hairy ape wandering around the timberline? Surely that one had died out with the Loch Ness Monster and the human face on the moon. But there had been a flurry of Sasquatch spottings in this forest during the past month. And no story was too stupid for the *National Whisper*, right? So here she was—desperately seeking Sasquatch.

She'd been here for three days, and so far all she'd managed to discover was sunburn, mosquito bites, and poison ivy. And seed ticks. She constantly wanted to scratch, including some places you couldn't scratch in polite society. But she hadn't given up. Every day at sunup, she had stumbled out of her motel room and plunged back into the forest, tracing and retracing the paths from which campers had made their sightings. It seemed like a futile, foolish quest, but by God, if there was a Sasquatch, Tess was going to be the one who found him.

After three days, she was about ready to give up. She had pored over her files, looking for something to give her an edge, something she had missed before. It was the third time through before she picked up on it—all the sightings had occurred at night. Could it be Sasquatch was a nocturnal beast? More related to the owl than the ape? Or could it be a survival instinct? She had read that grizzly bears now mostly traveled at night—to avoid humans. It was a classic example of natural selection; those that learned to move at night survived, while those that didn't—didn't. Could Bigfoot have evolved the same way? Even if it was a long shot, it merited a nighttime excursion. She just wished nighttime in the forest wasn't so incredibly . . . dark.

Up ahead, she detected a break in the brush. A few steps closer and she could see moonlight streaming through the tree branches. A few more steps and she was out of the woods.

It was almost as if she had stepped onto a foreign planet. Where before the path had been so thick with green she could barely move, the tableau now before her was so barren a stranger might wonder if anything had ever grown here or ever could again. Only when Tess lowered her eyes did she see the telltale signs of former life—low-cut stumps dotting the ground, the last remnants of thousands and thousands of trees.

Her eyes were diverted by faint traces of life, down the slope about five hundred feet or so. She saw a large tree cutter, one just like the dozens she had seen since she came to the forest. And beside the tree cutter, she saw two silhouetted figures. One was much larger than the other. Both were moving slightly; one had his arms raised above his head.

Tess strained her eyes, trying to see more clearly. Were they talking or arguing or what?

She started moving down the steep incline. She had to move carefully, one cautious step at a time. The ground was covered with branches and debris, and there was nothing to hold for support.

The larger of the two figures turned sideways as she approached; its profile was backlit by the moon. The silhouette was massive and irregular, wild and hairy—

Sasquatch?

Tess moved faster down the incline, still watching the spectacle below. She could hear a voice now, loud and angry, shouting, but she couldn't pick up any of the words.

Tess hit something—she never knew what it was—and started to tumble. She was rolling down the hill feet first, unable to stop herself, her camera bag alternately pounding the ground and her head.

She reached around on all sides, desperately grabbing for something to stop her fall. Her hands finally managed to light on a thick tree root half protruding from the dirt. She clamped the root and braced herself.

She felt like her arm was being ripped out of the socket, but fortunately, the root held. She stopped sliding. Slowly she lifted herself to her feet.

Sasquatch and the other silhouetted figure were definitely fighting—and not just with words. Blows were being exchanged. Sasquatch seemed to be getting the worst of it; the other figure was landing punch after punch. It was almost as if the poor beast didn't have his heart in it, didn't want to fight back. Sasquatch was getting creamed.

The other man landed a sharp blow, sending Sasquatch reeling backward against the huge mechanical tree cutter. The man picked up a long metal object—a crowbar, she thought, or maybe a tire iron. Sasquatch was pinned down and trapped. He was a goner—or so Tess thought.

Out of nowhere, Sasquatch raised his hairy arm, and this time it was holding a gun. She winced as the sound of a shot echoed through the clearing. She heard a sickening cracking noise as the other man crumpled to the ground. He must be dead, she thought, shot at such close range. But no—the fallen figure was moving, if slowly. He was still alive.

Sasquatch started running, away from both his opponent and Tess.

Tess kept moving cautiously forward. She didn't know what was going on, but there was bound to be a story in it. Maybe even a story for the *National Whisper*; after all, it did feature Sasquatch. And besides, this was a heck of a lot more interesting than traipsing through the woods.

The man left behind slowly climbed up to the cab of the tree cutter. What on earth? Tess wondered. Was he planning to chase Bigfoot in the tree cutter? She kept moving forward and was less than a hundred feet away when the man turned the ignition.

The night sky was suddenly illuminated by a hot white flash. An instant later, a huge booming sound rocked the clearing. The force of the explosion knocked Tess off her feet, left her clutching red dirt for dear life. She kept her head down while smoke and metal debris flew through the air.

What is happening? she wondered. She felt the radiant heat of the explosion warming her, and for the first time became frightened. What was she doing out here all alone, separated from police, doctors, any semblance of civilization?

Up on the tree cutter, she heard the man scream. He was still alive! She looked up, and her eyes widened with horror. He was burning, flames radiating from every part of his body. He stumbled away from what remained of the tree cutter and began running in circles, as if desperately searching for something, anything to take him out of his misery.

And then all at once his howling stopped. The burning man stood still for a final moment, then crumbled to the ground. The human being was gone, replaced by a heap of charred flesh.

Tess pulled herself out of the mud, trembling. What happened? she asked herself. What have I stumbled onto? And—as her reporter persona reasserted itself—why the hell aren't I taking pictures?

Idiot. She pulled the Nikon .35 millimeter out of her camera bag, turned it on, and peered through the viewfinder. It was much too dark. She knew the pictures wouldn't come out, even with the flash.

She also had a palm-size Sony camcorder in her bag. She remembered that when she had checked it out, Chuck, the guy in Property, had explained that it had a twenty lux rating—meaning it could take decent pictures in candlelight.

Maybe it could do some good here, she reasoned. She yanked it out of her bag and started recording. The tree cutter was still burning, like a fiery funeral pyre. She videoed the destruction, then panned over to tape what was left of the burning man.

She almost had the corpse in her viewfinder when she saw Sasquatch reappear. He was moving forward, making a beeline in her direction.

He'd seen her.

Tess turned and ran. She avoided the slope and moved in the other direction, barreling past the burning metal and heading toward the safety of the woods on the other side of the clearing. If she could just make it to the woods, there was a chance she might be able to lose him. Might make it back to civilization to file her story.

She couldn't be sure of much, but one fact was abundantly clear. Hairy Neanderthal evolutionary throwbacks didn't pack pistols. Plus, when he had run at her, Tess had seen a face illuminated by the light of the flames. The mask was clenched in his hand. The conclusion was inescapable—Sasquatch was a human being.

A human being she'd just seen kill someone.

The heel of her shoe dug into the soft loam of the earth. Her ankle twisted and she fell crashing to the ground. *No!* she told herself. You may not give up that easily! She pushed herself back to her feet, leaving a shoe behind. She didn't dare turn her head and look, but she could hear him behind her, hear him running, panting, grunting.

She had to keep moving, had to keep pushing herself. The other edge of the clearing was still hundreds of feet away. She had to make it. *She had to.* She could not give up.

All at once, she realized she didn't care about getting a story anymore. She didn't care about her clothes, she didn't care about her hair, and she didn't care whether she ever worked again at the *National Whisper*.

She just wanted to live.

And she felt absolutely certain that if Sasquatch got his hairy paws on her, she wouldn't.

ONE

* *

Paul Bunyan's Stepchildren

* 1 *

Ben Kincaid drummed his fingers on the card table set up inside the Magic Valley Mystery Bookstore. When he arrived, the table had held twenty copies of his first book, *Katching the Kindergarten Killer*. And now, an hour and a half after the book-signing began, the table still held twenty copies of *Katching the Kindergarten Killer*.

The owner of the bookstore, Fred Franklin, sauntered over to Ben's table. He was stroking his pet, a large black and white tuxedo cat. "Slow day for autographs, huh?"

"I don't seem to be getting much traffic," Ben admitted. "Maybe if you put me in the back next to the café."

"Nice try. We don't have a café."

"You call yourself a bookstore and you don't even have a café?"

Fred smiled. "What can I say? Magic Valley isn't really in the mainstream." He picked up one of Ben's books. "So I gather this is nonfiction? True crime?"

"Right."

He skimmed the summary on the dust jacket. "Mmm. Serial killer. Cut the heads and hands off his corpses. Pretty grisly stuff. Why'd you want to write about this?"

"I wrote about it because I lived it."

"You mean this really happened? Like, to you?"

"That's why I wrote it. I thought people might be interested in reading a firsthand account." He glanced at the unmoving door. "Guess I was wrong."

"Don't jump to any conclusions. It's early yet. Wait till people start getting off work. Folks aren't too used to book signings here in Magic Valley. I've been trying to get those publishers to send me an author for over a year, since I opened. And you're the first one I've gotten."

Lucky me, Ben thought. "It's been the same story every place I've gone. This is my eighth signing in six days. And every one of them has been dismal."

"Hey, at least your publisher is touring you. Most first-time authors don't get that." He stroked his cat, who responded by curling up against Fred's neck and pressing her wet nose against his cheek. "You should consider yourself lucky."

"If you say so."

"And it's gotta be better than practicing law, right? Every lawyer I know wishes he was doing something else."

Ben decided not to comment. "Nice cat you've got there. Think he'd like an autographed book?"

Fred laughed. "Margery isn't really the literary type. She's more the feed-me-stroke-me-get-out-of-my-way type."

"Sounds like my cat, Giselle."

"You an animal lover?"

"Well, the cat was a present from a friend. But yeah, actually, I am."

Fred looked up abruptly. "Oh, look, someone's coming in. Let me get out of the way." Fred skittered toward the back of the bookstore, cat in tow.

The woman who approached Ben's table was, in a word, bizarre. She was dressed in a helter-skelter, crazy-quilt fashion—wild bright colors, mismatched layers of clothing. Her steel-blond hair was just as wild; it jabbed out in straight lines like she'd just been electrocuted. She was inhumanly thin, almost skeletal—like something out of a grim Grimm fairy tale.

"Are you the author?" she asked.

"I am," Ben said, holding out his hand.

"Are you sure? You seem so young."

"Everyone says that."

"Except for the bald spot on the back of your head, of course."

"Of course." He picked up one of the books on the table. "Can I interest you in my new book?"

"Oh, I've already read it."

Ben did a double take. "You have?"

She grinned. "Don't act so surprised."

"Well, it's just—I'm not sure I've ever met anyone who's actually read my book before. Other than a close personal friend."

"Oh, I did. I read every word of it." She gazed deeply into his eyes. "And the whole time I read it, I couldn't help but think about you."

Ben coughed. "About—about me?"

She reached out and brushed his shoulder. "You were so brave. Chasing after the maniac the way you did."

"Well, I had to do something after that corpse turned up in my car. If I hadn't, they probably would've sent *me* up the river."

"And that horrible chase sixty feet up in the air—you must have nerves of steel."

"Actually, I was scared to death."

"It wasn't just the story you told. It was the way you told it. It was—inspirational." She took his hand and clasped it in both of hers. "I just wanted to hold the hand that penned all those magnificent words."

Ben cleared his throat. "Well . . . that's very kind."

She did not release his hand. She inched closer to the table. "I felt such a magnetism when I read your book. I kept thinking, 'This man must be someone very special.' "

"Oh, not really."

"I kept thinking, 'This is the man I want to spend the rest of my life with. This is the man I want to father my children.' "

Ben's lips parted. "This is—you want—"

She sidled next to him at the table, her steel bristle hair tickling his cheek. "So, tell me, Ben. I *can* call you Ben, can't I?"

"I suppose."

"Is there someone special in your life?"

"Uh . . . yes. Yes, there is. Most definitely."

Her face fell. "There is?"

"Yes. Several people, actually."

"Several?"

"Well . . . yes. There's my mother. And my sister."

"Silly. I mean like a girlfriend."

"I have some friends who are girls."

"You know what I mean."

"You want to know if I'm in a relationship?"

"I want to know if you're having sex. Because if you're not, have I got something special for you."

Ben's throat went dry. "I think perhaps you've made a mistake."

She wrapped her arms around him. "Don't fight it, Ben. This was meant to be."

Ben's face turned a bright crimson. "This was not—this is moving a bit too fast for me."

"Life is short. Why wait?"

"I really couldn't possibly—"

"When I read your book, I realized we had a connection, a bond that transcended the boundaries of time and space."

Ben scooted out of his chair. "I'm not prepared . . ." He tried again. "I'm just here to sign books, you know?"

The woman appeared crestfallen. "Just to sign books?"

"I'm sorry, but—yeah."

She pulled her copy out of her purse and dropped it on the table. "I guess some bonds are stronger than others." She sighed. "Perhaps in our next lifetimes."

Ben opened the front of her book, relieved. "Who should I make this out to?"

"Marjorie."

He began to write. " 'To Marjorie—' "

" 'To Marjorie, whom I have always loved—' "

Ben paused. " 'To Marjorie, whom I have always loved'?"

" '. . . in memory of that special night we shared, flesh to flesh, huddled close beneath the moonlight. I shall never forget you.' "

Ben applied his fountain pen to the title page. Why fight it? ". . . I shall never forget you." He signed the book and passed it back to its owner, then redirected his attention to a burly, bearded man making his way through the front door. He was carrying a jumbo-size banker's box, which, judging from the difficulty he was having carrying it, must be filled to the brim.

"Are you the author?"

Ben extended his hand, but the man still held the immense box. "I'm the one."

"Are you sure? You seem so young."

Ben sighed. "I have a very old portrait in my attic. Can I autograph a book for you?"

"Nah. I don't have time to read. I'm a writer."

"Ah. What have you written?"

"I'm glad you asked." The man dropped the weighty box on the end of Ben's table with a thundering thud. "I know you're probably very busy, but would you mind looking at my manuscript?"

"Your . . ."

"It's twenty-four hundred pages of rough first draft, but I know a competent editor could turn it into a masterpiece. So whaddaya say?"

The owner of the store had been right; after the sun set, traffic in the bookstore picked up. Ben had the pleasure of fielding a wide variety of comments and remarks:

"So, do you think you might ever write a serious book?"

"What's next, the Great American Novel?"

"My six-year-old here is also a writer."

"I've got a great idea for a book, but I'm just too damn busy to sit around typing all day long. Tell you what. I'll give you my idea, you do the writing, and we'll split the profits fifty-fifty."

"So, is this fiction? Or is it a novel?"

"I'm sorry, your name doesn't ring a bell. Have you done anything I should know about?"

"I don't mean to pry, but how much do you writers make? You don't have to give me any details. Just in round numbers. Six digits? Or seven?"

"Where do you get your ideas?"

Ben leaned back in his chair and smiled. "Cleveland."

When closing time finally rolled around, Fred reappeared, cat still in his arms. "Well, Mr. Kincaid, I want to thank you for coming out tonight to sign."

"It was my, um, pleasure."

"I'm going to give Margery here a can of Feline's Fancy. That's her favorite, you know."

Ben tickled the cat. "What a sweetie. Mind if I hold her?"

"Of course not." Fred transferred possession of the tabby to Ben's arms.

Ben stroked the cat's neck and back. She squirmed and rolled under his touch, loving every minute of it, purring loudly. "What a nice cat."

Fred grinned. "Actually, she's a monster."

"Excuse me?"

"She's horrible. I can't sit still for a moment but that she starts rubbing her wet slimy nose all over me."

"That's what cats do."

"She gets cat hair all over the store."

"It's shedding season."

"She's always whining for attention or food or to be let in or out. Just drives me crazy."

Ben held the cat tightly in his hands. "I'm surprised you ever took her into your home."

"She was a gift from a friend. At least I thought she was a friend. And she's never been in my home. She stays at the store."

"Even at night? When no one's here?"

"I've tried to get friends to take her on, but no one's that stupid. Pound won't have her. Frankly, I'm out of ideas."

Ben held the cat close to his chest. "Well, in time, I'm sure the two of you will grow close and—"

"So tomorrow I'm taking her to the vet for the Big Needle."

Ben's muscles clenched up. "For *what*?"

"I'm having her put to sleep."

"But she's still young. She's in perfectly good health."

"She's driving me insane."

"Let me try to find someone!"

"I've been down that road before, and I know she'll be back in my lap again by lunchtime."

"But you can't just kill her!"

Fred put a hand on his hip. "Hey, back off, chump. She's my cat and I can do anything I damn well please with her. Including putting her to sleep."

"I don't think the vet will—"

"I've already made the arrangements. Appointment's at ten in the morning. So I'll feed kitty her last meal, let her get a good night's sleep, and then . . ." He pantomimed pushing the plunger on a syringe, then acted as if he'd just received an electric shock. *"Bzzzzt!"*

Ben's lips moved wordlessly.

"Anyway, Kincaid, thanks again for coming to the store." He took the cat from Ben. "It's been great."

Ben stared blank-faced at the man. "Yeah. Great."

Even as Ben crept down the alleyway, he couldn't believe he was doing it. This was the kind of escapade Christina would concoct; she would spend hours trying to talk him into it, until finally he relented. But now here he was out by himself, doing it on his own.

Damn. Whatever she had, it must be catching.

But how on earth could he face Clayton Langdell and the rest of the gang at the Society for Prevention of Cruelty to Our Other-Than-Human Neighbors if he allowed this act of barbaric cruelty and species snobbery to take place? More to the point, how could he face Giselle? He had argued and argued with Fred, but nothing he had said had changed the man's mind. There was no other alternative. Ben normally wasn't one to meddle in other people's business, but some things were just wrong, and this was one of them. He had to do something.

Didn't he?

Navigating the town had been easy, even for a stranger, even in the dead of night. Magic Valley was a small northwest Washington town nestled at the foot of Mount Crescent. It had fewer than ten thousand residents, and the cabdriver had given Ben a thorough tour on his way in. Downtown was laid out on five streets: Main Street, which coursed through the center of the town, and the four cross streets, Lincoln, Garfield, McKinley, and Kennedy—one for each assassinated president. Most of the residences were to the north, between Main and the Magic Valley National Forest, site of the logging operation that supported most of the town.

Ben tiptoed past a pawnshop, a drugstore, a dry goods store, and a grocery. Almost all the businesses had yellow ribbons tied to the door or a lamppost. What was that all about? he wondered. Well, that was something he could ask about tomorrow, after this *Mission: Impossible* escapade was behind him.

He crept down the steps that led to the basement entrance of the bookstore. He had checked the lock on his way out; it wasn't the worst he'd ever seen, but he didn't think he'd have much trouble getting past it. Long ago his friend Mike Morelli, Tulsa homicide cop, had made him an expert on lockpicking. And there was no sign of a security system.

He scanned the street above him in all directions. He saw two men standing on a streetcorner two blocks away. Even from this distance, he could see one of the men was huge, with muscles rippling out of his tank top and shoulder-length jet-black hair. The two were having an intense discussion about something. Ben couldn't imagine what anyone could want to talk about at this hour of the morning. After a few more minutes, both men disappeared down a side street.

Ben waited until everything was quiet. He whipped out the simple two-piece metal lockpick he had acquired at the pawnshop not far from his hotel. He pushed the thin metal brace up, holding the trigger piece out of the action. Then he probed the interior of the lock with the longer ridged piece, trying to trip the tumbler that would open the lock.

He heard a distinct popping noise, then tried the doorknob. It moved.

Ben drew in his breath. This was the critical moment. If he took the next step, he would be committed to this course of action. This absolutely positively illegal course of action.

Slowly he pushed the door open. There was no alarm—or none that he could hear, anyway. That at least was a relief.

He shuffled inside, feeling a sudden surge of adrenaline. He had taken the decisive step now; best to just get it over with.

He pulled his flashlight out of his coat pocket and swept it across the bookstore. The card table at which he had sat before was gone, and the largely unsold stock of his book had already been loaded into a cardboard box, ready to be shipped back to the publisher for credit.

He tiptoed down the nearest corridor, passing Agatha Christie's entire life's work, the Sue Grafton alphabet books, and the endless array of lawyer books, all of which appeared to have exactly the same cover.

In the far corner, he found his prey.

"Hello, Margery," Ben whispered, crouching down to the cat's level. "We're going to do a road-show reenactment of *The Great Escape*. And I'm playing Steve McQueen."

To his relief, the cat did not struggle, hiss, fight, claw, or otherwise express her objections. Ben shoved the flashlight into his jacket, then scooped Margery into his arms. He was almost back up and running when he heard the rhythmic *click-click* sound behind him.

He didn't have to be a detective to know he was not alone. And he didn't have to be a weapons expert to know he had just heard someone cock a shotgun.

"All right, mister." A cranky, nasal voice emerged from the darkness. "Turn around slow and easy. And keep your hands up in the air where I can see them."

Ben raised his hands. As he did so, Margery jumped down. She skittered across the floor, returned to her comfortable cushioned bed on the floor, snuggled her head into her paws, and closed her eyes. It would seem Margery knew when to abandon ship. "Ingrate," Ben murmured.

"All right," barked the voice in the darkness. "Keep your hands in the air and move!"

* 2 *

When at last the Honorable Judge Tyrone J. Pickens entered his courtroom, he looked as if he was suffering the ill effects of a singularly hard night. Perhaps several hard nights. On closer examination, Ben thought, perhaps years of hard nights.

Pickens's craggy face was speckled and ruddy, his nose shiny. His black-rimmed glasses seemed to be in constant motion, on, then off, on, then off. His posture was slumped and his expression was grim. He looked as if he would rather be anywhere else on earth.

Of course, Ben could sympathize with that. He would also rather be anywhere else. But here he was standing in the Magic Valley county courthouse. Handcuffed to the sheriff.

Judge Pickens rifled through the papers on his desk. "Looks like we got us a breaking and entering, is that it?"

The woman up at the bench, who Ben gathered was the district attorney, nodded.

"Great," the judge murmured. "Just great. First good fishing day in months, and I've got me a goddamn breaking and entering. How many days to try this sucker?"

The bailiff standing dutifully to the judge's side cleared his throat. "This is just an arraignment, your honor."

Pickens's face brightened. "An arraignment? Hot damn. We can whip through this sucker in two minutes." He pointed his gavel in Ben's direction. "You the perp?"

Ben cleared his throat. "I'm the accused, yes, your honor."

"You got a lawyer?" He gave Ben the once-over. "No, I suppose you'll be wanting us to appoint one."

"Actually, I am a lawyer."

The judge did a double take. "You sure about that? You ain't exactly dressed for court."

"The sheriff didn't give me a chance to change before hauling me to the county jail."

"Oh, I get it. You're the perp and the lawyer."

Ben nodded. "That's it."

"You gonna represent yourself? That would probably be a big mistake, you know."

Thank you very much, Ben thought. "I will for now, at any rate."

"Suit yourself." He recalibrated his gavel toward the other table. "Granny, whatcha got on this man?"

Ben's eyes crinkled. Granny? As far as he could tell, the woman standing before the judge was in her late twenties, tops. She had a perfect hourglass figure and rich, full chestnut-brown hair that swished engagingly across her clavicle with every step she took. She was not tall, but everything she had was jam-packed into a package that Ben was having a hard time keeping his eyes off.

Granny?

"Your honor," she explained, "the accused was apprehended down at Fred Franklin's bookstore this morning about three A.M."

Judge Pickens began scribbling notes. "What was he after? Cash?"

"According to him, all he wanted was Fred's cat."

Pickens raised his glasses. "His *cat*?"

"That's his story. Had his own lockpick he used to get in. He was a pro."

The judge smiled. "I guess that makes him a professional cat burglar. Literally." Pickens slapped his knee and let loose with a ripsnorter of a laugh, then leaned back and wiped his eyes. "But seriously, is attempted cat theft a crime?"

"Breaking and entering is."

Ben stepped forward, as best he could while still handcuffed to the sheriff. "Your honor, could I please explain?"

Pickens didn't look up. "No."

"But I think I could clear—"

Pickens cut him off. "You will remain silent until such time as I ask you to plead, got it?"

Ben complied.

Judge Pickens returned his attention to the prosecutor. "So, Granny, this guy got any priors?"

She nodded. "I ran some checks this morning. Turns out he was arrested once before in Arkansas for brawling in a bar."

Pickens scrutinized Ben's thin frame. "This guy?"

"It's on his record. Tell you what else I found out. He really is a lawyer. And he often works for something called the Society for Prevention of Cruelty to Our Other-Than-Human Neighbors. Some kind of animal rights terrorist group."

Ben couldn't remain silent. "*Terrorist* group?"

"The accused is believed to have participated in any number of break-ins and underground activities, many of them masterminded by this animal rights group."

The judge's teeth clenched up. "Go on."

"According to the court records, the accused represented this group in twenty-seven different cases in one year alone."

Ben pressed forward. "They were my only client!"

Pickens ignored him. "Recommendations, Granny?"

"I think we've got enough trouble right now from political extremists without letting another one loose on the streets."

"I agree." Judge Pickens pushed his glasses up the bridge of his nose. "The court hereby finds sufficient cause to bind the defendant over on the charge of breaking and entering. Bail is set for fifty thousand dollars."

Ben jumped out of his chair. "Fifty thousand dollars? For a catnapping?"

"If you can make bail," the judge explained, "you may pay it to the clerk of the court on your way out."

"Are you kidding? I can't even come close!"

"In which case I hope you like prison food, because you're going to be getting a lot of it." He pounded his gavel. "Court is out of session."

"But wait! I haven't even—"

The sheriff laid his hand on Ben's shoulder. "Don't bother. It's over."

Ben saw that the judge was already off the bench. A second

later, he was out of the courtroom. And a second after that, Ben presumed, he was stepping into his fishing waders.

Ben peered pleadingly at the sheriff. "It was just a cat!"

The sheriff nodded as he tugged on Ben's cuffs and led him toward the back of the courtroom. "That's what they all say."

* 3 *

Sheriff Douglas Allen walked Ben back to the county jail cell where he had spent part of the night and morning between arrest and arraignment. "Sorry the accommodations aren't nicer. I've been trying to get the town to appropriate money for a new jail, but it's no go. People just aren't interested in spending money to make life comfier for the criminal element." He cleared his throat. "No offense intended."

"None taken." Ben resituated himself on the edge of the metal cot that passed for a bed. There was nowhere else to sit. "Mind if I ask you a question?"

Sheriff Allen grinned. "Let me save you the trouble. It's short for Granville."

"Granville?"

"Right. Usually a boy's name, but that didn't stop her pappy from passing it on to her. Actually, it's her middle name. Her first name's Rebecca, not that it matters. Everybody calls her Granny. Always has. Even when she was just a scrawny little thing."

"She's not just a scrawny little thing anymore."

"You noticed that, did ya?" Allen laughed again, and Ben found himself liking this man who kept locking him up in an eight-square-foot cell. "I saw the way your eyes peeled back when she strolled across the courtroom. Not that you're the first."

"I don't suppose she's . . ."

"Available? She is, although she doesn't normally consort with the criminal element." He stepped out of the cell and locked the door. "Let me give you a piece of advice about our stunning young prosecutor, if I may."

"I'm listening."

"You know about the black widow?"

"I know what it is."

"But do you know about the female's . . . mating habits?"

Ben shrugged. "Sure. Mates with the male, then eats him."

Allen nodded. "And do you know where the black widow learned its tricks? From watching that sweet little package you drooled over in the courtroom. Granny Adams taught the black widow everything it knows."

"I'll keep that in mind. But actually, that wasn't my question."

"It wasn't? Damn. This is gonna get me thrown off the psychic hotline. What was it?"

"I wanted to know about the judge. He seems a bit . . . how shall I say it? On the extreme side."

"That's Tyrone, for you. Always very extreme."

"Fancies himself a hanging judge?"

"Around here, we call Judge Pickens 'The Time Machine'—because whatever the crime is, he always gives the defendant the maximum time."

This was lovely to hear. "Even catnappers?"

"Don't believe we've had any precedent. But I can tell you what he did to Sonny Carlisle last week."

"Stiff sentence?"

"The stiffest. Sonny'd been drinking too hard out at Bunyan's. He shouldn't have been driving, but he was. Ended up smashing into two teenagers. Killed one of 'em. 'Course, it was negligent homicide, but that didn't slow The Time Machine down any. He gave Sonny two fifty-year sentences."

"Two?"

"You heard me right. One for each victim. To be served consecutively, not concurrently. When the sentencing was over, he glared down at Sonny and said, 'Your parole officer hasn't been born yet.' "

"Why did he go all ballistic when Granny painted me as some political extremist?"

All traces of the sheriff's smile faded. "Well, for that answer, why don't you ask these fellows in the adjoining cells? I'm sure they could explain it better than I can." And on that, he pivoted on the heel of his cowboy boot and left the cell block.

Ben hadn't even noticed that there were two people, a man and a woman, in the cells on either side of him. He didn't think they'd been there last night when he was first brought in.

"Hi," he said, waving in both directions. "I'm Ben Kincaid."

The woman to his left barely lifted a hand. "Cheers."

The woman's most eye-catching feature was her hair—lots and lots of it, wild auburn curls like untamed ivy. Even though it was cut chin-length, it radiated out from her head like a nun's habit. She wore large round eyeglasses with wire frames, which lent width to her otherwise thin face. Freckles dotted her cheekbones. She was dressed in jeans and a collarless shirt. She was attractive, Ben thought, in a practical, no-nonsense sort of way.

The man, similarly dressed in grubby jeans and a T-shirt, was equally uncommunicative. Ben's greeting evoked barely a grunt.

"Lovely place, isn't it?" Ben said, gesturing about the cell. "I'm thinking of coming back here every year."

He thought he detected a twitch on the woman's face that might roughly translate into a smile, but it was gone before he had a chance for closer scrutiny.

"Either of you know a good lawyer in the area? I'm a lawyer myself, but I'm going to need someone else to explain to the jury that my so-called crime was an act of conscience. It would sound too self-serving coming from me."

The woman's head lifted a notch. "You committed a crime of conscience?"

Ben nodded. "Right. Animal rights protest."

"No kidding?" Ben noted that her accent seemed more East Coast than Pacific Northwest. "I'm sorry. I figured you were in here for drunk and disorderly."

"Uh, no."

"Whaddaya know, Rick? He's one of us." She walked over to the side of her cell that adjoined Ben's and gripped the bars. "Animal rights, huh?"

"Yeah. Some heartless *Homo sapiens* species bigot was planning to kill his cat, basically because she'd become an annoyance. So I broke into his place to liberate the feline prior to her execution date."

The man on the other side approached the cell bars. "You committed a breaking and entering to save a cat? Maureen, I think this kid is definitely our kind of people."

"Amen to that." She stretched her hand through the bars. "My name is Maureen Williamson. My partner in crime is Rick Collier."

Ben shook both hands. "So what are you two in for?"

"Disturbing the peace," Maureen answered. "We staged a protest this morning on the courthouse steps, which supposedly violates a municipal ordinance—which I'm sure is unconstitutional, not that that kept them from using it to get rid of us. They'll probably let us cool our heels for a day or so, then release us, hoping we've learned our lesson."

"We've learned a lesson all right," Rick said, "but not the one those pigs had in mind."

Ben turned his attention back toward Maureen. "What kind of protest was this?"

"Rick and I are both members of Green Rage. Have you heard of us?"

A decided crease lined Ben's forehead. "Of course I have. You're an environmental group. A bit on the . . . extreme side."

Rick snorted. "Compared to what? The Rotary Club?"

"You're eco-terrorists."

"That's not true," Maureen interjected. "That's bad press generated by the logging interests."

Rick cut in. "Don't back away from the truth, Maureen. I'd rather we were eco-terrorists than some candy-ass sit-on-your-butt-and-negotiate Sierra Club group."

"It's a question of semantics. It's true that Green Rage does engage in some activities that are not strictly speaking legal, just as your actions last night weren't strictly speaking legal."

"Wait a minute," Ben said. "Rescuing a cat is hardly the same as—"

"You rescue cats; we rescue trees," Rick said. "I don't see much difference. Granted, we sometimes trash heavy equipment belonging to the logging companies. Tree cutters, that sort of thing. Sometimes we spike the roads to flatten their tires. Sometimes we spike trees—but we take every precaution to make sure no one gets hurt."

"Do you know how fast our forests are disappearing?" Maureen added. "If clear-cutting continues at the current rate, by the year 2020 there will be no forests left. Think about that—*no* forests. And 2020 isn't that far away."

"Still," Ben said, "there must be peaceful alternatives that don't put people in jeopardy."

Rick snorted, even louder than before. "Jesus! Listen to Pollyanna over there. And he calls himself an activist."

"I'm not any less an activist just because I don't want to risk hurting people."

"That's exactly half right," Rick said, jabbing his finger in Ben's direction. "You don't want to take a risk. But it isn't other people you're worried about. It's yourself. You don't want to upset your own cushy, complacent lifestyle."

Ben felt his dander rising. "You don't know anything about me. How can you—"

"I know your type. I've been dealing with you all my life."

"Boys, boys, boys," Maureen said, "this squabbling doesn't do anyone any good. Ben, the reason Green Rage moved into this area is because the loggers are on the verge of destroying what's left of the once-immense Magic Valley forest. There's a huge old-growth forest surrounding Mount Crescent that has been protected for decades, but earlier this year the Forest Service sold the lumber rights to WLE Logging."

"The worst in the business," Rick added. "WLE—We Log Eternally."

"They claim they won't cut the old-growth trees, but the fact is, they will. They already have. It's the strategy they've employed to destroy dozens of other forests. They lie, cheat, deny—and then when they're found out, they pay some trivial fine and reap a huge profit. We believe there may be some indigenous species in this forest that live nowhere else."

"Like Bigfoot?" Ben chortled.

Maureen ignored him. "A forest is more than a collection of individual trees. The forest is a complex living organism. Take away any element of that organism and the whole suffers. And eventually dies." She drew in her breath. "We believe some of the largest cedar trees left on this planet may be in this forest—bigger than the one in Forks. And these people want to cut them down just to make a quick and easy profit. It's obscene, Ben. We have an obligation to try to stop it."

"Trying to stop it is fine. Noble, even. But not if you resort to—"

"Ben, all over America, our trees are dying, because humans are killing them. It isn't just the cedars of the Northwest. It's the sugar bush of Vermont. It's the dogwoods of the Catoctin Mountains in Maryland. It's the aspens of northern Michigan and the forested hollows of Appalachia. We're killing the trees, ravaging our forests to provide pulp paper for advertising supplements and junk mail. We asked the government to stop it, and they refused. We asked corporate America to stop it, and they said, 'Go screw yourself.' Citizen groups just don't have the clout." She paused, folding her arms firmly across her chest. "I don't like breaking the law any more than you do. But it's like Edward Abbey says—at some point, you have to draw a line in the sand and say, 'Thus far and no further.' "

Ben shook his head. "Don't get me wrong. I admire your commitment. I just can't countenance any activities that risk lives."

"Destroying the forests risks lives—all our lives," Maureen said. "The forest is part of the worldwide organism. Everything is connected. If we take away the forests, we alter the composition of the atmosphere. How long do you think our species can survive after the trees are gone?"

" 'Sides, can't make an omelette without breaking a few eggs," Rick chuckled.

"Yeah. That's what Timothy McVeigh said, too."

"Ben," Maureen said, "surely you can see the difference between planting a bomb for the express intention of taking lives, and planting a spike to *prevent* taking lives—tree lives."

"Ends don't justify means." Ben sat down on his bunk, frustrated. This wasn't going at all the way he wanted. He decided to try to reboot the conversation. "So why were you protesting in front of the courthouse? Shouldn't you have been chaining yourself to some old-growth trees?"

Maureen's mouth twitched again, and this time he was almost certain it was a smile. "One of our members—our leader, in fact—has been incarcerated. Accused of a crime he didn't commit. And Judge Pickens has set a bail so enormous he has no chance of getting out before trial."

Somehow this didn't surprise Ben. "What's his name?"

"George Zakin. He goes by Zak."

Zakin, Ben thought. Zakin. The name seemed familiar to him. As unusual as it was, he should be able to remember where he'd heard it. His memory must be in low gear.

"What's he charged with? Destruction of property?"

"Far worse," Maureen answered. Her eyes fell, and her voice grew somber. "Murder. In the first degree."

* 4 *

"Murder?" Ben's jaw literally fell with surprise. "What did he do?"

"He didn't do anything. He's accused of planting a bomb in a tree cutter rigged so it would explode as soon as a logger turned the ignition."

"And someone was killed?"

"Yes. Horribly. In flames."

"Good God! Surely that's proof enough of why your extremist tactics are unacceptable."

"But we didn't do it!" Maureen said. "Zak didn't do it. We're being framed."

"Who would want to do that?"

Rick pressed his face between the bars. "Who wouldn't, chump? This whole one-horse town is supported by the logging industry, which is busy replacing humans with more efficient machines and blaming Green Rage for the layoffs. We're like the Antichrist around here."

"Surely they understand—"

"All they understand is that they're out of a job, or might be someday soon. Some of these families have worked in the logging industry for generations. They literally don't know anything else. It's as if we marched into town and wanted to burn down their church."

"It's pathetic," Maureen said. "People consider us terrorists. But we've been assaulted right and left since we moved into this area. We've been beaten up, had our camp destroyed, had our personal belongings stolen. We can't even walk down the street alone; we always travel in groups. Have you seen those yellow ribbons all around town?"

"Yeah," Ben said. "I have."

"That's WLE's Nazi-like yellow ribbon campaign. Businesses are supposed to display the yellow ribbons to show solidarity with the logging management against the so-called environmental threat. Anyone who doesn't display the ribbons could find themselves on the wrong end of a boycott or out of work or with a store that's been burned to the ground. Truth is, we're not the terrorists—they are."

"Still, it's hard to believe anyone would frame your leader for murder."

"If they thought it would get Green Rage out of their forests, I'll bet half the people in this town would do it. And someone did."

"The police must have some evidence."

"Of course they have evidence. Otherwise the frame wouldn't work. But I know this for a fact. Zak is not responsible for that logger's death." She stopped for a moment, catching her breath. "You know, Ben, if you're a lawyer—"

Ben held up his hands. "Wait just a minute. I'm just passing through."

"We've been searching desperately for someone to take Zak's case, but of course none of the locals will touch it with a ten-foot pole. The court appointed some schmuck, but he doesn't exactly have his heart in it. If you took over the case—"

"Stop right there. I can't do it. I'm in the middle of a book tour. Also, I'm in jail."

Her eyes widened. "A book tour? You're—a writer?"

"Well, it's only my first book."

"Nonfiction?"

"Yes."

"Ben, that's perfect! You're—you're exactly what I've been looking for."

"I am?"

"Yes! You're perfect. Zak needs someone to take his case. Someone who's committed to the cause, to the truth. Someone who cares whether justice is served. And Green Rage needs a scribe. You could wear both hats!"

"I'm not sure I follow."

"You're a writer. You must know how important publicity is. God knows the logging companies have their propaganda machines working full-time, painting us as black, evil marauders. You've been exposed to it yourself—as soon as you heard the name Green Rage, you thought eco-terrorist. That's what the loggers want."

"Or perhaps it's just the truth."

"But you could change all that. You could expose the world to our point of view. Make them see things the way we do. Make them understand that time is short, that if we don't take action now, it will be too late." She looked at him eagerly. "What do you think?"

"I don't see how—"

"Aww, forget it, Maureen," Rick growled. "Look at this chump. He's not going to stick his neck out for us or anyone else. He's got his comfy little lawyer world. Probably a nice swimming pool and a big screen TV. He's not going to put himself on the line for us."

"That's not fair," Ben protested. "You don't know—"

"Please consider it, Ben," Maureen implored. "You don't know what a difference this could make. I can't explain it totally. I—I just have a sense that if you were on our team, sending the world our battle reports from the front lines, that might be just what we need to win the day. And God knows Zak needs you. If you don't help, he's going to end up railroaded, spending the rest of his life in prison. Or worse."

Ben didn't answer. She was staring at him, waiting for a response that wasn't coming.

"Please, Ben. I don't mean to pressure you, but I think you could be the best thing that happened to the environmental movement since Rachel Carson. You could make all the difference."

Her words had an unmistakable appeal. As his assistant Christina McCall had pointed out on any number of occasions, he was a total sucker for an underdog. He had certainly represented unpopular clients in the past; in fact, he considered it an attorney's duty to do so. But this was different. This wasn't simply a difference in opinion or belief. These people were *terrorists*.

"I'm sorry," Ben said. "I hear what you're saying. But I can't do it."

Maureen's face fell. She eased away from the bars, back into her own cell. She said nothing, but her disappointment was evident.

"Don't worry about it," Rick said. "You'll be a lot more comfortable back in the safety of your La-Z-Boy recliner."

Ben bit back his response. Rick wasn't being fair, but of course, there was no reason why he should be. Maureen had played fair, and look what it got her.

Nothing. Absolutely nothing.

Ben stretched out on his cot. He knew he was making the right decision. He was almost proud of himself. For once he wasn't running off on whatever half-baked quest fell into his lap.

But he couldn't quash the tiny voice in the pit of his brain that kept saying that maybe, just maybe, he was making a mistake. The tiny voice of doubt.

And guilt.

You have a unique opportunity here, Maureen had said. You could make all the difference.

Ben rolled over, buried his face in the pillow, and closed his eyes. But he felt certain he wasn't going to get any sleep.

* 5 *

Tess O'Connell rushed back to her hotel room and slammed the door shut behind her. With lightning speed, she turned the deadbolt, slid in the chain lock, and pulled a dresser in front of the door.

She wasn't taking any chances.

This was the first time she had ventured out of her hotel room since the night of the murder. When she looked back on it now, the whole episode seemed like one extended nightmare—far too chilling and extraordinary to be real.

Except it was. She knew it was. Every time she closed her eyes, it came back to her, insistent and unbidden. Like a nightmare.

She still wasn't sure how she managed to elude that monster who had chased her away from the scene of the explosion. He had to have known the forest better than she did. All she did was run, not stopping, not checking directions, just running. Maybe he hurt himself, maybe he had to stop to do something. She didn't know. All she knew for sure was that somehow, against all odds, she had managed to give Sasquatch the slip.

Whoever he was. Behind the mask.

When she finally made it back to her hotel, she had locked the doors, crawled under the covers, and holed up for days.

She hadn't even let the maids in to clean. She made room service leave trays outside her door. She was that scared. She didn't want to see anyone, didn't want anyone to come near her. Her boss at the *Whisper* kept phoning, leaving messages, but she didn't return the calls.

It was almost a week before she regained some semblance of the patented O'Connell chutzpah, before she felt she might be able to venture into the hallway without meeting Sasquatch at the first corner. Slowly, as the days passed, her terror began to fade, replaced by something altogether different.

The scent of a story.

For once in her life, Tess had the inside track on something big, maybe even bigger than anyone realized. She had seen what no one else had seen; she knew what no one else knew. What's more, she had evidence.

The videotape.

Unfortunately, when she replayed the tape in the camera it was too dark to make out, and the rooms at the Magic Valley Holiday Inn did not come equipped with VCRs. The hotel management wasn't able to provide her with one, either. Here she was, a reporter holding critical evidence in her hands—that she was unable to view. She realized that if she was going to see this, she was going to have to leave the room.

It hadn't been easy. But eventually, as the panic eased, she began to think about her station in life and what this tape could do to improve it. She had never meant to end up stuck at some low-rent tabloid. She had studied journalism at UCLA. She'd had ambitions, visions of Pulitzers. She wanted to be known as a serious investigative reporter. But at the time of her graduation, there had been a hiring freeze at all the newspapers. The industry was in a slump. It was beginning to look as if her only career opportunity would involve "hold the pickles, hold the lettuce."

Until she found the opening at the *Whisper*. And so she began her career of stalking celebrities and searching for the truth about crop circles and cow mutilations.

And Sasquatch.

She had seen the job as temporary, a stopping place until other prospects opened up. But when positions at the real papers did open up, she found herself tainted by her contact with the *Whisper*. "Oh, you're *that* kind of reporter"—and the interview would come to a swift conclusion. After a while, she developed evasive responses, but to no avail. The journalistic community was small and close-knit. Secrets were hard to keep.

And so her temporary stopover became an eight-year stint. With no end in sight. Eventually she had resigned herself to her fate.

Until the tragic last night of Princess Diana. Tess wasn't involved in that tragedy, thank God, but afterward the thought of having anything to do with this sort of journalism made her sick. Problem was, she still had to eat. And she couldn't figure out a way to make a name for herself in legitimate journalism.

Until now. If she could crack this murder, everything could change. This story had it all—murder, mayhem, sex appeal. This could be the lucky break that transformed her from Tabloid Mary to Diane Sawyer.

And so she took the plunge, left the safety of the Holiday Inn, and sought out the nearest place she could rent a VCR. Hadn't been hard, as it turned out. Even a one-horse town like Magic Valley had a video store on every block, and they all rented out VCRs. They even had a gizmo that converted the Video-8 tape from her recorder to a regular VHS tape.

It had taken her ten minutes to install the damn thing, to disconnect the rip-off pay-per-view machine fused into the hotel TV and connect her VCR, but at last she had everything ready. She could feel her anxiousness; her mouth was dry and her hands were wet, both from anticipation of what might lie on that strip of magnetic tape.

She pushed the Play button and the images flickered to life. The TV screen was bathed with vivid yellow and red. The tree cutter had already exploded; it was now just a raging mass of twisted, melting metal, fused together like the core of a nuclear furnace. The victim had already collapsed on the ground, all charred flesh and cinders.

She watched for almost a minute as the camera panned and scanned the horizon, showing the devastation of the clear-cut forest, brought into sharp and haunting highlight by the raging inferno. Several times she thought she detected a trace of movement in the distance, but it was hard to be sure. Was there really someone there, or was it an illusion created by the flickering of the flames? It was impossible to be sure.

Impossible—up to a point. Shortly thereafter, a large hairy figure began moving in a direct line toward the camera. It was tiny at first, barely discernible except as a point of movement. It came steadily closer until, even in the darkness, she could tell it was Sasquatch—or more correctly, someone dressed as Sasquatch. Sasquatch with his mask removed.

She couldn't make out the face yet, but he kept running closer, closer and closer, faster and faster. She could almost see it and then—

And then the picture changed. The camera moved every which way at once, moved so quickly she could make out nothing. And then all she saw was the ground, moving fast.

Tess knew what had happened. She had seen Sasquatch coming toward her and panicked. She had turned and fled for her life—just an instant before the monster's face would have been visible on the tape.

She punched the Stop button, cursing under her breath. And so, when all was said and done, she had nothing. Her big chance for success, her opportunity to bolt from the sleaze market, had dissipated.

She felt a stinging in her eyes. It had been stupid to let herself fantasize. She should have known something would go wrong—didn't something always go wrong? Face it—she was going to be spending the rest of her life with the ninety-five-year-old grandmother who gave birth to twins. There was no escape.

She slapped herself hard on the side of the face. Stop feeling sorry for yourself, damn it, and *think*! Suddenly she realized she knew a hell of a lot more than anyone else did about this case. She was the only living eyewitness—not counting the killer. She was the only one who knew exactly how it had happened. And she was the only one who knew there had been a fight preceding the explosion.

A fight. That was the key—it had to be. She had read in the paper that the victim was a logger, which made sense, since he knew how to start the tree cutter. If he was a logger, then who would be fighting with him? Who would be having an argument in the dead of night, at the site of a massive clear-cut?

Green Rage, that's who.

She knew that the police had arrested the leader of the group and charged him with the murder. But she didn't believe he was guilty; he didn't look anything like the person in the Sasquatch suit. The height and weight were all wrong. The police were just latching onto the obvious suspect, as they always did. They were assuming the bomb had been planted in advance, that it was part of a Green Rage terrorist strike, that the logger had just had the misfortune to be the person who turned the ignition that night.

Tess knew better. She knew the killer had been there all along, including when the bomb was triggered. She knew the two men had fought. She didn't know what they had fought about, but given the circumstances, it seemed more than reasonable to assume it had something to do with the destruction of the national forest.

She pushed herself off the bed, grabbed her notebook, and started making plans.

Somehow she would have to infiltrate Green Rage. The only way to learn what she wanted to know would be to gain their confidence, their trust. If she could get them talking, she might uncover the clues she needed.

Of course she would, she told herself. She was a reporter, wasn't she? A real reporter.

But to do this, she would have to venture outside. And longer than it took to get to the video store, too.

But what could happen to her? She had just been silly, hadn't she? Paranoid? After all, she had nothing on the killer, whoever he was. He or she. There was no reason to go after her. Hell, the creep probably never even saw her face.

Probably.

She laughed, trying to convince herself. Probably didn't have the slightest idea who she was.

Probably.

Enough. She was going to do this. No one and nothing was going to stop her. This might be the last chance she had to make the Pulitzer committee sit up and take notice. Or at least to get a job she didn't have to lie about when she called her mother. She wasn't going to let it pass her by.

Her eye moved unbidden to the draped window. She wasn't going to blow this opportunity, damn it. She wasn't.

No matter what the consequences.

Sasquatch peered through his binoculars at the draped window of the Holiday Inn room. Of course, the Sasquatch getup was not being worn at the moment, but the brain behind the mask had begun to think in those terms. It seemed a good label. Or perhaps—The Artist Formerly Known as Sasquatch.

After the night of the murder, after the woman escaped, Sasquatch had paced the streets of the city, but after several days without spotting her, he became convinced she must have fled town. What a relief it was, then, to see that familiar face strolling out of a video store this afternoon.

And how grim to see her toting a VCR. Sasquatch didn't have to be a genius to figure out what that was for. She had been carrying a video camera; it was the main reason Sasquatch had charged her. If anyone studied it closely—well, best not to even think about it.

Sasquatch had to get that tape. And her, too.

Sasquatch folded the binoculars and tucked them into a coat pocket. Best not to attract any attention. Best to keep a low profile. Best not to let anyone draw a connection between Sasquatch and that woman, whoever she was.

Because there was a good chance Sasquatch was going to have to kill her.

* 6 *

Ben was not having a good night. He had always been a vivid dreamer, but tonight's show was even more vivid than usual. Some of the dreams were standard-issue material: showing up in court in his underwear; being seduced by his childhood babysitter. But some of them were new: seeing his old Episcopal Sunday-school teacher shaking her head in disappointment; being tried in the Court of Celestial Appeals for murder—the murder of hundreds of thousands of old-growth trees. He even dreamed he'd been thrown into jail and was thrashing about on a rock-hard metal cot. Except—

His eyes opened.

Damn. That one was true, wasn't it?

"I knew you were looking for a new *pied-à-terre*, Ben, but I really think you should have consulted me before you made this selection."

The voice was very familiar. Even before he rubbed the sleep out of his eyes, Ben knew who was standing on the other side of the metal bars.

"Good morning, Christina. About time you showed up."

"Hey, I made the best time I could. I booked the first available flight *tout de suite*, after I played your rather desperate-sounding message on my machine."

"You'd be desperate, too, if you got only one phone call and you used it chatting with someone's answering machine." He peered blurry-eyed through the cell bars. She was wearing an all-combat ensemble—green fatigue pants with a flak jacket draped over a khaki shirt. Plus a kelly green hairband in her expansive red hair. "I thought you were trying to dress more conservatively. Now that you're a serious law student."

She checked herself. "What're you talking about? This *is* conservative. Besides, you're the one who dragged me out to the great Northwest. Everyone dresses this way."

"Maybe in the Montana Militia, but not around here." He forced himself to his feet. "Have you figured out a way to make my bail?"

"I figured out it was impossible, even if we sold both our combined assets for twice their worth. So I tried something else."

"Which was?"

"Getting the bookstore owner to drop the charges."

"Fat chance of that. He's—"

"—already agreed to do it."

Ben's eyes widened. "He's—"

"—already agreed." She fluttered her eyelashes. "Would I lie?"

"But—"

"The only thing that man ever wanted was to get rid of the cat. Unfortunately, after you made such a *cause célèbre* of it, the vet canceled the appointment, and none of the other vets in the area would euthanize the cat either."

"Tough luck."

"So I told him I'd take care of it. If he dropped the charges. Which he did."

Ben was flabbergasted. "Christina, you're a miracle worker. I'm eternally in your debt."

She smiled. "Truth is, he was beginning to feel guilty. He was glad to let someone else execute the cat for him."

Ben blanched. "Christina, you didn't!"

"No, of course I didn't."

"Then what?"

"I called an old friend of mine from TCC who knew a gal who had a sister whose husband was from Seattle. The husband in Seattle had a friend whose niece lives in a tiny burg not far from Magic Valley. The niece has a girlfriend who knows a girl from college who's getting married. The girl who's getting married is the youngest of seven daughters, and once she moves out, her mother's going to be all alone in her house. The mother lives in Magic Valley. She agreed to take the cat." She beamed. "Follow that?"

"Not remotely, but please don't repeat it. My head is already throbbing." He took a step back. "And you did all that in a day?"

"Well, I would've been faster, but the air phones on my flight didn't work."

Ben grinned. No wonder he liked Christina so much. In the years they'd been working together, she'd proved invaluable. She was a brilliant legal assistant, and now that she was in law school, she could function equally well as an intern and legal researcher. Most important, he had learned to trust her instincts. She was keenly intuitive and had a better understanding of people than he ever would. And now, for the capstone of her career to date, she'd produced his get-out-of-jail-free card.

"When can I leave?"

Another voice harkened down the corridor. "Whenever you want, Mr. Kincaid."

Sheriff Allen was moving toward them.

"In that case," Ben said, "I'll go now."

"Thought you might feel that way." He pulled the jangling cell keys out of his pocket. "This little lady's got you all fixed up. Never seen anyone come to town and get things done the way she did. She's got a lot of spunk." He grinned. "I like that in a woman."

"Christina's the best legal assistant I've ever had."

Allen tipped his hat. "That's high praise, I expect."

"Not really," Christina explained. "I'm the only legal assistant he's ever had."

Allen began unlocking Ben's cell.

Ben heard stirrings from the cell to his left. Maureen was awake and on her feet. "Looks like you grabbed the brass ring, Kincaid."

"No need to display your penal envy," Allen said as he slid Ben's cell door open. "You're getting out, too."

Rick pressed against the bars on Ben's right. "We are?"

"Yup. Judge says twenty-four hours is the most we can hold you for disturbing the peace. But let me tell you something. I got no feelings about your cause for or against. But if you and your people go on stirring up trouble around here, I will come down on you—hard."

Maureen nodded. "Thanks, Sheriff."

Allen unlocked Maureen's and Rick's cells. " 'Fore you all go, I wonder if I might, um—" He cleared his throat awkwardly. "I wondered if I might have a word with Miss, uh, is it Christina?"

Christina turned, surprised. "That's my name."

"You think you're going to be hanging around town for a spell?"

"Well, I couldn't get us a flight out of here until tomorrow."

"I just wondered if, you know, if you and this guy ain't hitched or anything—"

Christina's eyes expanded.

Allen cleared his throat. "I wondered if you wouldn't mind having lunch with me."

Christina appeared momentarily perplexed. She glanced at Ben. "Is that a problem?"

Ben shrugged. "Not with me."

"Then it's a date."

A *date*? Ben thought. He just invited her to lunch, for Pete's sake. Was that a date?

"Now," Christina said, "if it's all right with the rest of you, I'd like to get the hell out of here. Jails and I are . . . not bosom buddies."

Ben knew what she was talking about. Christina had spent a horrible period locked up in a tiny, dirty jail cell several years ago when she was falsely accused of murder. The incident had left emotional scars. She had nightmares about finding herself shut up behind bars again. Just the thought of it was enough to make her break down like a baby.

Allen led the four of them down the corridor. Ben thought he detected a certain bounce in the man's boots that hadn't been there before. And they hadn't even started the lunch date.

"Welcome back to the free world," he said, opening the outside door. "Now stay out of trouble, you hear?"

Ben heard, all right. Loud and clear.

* * *

Maureen started at Ben again the instant they stepped out of the jailhouse. "Seriously, Ben, think about my invitation. This could be a unique opportunity for you to be a potent force for good."

Ben waved his hands in the air. "I'm sorry, no. I'm not going to become known as the mouthpiece for terrorists."

"Then forget about the book idea. Just take Zak's case. He needs a lawyer who knows the ropes. Who has experience with capital murder cases."

Christina's ears pricked up. "A case? They're offering us a case?" She grabbed Ben's arm and lowered her voice. "Ben, this could be just what we need."

"Believe me, it isn't."

"Ben, we haven't had a paying case for months. We haven't had a case that paid well since Wallace Barrett, and that money ran out a long time ago."

"Trust me, Christina. This isn't the answer."

"Look, maybe you don't need the cash, but I'm paying tuition at TU, and that bill is larger than the GNP of some industrialized nations."

"Christina, this wouldn't be a moneymaker. More like a pro bono case. With some serious negative ramifications." He turned back toward Maureen. "I'm sorry. I'd like to help. But it's out of the question." He extended his hand. "I just can't do it."

Maureen took his hand and clasped it. Her eyes seemed much softer than they had before. "I'm sorry to hear that," she said. "I'm disappointed and—well, just very . . . sorry." She turned quickly and headed down the sidewalk. Rick followed a beat behind her.

Ben and Christina watched as the pair passed out of sight. "Are you sure about this?" Christina asked.

"Absolutely," Ben replied. "It's for the best. Really." He started walking in the opposite direction.

Ben hadn't moved ten feet when he heard a piercing shout from down the street. *"Maureen!"*

"What's that?" Christina asked.

Ben whirled around. "Stay here." He raced down the street and rounded the same corner he had seen Rick and Maureen take a few moments before. Following the sounds of struggle, he ducked into a side alley behind a closed dry cleaning store.

There were three of them—big burly thugs, the kind you knew immediately couldn't possibly be good for anything in the world except inflicting pain. One of them had a chain wrapped around his fist and was using it to pummel Rick. Another one had Maureen pinned against the wall, her face stricken with terror. The third seemed content to fold his arms, supervise, and sneer.

"Well, now," the third man said. "Let's show these two tree huggers what rage really is, whaddaya say, boys?"

* 7 *

Before Ben had a chance to think, much less act, the metal chain whipped around in a deadly spiral. Rick turned away, but had no room to maneuver. The chain crashed down on his back. He cried out as he fell to his knees. His assailant grinned and brought the chain around again.

Maureen was struggling for all she was worth, but her attacker had her pinned against a brick wall, his arms on either side and beneath hers, leaving her nowhere to go. The man outweighed her by at least a hundred pounds and was much stronger. He snapped his hand back for a sudden slap across the side of her face. Maureen's head banged against the brick wall, then went limp.

"Stop!" Ben shouted. He knew that probably sounded incredibly unthreatening to these toughs, but he hoped it might slow them down a few beats. He had to think of something. But what could he do?

"Lookee here," said the man with the folded arms. "Another tree hugger. Looks like I'm gonna get to do some poundin' myself." He started toward Ben, not in a hurry, making it all the more frightening. There was something about the man, something in his calm, powerful manner, that made him absolutely terrifying.

"I've called the sheriff's office," Ben said, trying to suppress the stutter in his voice. "They're on their way."

The man shook his head, still moving toward Ben. "There's no pay phone on this block. You haven't had time."

Without thinking, Ben whipped his checkbook out of his back pocket. He just hoped it was dark enough back here to get away with this. "I used my cell phone. They're on their way. Won't take them a minute to get here."

"You're bluffing."

"It's true," Maureen said, bringing as much strength to her voice as she could muster. "It's standard Green Rage operating procedure. First sign of trouble, call the cops."

"Listen!" Ben said. "I hear them coming."

Somewhere in the distance, they heard the sound of a door slamming, followed by the sound of feet moving quickly on the pavement.

"Damn it all to hell," the man swore, throwing down his big muscled arms. "Let's get out of here, boys."

The man with the chain stopped in mid-swing. The brute hovering over Maureen stepped away, but not before cracking her one more time across the jaw.

"We'll be back," the leader said. "This is just a reprieve." He started to go, then whipped around suddenly, lurched forward, and drove his fist deep into the soft part of Ben's stomach. Ben doubled over and fell to the pavement.

"That's to remember me by," the man growled. He and his two accomplices disappeared in the darkness of the alleyway.

"Are you all right?" Maureen said, rushing toward Ben. Her eyes were full of concern.

Ben wasn't entirely sure. His gut felt like it was on fire; he couldn't seem to stand up straight. "Am *I* all right? What about you? And Rick?"

"Rick!" She ran back the other way, then knelt by her friend. Ben could see that he was conscious, although he seemed to be having a hard time moving.

He was suddenly aware that Christina was standing behind him. "Didn't I tell you to stay put?" he asked.

"What of it?"

Ben smirked. "I assume you provided the sound effects—the slamming door, the rushing feet."

"Seemed like the least I could do. Nice bluff about the cell phone. Who knows? If you'd take more cases maybe you could afford a real one."

Ben tried to push himself to his feet, but every time he moved, his stomach felt as if stitches were being ripped out.

"I think Rick's okay," Maureen said. She sat on the ground beside Ben. "At least in the sense that he's not going to die. But I want him to go to the hospital."

"No hospitals," Rick said emphatically. "Doc can take a look at me when we get back to camp."

"Doc's our medic," Maureen explained. "A member of our group. We've been trying to make ourselves self-sufficient by recruiting people with professional training. You know, so they can help out when the need arises, without our having to bankrupt ourselves hiring outside assistance. We've covered most of the major fields, except of course . . ."

"Law," Ben said, finishing her sentence.

"Yeah. Most of the lawyers we've talked to seem more interested in summer cottages on Puget Sound than helping a group of . . ."

"Eco-terrorists," Ben said, filling in the blanks.

"Environmental warriors," she replied, then all at once broke out in a grin. "Anyway, we've got to run before more of these hoods appear. You can see what we're up against. Like I told you, they're everywhere. It's not even safe for us to walk the streets." She turned suddenly; Ben realized she was fighting back tears. "Thanks for the help. You're pretty quick on your feet, and if you don't mind me saying so, and I—well, never mind. I hope we see you again sometime."

"I'm in," Ben said.

Maureen stopped short. "You're—I'm sorry?"

"I'm in. I'll help."

"Do you mean—"

"I mean, you need a lawyer. Well, here I am."

Maureen grasped both his arms. "That's wonderful. That's—"

Ben cut in. "But I won't do anything illegal. So don't ask."

"No, of course not. Are—are you sure about this?"

"I'm sure."

Overcome with enthusiasm, Maureen threw her arms around him and hugged him tight. Ben felt a sudden rush that he knew had nothing to do with the acquisition of a new client. "That's so wonderful! This is the biggest break we've had in months!" She hugged him again, overcome with enthusiasm. "Mr. Kincaid, I think this could be the start of a beautiful friendship."

TWO

* *

Counter Friction

* 8 *

Tess parked her Jeep Cherokee in the only opening in the gravel-covered parking area. The place was packed—by Magic Valley standards, anyway.

She wasn't surprised. There were only two bars in Magic Valley, and this one—Bunyan's—was the only one that stayed open after midnight. For the crowd that wanted to drink into the wee hours of the morning, this was the place to be.

She crossed the parking lot, passing between two rows of pickups, mostly red, a few blue or green. A bumper sticker caught her eye: KILL AN OWL, SAVE A LOGGER.

She shook her head. Those Green Ragers had to be crazy to hang out here. Not that there were a lot of choices.

She opened the front door of Bunyan's. A thick cloud of smoke hit her so hard she almost choked. Her eyes stung; it was several seconds before she could see anything. When she could, she didn't see much she liked.

The place was filled with men, most of them tough, bearded, and sizable. Not the kind you'd expect to see at the Friday-night poetry reading. Excepting the waitresses, she saw only a couple of women. The place was decorated with logging memorabilia—rusted hacksaws and chain saws, sepia-toned photos of logging operations throughout the century. One wall displayed a huge neon image of Paul Bunyan—one hand on his trusty axe, the other on Babe the blue ox.

She scanned the bar till she found the guys she was looking for. There were two of them, both seated at the bar. They both had long hair; one of them wore an earring, although these days that wasn't uncommon even with the loggers. They were younger than most of the rest of the men in the bar.

She knew one of them—Rick Collier. He was one of the top men in the local Green Rage hierarchy, second in command to George Zakin, the man currently under lock and key. She didn't know the other man, but since he was deep in an animated conversation with Rick, she thought it a good bet that he was also a member of Green Rage.

And as luck would have it, there was an empty barstool beside Rick. Although, upon reflection, she thought it probably was not luck but the fact that no one else in the bar wanted anything to do with them.

She sashayed up to the empty bar stool, consciously ignoring the leers she received from the men she passed. Most of them probably thought they were giving her a compliment, but from her perspective, all they were giving her was the creeps.

She took the empty stool and ordered a gin and tonic. While she waited, she tried to eavesdrop on the discussion to her immediate right.

"Can we trust him?" the man she didn't know asked Rick.

"I think so," Rick answered. "To a point, anyway. He's probably at the dilettante stage. He'd like to think of himself as an activist, committed to the cause. But he's probably not ready to take any risks."

"How much can we tell him? How much should he know?"

"Nothing about anything illegal, that's for sure. He's still processing. Let's not get his panties in a twist over some penny-ante act of ecotage."

There was a pause before the other man asked the next question. "Do you think he suspects?"

"Naw," Rick said confidently. "Not a chance. He's clueless."

The two men fell silent. Tess supposed this was her opening. She took a cigarette out of her purse, pressed it to her lips, and tapped Rick lightly on the shoulder. "Do you know if smoking is permitted?"

He peered at her through the smoke-filled air. "If it isn't, you'd better run, 'cause this shack must be on fire."

She smiled seductively. "Got a light?"

Rick shook his head. "Sorry. I'm not into self-destruction."

She set the cigarette on the counter and leaned closer to him. "What are you into?"

"Why do you want to know?"

"Tsk, tsk. Answering a question with a question. That's a bit defensive."

"I've learned to be." He started to turn back to his companion. "If you'll excuse me."

Tess laid her hand on his shoulder and gently brought him back around. "Please don't. I'm all alone here, I don't know anyone, and I'd really like some company."

Rick's expression was decidedly unsympathetic.

"My name is Tess. What's yours?"

"Rick. But then, you knew that already, didn't you?"

Tess pulled up, startled. "Wha—what do you mean?"

"You know exactly what I mean. Who sent you?"

"Sent me? I just—this was the only place open—"

"Uh-huh. Right. Look, if you're snooping for information, just ask. Chances are I won't tell you squat, but at least we'll save time and you won't have to demean yourself by pretending to come on to me."

Tess pressed her lips together. Some investigative reporter—it hadn't taken him two seconds to make her. It was time to retrench.

"Look, I'm sorry," she said. She cast her eyes downward. "I didn't know how to approach you. I just . . . wanted to talk."

"On whose behalf?"

"Just—for me. I wanted to get to know you."

"Like I said, if you'll excuse me—"

"Please wait." She held up her hands and put on her most pathetic expression. "I want to help you." She glanced at his companion. "All of you."

Rick let out a guffaw. "I'm sure. Now I've heard everything."

"It's true." She glanced around the bar, as if checking for spies, then lowered her voice. "I know about the Cabal."

Rick's eyebrows formed a broad ridge over his eyes. "What are you babbling about?"

"You heard me. I know about them. And I think I have information you could use."

"And just what is it you think this Cabal is?"

"The Cabal is a secret organization formed and funded by a consortium of major logging companies. From what I understand, each of the eight largest companies kicked in a million dollars. They hired a man to lead it, a former CIA operative experienced with dirty tricks. His name is Amos Slade." She paused. "Although those who know him call him the Prince of Darkness."

"And what is it you think this so-called Cabal is supposed to do?"

"The Cabal was formed for one reason and one reason only—to screw the environmental groups, particularly the so-called eco-terrorists like Green Rage."

"And why would they want to do that? We haven't stopped the logging, as any fool can see."

"No, but you have made it more expensive. Most analysts estimate that eco-terrorism costs the logging industry about twenty million a year in lost equipment, derailed plans, overtime, and other related costs. I suppose compared with that, the cost of funding the Cabal seemed pretty minor."

"So far you haven't told me anything I don't already know."

"Do you know they're planning to strike? Strike and strike hard." Tess tried to keep her eyes locked firmly on his, tried not to give any hint that she had segued from known fact to pure fiction. She had learned about the Cabal, or at least heard rumors about it, during her preliminary research before coming out here. What she didn't know—had no way of knowing—was what the Cabal planned to do next. Although any educated guesser could anticipate that a strike against Green Rage was imminent.

Rick was obviously unconvinced. "Lots of people have heard about the Cabal. That doesn't prove you have any inside information. How do I know this isn't all some fantasy you've cooked up?"

"They've already hit you, haven't they? Twice, from what I heard."

"How do you know that?"

"Because I know what I'm talking about. Don't I?"

Rick hesitated before speaking. "There have been two raids

on our camp out in the forest. Minor property damage. No one was hurt."

"Those were just warnings—warnings you didn't heed. The next attack will hurt."

Rick batted a finger against his lips. "When will they strike?"

"I can't say exactly. But I know it will be soon."

"And how do you know all this?"

Tess lowered her head. If ever in her life she was going to give an Oscar-quality performance, it had better be now. "I—I'm having a relationship with a man in Slade's organization. One of his most trusted advisers."

"A relationship?"

"An . . . intimate relationship."

"You're sleeping with someone in the Cabal? And you're talking to me?"

"Please try to understand. I'm not a bad person. At least I don't think I am. I want to do the right thing. And I'm sympathetic to your cause."

"I'm supposed to believe that some Cabal piece of ass is a secret environmentalist?"

"It's true! I mean—" She paused, trying to create the right effect. "I suppose I wasn't at first. I'd never really thought about it—forests, trees, nature. Truth is, I never spent much time outdoors. But then when I got involved with John and started seeing what those loggers are doing, I was horrified! They're just destroying everything. At the rate they're going, soon there won't be anything left. And they know that! But they don't care."

Rick's jaw was set, but if Tess wasn't mistaken, his hard exterior had softened just the tiniest bit. "I still don't understand what it is you want."

"I want to join you. I want to be part of your work." She sat up straight. "I want to join Green Rage."

"Have you broken it off with this—what's his name? John?"

"No, I haven't."

Rick rolled his eyes. "I don't believe this." He nudged his companion. "Let's get out of here."

"Wait. Please!" She grabbed his shirt sleeve and literally held him down on his stool. "Don't you see? This could be perfect."

"What could be?"

"Me." She leaned closer to him and lowered her voice. "Don't think of me as a Cabal insider. Think of me as Mata Hari."

"You're saying—"

"That's right. I'll stay with John, much as he disgusts me. I'll learn whatever I can. And I'll report back to you."

Rick chewed his lip for a moment. "And in return?"

"Nothing. All I want is to be part of Green Rage. To spend time with you. To help you with your work. I want to run with people whose hearts and minds are in the right place. I want to be a part of something that matters."

Rick continued to ponder. "I'll have to talk to Maureen. Some of the others. They'll want to meet you."

"I understand."

"I don't know what they'll say. We haven't been receptive to new members, other than those we recruited ourselves. We're too worried about being infiltrated by loggers or the Cabal."

"I understand. I'll do whatever you want me to do."

Rick shook his head. "An inside line on the Cabal. Damn. It's almost too good to believe." He stared at her another long moment. "You'll have to give me an address or phone number."

"No problem." Tess smiled, and for once, her expression without reflected her feelings within. She had him hooked now. It was just a matter of time—and she was betting it would be a short time—before she'd be in like Flynn with Green Rage. Once she had their confidence, it should be a cinch for an old pro like her to find out what she wanted to know.

Like who was wearing the Sasquatch suit the night of the murder.

Sasquatch was sitting in the back of the bar, drinking alone. Sasquatch had seen Tess make her grand entrance, watched her cozy up to Rick Collier and initiate a conversation. Although Sasquatch didn't know exactly what they were talking about, it didn't take a genius to figure out what she was trying to do.

She was trying to worm her way into Green Rage.

She was trying to find the killer.

Wouldn't she be surprised to know that killer was sitting barely ten feet away, downing a tall cool one?

Sasquatch turned slightly so she wouldn't have a clear view of him. There was no telling what she knew anymore. Best to assume the worst—that she'd gotten a good view and it was recorded for all time on Video-8 tape. But if so, why all this subterfuge? Why all the investigation? Why hadn't she gone directly to the source—or contacted the police? There was something strange going on here.

Sasquatch lifted a beer bottle, polishing it off. It could be that she was just swimming in the dark, that she didn't know a damn thing. And if so, fine.

But it was also possible she knew everything, and she was just biding her time, filling in the gaps in her story. If that was it . . .

Sasquatch sat grimly in the booth, clutching the empty beer bottle with both hands. Things had come too far. There was too much invested to let her bring it all crashing down now. If she knew . . .

The secret would have to die. With her.

* 9 *

While Ben waited for the sheriff to arrive the next morning, he strolled around the jail and courthouse complex. The building was weather-worn yellow brick, like most of the downtown edifices. Climbing ivy decorated the west wall, adding a splash of color to the otherwise monochrome facade.

The parking was in the back, and there was a good deal more of it than Ben would have guessed. What most surprised him, though, were the two helicopters in the rear, each with its own helipad. Ben had spent enough time with his cop friend Mike Morelli, who was the pilot and co-owner of his own copter, to know they were expensive pieces of equipment—not something you'd expect to find in a tiny town like Magic Valley.

Eventually Ben saw Sheriff Allen pull into the parking lot. He followed the man to his office.

Allen was obviously surprised to see him. "Granted, I was expectin' to see that cute little friend of yours come lunchtime, but I didn't expect to see you again come hell or high water."

"I can imagine. I thought you opened up at nine. I've been waiting since then."

"Oops. Sorry about that. Had some business to take care of. Deputy Hardin was supposed to be in. Guess he got called out."

Ben nodded. "It's all right. Out catching bad guys?"

"I wish. Nah, I was on the phone with some hospital bureaucrat in Seattle. My mother's in a cancer treatment center there."

"I'm sorry to hear that."

"You and me both. She's been there four years. It's all that's kept her alive. But it's just about killed me."

"Are you her only child?"

"Nah. Got me a sister here in town. But she's—well, not too good in the head. So I've got to take care of Mom myself." He waved his hand in the air. "But I'm sure you've got problems, too."

"I saw two helicopters out back," Ben said. "Mind if I ask what they're for?"

"Mountain rescues, mostly," Allen explained. "When we need to get up there in a hurry. Or when conventional approaches don't work—like after 'bout thirty feet of snow."

"You have pilots?"

"I fly one of those little birdies myself. So do two of my deputies. We don't use 'em all that often, but they're nice to have for emergencies." He jingled the keys dangling from his belt. "Anyway, I'm sure you didn't come here to engage in friendly chitchat. What can I do for you?"

"I've been asked to represent George Zakin. As his attorney."

The sheriff pushed his hat back. "You're representing Zakin? I thought Bruce Bailey drew that short straw."

"Bruce has agreed to step down, since he's never tried anything more serious than a drunk and disorderly. Although technically, he will serve as local counsel."

"Does Judge Pickens know about this?"

"He will as soon as he reads my entry of appearance and application for admission *pro hac vice*."

Allen slid out of his chair, shaking his head. "Mister, it's not for me to tell a stranger what to do. But I think you're asking for a whole passel of trouble."

Ben nodded. "Story of my life."

"Mind you, I've got no problem with wanting to protect the environment. But those Green Rage people think it's acceptable to break the law. What's worse, they like to plant bombs. I had to go off to some special bomb school in L.A. just to get educated enough to deal with these characters." Allen fingered the rim of his hat. "I don't care nothing about their politics. But if they break the law, they're criminals. Period."

Ben could see he was unlikely to find much sympathy here. "Can I see my client?"

"Suit yourself. I got him in a private cell in the back." He unclipped his ring of keys from his belt. "Follow me."

It had been bothering Ben all night. He had never been good with names, but George Zakin was so distinctive, he knew it couldn't be a coincidence. He'd heard the name before. Unfortunately, he couldn't for the life of him remember where.

Until he saw the man's face.

"George Zakin," Ben said, thinking aloud. "Zak. Of course." He stepped into the cell and waited until the sheriff had closed the door behind him. "I represented you back in Tulsa. The chimp case. How long ago?"

"Been a good many years, counselor." Zak grinned. "Maureen told me you were coming."

"Six years," Ben murmured, still thinking backwards. "Six years if it was a day."

Zak's long black hair was pulled back in a ponytail. Looked as if it hadn't been washed in many moons. He had a scruffy beard that masked a rough complexion. His blue jeans had holes in at least three places. "You were just getting started back then."

Ben nodded his head, remembering. "I was. I didn't know what I was doing."

"Maybe not. But you got me off."

"You were up for first-degree murder that time, too."

"Yup. Strange world, ain't it?" He laughed softly. "I 'bout blew a gasket when Maureen told me who she'd lined up to handle the case. Who'da thunk?" He motioned, inviting Ben to the lower bunk, the only place to sit. "And look how far you've come. Now you're the experienced defense attorney. And a writer to boot."

"You've come a long way yourself," Ben said. "From animal rights to environmental . . . activism."

"Both worthy causes," Zak said firmly. "But I realized that the forests are the emergency cause at this juncture in history. You may have heard—I had a bit of a falling-out with Clayton Langdell and the rest of the gang in the animal rights group."

"I hadn't."

"But it worked out for the best. This is where I belong."

"In jail?"

He laughed. "No, I mean with Green Rage. These are the people who know what's really happening to the world. And they aren't afraid to do something about it."

Ben overlooked the last bit. Green Rage's tendency to "do something about it" was the part he was trying to forget. "How long have you been with the group?"

"More than three years now."

"And you're the leader?"

"Of the local chapter." Zak shrugged. "What can I say? I was born to lead."

"There must be more to it."

"I had a lot of experience from the chimp raids and whatnot that Green Rage found invaluable. Believe me, after figuring out how to break into some of those high-security research labs, spiking trees and putting sugar in Mr. Ranger's gas tank is a cinch." He leaned forward eagerly. "So you're going to take my case?"

"Only if you want me to. This isn't a mandatory assignment. You have the right to pick your own attorney. If you don't want me, just say the word and I'm out the door."

"What, are you kidding? Before, I was headed for trial with some nerd who couldn't beat a traffic ticket. Now I'm with my old buddy, the lawyer with a proven track record. This is a dream come true."

"Still, it could focus the prosecution on your prior arrest—"

"Ben, I was looking at doing twenty, thirty years in the state pen, easy. Maybe even the death penalty. Until now. I know what you can do. I've seen you do it."

"All right, then." Ben pulled out a legal pad and tried to make himself comfortable. "Why don't you tell me what happened?"

Zak spread out expansively on the other end of the cot. "I gather you know about Green Rage—what we're doing and why."

"I've got the general idea. The immediate goal is to prevent the clear-cutting of the Crescent National Forest."

"Right. The federal government and the Forest Service already sold us out. Green Rage is the last line of defense. We've been busting our chops trying to come up with some way to stop the destruction."

"Monkeywrenching?"

"You bet. Whenever and however we can. Tree spiking. Road blockades. Sugar in the carburetor. We've also tried to come up with a legal solution."

"Like what?"

"Well, the only way we could get an injunction would be if we found some endangered species that's indigenous to the forest—a species that would be threatened by the clear-cutting. You know, a snail darter or spotted owl or something."

"But you couldn't find a conveniently endangered species."

"Right. And frankly, given the current political climate, I'm not sure a snail darter would be enough to do the trick. There's too damn much money to be made out there. We need something sexy."

"Like the largest cedar tree in North America?"

"Exactly. We kept hearing rumors about the damn thing from campers and hunters, but we never could find it. And we heard other rumors that were even more exciting."

"Such as?"

Zak grinned. Ben remembered that he could be incredibly charismatic when he wanted to be. "Bigfoot."

"You're joking."

"I'm not. Haven't you read the newspaper articles?"

"I don't read those kinds of newspapers."

"Some of them have been in legitimate papers. There've been several sightings in the last few months. People come down out of the forest and swear they've seen a huge hairy manlike beast walking—or running—upright in the forest."

"That's preposterous."

"That's what I thought at first. But the stories just kept coming."

"Crackpots."

Zak laughed. "I gather you're not a student of cryptozoology."

"I don't even know what it is."

"Cryptozoology. The study of legendary or imaginary animals, and specifically the determination of whether they actually exist."

"If Bigfoot existed, he'd be in a zoo by now."

"Says you. Did you know the mountain gorilla was believed to be a mythical animal—till it was discovered and photographed by explorers? And that wasn't until the early twentieth century."

"Nonetheless, no one with half a brain is going to believe there's really a Bigfoot. Much less a federal court."

"Granted, we would need a lot of proof. But you're wrong to assume that no one sensible would believe it possible. A scientific team working out of Mount Hood has spent three years and more than half a million bucks searching for Sasquatch."

"You're joking."

"I'm not. It's called the Bigfoot Research Project. Fellow named Peter Byrne ran the whole thing. Using grant money from Boston's Academy of Applied Science. They rigged the forests with underground sensors that would detect the movements of any large creatures."

"So did they find any Bigfoots? Or should that be Bigfeet?"

Zak smirked. "No, they didn't. But their operation has given this whole Sasquatch thing a great deal more credibility."

"And this interested Green Rage?"

"You'd better believe it." Zak leaned forward, gesticulating energetically with his hands, like a storyteller spinning yarns over a campfire. "Forget the snail darter. If we could prove the forest was the habitat of Sasquatch, those loggers wouldn't stand a chance in court."

Ben's eyes narrowed. "I'm beginning to get the picture. You faked the Bigfoot sightings. You dressed up in a costume and ran around some drunken fishermen or something."

"Ben, Ben, Ben. I didn't dress up in any costume. When did you become so cynical? This isn't the Ben Kincaid I knew back in Tulsa."

"It isn't?"

"Hell, no. Back then, you were—well, if anything, a bit on the naive side. People used to joke about it, down at the courthouse. Seemed like you'd fall for anything." He folded his arms. "But at the moment I'm detecting a distinct lack of acceptance. What happened to you?"

"Everybody grows up," Ben murmured. "I've had some . . . distinctly eye-opening experiences since you saw me last. But let's get back to your story."

"Right. So anyway, we were looking for this tree, we were looking for Sasquatch. And we were trying to buy ourselves time with the usual monkey-wrenching tactics."

"Like planting lethal spikes in trees marked for cutting?"

Zak frowned. "We never spiked trees without telling the loggers."

"I know you've blown up equipment."

"What of it? Those goddamned loggers have blown up people. *People!*" He pushed himself off the bunk and began pacing in an agitated circle. "Do you know who Judi Bari is?"

Ben shook his head.

"She used to lead Earth First! She was making real strides, stopping the clear-cutting of the coast redwoods. First, the loggers ran her off the road and threatened to beat her up—while she had her little girl in the car. Then they put a bomb in her car. Blew up right beneath her. Thousands of nails were projected into her body at hundred-plus velocities. She didn't die—although at the time she wished she had—but she'll be crippled for life."

"If she was attacked, I'm sure the law enforcement people will—"

"Are you joking? They never even investigated. They said she must have planted the bomb herself."

"What?"

"You heard me. The FBI accused her of making the bomb herself. Said she left it in her car by mistake or it exploded prematurely. They never investigated other possibilities, even though she had just been assaulted a few weeks before."

"Still—that must be an extreme case."

"She's not the only one. Leroy Jackson, a militant Navajo who fought to save a sacred forest of ponderosas in the Chuska Mountains, was found dead under his pickup. Ranchers tried to push conservationist Dick Carter over a cliff in Utah. Jeff Eliott's logging-town home was burned to the ground after he joined Earth First! A bulldozer operator in Siskiyou National Forest buried five blockaders in dirt. A truck driver ran over Dave Foreman, another former leader of Earth First! Buzz Youens, an opponent of logging in the Apache National Forest, disappeared after threats on his life by loggers. His decaying body was found a year later—handcuffed to a tree. He'd been shot."

Ben stuttered. "I—hadn't heard."

"Of course you hadn't. They don't want you to hear. Face it, Ben, the news media are controlled by the big business interests that pay their bills. Every time we walk into Magic Valley, we think, 'Is this the time? Is this when the loggers get us like they did Judi? Is this the time I get blown up or beaten or burned alive?' "

"I think we're wandering a bit from our subject."

"I just want you to understand what we're up against. They have the strength, the resources. The money. And the cold-blooded willingness to use them to protect their precious bottom line." His face twisted up with disgust. "We're kids on the playground next to those butchers."

"Nonetheless, you have participated in illegal activities."

"Yeah, me and Gandhi. For a good cause. I believe what Thoreau said: 'Let your life be a counter friction to stop the machine.' And," Zak added, "I've never hurt anybody."

"Then you didn't—"

Zak looked directly into Ben's eyes. "Didn't kill that logger? Of course I didn't. Did you think I did?"

"I—" Ben coughed. "Well, I couldn't be sure until . . ."

"Ben, listen to me. I didn't kill Gardiner. I didn't bomb that tree cutter. I don't know what happened out there."

Ben listened to Zak's words and stared deeply into his eyes. He wanted to believe him. He wanted the relief, the absolution that would come from knowing this man he had put back on the streets had not committed murder. But that assurance was not coming easily.

He continued questioning. "Why do the police think you did it?"

"I'm the obvious suspect. And police love obvious suspects."

That part was true enough. "Why did they think of you?"

"I'm the leader of Green Rage. Green Rage is the group they most want to get rid of. Therefore, cut off the head—"

"There must be something more."

Zak hesitated. "I—have worked with bombs before. I know a fair amount about them. In fact, I have—" He drew in his breath. "Well, I might as well come out with it. I have a felony conviction. Conspiracy to make a destructive device."

Ben pressed his hand against his brow. "Oh, God."

"It was all trumped up. We were going to blow up some tree cutters, that's all."

Ben stood. "So when some poor logger was killed in a tree-cutter explosion—"

Zak tilted his head. "You got it. Obvious suspect."

Ben frowned. He had been reluctant to take this case in

the first place, and he was already beginning to regret it. "Did you know this logger?" He checked his notes. "Dwayne Gardiner?"

There was a moment of silence before Zak answered. Was it hesitation or was he just catching his breath? "No, I didn't know him. Why should I? I don't hang out with loggers."

"Do you have an alibi? For the time of the murder?"

Zak shook his head. "I was in the forest. Searching for that tree. Or Bigfoot."

"There's no one who can vouch for you?"

"There is. Another member of Green Rage—her name is Molly. She was with me all night long. We're—" He grinned. "I expect you can figure it out. Anyway, I'm sure she'll testify."

"Well, that's something. What else do they have on you?"

Zak shrugged. "That's all I know. You think there's more?"

"They can't be basing this prosecution solely on your prior record. I'm going to have to chat with the prosecutor. Is there anything else relevant that you haven't told me?"

"I don't think so."

"Don't just think. Be certain."

"Okay, I'm certain."

Ben leaned closer. "Listen to me, Zak. I'm your lawyer. Anything you tell me is absolutely privileged. I can't repeat it, and even if I did, no one could use it against you. But if there's more bad evidence out there—and there must be—I need to know about it. If I know the strikes against us, I can prepare for them, soften the blow. If I get blindsided, you'll just be hosed. So tell me what you know. Tell me everything."

"I have," Zak insisted. "I've told you everything. There's nothing more."

"I hope to God that's right." He started gathering up his belongings. "I'll be in touch."

"Ben." Zak grabbed his arm, brought him back around till they were face-to-face. "Ben, I did not kill that man. I'm telling the truth. I had nothing to do with it."

Ben stared back at him. He had rarely seen such an earnest expression in his life. How could he not believe him? "All right then. I'll do everything I can to help you. Let me get to work."

Zak released his arm. "I really appreciate this, Ben. Really." His wide-eyed grin returned. "Hell, I haven't felt this good since I was arrested. I'm back in the hands of Ben Kincaid. Hallelujah! The man who saved me once will do it again. I know you will. Hell, if it hadn't been for you, I wouldn't be standing here now!"

Yes, Ben realized, that was absolutely the truth. If Ben hadn't gotten him off the last time he was charged with murder . . .

But, Ben thought, as the sheriff opened the cell door, there were some things he preferred not to dwell upon.

* 10 *

Ben wandered around the Magic Valley county courthouse for a full fifteen minutes before he finally acknowledged that he was not going to find the district attorney's office on his own. Although it went against every male bone in his body, he relented, went against instinct, and asked for directions.

The D.A.'s office was in the basement, as it turned out—not exactly the first place you would look. Once he stepped through the double glass doors, though, he recognized all the advantages of the location. It was private and quiet—much more so than the rest of the courthouse, which was playing host to a dozen different civic functions at once. Even better, the space was expansive—more than sufficient to provide adequate room for the staff and spacious offices for those at the top of the totem pole.

And the face at the very top of the totem pole was Granny's. If Ben didn't know it before, he certainly knew it when he saw her office—more than twice the size of any of the others, decorated in an upscale, high-gloss style that would have fit nicely into any of the many Tulsa law firm offices Ben had visited.

"So you're taking on the Gardiner case." Granville Adams—Granny, at least to her friends—slid out of the chair behind her desk. She was not tall, but what she lacked in height she made up in bearing. Ben had rarely met anyone who so immediately impressed him with such self-confidence. She walked right up to him—closer than most would, intentionally violating his personal space. The fact that she was devastatingly, almost aggressively attractive made the intrusion all the more difficult to ignore.

"Word travels fast in a small town."

Her lips turned up, something between a grin and a smirk. "Word travels to me, anyway. There's not much goes on around here I don't know about."

Ben didn't doubt it for a minute. "I came by to see what you could tell me about the Gardiner murder."

She arched an eyebrow. "And what makes you think I would be inclined to tell you anything?"

"Oh, I don't know. The United States Constitution, maybe?"

Again with the smile/smirk. "If you're asking for any potentially exculpatory evidence in the prosecution's possession, I'll provide it at our earliest convenience. If you're asking me to explain the prosecution case to you, forget it."

So, Ben thought, she was going to be one of *those* prosecutors. Why was he not surprised? "I'd like that evidence as soon as possible. And all your exhibits. And a list of witnesses you intend to call at trial."

"I'll do what I can. But no promises. We're very busy."

"That's not good enough. I've already missed the preliminary hearing. The case is set for trial. I barely have time to make the essential motions. I certainly don't have time to mud-wrestle you over fundamental discovery issues."

"Mud-wrestling, huh?" Her golden eyebrows danced just beyond Ben's nose. "Sounds kinky."

Ben swallowed. What was it the sheriff had compared her to? A black widow? "If you don't comply, I'll be in the judge's office first thing in the morning making motions for sanctions. And a continuance."

She held up her hands. "Calm down, calm down. No need to use those big-city tactics on me. I'm just a small-time country prosecutor, remember?"

Yeah right, Ben thought. And Lucretia Borgia was just a bad cook.

"Take a seat, Kincaid. Let's talk turkey." She pointed toward a plush cushioned seat and positioned herself behind her desk. "I know you're not from around here. What's your interest in this case, anyway?"

"I don't have one," Ben answered. "I'm just a lawyer representing a client."

"Your newfound friends aren't very popular around here; I hope you know that. Those yellow ribbons are in the windows for a reason. Once people find out you're with Green Rage, you'll be a pariah, too. I doubt if Emma will let you stay at her place any longer."

Ben tried not to react. She knew where he was staying. "I've been invited to stay at the Green Rage camp."

She twisted her neck. "Don't think I'd recommend that, Kincaid. That campsite has been hit twice already, and I suspect the next attack is just a hairbreadth away."

"Attack? By whom?"

"Don't know. If I did, I'd file charges against them, wouldn't I?"

"So you make it a point not to know."

Her face turned stern. "Are you accusing me of something, Kincaid?"

"No." Not yet, anyway. "Well, I appreciate your concern, but I'll be fine. I probably need to stay in town. I'm sure I can find someplace."

"You know you're not going to make any money off this case, don't you? Those tree-hugging hippies don't have much cash. What little they do have, they spend on bomb ingredients."

"Maybe I just need the practice."

"Or maybe you don't care about money, 'cause you've got a rich mommy back in Oklahoma."

Ben's eyebrows knitted together. "How do you know—"

"What do you take me for, Kincaid—some rank amateur? I may not live in a big city like you, but don't mistake me for a rube or you'll be very, very sorry." Her face relaxed. "I had you checked out the second I heard you were taking the case. It's all part of the game."

"The game? Sounds more like invasion of privacy to me."

She dismissed his remark with a wave of the hand. "Do you know anything about the logging industry, Kincaid?"

"I know they cut down a lot of trees."

She leaned back in her chair, pushing her feet against her desk. The hem of her already short skirt slipped up her thighs. "They do a hell of a lot more than that. The logging industry made this town. Without logging, Magic Valley wouldn't exist."

"You mean this area would all just be a huge, untouched, virgin forest? That'd be a shame."

"What I mean is, there'd be several thousand people with no way to make a living. Once upon a time, this area was one of the most poverty-stricken, economically depressed parts of the country. Starvation and malnutrition were rampant. Logging changed all that."

"I really don't see what this has to do—"

"Everyone who lives here is indebted to the logging industry. Everyone. It's our lifeblood. It runs through our veins." She sat upright. "So you can imagine how we feel when a pack of would-be anarchists who don't even live around here stroll into town and start spiking trees and blowing up equipment, trying to shut the logging operations down. From our perspective they're like vampires."

"I really don't see the connection with the Gardiner case."

She shrugged. "You've chosen sides, Kincaid."

"All I've done is—"

"You may not realize it yet, but you've made your choice. A very dangerous one. And I suspect you've done it because you're basically a good-hearted person who's only heard one side of the story."

"I'm here to try a lawsuit. Not to get involved in local politics."

"Let me do you a favor, Kincaid." She scribbled an address on her notepad. "My father has worked for WLE Logging all his life. He's one of the top foremen at their sawmill just north of here. I'll tell him you want to make a visit."

"That's not nece—"

"I think it is. You need some perspective. After all, you're an officer of the court. And you've aligned yourself with people who are avowed lawbreakers."

Ben bristled. "If they break the law, it's for a reason. In the great American tradition of civil disobedience."

"As best I recall, Thoreau never blew anyone up." She tore the top sheet off her notepad. "Look, if you're going to jump into the boiling cauldron, you ought to at least have some clue what's cooking." She handed the address to him.

Ben reluctantly took the piece of paper. "Could we possibly talk about the case now?"

Granny grinned, damn near irresistibly, Ben thought. "What do you want to know?"

"Why did you arrest my client for this murder?"

"Because he did it."

"Could you give me a little more?"

"He had motive, means, and opportunity. Call me simple-minded, but I think that's enough to bring charges."

"The motive, I assume, would be Zak's hostility toward the loggers and the logging industry at large."

She did not quite look him in the eye. "At the very least. And he certainly had the means. Those Green Rage nuts make no secret of the fact that they're stockpiling bomb components. To the contrary, they advertise the fact to terrorize the loggers. Every time I turn around they've torched another tree cutter or eighteen-wheeler. Those people are insane."

"It isn't insane to want to keep the forests from being flattened."

"Oh, yeah? And how about dressing up in a Sasquatch suit?"

Ben reddened a bit. "I don't know that the Sasquatch sightings had anything to do with Green Rage. For all I know, it could be a logger plot to make Green Rage look ridiculous."

Granny leaned back and laughed. "Yeah, right."

Ben tried to bring the conversation back to the case. "What about opportunity?"

"In case you don't know it, your man admits he was in the forest around the time of the murder, although he says he was just smooching with some Green Rage floozy. I agree that he was in the woods—planting the bomb that killed Dwayne Gardiner."

"Even if Zak planted a bomb on the tree cutter, and Gardiner had the misfortune to set it off, that wouldn't be first-degree murder. It's just bad luck that Gardiner was around when the bomb went off."

"I disagree with you. First of all, planting bombs is a felony, and if someone gets killed in the perpetration of a felony, he can be charged with felony murder, which is a first-degree murder charge in this state. But it doesn't matter." She paused, allowing Ben to wonder for just a moment. "Because the autopsy report showed that Gardiner had been shot."

"What? But I thought—"

"Yes, the body was caught in the explosion and burned. We almost didn't do an autopsy, especially since the fire didn't leave much to be examined. But being the dutiful soldiers we are, we did the tests. And it turned out the man had been shot."

"Then he was already dead."

"We don't think so. The gunshot appears to have caught the poor man in the shoulder. I'm sure it hurt like hell, but it wasn't fatal. It was the explosion that killed him. Nonetheless, the fact that he had been shot just before the explosion tells me there was a second person present—a second person with the express, premeditated intent to kill him." She folded her hands on the desk. "And that, Charlie Brown, is why Zakin has been charged with first-degree murder."

Ben couldn't argue with her logic. He would've drawn the same conclusions himself. "Anything else linking Zak to the murder?"

"Tons. Footprints. Fingerprints. You name it." She leaned forward. "Seriously, Ben—and I'm just talking lawyer-to-lawyer now—I don't want to jinx your good deed for the day, but you're gonna lose this case. We've got that murderous zealot dead to rights. And let me tell you, when the sentence comes down, it's not going to be pretty. Judge Perkins has a reputation."

"I've heard."

"Then you know he won't let Zakin off with a life sentence. That boy's gonna fry."

Ben squirmed in his seat. "Appreciate your sensitivity."

"With all due respect, Ben, the smartest thing you could do is drive your rental car back to the airport and get the hell out of here. This town is on edge. Everyone's afraid Green Rage will succeed in closing down the logging and they'll all be out of jobs. Plus we've got a drug problem like we've never had before. One of those new designer drugs—about ten times more potent than crack—is all over town. We call it Venom because it's deadly poison to the people who use it. Screws up their head. Tears them apart."

"And this just happened?"

"In the last few months. It came out of nowhere, and the next thing we knew it was everywhere."

"I'm sure that's—"

"The point is, Magic Valley is a tinderbox, Kincaid, and you don't want to be caught in the middle when the explosion comes."

Ben pushed himself out of his chair. "I will expect you to send me any exculpatory evidence. And all your exhibits. And your witness list."

She sighed. "You'll get it. You'll get it." She slid out from behind her desk and sashayed across the office till she was standing even closer to him than before. "And then maybe, when this unpleasant mess is all over, you and I can relate to one another on a more . . . personal basis."

Ben coughed. "What do you—"

She leaned closer. "Like I said, I've done some checking on you, Mr. Kincaid. You're an impressive individual." She touched his shirt, only for an instant, but more than long enough to send an electric charge coursing through Ben's body. "I'd like to get to know you better."

Ben took a step backward, bumping into the chair. "I'd better go," he said, trying hard to modulate his voice. "I've got a lot of work to do."

As he passed through the door, he caught a last fleeting glimpse of her, a look of sly amusement on her face, wiggling her fingers. "Stay in touch."

* 11 *

Compared to the expansive layout of the district attorney's spread, the public defender's office was a hole-in-the-wall in a separate building half a mile from the courthouse. Ben supposed he should be pleased that a town this small even had a public defender's office, but he couldn't help wondering how an operation this size could possibly do battle against an operation like the one he had just visited.

The outer office was just as small as he had imagined it would be—four desks crowded together in a room probably intended for one. Everyone was so busy they didn't even look up when he entered.

Ben approached the desk closest to the door, where a woman in her mid-thirties was attempting to organize pleadings in an oversized black notebook. He cleared his throat. "I'm looking for a woman named Christina McCall."

The woman gazed blankly at him.

"She's about so high"—he held his hand maybe four feet off the ground—"with lots of curly red hair—"

"Ah. She's in the room in the back. The sucker's office."

"The, uh—excuse me?"

Her eyes had already returned to the pleadings. "This is a small office, as you may have noticed. Us four girls are all administrative. We don't actually have any lawyers on staff. Can't afford them. Judge Pickens appoints lawyers as necessary. We call 'em the suckers."

Ben's chin raised. "And so the room in the back—"

"They usually need a place to review files and prep and whatnot. 'Fraid that's the best we have to offer."

"They work in this cubbyhole all through the trial?"

"Trial? I suppose they would." She leaned toward the woman at the desk closest to her. "Imogene, when was the last time one of the suckers actually took a case to trial?"

Imogene thought for a moment. "Been three years now. Stanley Boxleiter. Convenience store holdup. He got creamed."

The woman glanced back at Ben. "There you have it."

Ben frowned. "I get the impression this office doesn't have a tremendous win-loss record."

"What can you expect from conscripted defense lawyers? Some of 'em aren't even familiar with criminal law. They take any plea bargain that's offered." She snapped the binders shut on the black notebook and closed it. "But the real reason is Judge Pickens. The Time Machine. He's . . . how shall I say it? A strong believer in law and order."

"Favors the prosecution?"

"That would be one way of putting it. At any rate, he's never had any problem listening to Granny talk. I've seen some poor suckers who never managed to finish a sentence." Her hand suddenly moved to her mouth. "Omigosh. You must be that fellow from out of town who's representing the terrorist?"

Yes, Ben thought, I'm the *sucker* who got that case.

Her eyes lowered. "You may want to consider a change of attire, at least when you go into court."

"What, I should wear a football helmet?"

"I was thinking more like a bulletproof vest."

Ben weaved through the crowded desks and found the closed door in the back. He pushed it open and stepped inside . . .

. . . and three steps later, his nose was pressed against the opposite wall.

"Welcome to Chateau Kincaid. Kinda cozy, huh?"

Christina sat behind the desk by the north wall. It was a small desk, but it was the only desk that could possibly fit in this tiny office.

"This is where we're supposed to work?" Ben asked. "This is impossible."

"You're being negative. Don't think impossible. Think . . . challenging. Quaint. Intimate."

"No one needs to be this intimate. My jail cell was larger."

"If you'd like, I could revoke your bail."

"Very funny." Ben took a folding chair that was leaning against the wall, unfolded it, and sat. "Christina, you know I'm not accustomed to a plush workspace, but this is ridiculous."

"Maybe so, but it's all we've got. Our client can't afford to rent office space for us, and last I looked our firm coffers weren't overflowing either. It's going to have to do."

"Swell." Ben crossed his legs and tried to pretend he was comfortable. "What have you managed to find out?"

"Nothing you probably don't already know. But I haven't had a chance to read the files yet. I will. The murder occurred on July thirteenth. The victim, Dwayne Gardiner, was shot. Soon after, he was caught in the explosion of a huge piece of logging equipment, a tree cutter. He burned to death."

"Any witnesses?"

"None have turned up. The case against our client is based on his hostility toward loggers and his known proclivity for torching logging equipment, although I have a hunch there might be some forensic evidence pointing toward him as well."

"There must be," Ben said. "There wouldn't be a case otherwise."

"My thinking exactly. And we have to anticipate that there may be other connections as well. Our client has been in town for at least six months now, since the injunction fell and WLE Logging started building roads to get into the old-growth forest. It's entirely possible Zakin knew the victim or had some other tangential connection."

"I've talked to Zak. He says he didn't know the guy."

"Really? Well, the prosecution must have something."

"Agreed. We have to figure out what it is." He paused, relishing the pleasure of dropping a bombshell he knew and she didn't. "By the way, Zakin is a former client of ours."

"Right. The Chesterson Chimp case."

"You remembered?"

She looked at him incredulously. "Of course I did. I knew who he was the instant I heard his name. How many George Zakins did you think there could be?"

"I can't remember the name of every client."

"I can remember that one. So how is he?"

"Oh, about the same. He's changed location and cause, but that's about it."

"I remember we believed he didn't kill the research doctor in the Chesterson case. What about here?"

"He says he didn't do it. And I think he's telling the truth."

"You're a horrible judge of character."

"Don't remind me." Ben glanced down at the desk, which was covered with file folders on all but one corner, which held the telephone—a big black old-style phone with a dial.

"Is the phone connected?"

"It is," Christina replied. "Unfortunately, there's no budget for phone calls."

"Meaning?"

"It's your nickel." She picked up the receiver and handed it to him. "Wanna phone home?"

"Right." Ben took the receiver and dialed his office in Tulsa.

Someone picked up on the seventh ring. "Ben Kincaid Law Office."

"Hey, Jones, stop messing around on the Internet and get to work."

"Boss!" Ben heard some clicking noises on the other end that sounded suspiciously like a modem switching off. "How did you know?"

"Lucky guess. Is Loving there?"

"I'll put him on."

Ben heard some garbled shouting in the background. A few moments later, someone picked up an extension phone. "Skipper, is that you?"

"It's me, Loving."

"How're ya doin'? How's the book tour? I kept tellin' Jones you'd call soon. It's not that he's forgotten about us, I told him. It's just that he doesn't have time, what with fending off autograph hounds and appearing on talk shows. Right?"

"You hit the nail on the head."

"Where are you?"

"In Washington State. Tiny place called Magic Valley."

"So you're making time for the little people, too. I think that's great."

"Look, both of you—there's been a surprising development. I've taken a case up here."

"You have?" Jones said. "What a hustler you are, Boss. What kind of case?"

"Murder. First degree. Anyway, Jones, I need some research, and I need it quick. We've already missed the preliminary hearing."

"Say no more, Boss. I'm on it." He hesitated a moment. "Can I, uh, do it from here?"

"With the Internet and fax machines, I don't suppose it much matters where you are. Got some pressing engagements?"

Loving made a deep chortling noise. "He doesn't have any engagements. He just doesn't wanna leave his sweet patootie."

"She is *not* my sweet patootie!" Jones barked.

Ben smiled. "So, Jones, you and Paula are still going hot and heavy?"

"Well, they're still going," Loving said. "I doubt if it's very hot."

"Butt out, buster!" Jones fired back. "I'll have you know we are very hot."

"Uh-huh."

"We're like spontaneous combustion. Steam practically rises every time we—oh, why am I telling you this, anyway?"

"My sentiments exactly," Ben said. "Could we steer this conversation back to the matter at hand? I'm also going to need an investigator."

"Say no more, Skipper," Loving said. "I'm on the first plane out."

"You're sure you don't mind?"

"Of course not. I haven't let some librarian wrap a ball and chain around me."

"Loving," Jones barked, "you're a sexist cretin."

"Jones," Ben interjected, "could you drop by my apartment after work this evening and pass the word along to Joni?

She's keeping an eye on my cat and Mrs. Marmelstein. Tell her I'm sorry, but I'm going to be gone a little longer than I anticipated."

"Will do, Boss."

Loving guffawed. "If Paula will let him out of her sight long enough."

"Loving!"

"Well, boys," Ben said, "it's been a real, um, pleasure talking to you. Christina will fax you the details on the case. Stay in touch." He hung up.

"Everything status quo back home?" Christina asked.

"Totally," Ben said. "A little too much so, actually."

Christina pushed out from behind the desk. "Well, I have tons of work to do, and so do you. But we're not going to get it done tonight. Maureen wants us to come to the Green Rage camp."

"Why? I told her I'm not going to do anything—"

Christina held up her hands. "She's not expecting you to torch any heavy equipment. She just wants the rest of the group to meet you. She wants their approval of your involvement."

"Approval? Why?"

"I gather they're a little guarded about who they let in the organization."

"What, they're afraid I might learn the secret handshake?"

"No, they're afraid of FBI agents and logging company spies."

"Look, I'm not joining Green Rage. I'm just acting as defense counsel."

"Just the same, the location of their camp is secret. They're going to pick us up, blindfold us, and take us out there."

"*Blindfold* us? Christina, are you thinking maybe taking this case wasn't the brightest thing I ever did?"

She laid her hand on his shoulder. "Don't worry about it, Ben. I'm used to it."

* 12 *

Rick showed up at the appointed time—with the blindfolds. After a token effort at talking him out of the cloak-and-dagger routine, Ben and Christina submitted. As far as Ben was concerned, this was taking security measures way over the top, but Rick insisted.

The blindfolds were thick and black, perfect for keeping out all traces of light and clinging close to the face, eliminating that peephole down the line of the nose available with most blindfolds. Once they were securely vision impaired, Rick loaded them into the backseat of his Jeep. At least Ben assumed it was his Jeep. It could've been a San Francisco trolley car for all he could tell.

At first Ben attempted to keep track of the directions—first a right turn, then a left, drive for about a mile . . . but it was pointless. After ten minutes, he was hopelessly confused, and he'd been told it would be a good half hour before they arrived at the Green Rage camp. He couldn't retrace their trail even if he wanted to. And honestly, why would he want to? If they didn't want him there, he didn't want to be there.

After fifteen minutes or so (he couldn't see his watch), Ben sensed they were entering a different environment. He couldn't explain exactly how he knew, but he knew. A difference in the climate, perhaps, but it was more than just temperature. There was something about the air itself—the thickness, the crispness. The smell. And the sounds—

"We've entered the forest," Rick said. His voice came from the front of the Jeep, whipped back like the wind rushing in Ben's face. "Another fifteen minutes or so and we'll be at the camp."

"I thought so," Ben said. "Everything seemed different somehow."

"You've entered a different world," Rick answered. "You've left behind the artificial world of the city—concrete, smog, Burger King. You've entered the forest primeval—pure, natural, untouched. At least for the time being."

Ben and Christina sat in silence as they rode the rest of the way. Time seemed to pass more slowly. Ben paid more attention; he soaked in the sweet scent of pine, the musty smell of the earth.

Eventually Rick brought the Jeep to a stop. As the engine died, Ben could hear the soft play of voices, not far away. And a million other sounds as well: birds singing, the wind whistling through the trees, the chirp of the crickets, the mournful cry of the hoot owl.

"We've arrived."

Ben felt the rise of his seat as Rick jumped out of the front. He felt fingers brushing against his face, and an instant later, he could see again.

Ben stepped off the Jeep and did a full circle, absorbing his new surroundings. The sun was setting, but he could still see clearly. It was green everywhere he looked, green and more green. They were surrounded by an enclosure of trees, tall pines that stretched up to infinity—or at any rate a good deal higher than Ben could see.

A row of small blue nylon tents nestled just inside the clearing. A stone circle told Ben where the campfire had been and would likely be again. There were a few boxes, shirts, plates, and other signs of humanity strewn about, but not many. It appeared to Ben that they had made a genuine effort to leave the area undisturbed.

"So this is the big secret terrorist camp?" Christina said. "How disappointing. I was expecting something out of a James Bond movie."

Rick laughed. "We like to keep things simple. All we need is a base of operation, a place to stow our gear. Creature comforts we leave for someone else. Besides, it's important that we be able to pack up and move at the drop of a hat. The logging company has people searching for us at all hours of the day. And that's in addition to whatever Slade and the Cabal might be doing."

The Cabal, Ben thought. Zak had told him about that, but he had suspected it might just be a fairy tale Zak cooked up to make his situation seem more dramatic. Or just a paranoid fantasy. Well, if it was, it was a shared fantasy.

"Let me introduce you to some of the rest of the group." Ben saw people emerging from the edge of the forest or out of tents.

"You've met Maureen, of course." Ben nodded in Maureen's general direction. She looked just the same as before. It was possible she'd changed to a different flannel shirt, but he couldn't be sure.

"Of course," Ben said. "One never forgets one's cellmates."

"She's our communications expert. Everything from ham radios to e-mail."

Rick continued moving down the line. "And here's another distaff member of the Green Rage team. Deirdre Oliphant. Excuse me, *Dr.* Deirdre Oliphant."

Ben shook her hand. "A medical doctor?"

She shook her head. "A scientist." If so, Ben thought she was about as unscientist-looking as anyone he had met in his life. She had long silky blonde hair and a tall hourglass figure that could easily have graced the cover of a fashion magazine. "I'm a dendrochronologist," she explained.

"Oh," Ben said. "Wonderful." He shot a quick glance at Christina. "Should I pretend I know what that means?"

Deirdre laughed. "It's really very simple. I study trees. My speciality is determining their ages."

Christina nodded. "Counting their rings and all that?"

"Exactly. Except that it's a little more complicated than that, especially with the older trees. We have to use other techniques, like extracting core samples, to date trees without cutting them down."

"Is this speciality greatly in demand?" Ben asked.

"It is with us," Maureen interjected. "It's crucial to our work. We can occasionally get government support for preserving old-growth trees."

"You wouldn't believe how old some of these trees are,"

Deirdre explained. "Beyond these pines is a dense forest of cedars that go back hundreds of years. Of course, there are redwoods in California that go back thousands of years, but for cedars, five hundred years is awesome. Can you imagine? These trees were here when Beethoven was taking piano lessons."

"Impressive."

"My holy grail is to find a cedar larger than the current recordholder in Forks, a town a few hours south of here. If I can find that, it could save the forest."

Ben gazed about, awed by the thought of the living history all around him. It went back to what he was feeling before. Even though he couldn't explain it, he had a sense of tranquility, of timelessness. Of constancy through the ages.

"The next fellow in line," Rick continued, "the one doing the Santa Claus impression, is Doc Potter. I think we mentioned him before. He's our medic and the senior member of the team."

Ben shook hands with the gentleman, who sported a bushy snow-white beard. Ben guessed him to be in his mid-fifties, considerably older than the rest of the group.

"I'd like to think people whose only goal is preserving forests wouldn't need a medic," Doc said. He had an open, avuncular manner that Ben liked immediately. "But experience has proven that we do. This is the seventh Green Rage team I've been part of."

"It must be exciting work," Christina said.

"Yes, it's exciting." He glanced at his compatriots. "Sometimes it's a wee bit too exciting. You may have heard about the incident in Oregon a few years back. Loggers came in the night, grabbed some environmentalists, dragged them out of their tents. Beat them up pretty badly. And by the time they got to a hospital, one of them had bled to death. Since then, we've always had a medic with every away team."

"Sounds like what you need is a pack of thugs or attack dogs."

"Don't think we haven't considered it," Rick said. "Unfortunately, we couldn't keep dogs out here. And Slade has all the thugs." He took another step down the line. "Let me make a couple more introductions, then we'll give you a rest. This is the lovely Molly Evans."

Ben thought Rick's manner altered as he came into Molly's presence, although he would be pressed to explain just how. Molly had short bobbed brown hair and a clean honest look. Which pleased him since, if he recalled correctly, she was going to be his ace alibi witness. "You were out in the forest with Zak the night of the murder."

Molly's round brown eyes glanced quickly at Rick, then back to Ben. "That's right. I was with him. We were . . . um, talking."

"That's fine," Ben said, smiling. No need to embarrass her now. They could get into the details later. "And you're willing to testify?"

"Can't say that I'm looking forward to it," she said honestly enough, "but I feel I have an obligation to Zak."

"I understand," Ben answered. "And I appreciate it."

Rick nudged Ben to the end of the line. "This is our resident radical, Al Billings."

Ben shook hands with the robust man sporting the red beard and earring. "I thought Zak was the resident radical."

Rick laughed. "Zak believes in monkey-wrenching logging equipment. Al here favors targeted nuclear bombing."

"That *is* radical."

Al grinned, toothy and earnest. Ben had the impression he had heard Rick's teasing before and had learned to be good-natured about it. "Rick exaggerates a bit. But the fact is, WLE and Slade and the Cabal aren't pulling any punches, so why should we?"

"If you try anything too extreme, public sentiment will turn against you," Ben said.

"Hasn't that already happened? All our tactics to date have been kindergarten stuff, just pranks—but we've already been painted black as night by the loggers and the media. I say it's time we did something to deserve our reputation."

"Al is a little high-strung," Rick explained, "but he makes dynamite gumbo, which is the real reason we keep him around."

"Have I met all the leaders of the group?" Ben asked.

"Just about," Rick answered. "All but—" Rick stopped short. Ben saw Maureen shoot him a stern look. "I mean, that's all."

"Rick," Ben said, "you guys are going to have to level with me."

"You have met all the current leaders," Maureen explained. "What Rick is stumbling around is that one of our leaders left, just a few days ago. Her name was Kelly. Kelly Cartwright."

"Why did she leave?"

"Oh, it's too complicated to explain. And it's all political. Nothing to do with this case."

Is that right? Ben wondered. Then why didn't you want Rick to tell me about her? "Where is she now?"

"I don't know exactly. I heard she joined some kind of camp in Oregon. I could probably track down an address if it's really important to you."

Al interrupted. "Rick, we need to talk." He glanced at Maureen. "About the woman. She's here. I've got her in a tent."

"Later." Rick guided Ben and Christina toward the campfire. He pointed toward the nearest boulder and suggested that Ben sit down. Not exactly a recliner, Ben thought, but he could probably get used to it.

The rest of the group joined him around the campfire. Maureen took the lead in the conversation. "As most of you already know, the new kid in town is Ben Kincaid. He's a lawyer, a right-minded activist, not to mention a distinguished published author, and he's agreed to represent Zak in this upcoming trial. He's represented Zak before; they have some history. He's also considering doing some writing about our group and the efforts we're making to prevent this whole forest from being leveled. I want every one of you to give him your utmost cooperation. Anything he needs, he gets."

"Is he one of us?" The question came from Al, who was seated on the other side of the campfire.

"I'm not sure what you mean."

"Has he joined Green Rage? Is he standing with us or is he on the outside looking in?"

"I haven't joined Green Rage," Ben answered. "I'm sympathetic to the cause. But that's really irrelevant to my work as a lawyer. I don't have to agree with everything my client believes to represent him."

Al threw down his cowboy hat. "Man, that's just not good enough."

Maureen cut in. "Al, listen for a minute."

"I'm listening, Maureen, but I don't like what I hear. There's no way I'm going to spill my soul to someone I don't know who isn't even in the group. For all I know, he could be a Cabal plant. Or a Freddie."

Ben glanced up at Maureen. "Freddie?"

"Forest ranger. It's a nickname." She glanced over at Al, who was on his feet and pacing. "Not a very flattering one."

"Aren't the rangers on your side?" Ben asked.

"You'd think so, wouldn't you? But no, the rangers side with the loggers almost every time. They're part of the establishment. Do you realize that fifty percent of the clear-cutting in this country is taking place on national park land? True. The government is selling the country out from under us. And the rangers are being paid to go along with the sellout." She looked back at Al. "Look, it's this simple. Do you want Zak to go to prison? Or worse?"

Al pursed his lips together. "No."

"Then cooperate with Ben. We've checked him out, and we think we're damn lucky to have him. More important, we think he's just about Zak's only hope of beating this trumped-up charge. We have to do everything we can to help him."

"You can do whatever you want to do," Al said. "It ain't gonna help."

"And just what is that supposed to mean?"

"I mean, Zak's got his dick in a ringer and he ain't never gonna get it out." There was a chorus of groans and disapproval. "You clowns are just kidding yourself. We all know what's really going down here. Why are we afraid to say it?"

"I'd like to know," Ben interjected. "What's really going down here?"

"It's the Cabal, man. They set this whole thing up. They'd do anything to get us out of the forest. They killed that logger and they framed Zak."

Ben arched an eyebrow. "I see. It's all a conspiracy."

"Don't patronize me, man. I don't have to put up with that." He took a step toward Ben, but a sharp look from Maureen stopped him in his tracks. "I'm not talking about alien abductions here. But it is a fact that the logging companies have poured a ton of money into stopping us and other groups like us. The Cabal has more operating cash than they know what to do with. Framing Zak would be a piece of cake for them. Put some money in the right hands, plant a little false evidence, and presto! Zak's on his way to Death Row."

Christina edged into the conversation. "But why would they go after Zak?"

"He's been the driving force of this group since he joined, and they know that. Cut off the head, and the body withers." He paused for breath. "Same reason the Mob killed Jack Kennedy."

"Sit down, Al." Maureen's directive was echoed by several other groans and *oh, mans*. "This isn't getting us anywhere."

"I'd like to talk to each of you," Ben said. "I'd like to know everything you know, everything there is to know about Zak. Who was with him the day of the murder, who saw him where. Did he ever talk about the loggers, the victim, planting explosives."

"Zak talked about explosives every day of his life," Doc said. "It's what he did. More than once I had to treat him for a burn because he spilled some chemical or another on himself."

"Of course," Deirdre suggested, "that could be exactly why the Cabal would use that M.O. to kill the logger. The use of a bomb guaranteed the cops would come looking for Zak."

"All this speculation is getting us nowhere," Ben said. "I need to know the facts. Who knew Zak best?"

Ben noticed several false starts before Maureen finally spoke. "We all knew him, Ben. Intimately."

Al swallowed a smile. "Yeah. Especially the women."

Molly shot him a killing look.

Doc chimed in. "What about you, Deirdre? You knew Zak rather well, didn't you?"

Deirdre flushed. "Zak and I spent a lot of time . . . talking."

Ben saw Al cover his mouth, as if he was about to burst out laughing.

"I don't know if you know this yet," Deirdre continued, "but Zak has an enormous brain. He was always asking questions, helping me date trees, trying to learn something new. He was very interested in my work."

Al's laughter finally burst out explosively. "The only thing he was interested in was getting into your pants!"

"Al!" Maureen's eyes were like lasers cutting across the camp. "If you can't be helpful, maybe you should go for a walk. Preferably over a cliff."

"All right, all right." He waved his hand at her. "I know when I ain't wanted, man." He ambled over into the forest and in a matter of moments had disappeared.

"Zak isn't the only subject I need to know about," Ben explained. "I want to know everything there is to know—everything that's factual—about this so-called Cabal you all seem so paranoid about."

"The Cabal is hell on wheels," Rick muttered. "And its leader, Slade, is the fuckin' Prince of Darkness."

That again. "Did you get that, Christina? Prince of Darkness."

She nodded. "Do we have subpoena power over a foreign potentate?"

Ben smiled. "If you people want me to believe there's some gigantic high-powered conspiracy out to get you, you're going to have to work a lot harder. Why would anyone want to do this?"

Maureen looked at Ben squarely. "In a word, money."

"The conspiracy you're describing sounds like it would be expensive, not profitable."

"You have to understand the big picture. Ben, what do you think is the main purpose of our monkey-wrenching activities?"

He shrugged. "I assume you're trying to scare people off. Threaten the loggers with their lives."

"Wrong. That's the way the media plays it, that's the line the logging conglomerates feed them, but that isn't the truth. We take every possible precaution to make sure no one is hurt by our activities, and so far we've been successful. Monkey-wrenching is about money."

"I'm afraid I don't get it."

"Let's take tree spiking, for example. Tree spiking is not about trying to hurt loggers. Tree spiking is something we do when we hear that another expanse of old-growth forest is about to be sold for logging. Basically, we hammer a nail or some other large piece of metal into a tree. We then warn the Forest Service or the timber company bidding on the sale or both. At that point, if the Forest Service still wants to sell the forest, they have to send a crew out with metal detectors and crowbars to remove the spikes. It's a lot of trouble and expensive. In many cases, the Forest Service simply cancels the sale. If they do proceed, many logging companies will not bid, because they know that if a spike runs through their lumber-mill, it could damage the blade of the saw and cost them thousands of dollars. Toss in some sabotaged tree cutters or haul trucks, and before long the profit margins start shrinking. And since profits are the raison d'être of big corporations, the trees don't get cut. Not because the loggers have decided to perform a service for humanity, but because our efforts have simply made it too expensive."

"But tree spiking still creates a danger that someone will be hurt."

"We always discourage spiking trees at low levels, where it could strike a chain saw and hurt a logger. We spike up higher than they can reach."

"Wait a minute," Christina said. "I remember hearing about some logger who got hurt by a spiked tree."

"But do you know what actually happened?"

"Well . . ."

"Here's the facts. In 1987, a band saw in a Cloverdale, California, mill struck an eleven-inch spike and shattered, sending pieces of blade flying across the room. One section hit a logger named George Alexander and broke his jaw. Instantly, the media jumped on the bandwagon denouncing eco-terrorists without doing the least investigation of the bill of goods they were being sold by the logging corporation. The truth is, that band saw shouldn't have shattered like that just because it hit a spike. It was cracked, wobbly, and due for replacement, but it hadn't been replaced because the company didn't want to spend the money. Alexander himself said he almost didn't go to work that day—because he was concerned about the dangerous condition of the band saw, which he had been complaining about for weeks."

"Still, if the environmentalists hadn't spiked the tree—"

"But did they? The spike was not in an old-growth tree. It came from a nonwilderness tract. There were no environmental groups protesting the harvesting of those trees. The protest came from local area residents, who were concerned about the noise, truck traffic, and erosion damage the logging was causing. Weeks after the incident, the police admitted their chief suspect was a local conservative Republican in his mid-fifties who owned property near the logging site. And the logging company later admitted they had received warnings and threats—from local residents. Of course, none of that was reported in the press."

"It's hard to imagine someone other than an eco-group spiking trees," Christina said.

"Excuse me," Rick said, jumping in, "but who do you think invented tree spiking? Loggers, that's who. Loggers invented it around the turn of the century during the labor wars with the big logging companies here in the Pacific Northwest. We just borrowed a trick from their toolbox." He paused. "Look, I wish we could get our work done with hugs and kisses, too, but at some point you've gotta face facts. It's like B. Traven said: 'This is the real world, muchachos, and you are in it.' "

"We're getting off the subject again," Ben said. "If anyone knows of anything that might help Zak or might possibly be relevant to the trial, please come tell me."

"We will," Maureen said, speaking for all of them. "Anything else we can do for you?"

"Yes. Stay out of trouble."

"What's that supposed to mean?"

"I think you know. No spiking, exploding, or any other illegal activities until this trial is over."

"Are you saying we should turn the forest over to the loggers? Maybe just roll out a red carpet?"

"I'm saying that jurors are influenced by pretrial publicity, okay? Even the most fair-minded soul can't help knowing what he knows. If there's a lot of bad press about Green Rage, it won't help Zak at trial."

Rick looked aggravated. "We can't just sit on our hands!"

"I didn't ask you to give up. I asked you not to do anything illegal. Magic Valley is already in turmoil. It's the worst possible setting for the trial of an environmental activist accused of murdering a logger, and my chances of getting a change of venue are slim. Any aggressive activity by Green Rage will only make the situation worse."

"Sorry," Rick said. "We can't afford to lay low. They could level this whole forest before the case goes to trial."

Doc nodded. "I agree."

"People, be reasonable!" Christina pleaded. "Do you want to see Zak convicted?" She appealed to Deirdre. "Deirdre, you're a scientist. You're used to thinking logically. Talk to them."

She shook her head slowly. "I'm sorry. I agree with them. If we lay low, this forest will disappear."

"Then you'll plant new trees."

"You can plant new trees," Deirdre said, "but you can't plant a forest."

"I don't know what you mean."

"It's been proven scientifically a dozen times over. Once a forest is gone, it's gone. Trees may be a renewable resource, but forests are not. Replacement trees, set out in rows, all the same size and species, are less able to resist the drought and cold, insects and diseases, because they grow in simplified strands, not in the vigorous, complex ecosystems that evolved naturally over eons."

"Trees are trees—"

"Scientists have performed several studies in the aftermath of clear-cutting, focusing on the herbaceous layer—the shrubs and plants that are sheltered by forest trees—the forest life forms most sensitive to disturbances. Their conclusions are uniform. The forest doesn't—won't—grow back. You see, the loggers engage in monoculture; they see the forest as nothing but trees to be harvested. In truth, the forest is a complex organism filled with varied but interdependent life. Once that organism is disturbed, it becomes vulnerable to disease and extinction. In areas where clear-cutting occurred decades ago, species and foliage have drastically declined. On average, less than half of the species returned, and only a third of the plant life. The conclusion is inescapable—forests don't grow back."

"It's true," Rick said. "I grew up in Vermont. It used to be almost entirely covered with trees—till the forests were clear-cut almost a century ago. We used to have white pines reaching two hundred feet in height. Black walnut trunks five and six feet through the middle. Chestnuts spread two hundred feet from one branch tip to the next. And what do we have now? A forest of sticks."

"I grew up in Michigan," Doc said. "The great pines that used to grow there disappeared after they were clear-cut. They were replaced—*when* they were replaced—by oaks and aspens, which are being devoured by the gypsy moths so prevalent now that it's dangerous to drive during the caterpillar season—the roads are slick with mashed corpses of the larvae. Changing the forest composition totally ruined the ecosystem."

"And," Deirdre said, "we haven't even factored in other human activities that are killing trees and making regrowth difficult. Air pollution. Acid rain. Ozone depletion. The bottom line is that when the evolved, biologically rich ecosystem that created the original forest is destroyed, it's destroyed forever."

Ben felt an intense gnawing in the pit of his stomach. "I hear what you're saying," he said levelly, "but a man's life is on the line. We can't risk a human life to save some trees."

"Right," Doc said. "Because we humans are always more important than any other living thing on the planet."

"I don't mean that," Ben said. "But—"

"Ben," Deirdre interrupted, "can I show you something? It's just a short walk."

Ben pushed up to his feet and followed her out of the

clearing, Christina close behind. He was happy to leave that scene. It was frustrating and . . . disturbing. In the extreme.

They had walked barely five minutes when Deirdre began speaking again. "All of the trees in this area are old growth. They go back hundreds of years. Every limb brushing your shoulders is older than you, older than your parents, older than their parents. Some of them are older than Columbus."

They continued walking. "When WLE Logging first got the rights to cut in this area, they made a public announcement that they would cut no old-growth trees. They got all kinds of great PR—even a pat on the back from the mayor." She continued walking, touching the leaves on the branches as she passed. "We were relieved. Maybe for once someone would do the right thing without being economically blackmailed. Still, Zak wanted to be sure. So he led a team into the forest."

She paused, and Ben noticed her lips trembling a bit when she spoke again. "And this is what they found."

All at once Ben emerged from the forest and stepped into an enormous clearing. It was as if he had stepped onto the landscape of a different planet. Where before, everything had been green, verdant, and alive, now suddenly his surroundings, as far as his eye could see, were barren, bleak, and dead.

It took several moments before the full impact of what he was seeing hit him. His eyes slowly lowered.

"Oh my God," Christina said breathlessly.

There were stumps on the ground, one after another, an endless sea of severed trunks. Ben thought about counting, but it was impossible. Hundreds upon hundreds of trees had been felled, leaving behind only stumps wider than he could reach. Acres and acres of land had been leveled, flattened. There was no cover, no plant life, no animal life. Nothing green. It was as if an invading army had marched through and destroyed everything in sight.

Ben didn't need to be a dendrochronologist to know that these trees had been around for hundreds of years. And now there was nothing left but broken branches and dead stumps.

"And," Deirdre added quietly, "this entire area was clear-cut—in three days."

Ben knelt down and touched the stump closest to him. "This is something I will write about," he said. "People should know what's happening out here."

"You're right," Deirdre said, nodding her head. A single tear dropped from her eye. "I just hope someone is listening."

* 13 *

Tess closed the magazine and tossed it onto a sleeping bag. She'd been in this tent for over an hour now, all by herself, waiting. She'd read through that issue of *Outdoor* magazine three times, and it hadn't interested her the first time. She'd started talking to herself, subvocalizing animated conversations with everyone she knew. She was going stir-crazy.

Since she'd come back to the camp with Maureen and Al, she'd been treated like a potential leper, shuffled off to the side, isolated. She could understand that they wanted to be cautious, but enough was enough already. How long did they need to get their act together and decide what to do with her? How long could she stand being cooped up in this stupid tent?

Of course there was more at stake than just her personal discomfort. If she wasn't allowed to circulate, if she couldn't talk to the members of Green Rage and get to know them, earn their confidence, she was lost. She would never get the information she needed, never be able to crack this case.

She didn't have forever, either; she knew that. Rudy had been constantly calling her hotel room, asking where the hell she was and what she was doing and where was his story on Bigfoot, anyway? She could blow him off for a while without serious consequences, muttering vague promises about a really big scoop she was tracking, but that wouldn't last forever. For that matter, neither would her travel advance.

She watched the shadows as they flickered on the outside of the tent. The movement and muffled voices provided her only hint of what might be taking place outside. Some time earlier, the group had assembled and held some kind of meeting. No doubt she had been on the agenda, but she knew she wasn't the only action item. There was another stranger in their midst, someone else whose worthiness was being judged. And Green Rage had many plans afoot; she had heard enough words like *immediately* and *tonight* to realize that some of them were imminent.

Al had asked her to wait in the tent till he returned, but that didn't mean she had to do it. She could rebel; it's not like he was her father or anything. Still, she was trying to gain their trust, and she thought the best way to do that was to be cooperative. Earnest. Act as if she was desperate to please them, like she wanted to be one of them more than anything else in the world.

And then a little voice inside her head said, Once you have their trust, you'll betray it. You'll take their secrets and smear them across the pages of the *National Whisper*. Or maybe even a real newspaper. You'll get your Pulitzer, and they'll get five to ten.

Tess pushed the voice out of her consciousness. That kind of thinking would get her nowhere. She needed to focus on the task at hand. Which at the moment was waiting.

She was preparing to plunge into *Outdoor* magazine for the fourth time when Al finally reappeared. He unzipped the entrance to the tent and poked his head through. "We're ready for you," he said.

She couldn't help noticing that he wasn't smiling.

Tess crawled out of the tent and followed Rick to the circle of stones in the center of the clearing. She saw only six Green Ragers present. The others must have gone elsewhere. Secret mission, she suspected.

Rick introduced Tess to those present and gave her a smidgen of information about their backgrounds. "I've told everyone what you told Al and me in the bar about your . . . background. Why you'd like to join our cause."

"Good," she said. She was mentally deliberating on what

character she should be playing. She thought it best to seem a little timid, lacking in confidence. Perhaps even a bit in awe of them. "I appreciate that."

"But there's a lot more we'd like to know." Tess remembered that the woman speaking, the one with the curly brown hair and the round wire-frame glasses, was called Maureen.

"Just ask," Tess said, letting her lips tremble slightly. "I'll tell you anything you want to know."

"We are of course interested in the activities of the Cabal, and intrigued by the possibility of having an inside line on what Slade might be planning next. I'm sure you anticipated that."

Tess decided that her character, who was after all the mistress of a paid thug, should not be too terribly bright, so she didn't show any sign of picking up on the suggestion Maureen was making.

"We know Slade is in Magic Valley. He's been spotted. We were not aware he had any . . . associates with him."

"You don't think he made those raids on your camp himself, did you?"

"No. But hiring paid muscle is one thing. My understanding is that the man you're having the liaison with is somewhat higher in rank."

"John is Slade's right-hand man. Any time Slade wants something important done, John is the man he calls."

"I was not aware of John."

"Most people aren't. Slade is the sort of man who likes to take credit for everything himself. At the same time, he doesn't want any trails leading back to him. So whenever he needs something done that's . . . less than legal, he talks to John."

"And John talks to you?"

Tess allowed herself a slight smile. "He does have a habit of gabbing on when he's"—she giggled—"excited. And after."

Maureen stared at her with a near-stony visage Tess found difficult to read. Was she doubting Tess, or appalled by this nonfeminist dinosaur? Or just trying to figure how best to use her? "So," Maureen said, "you've known about some of the Cabal's activities even before they happened."

"That's right."

"Such as?"

"Well, I know they raided your camp twice, even though I don't believe you reported it to the police."

"There's been a lot of talk about the raids in town," Al said abruptly. "She could've picked that up from anyone."

"But she also knows about that Cabal," Maureen said. "And Slade. And that is not common knowledge."

"Not common, but not unknown, either," Al insisted. "If she did some serious research, she could have found some of the articles other environmental groups have written about it."

"Please believe me," Tess said, plastering on her most earnest smile. "I wouldn't even know how to do this . . . research. All I know is what I've been told by John." She took a deep breath. "And it horrifies me. That's why I want to join you."

"I'm sorry," Al said, "but we can't afford to take the risk. She could be a cop."

"She isn't a cop," Maureen said. "I'm certain of that." She peered directly at Tess. "Are you?"

"No," Tess said firmly. "I'm not."

"Or worse," Al continued, "she could be a Cabal plant. That would explain how she knows so much about them."

"It's possible," Maureen said, batting her finger against her lip. "But I just don't think so." She glanced at Rick. "Do you?"

"No, I don't." Rick leaned toward Maureen and whispered a few words in her ear. Maureen nodded. "I'm more concerned about your level of commitment."

Tess frowned. "What do you mean?"

"I mean, you may feel all dedicated to the cause now. It may seem like a cool, exciting thing to do, in a dilettante-ish way. But when the heat is on, and it doesn't seem so fun and exciting anymore, you may wither. It's one thing to talk the talk, but quite another to actually walk the walk. We can't use someone who's going to crack up and run the first time she sees something dangerous or illegal happen."

"I'll do whatever you want me to."

He peered down at her. "Are you sure about that?"

"Yes," she said, without hesitation. "Absolutely."

"All right," Rick continued, "here's what we're going to do. We've got a little . . . activity planned for tonight. We considered postponing it, but the group consensus is to proceed."

"And?"

"And you'll come with us. If you follow through on this and still want to be part of Green Rage, then I think you'll be in for the long haul. More to the point, if you've participated in an illegal act, then you have as much to lose as the rest of us—if someone talks to the cops or the Freddies."

"I understand. Security in shared risk."

"That's exactly right. Will you do it?"

Tess never let her eyes break from his. "I will."

Al rose abruptly and threw his hat onto the ground. "Not again! This is insane!"

"I've made my decision," Rick said.

Al muttered a few words Tess didn't understand, then stomped off into the forest.

"First, I'll fill you in," Rick said. "Then I'll take you back into town so you can get whatever gear you'll need to spend the night in the forest. If you have to make some excuses to John, you can do it. At any rate, you need to meet me at Bunyan's by nine. I'll pick you up and bring you back out here."

"Got it," Tess said, trying to suppress her excitement. "Can you tell me the plan?"

It looked like she'd succeeded. He was going to take her into his confidence.

"Yeah," Rick said, leaning close to her and lowering his voice. "You'll need to know. Here's what we're going to do."

* 14 *

They placed Tess in the middle of the chain of four, with Maureen and Rick in front of her and Al behind her. She preferred to think it was so they could make sure she didn't get lost. But she suspected that at least part of it was that they still simply didn't trust her.

It was the dead of night, well after three A.M. She was reminded how forbidding the forest could be at this time of night. Every other step she tripped over something she couldn't see and felt something brush against her she couldn't identify. A voice deep inside her told her to run, to flee, to get the hell out of Dodge. But she had to fight her panic down, to suppress those natural instincts.

This was a test. They were trying to determine whether she had what it took to be part of their group. She couldn't fail the test, not if she hoped to become a member and get the inside scoop she needed to crack the murder. She had to persevere.

"We wait here," Rick whispered. They hunkered down in a grove of trees on the crest of a small hill. Maureen and Al both sat, propping themselves against large tree trunks. They at least seemed to know what they were doing.

"Where are we?" Tess asked timidly.

"Near Northwest 14," Rick said. He pointed toward a large section of tall trees on the opposite side of the clearing—NW14, on the surveyors' maps.

"I thought we were going to spike the trees," Tess said. "It's already after three."

"We wait," Rick said firmly, and he rested himself on a large rock beside Maureen.

Tess didn't understand, but she saw no point in arguing. She found a soft spot in a pile of leaves, sat down, and waited.

It was more than half an hour later when Rick rose to his feet, brushing the dirt off the back of his jeans. "I think that's long enough."

Tess was startled by the sound of his voice. There had been no conversation during the waiting period—for security reasons, she assumed. And given the lateness of the hour and the length of time she'd been hiking, she had all but fallen asleep.

Tess pushed herself up, wiping her eyes. "Mind telling me what's going on? You told me we were going to spike trees. Said we would start around three. Wasn't that the plan?"

"That's what we told you," Rick said. "But that wasn't the plan."

"I don't understand."

"Don't take this the wrong way," Maureen said gently. "But we had to be sure we could trust you."

"So you *lied* to me?"

"We gave you false information about our plans," Al explained. "Then we took you back to town and made sure you had a chance to report, if that was your intent."

"You thought I was working for the cops?"

"Or worse, the Cabal." Maureen laid her hand gently on Tess's shoulder. "You have to understand—we know the Cabal has tried to infiltrate our group. And we feel certain they'll try again. We had to be cautious."

"So you fed me false information."

Rick nodded. "And then we came out here, near the place where we told you we would spike, and waited. There's really only one practical way into Northwest 14, and I could watch it perfectly from here. If there had been any cops or loggers or Cabal thugs coming to catch us in the act, I would've seen them."

Tess's lips parted. "You laid a trap."

"Correction. I waited to see if there was a trap. There wasn't. You didn't talk."

"I could've told you I wouldn't." She frowned. "But I guess you had to see it for yourselves. You had to be cautious."

"But no longer," Maureen said. "You've passed this test, and there won't be any more. You're a member of Green Rage now." She squeezed Tess's shoulder affectionately. "Welcome to the club."

"Swell," Tess said. "Do I get the secret decoder ring now?"

They laughed.

"Even better," Al said. "You get to be a real-life terrorist."

Maureen slapped his shoulder. "Stop that. You're worse than the press. We are not terrorists."

"I'm not interested in semantic games," Al said. "We blow things up for political reasons. You choose your own label."

"So," Tess asked, "are we going to spike those trees now?"

"Nah," Rick answered. "That was never on the agenda. Those trees in Northwest 14 aren't old growth, and besides, we spike only before clear-cutting begins, when there's still time to back the loggers off. No, we have a different plan. We need to walk a little more."

"Not as much as before, I hope," Tess said.

"Just about ten minutes."

Tess followed Rick as he led them on another hike through the dense dark forestland. When he finally stopped, she could see they had reached the site of an ongoing logging operation. Fallen trees lined the perimeter. Heavy machinery dotted the landscape.

"I thought the current logging was taking place south of here," Tess said. "Near the river."

"It's supposed to be," Rick said. "These are old-growth trees, four and five hundred years old. The trees lining the perimeter have been marked by the Freddies with a blue X—that means do not cut."

"So why is all this equipment out here?"

"Why do you think? They're cutting the trees, anyway—even though it's against the law and contrary to their own press-release BS. Al found out about it last night while he was scouting. It's a renegade operation. They send a small team out here while the main team stays where they're supposed to be. Acting as cover."

"But why? When they have the other trees?"

"Because they want them all," Al answered.

"It's more than that," Maureen added. "When loggers work the smaller trees, they may have to cut all day before they make their quota. When they work these huge old-growth trees, one tree alone may be sufficient to fill a huge eighteen-wheel transport truck. They get more done in less time. Which translates to higher profits."

"You should call the police," Tess said. "Or maybe the Forest Service."

"We've tried that route before," Al said. "By the time any of those so-called officials take action, this forest will be leveled. The logging company will be fined—maybe—and perhaps reprimanded. But they won't care, because they'll still have their grossly inflated profits, which will far exceed any fine levied. And the trees will be gone."

"That's just horrible," Tess said. "Someone has to do something."

"Our thoughts exactly," Al replied. "Someone has to speak for the trees, but no one in officialdom is doing it. So we've elected ourselves."

"What are you planning to do?"

Al crouched down and pointed. "See that huge piece of machinery down there?"

Tess followed his finger. She saw a large metal machine, five wheels on each side, with a cab in the center, and two great robot arms at the front with sharp pincer blades at each tip.

"That's a tree cutter. One of the great myths the logging companies like to perpetuate is that trees are felled by stout-hearted manly men. But the truth is, today, most trees are felled by big machines like that one. They're much more efficient. That thing can take down a twelve-inch tree all by itself. It grips it with one claw arm, cuts it with the built-in saws in the other, and carries it to the transport truck. No crash. No *Tim-berrrrrr!* And no manly men. Unless you count the one sitting in the air-conditioned cab with the FM radio."

"That's the real reason there are fewer loggers working every year," Maureen explained. "That monster can outwork twenty men with chain saws. And it doesn't get tired. And it doesn't require Social Security payments or health care coverage. Guess which the big logging companies prefer?"

Tess felt a tightness in her jaw. "How many weeks will it take that machine to clear-cut these old-growth trees?"

"Weeks?" Rick laughed. "Try days. Three, I'd guess. Maybe four at the outmost. Which is why we couldn't afford to wait until after Zak's trial."

For once Tess couldn't think of a thing to say. "That's wrong."

"No argument from me," Al said. "But I'm going to set it right again." He reached into his backpack and pulled out a gray hand-sized object.

Tess didn't have to be a demolitions expert to realize that it was some kind of bomb.

"What are you going to do?"

"What do you think? I'm going to take that monster out."

"People could be hurt."

"Not if I do it now. When no one's around."

"But when they start the ignition—"

"Despite what you may have heard, we don't use trigger bombs or movement bombs or anything else that's designed to harm some unsuspecting operator. All we do is take the thing out, so it can't be used to kill any more trees."

"Surely the company will just replace it."

"Maybe. But they cost hundreds of thousands of dollars. They might decide this forest has become too expensive for them. Especially if we do it again. And again. And again."

"Hundreds of thousands of dollars?" Tess said. "We could be charged with grand larceny. Arson."

"Only if we get caught. Excuse me."

Al crept down the side of a small slope and entered the clearing. He moved slowly at first, making sure no guard had been posted and no drunken loggers were hanging about. Once he was certain the coast was clear, he moved more quickly. He walked directly to the tree cutter and planted his bundle at the base. He fiddled with it for a few moments, turned, and ran.

"Get down!" he shouted.

Tess and the rest fell back into the trees. They crouched

down and covered their heads. Al caught up to them and dived forward. *"Hit the deck!"*

An instant later, the tree cutter exploded. Tess heard the explosion before she saw it. It was as if a sonic boom had sounded inside her eardrums. Even with her head hidden under her arms and buried in the soil, she could feel the intense surge of heat radiating outward. When at last she looked, she saw a raging inferno where a tree cutter once had been, a ball of flame that seemed to spew forth from the bowels of the earth itself.

Pieces of machinery fell to earth all around her. Flames continued to devour the steel contraption. "Are you all right?" Maureen asked.

Tess nodded. "I'm fine. Just a little shaken up." She couldn't tell them the truth—that she had seen one of these things explode before.

Suddenly Tess's ears were alerted to another sound—voices. They were coming from the clearing on the other side of the burning machine.

"Oh my God," Maureen said. "Someone's here."

"They've seen us," Rick said, clenching his teeth. He looked down at his friend. "Al, are you all right?"

Al pulled himself up to his knees. A trickle of blood lined the side of his face. "I'll make it."

The voices were coming closer. In the flickering light provided by the inferno, Tess saw three figures racing forward. Three angry figures. And at least one of them was holding a gun.

"Let's go!" Rick shouted. They turned and ran, heading back the way they came, this time not in any orderly fashion but all at once, helter-skelter, trying to make as much time as possible.

Tess ran as fast as she could manage, trying not to trip, to fall, to hit anything. She wasn't sure which prospect scared her more: that the people chasing them would catch her or that her newfound friends would leave her alone in the dark forest.

She didn't have time to weigh the grim possibilities. She just tried to stay on her feet and to keep them moving.

A gunshot erupted over their heads.

"Run!" Rick cried. And Tess ran, with every ounce of energy she could muster.

But the voices were gaining on them.

* 15 *

The instant Ben entered the courthouse the next morning, he knew something had happened. There was a buzz in the air; every staffer in sight flittered from one ear to another, whispering, shaking heads, doing everything but their jobs. He saw it in the elevators, in the filing room—even in the men's room. Some tidbit of information was circulating from one person to the next with great alacrity. Unfortunately, no one seemed inclined to share this tidbit with Ben.

For that matter, Ben noticed, no one seemed inclined to share anything with him at all. The word was out, he supposed. He was representing the eco-terrorist, and his stock was valued accordingly. If people spoke to him at all, it was in clipped, essential monosyllables. No one got chatty. Most turned away.

When Ben arrived at the courtroom, Sheriff Allen had already delivered his prisoner—Ben's client—to the defendant's table, in handcuffs and coveralls.

"Morning," the sheriff said, tipping his Smokey the Bear hat as Ben approached.

"Same to you," Ben said, relieved to hear someone actually talking to him. "Thanks for escorting Zak."

"It's my job." He didn't move away. Ben could tell there was something else on his mind. Allen shifted his weight awkwardly from one foot to the other. "Uhh . . . look, Mr. Kincaid—"

"Call me Ben." He wasn't going to give up a chance to get

friendly with someone local. He probably wouldn't get another one.

"Well . . . Ben, then. I was wondering . . ."

Ben instinctively glanced at his watch. The hearing could start at any moment. "Yes?"

"I was wondering . . ." He cleared his throat. "Wondering if maybe you've set up any office space yet?"

"We've got some temporary space in the back of that closet you call the public defender's office. Why? Planning to make an arrest?"

"Well, no." He fingered the brim of his hat. "Actually, I was hoping to drop by and ask that sweet little legal assistant of yours out to lunch."

"Didn't you have lunch with her yesterday? And the day before?"

"Well, yes. Yes, sir, I did. But I didn't get enough of her." He let out a sheepish grin. "I haven't seen anything like her come to Magic Valley for a good long time. She's a regular ball of fire!"

"Isn't she, though." Ben pursed his lips. "We're going to be very busy. We have a murder trial to gear up for."

"Oh, I know, I know. But I figured, she's gotta eat, right?"

"Yeah, right."

"Unless you've got some objection . . ."

"What am I, her father? What Christina does in her spare time is her business. I need to speak to my client now."

"Understood." Sheriff Allen tipped his hat, then headed toward the back of the courtroom.

Ben slid into the chair next to his client. "How's it going, Zak?"

Zak brushed his hair out of his eyes and grinned. His hair seemed particularly limp and dirty. They probably don't supply Johnson's baby shampoo in the slammer, Ben thought.

"I'm all right," he answered. "Jail time is no walk in the park, but I'm used to it. How's my case coming? Got any leads?"

"Not yet. But I have managed to get the Green Rage seal of approval."

"Well, that ain't no small feat."

"Zak, I need to talk to you about something."

"What's up?"

"I had a talk with the prosecutor yesterday, and it was . . . disturbing. She seems very confident about her case against you."

"Does that surprise you? She's got her career on the line. She doesn't want me messing up her win-loss record."

"Maybe so. But she also intimated that she had a lot of evidence against you that I don't know anything about. Do you know what that might possibly be?"

"Sorry, counselor. No idea."

"Think hard, Zak. This is important."

He spread his arms. "I'm telling you, I don't know."

"She seemed pretty secure about her theory of motive, too, although she didn't care to share it with me. Any ideas?"

"Oh, hell, that's not hard to figure. She's going to say I am a crazed zealot eco-bandit, some tree-loving nutcase who thought he had the right to kill to further his cause. Isn't it obvious?"

"Maybe. I just don't want to be caught flat-footed. It's important that you tell me everything, the good and the bad. If there's something you've held back, please tell me now."

"Relax, Ben. There's nothing. Nothing at all. The woman was probably just jerkin' your chain."

"And you didn't know Dwayne Gardiner?"

"Right."

Ben eased off, but he still wasn't satisfied. He wasn't sure exactly why, but the whole situation left him with a very uncomfortable feeling.

"All rise."

The bailiff brought everyone in the courtroom to their feet. Ben saw that Granny had slipped in at the other table while he was talking to Zak.

"Court is now in session. The Honorable Judge Tyrone J. Pickens presiding."

The judge took his seat at the bench, then peered out into the courtroom. "Well now, looks like old home week, doesn't it?" He adjusted his glasses and scowled at Ben.

"What'd you do this time, son? Rescue a lobster from a seafood restaurant?"

"Uh, no, sir." Ben cleared his throat. "Actually, I'm not the defendant."

Judge Pickens pulled a face. "You're not? Then what're you doin' here?"

"I'm counsel for the defendant." He gestured in Zak's general direction.

"You're a lawyer?" Pickens's eyes widened. "Oh, that's right. You represented the animal freaks."

"Not freaks, your honor. They're people concerned about the unethical treatment of living creatures."

Pickens sighed. "I can see this is going to be a fun trial." He took the papers handed to him by the bailiff and skimmed them quickly. "So you're representing this George Zakin?"

"That's right, your honor."

"I see. You've regressed from varmint hugging to tree hugging."

"Your honor, I must ask you not to prejudge—"

"I'm not prejudging anything, son." He jabbed the gavel in Ben's direction. "When this trial begins, I'll be entirely fair and impartial. Doesn't mean I have to forget all common sense in the meantime." He shifted his gaze to the other side of the courtroom. "You prosecutin' this one, Granny?"

"I am, sir."

"How long is this going to take?"

"I can't speak for my esteemed opposition," Granny said, swishing her head so that her radiant hair danced around her shoulders. "But our case won't take more than a week. Probably less."

"A week? Damn." He tossed his bifocals down on the bench. "Don't you people know it's fishing season?" He looked up abruptly. "Oh, excuse me, Mr. Defense Attorney. You probably object to fishing, too."

"Catch and capture, or catch and release?"

"Catch and *release*? What would be the point of that?"

Ben shrugged. "I never understood the point of fishing to begin with."

"Mr. Kincaid, I fear you and I are not going to get along."

He flipped a page in his desk calendar. "We'll start the trial Monday of next week. Any motions I need to hear?"

"I've filed a motion to be admitted to practice before this court *pro hac vice*," Ben said. "It's been endorsed by—"

"Right, right, granted." Judge Pickens grimaced. "I don't suppose I can keep you out of the courtroom, however much I might like to. You death-qualified, boy?"

"Several times over, your honor."

"Good thing." He looked up. "You going for the death penalty, Granny?"

"You better believe it," she answered.

"Figured as much." Eyes back to Ben. "So you stay on your toes and handle this thing right. Understand, son?"

"Perfectly."

"I don't want the appellate boys hassling me about incompetent counsel. Anything else I can do for you?"

"I haven't received all of the prosecution's exhibits."

Granny looked incredulous. "He just entered his appearance yesterday!"

"But the case has been on the docket for weeks. We specifically requested the medical examiner's report."

"Couldn't lay my hands on it," Granny said. "Given the short notice. I'm sure it'll turn up."

Yeah, right, Ben thought. She was withholding the report for a reason. And he'd have to figure out what that reason was without any help from her.

"Any other motions?"

Ben stepped forward. "Yes, your honor. I've filed a motion for change of venue."

"You got somethin' against my courtroom, son?"

Heaven forbid. "No, your honor. But I have become aware that there is a certain local hostility toward the group my client leads."

"After stunts like they pulled last night, what do you expect?"

What had happened? What did everyone in town except him already know about?

There was an awkward pause. "You do know what happened last night, don't you, son?"

Ben bit down on his lower lip. "Well, actually . . ."

"Someone used plastic explosives to blow a two-ton tree cutter to kingdom come. That's a three-hundred-thousand-dollar piece of machinery."

Ben's jaw tightened. So they went ahead with their plans, anyway. *Damn!* "Do we know who did it?"

"Of course we know who did it!" the judge bellowed. "And so do you. I don't know if we'll ever be able to prove it, but we sure as hell know who did it."

"Your honor," Ben said evenly, "I think this incident, and the hostility it's obviously generating, strengthen my argument for a change of venue. My client can't possibly get a fair trial here."

"Well, now, whose fault is that? Did we ask your little friend to come to town and start blowing things up? Did we ask him to get everyone so worked up they don't feel safe in their own homes? Don't know whether their next paycheck might be their last?"

"Your honor—"

"From where I'm sitting, it looks like he decided to come here and cause all this trouble. He's made his bed. Now he can lie in it."

"Your honor, that's hardly the legal standard—"

"Are you challenging my ruling?" Judge Pickens thrust the gavel forward with such strength Ben expected it to come sailing toward his head. "Because that's one thing I will not tolerate in my court!"

"Yes, sir." Ben knew that if he wanted to appeal, he'd have to do it in writing, to a higher court.

"And while we're at it, let me point out to you, son, that your predecessor already made a motion for change of venue that was denied, as you'd know, if you'd read the file."

"I did know, but—"

"And for that matter, he also made a motion for dismissal of charges, for pretrial release on bail, and for suppression of evidence of terrorist activities, all of which I denied. So don't bother trying again!"

"Yes, sir."

"Is there anything else?" Pickens waited not a tenth of a

second before pushing himself to his feet and stomping out of the courtroom.

"Court is out of session," the bailiff announced, just in case there was someone too stupid to figure it out for themselves.

Ben turned back toward his client, but not so quickly he didn't catch sight of Granny at the next table. She flashed him a confident smile that was all too easy to read. She'd come out of this hearing way ahead—and she'd barely said a word.

Zak tugged the sleeve of Ben's suit. "Did that go as bad as I think it did?"

Ben tried not to seem unduly concerned. "This is just a pretrial hearing. Judges love to blow off steam when there's no jury looking on. The trial will be different."

"Glad to hear it."

Sheriff Allen came forward to collect his prisoner and escort him back to his jail cell.

Ben collected his materials, loaded his briefcase, and started out of the courtroom. On his way, he noticed for the first time a man sitting in the back row of the gallery. He was middle-aged, balding, slightly overweight, but immaculately dressed in a well-tailored suit.

And he was smiling. As if the hearing had been everything he'd dreamed it might be.

Ben couldn't help but wonder who the man was. And there was one way to find out . . .

He extended his hand. "I'm Ben Kincaid."

The man in the back row took the hand and squeezed. "I'm Amos Slade," he replied.

Ben froze. *Slade?* The man he'd heard so much about? The boss man for the infamous Cabal?

Ben tried to shake a few words out. "I—I think I've heard your name mentioned."

Slade chuckled. "I'll bet you have."

"Are you—working for the logging companies?"

Slade's eyes narrowed slightly, but they remained constantly focused on Ben, never wavering. "I'm . . . an independent contractor. I run a consulting business."

"Consulting with logging companies, right?"

Slade shrugged. "At times."

Ben withdrew his hand before the trembling became too apparent. Maybe it was just the influence of what he'd heard at the Green Rage camp, but somehow this man seemed to radiate evil. "I'd—like to talk to you sometime soon."

"I'd welcome the opportunity. These days I'm down at the WLE sawmill, just outside of town. Drop by any time."

"Thank you. I will." Ben walked out of the courtroom. He knew it was irrational, but he couldn't get away from that man fast enough. Every second he stood before Slade, he felt as if he was being evaluated, sized up. Like a shark eyeing a guppy.

The Green Ragers had said Slade was devious, corrupt, unprincipled. And now he believed it. Maybe it was just his overactive imagination, but when Ben looked into those eyes, he thought he saw a man who was willing to do anything to eliminate obstacles that obscured his goal.

Or people who stood in his way.

* 16 *

The medical examiner pulled the slab drawer out of the morgue wall, then whipped the pale green sheet off the corpse with a flourish. "Ta-da!"

Ben Kincaid's face started turning the same color as the sheet. He covered his mouth with his hand, then pinched his nose.

"He's been in the deep freeze for a good long time now." The medical examiner was a middle-aged man named Larry Tobias, with a chubby midsection and a perpetual friendly smile. "There shouldn't be any smell."

"There is," Ben said, trying to talk without opening his mouth.

"Huh. Guess I've gotten where I don't notice anymore." He

observed the distressed expression on Ben's face. "You did say you wanted to see him, didn't you?"

"I did," Ben whispered. "I must have been out of my mind."

Tobias grinned. "First time to see a stiff, huh?"

"No," Ben answered. "But it's one of those special pleasures that retains its potency through the years." Like it or not, Ben realized, he was here, and he had asked to be here, so he'd better make use of the time. He forced his eyes downward to the desiccated remains of Dwayne Gardiner.

His skin was black, charcoal black, where there was skin at all. Most places he had been scorched to the bone—more skeleton than corpse. The body was so grisly and inhuman it hardly seemed real—more like something that should be dangling from a string in a Halloween haunted house.

"What can you tell me about the cause of death?" Ben asked, looking away.

"Three guesses," Tobias replied, chuckling amiably. "He burned to death. Although it's possible that cardiac arrest killed him before the flames did."

"Cardiac arrest?"

"Brought on by fear and panic and pain. I don't know—maybe I just want to believe it. Anything that brought an early end to his suffering would be a mercy. No one needs to be conscious for every moment of burning alive."

Ben didn't doubt it. "The prosecutor told me Gardiner also suffered a gunshot wound."

"Right. Just below the shoulder. Not that bad, all things considered, although it could've been fatal in time if it hadn't been treated. But the fire killed him before that became an issue."

"How can you tell?"

"It's easier than you might think, even with a corpse that's been as thoroughly destroyed as this one. Live tissue that's been burned has a whole different look, feel, and consistency than dead tissue. If he was already dead before he burned, for instance, there would be no formation of hard scabs—what we call eschar. But as you can see, the scabs are everywhere—where the skin hasn't been burned away altogether. So he wasn't dead when he caught on fire."

"What else can you tell me?"

"I think the fire followed the shooting very closely in time—maybe as soon as a minute after."

Ben tried to imagine the scenario in his mind. First, the assailant shoots him at point-blank range. Then, just for good measure, he blows him up. "Seems like overkill."

"Yeah. Especially since they were out in the heart of the forest. Gardiner may have still been able to move after he was shot, but he certainly couldn't make it back to town. Without assistance, he would've died out there. Setting him on fire was unnecessary."

"But he wasn't set on fire," Ben noted. "Not as such. The tree cutter had been bombed, and he was caught in the explosion. Would Gardiner have been able to start the tree cutter even after he was shot?"

Tobias shrugged. "It's possible. There are stories of people suffering mortal wounds—even losing limbs—and still driving themselves to the hospital."

"But why would he want to start a tree cutter? Surely the clear-cutting could wait until after he'd been to the hospital."

"You're out of my field of expertise now."

"Maybe it was self-defense. Maybe he was planning to run over his assailant or snap him like a twig in those huge claw arms. Or maybe he was just going to drive the thing back to town, and that poor unfortunate soul made the mistake of starting the tree cutter and—"

Tobias looked up. "Boom."

Ben nodded. "I haven't seen your report yet. Are there any other points of interest? Distinguishing characteristics or oddities?"

"I'm afraid I didn't find all that much. Fire is the great destroyer. It doesn't leave many traces behind for forensic detectives to follow."

"I can imagine," Ben said, forcing himself to gaze once more at the charred remains. It seemed miraculous that any determinations could be made from a corpse in that horrible condition.

"There was one detail you might want to know about," Tobias said. "One thing you wouldn't normally expect to see. Did Granny tell you about the bite?"

Ben raised an eyebrow. "No, she certainly did not. Did you find a bite mark?"

"Sure did." He pulled out the corpse's right arm and pointed to a shallow, barely noticeable indentation on the right forearm. "Least that's what I think it is. Missed it the first two times I went over the corpse. Almost missed it the third. After burning, it's hard to see anything."

Fighting his instinctive revulsion, Ben crouched down and took a closer look at the blackened limb. He did see a few slight impressions, but he could never have identified them. "Not much there, is there?"

"Maybe not. But Granny was really excited when I told her about it."

That caught Ben's attention. "She was, huh?"

"Oh, you better believe it. She started jumping up and down, dancing around the morgue. Kept giving me these great big bear hugs, which as you can probably imagine was not an altogether displeasurable experience."

Ben didn't laugh. His mind was already a million miles away. What was Granny so excited about? He couldn't believe this vague bite mark would be adequate to identify the assailant. "I'd like copies of anything you sent to Granny."

"Sure, you're entitled. I couldn't figure out why the first lawyer on this case didn't ask for them."

"Criminal law isn't his strong suit. That's why he—" Ben stopped in mid-sentence. His mind suddenly flashed on something he had seen in the file yesterday afternoon. It hadn't meant anything to him at the time, it seemed like a standard prosecution request for exemplars. Hair exemplars, blood exemplars—

And dental exemplars.

Of course, Ben's predecessor saw no reason to object. So Zak had bitten down on a soft substance, probably wax, and left an impression of his teeth. Which Granny now had in her files, ready and waiting for trial.

Ben thanked the medical examiner and left the building. As he headed back toward his temporary office, he couldn't shake the feeling that he was way behind, that he was playing catch-up and coming up short. And if he didn't get up to speed soon, before the trial began . . .

It would be too late. Especially for Zak.

* 17 *

Peggy Carter was surprised to find the rest of the prosecution team already assembled in the conference room when she arrived. Judging by their posture and the expressions on their faces, they had been waiting for a good long time.

Granny was sitting at the head of the table, as indeed she always did. "Glad you could make it, Peggy."

"I just found out about the meeting. I was in the library when the memo—"

"Sit down, Peggy." Granny pointed toward an empty chair at the end of the conference table. "We've waited long enough."

Peggy did as she was told. This was the way it always was with Granny. No chance to explain, no hope for redemption. Just a quick fix of guilt and on with business.

Peggy had been at the D.A.'s office for over a year now. And every day she came to like her esteemed boss a little less. When she had first signed on, she had been excited at the prospect of working under a fellow female, a serious-minded career woman who had broken through the glass ceiling against all odds and even gotten herself elected D.A. What had originally seemed like a breakthrough for the cause, though, now only seemed like another day in hell.

She wanted to quit, but at the moment, that just wasn't an option. She had a twelve-year-old daughter at home, a daughter who depended on her single mom for her support. They were in debt and overextended. They couldn't afford an interruption in income, even a brief one. And Peggy knew that if she gave up this job, the interim before she got her next would likely be more than brief. In Magic Valley, employment opportunities were none too extensive. Most of the logging corporations had in-house counsel departments, but none of them were hiring. There were no other large businesses or industries in the area. She could go into private practice, but she knew she'd never be able to pay the bills on what she'd make. And moving was too expensive even to contemplate.

So that left the D.A.'s office. Which at the moment meant working under Granville Adams. At least until the next election.

"As you probably already know, the Zakin trial has been set for Monday. Needless to say, I want every one of you giving this case your full-time attention, and then some. Understand?"

Nods all around. In addition to Peggy and Granny, there were two other staff lawyers in the conference room, Kip Farmer and Troy Potter, neither of them superstars. But Granny didn't really want superstars on her team. *She* was the superstar; what she wanted from others was simply blind obedience and a willingness to perform the grunt labor trials required but that she was much too important to do herself.

"How's the forensic end of the trial shaping up?"

Kip Farmer coughed into his hand. "Everything seems to be in tiptop shape. We've sent the fingerprints to the lab, and they've come back with precisely the results we wanted."

"Funny how that happens so often, innit?" Granny grinned. "What else?"

"Footprints have been checked and double-checked."

"What about the bite mark? Did you get the expert I wanted?"

"I did. In fact, I had a long chat with him on the phone this morning. He's perfect—got credentials up the wazoo. Plus he's white, handsome, and speaks in complete sentences."

"Yes," Granny said impatiently, "but is he a good expert or a bad expert?"

Kip stammered. "Uh . . . I'm . . . uh, not sure what—"

"A good expert is an expert who understands he has an obligation to say anything we want because we're paying his vastly inflated fee. A bad expert is one who insists he has an obligation to the truth, whatever he perceives it to be."

Peggy spoke timidly. "Don't we have an obligation to the truth, too?"

Granny dismissed the remark with a wave of her hand. "Of course we do. Is there anyone here who doesn't think Zakin committed this crime?" She waited a beat, as if someone might dare respond in the affirmative. "That being so, we have an obligation to get a conviction. And we don't want our work screwed up by some expert who decides to wrestle with his conscience during cross-examination. Got it, Peggy?"

Peggy bit her tongue. Stupid, stupid, stupid . . .

"What about on the personal side, Troy? Have we got motive sized up?"

Troy leaned forward a bit. "I think so, yes."

"Don't think, Troy. Know."

He corrected himself. "I, uh, know so. I'm certain."

"You'd better be."

"I've reviewed Grayson's testimony several times now. I think—er, I know he'll deliver what you want and more."

"Good. Very good." Her face curled up in a smile. "I can't wait to see Kincaid's face when he takes the stand."

Troy seemed disturbed. "But—um—can I ask one question?"

"Just one, Troy."

"Aren't you going to have to put his name on your witness list? And when defense counsel sees his name—"

"In the first place, I'm going to delay submitting a list until the last possible moment. Judge Pickens is on our side, so honestly, what's Kincaid going to do about it? In the second place, I have to list the witnesses' names, but I don't have to give a detailed description of what I expect them to talk about. I think I can mislead Kincaid into thinking he's being called for one reason, then sock it to 'em when he's on the stand."

Peggy stared down at the conference table. Was this ethical? But she knew better than to ask the question aloud. She'd only get the same treatment she'd gotten a few minutes before.

"Well, team," Granny said, clapping her hands together, "it sounds as if we are in fine fettle. If there's nothing else—"

"I have something," Peggy said.

All eyes turned to her end of the table. "Oh?"

Peggy swallowed. She didn't want to speak. She'd much rather let the moment pass and retreat to the safety of her office. But there was an issue that had to be raised.

"I've been reading some disturbing reports," Peggy said, trying to pretend she didn't feel Granny's eyes burning down on her. "Some from the DEA, some from local law enforcement agencies. We've got a drug lord in town—a major player. One Alberto Vincenzo."

Granny's annoyance was apparent. "Does this relate in some way to the Zakin case?"

"I think it might." Peggy pulled a photo out of a file folder. "This is Alberto Vincenzo." It was a waist-up shot. Vincenzo was a big man, with long stringy black hair and a scar above his right eye. His face was defiant; his shoulders and chest rippled with muscles. He looked scary.

"Vincenzo has been in Magic Valley for at least a month, maybe longer. We don't know what he's doing here. But given the fact that we've seen a huge spike in the distribution and use of Venom, it isn't hard to put two and two together—"

"I'm sure this little lecture is fascinating to Kip and Troy," Granny said, "just as it is to me. But what the hell does it have to do with this murder case?"

Peggy tried to be brave. She had made a cardinal mistake—she had taken the spotlight off Granny for too long. This was Granny's show, and she expected to be the star. She didn't like upstarts.

"We all know the wife of the murder victim was concerned about his behavior in the weeks just prior to his murder. She reported violent mood swings, reckless behavior, extended periods of sleep followed by extended periods of sky-high alertness. In short, exactly the symptoms associated with this new designer drug."

Granny's face became set and positively grim. "What are you implying, Peggy? Do you think we arrested the wrong man?"

"No, I'm not saying that. But if Gardiner was using this new drug being distributed by Vincenzo, then Vincenzo is a potential suspect."

Granny's face burned red. "So I guess you think we should release our local eco-terrorist, against whom we've already got an ironclad case, and go chasing after your drug lord."

"No, of course not." She drew in her breath. "All I'm saying is that Vincenzo is a potential suspect. As such, any evidence pointing to Vincenzo is exculpatory as to the guilt of Zakin. Therefore, applying the standard of *Brady* v. *Maryland*, we have an obligation to inform defense counsel."

Granny gaped. "To do what?"

"To give Zakin's lawyer everything we've got on this Vincenzo creep. I'll be happy to take care of it if—"

"No." Granny laid her hands firmly on the table. "That is not going to happen."

"But the law requires—"

"The law requires us to turn over any potentially exculpatory evidence. But this half-baked theory of yours isn't exculpatory. It doesn't make the case against Zakin any weaker. It just creates the possibility of a wild-goose chase and a distraction the defense can use at trial to confuse the jury."

"He has a right to know about any potential suspects."

"Who considers this . . . Vincenzo a suspect? I don't. Do you?"

Kip and Troy both shook their heads rapidly.

"However tenuous," Peggy said, "there is a potential connection."

"Am I to inform defense counsel of every criminal in town? Or in this case, every potential but as yet uncharged criminal? I don't think so."

Peggy didn't know what to say. The law was clear. But Granny seemed determined to ignore it.

There was a long and very unpleasant silence.

"Give me the Vincenzo file, Peggy."

Peggy reluctantly complied.

"I'll refile this. Where it belongs."

Yeah, Peggy thought. Like in the incinerator.

"If we had any hard evidence pointing toward this drug

kingpin," Granny continued, "I'd agree with you, Peggy. But I will not feed the defense an escape hatch by creating a connection that doesn't exist. We have an obligation to produce evidence, not to invent theories." She leveled her gaze, finding Peggy's eyes and fixing upon them. "And furthermore, my dear, let me tell you something that *is* the law. Granny's law, if you will. I expect—no, *require* absolute loyalty from my staff. Do you understand what I'm saying?"

"Yes, ma'am."

"If you're with me, I want you with me one hundred percent. Otherwise, you can get the hell out."

Peggy pressed her lips together.

"I'm waiting for an answer, Peggy. Are you with me?"

"Yes, ma'am. One hundred percent."

Granny waited a good long time before she released Peggy from her penetrating gaze. "Good. I'm glad to hear it. I was beginning to wonder."

Peggy tried to read the expression on the dragon lady's face. Did she still wonder? Did she still have doubts about Peggy? If she did, that could be fatal to Peggy's employment status.

Granny spouted a few more "go, team, go" platitudes, then walked briskly out of the conference room. Peggy noticed that Kip and Troy both left without saying a word to her. She had obtained pariah status; none of the suck-ups would have anything to do with her till they were sure she was back on Granny's good side.

She was relieved that the meeting was over but disturbed at the result. She knew damn well they were obligated to produce the Vincenzo evidence. True, the evidence against Zakin was enormous, but courts had made mistakes before. And with someone like Granny in charge, anything could happen. What if this suppression of evidence caused an innocent man to be convicted, even executed, for a crime he didn't commit?

And if she participated in the suppression of evidence, she would be just as liable—just as guilty—as Granny. In fact, if it were to ever come out, Peggy wouldn't be surprised if it didn't turn out to be all her fault.

But what could she do? Granny had made her decision and would never reconsider it.

And she couldn't cross Granny, could she? If Granny ever found out . . .

Peggy ran to her office and slammed the door behind her. There had to be something she could do, something that allowed her to keep her job, keep paying the bills, not be disbarred, and still not commit a sin a thousand rosaries couldn't wash away.

But what was it?

* 18 *

Ben was hard at work at the tiny desk in the closet they were currently calling his office when he heard a knock at the door.

Who was that? he wondered. Couldn't be Christina. She never knocked. "Come in."

The door opened, and a strapping mountain of a man stepped inside.

"Loving!" Ben rose to greet his investigator, shaking his powerful hand. Loving probably outweighed Ben by a hundred pounds, and it was all muscle. Strength radiated from every part of his body. Ben had first met Loving on the wrong side of a gun, but he had somehow parlayed that unfortunate confrontation into a close working relationship and friendship.

"You weren't kidding when you said you'd make good time. I can't believe you're already here."

Loving shrugged awkwardly. Nothing like watching a mountain-size man act sheepish. "Aw, it wasn't nothin', Skipper. Just pulled a few strings at the airlines."

Pulled a few strings? Ben wondered. Or bashed a few heads?

"Talked to your cop buddy Mike Morelli before I left. He

wanted to come, but he's buried in some triple homicide shoot-out on the Fifteenth Street bridge. He said to call if you need help."

"I'll keep that in mind."

"And Jones has been burnin' the midnight oil, running up his Internet bill tryin' to get you background info. He says he'll be FedExing you a report tomorrow morning."

"Excellent." Ben smiled. "We've already got a trial date hanging over our heads, and it's not far away, either. I'm going to try to meet all the key witnesses, but I can't possibly do everything that needs to be done in the time remaining."

"That's why I'm here, Skipper. Just tell me what to do."

"Great. My primary concern right now is the victim, a logger named Dwayne Gardiner. The prosecution is trying to paint the killing as politically motivated—an eco-terrorist takes out a tree killer. But Gardiner was also shot *before* the explosion that burned him to death. That seems unnecessary, especially if the only motive was stopping the clear-cutting."

"You wanna know why he was shot first."

"You read my mind. There are a bunch of bars and pool halls and such where the loggers congregate during their off-hours. I'd like you to hang around, see if you can get to know these men a little."

"And see what I can find out about this Gardiner."

"Exactly. You never know what you might turn up. Anything could be useful."

"Got it. Anything else?"

"In time. I suspect I'm going to need someone to do some digging into Green Rage. See if there are any secrets I need to know about. They just lost one of their top members. I'd like to know why."

"Can't you just ask your client and his pals?"

"I can ask," Ben said. "But I can't always be sure about what I'm being told. Anyway, first things first. See what you can learn about Gardiner—"

Christina burst through the door. She was carrying a huge cardboard box, practically big enough to hold a refrigerator. She smiled and greeted Loving.

"What's that?" Ben asked. With the three of them and the

box in his pseudo-office, there was barely enough room to move. He was beginning to feel distinctly claustrophobic.

"These are the prosecution's exhibits," she answered. "The ones that can't be photocopied."

"When can we expect the ones that can be photocopied?"

"They say they're still working on it. Which is to say, they're taking their time and will push it just as long as they think they can without causing you to run to the judge."

Ben peered at the huge box. "This seems like an odd way to produce physical evidence."

"I think it would be fair to say this is the way calculated to be least convenient to the defense," Christina replied. "Some of the clerks in the filing office gave me the skinny. Granny's put the word out—she wants everyone to be as uncooperative and obstructive as possible, within the letter of the law."

"But why?"

"Because she wants to win, Ben. She wants to win big."

Ben peered over the edge of the box. "Anything in here of interest?"

"Oh yeah." Christina reached inside. "Here's something the cops found after the murder—in George Zakin's tent." She pulled out a huge mess of cloth and fur; to Ben, it looked like a wadded-up throw rug.

"I don't follow. What is it?"

Christina shook it out to its full length. It was as long as a tall man, covered with black hair and fur—with a zipper up the back.

That was the first thing Ben noticed. The second thing he noticed was the mask, apelike and entirely black.

And the third thing he noticed was the abominable smell—worse than the worst skunk that ever walked the face of the planet. What was it?

Ben slapped his forehead. Of course. It was a Halloween costume.

Sasquatch.

"Why didn't you tell me?"

Zak ran his fingers through his long, unkempt hair. "I just

didn't think it was important. I didn't want to confuse the issues."

"Confuse the issues? What the hell are you talking about?" Ben grabbed him by the shoulders and shoved him back onto his cot. "You're on trial for murder!"

"It's just politics, man."

"Let me give you a news flash, Zak. I've spoken to the prosecutor personally, and I don't think she's remotely interested in politics, except maybe her own reelection. What she cares about is preserving her win-loss record and seeing you jabbed with a lethal syringe!"

"She's just a pawn, Ben. There are larger forces at work here."

"Larger forces? What are we talking about here? Global conspiracies? Covert government operations? 'Cause I'd really like to know."

"Don't be patronizing. I'm talking about the Cabal. The million-dollar mob. Their dirty tricks make our monkey-wrenching tactics look like kid stuff."

"I think we're getting a bit off the subject. Why did you lie to me about the Sasquatch suit?"

"I didn't want Green Rage to get distracted. I didn't want to feed Slade and the logging machine any ammunition."

"So you lied to your lawyer."

Zak extended his hands. "Look, the suit was no big deal. I never even wore it."

"Someone did."

"You're assuming all those rubes who reported seeing Bigfoot saw someone wearing my suit. For all I know they saw the real thing."

"Give me a break."

"It wasn't even my idea. Some of the other nitwits in the group bought this Bigfoot suit, and they'd been running around in it before I even showed up here. I thought their suit looked particularly stupid and unconvincing, so I got my own. It was a first-class outfit. Very handsome and manly. Bigfoot had a bright red nose, like Rudolph or something. But Green Rage put the kibosh on that particular program, so I never got to wear it. Never even showed it to anyone. In fact, I threw it away."

"The cops found it in your tent."

"Not my suit. That's the original one. The boring number Green Rage had before I made the scene."

"Why would it be in your tent?"

"I don't know. I didn't put it there."

"The prosecution has tested it. They've found traces of sweat and skin flecks. They say it was worn—recently."

"Not by me."

"Then who?"

"How should I know? Our camp was hardly a high-security compound. Anyone could've gotten in there and gotten the suit. And put it in my tent when they were done."

"Now you're sounding paranoid."

"You have no idea what these Cabal people are capable of. I do." He leaned forward, arms outstretched. "It's just a stupid suit. It doesn't matter."

Ben wanted to beat his head against the cell bars, but he managed to exercise some measure of restraint. "The prosecution knows someone was behind all the Sasquatch sightings. You had the perfect motive. And now they find the suit in your tent. They're gonna tell the jury you're Bigfoot."

"And that makes me a murderer?"

"Granny's theory will go something like this: First, the fact that you were prancing around in a Bigfoot suit explains why you would be out in the forest late at night."

"I was always out in the forest late at night."

"But they need you to be doing something you shouldn't. That's how they get to motive. They'll say you were trying to instigate false Bigfoot sightings—and maybe planting a few bombs on logging machinery for good measure. And this logger, Dwayne Gardiner, spots Bigfoot and decides to have a few words with the prehistoric beast. Maybe even take him back to camp to see his boss. You panic and shoot him. But to your horror, he doesn't die right away. So you put him on the tree cutter and blow him to kingdom come."

"That isn't right. It didn't happen that way."

Ben arched an eyebrow. "Then how did it happen?"

"I—I mean—I wasn't there."

Ben took a few short steps until the two men were standing very close to one another. "Now listen to me, Zak. And listen good. I will not put up with this."

"You're not backing out, are you?"

"I can't back out. It's too close to trial. The judge wouldn't let me quit even if I asked. But I can tell you this." He planted a finger square in Zak's chest. "I will not put up with any lying. You must tell me everything, the good and the bad. I've never had a case that didn't have some bad facts and I probably never will. But if I know about them in advance, I can prepare. I can be the one who tells the jury about it up front, to soften the impact. But I can't do any of that if you don't tell me the truth!"

Zak held up his hands. "All right, man. I got it. It won't happen again."

"And to make sure it doesn't, Zak, let me ask you again. Is there anything else you haven't told me? Anything that might be potentially damaging to us at trial? *Anything?*"

"No, man. Nothing. Definitely not."

"Be sure, Zak. Be absolutely sure."

"I am. I am."

Ben waited a long moment before speaking again. "I'm warning you . . ."

"There's nothing else, man. I promise. And if I think of anything later, I'll call you."

"You do that." Ben reached through the bars and rapped on the outer wall—the signal to the sheriff that he was ready to leave. "How am I going to explain this to the jury? I don't suppose we can say you were preparing early for trick or treat?"

Zak tilted his head to one side. "Well . . ."

"Or maybe you'd been invited to a masquerade ball?"

"I don't think so."

"Or maybe you were satisfying your angora fetish."

Zak gave him an unamused look.

"Well, I'll keep working on it. Can I ask you one more question?"

"Sure. Shoot."

"I may be sorry I asked, but"—Ben's face squinched up—"why does the suit smell so bad?"

"That's easy. Most of the reports of close encounters with Bigfoot have mentioned his tremendous stench. Really horrible—worse than dead animals that have been left out in the sun. It's a Bigfoot calling card."

"And you wanted to be authentic."

"Of course." Zak shrugged his shoulders. "What's the point of having a fake if it isn't real?"

* 19 *

Ben approached the sawmill with considerable trepidation. Maureen had warned him he would feel this way, but he hadn't believed it until he arrived. After all, he was an impartial participant. He was a lawyer representing a client, conducting an interview relating to a murder case. He was not necessarily involved in the political issues that underlay the conflict.

He just hoped everyone else understood that.

He parked his rental car and started up the dirt path that wound toward the main building—a huge log-and-sideboard structure at the edge of the Crescent National Forest. As Maureen had explained to him, the sawmill had been there since the 1950s, processing tons of lumber on a daily basis for any number of logging sites.

Even from a good distance away, Ben could hear the teeth-grinding sound of the sawmill at work. It was a shrill, piercing sound, like a dentist's drill magnified a thousand times over. Except instead of opening a root canal to save an abscessed tooth, it was splitting, pulping, and destroying hundreds of years and thousands of acres of wild growth.

Ben brushed shoulders with several loggers making their

way out of the main building. He was pleased to see that, contrary to stereotype, they did not all wear flannel shirts. Jeans and T-shirts seemed more the current fashion. But then, it was still summer. Maybe the flannel came out later in the year.

He saw a group of loggers off to one side whispering. One of them glanced at Ben, then lowered his head into the communal huddle. If I were a paranoid man, Ben thought, I'd think they were talking about me.

And then he saw one of the men in the huddle jerk his thumb in Ben's direction.

That settled it. Paranoid or not, Ben was the topic of conversation.

Ben was so busy watching the huddle that he almost walked right into the man standing directly in front of him.

"Oops!" Ben put on the brakes at the last possible minute. "Sorry about that."

The man didn't move. He didn't smile, either. "You don't look like you belong here. Got some ID?"

"What is this, a gestapo camp? You need ID just to get in?"

"We have to be careful. There are terrorists in the area who would love nothing more than to see this mill blown to bits."

"Well, I can assure you I'm no terrorist."

"Didn't I see you at the courthouse?"

Ben's heart skipped a beat. "Courthouse? Me? You must be thinking of my older brother."

"No. It was you." He placed his fists firmly on his hips. "You're the lawyer. The one who's representing the killer."

Ben swallowed a big gulp of air. "Yes, I'm a lawyer. And I'm here on official business." He noticed that the larger group of men at the side were slowly edging in his direction. "So if you'll please just step aside . . ."

"You've got some nerve, showing your face here. After what happened to Dwayne."

"Look, I wasn't even in town when Dwayne was killed."

The huddled men—there were five of them—pulled up behind Ben. One of them, wearing a red baseball cap with CATERPILLAR printed across the front, spoke. "Who is this creep, Jerry?"

"He's one of those Green Rage assholes."

"You're kidding." Strong hands clamped down on both of Ben's shoulders. "Here?"

"It isn't true," Ben protested. "I'm not a member of—"

"He works with them," the first man—Jerry, apparently—explained. "Helps them do their dirty business."

"No shit," Caterpillar man said. The others pressed close on all sides. "What were you planning? To bomb the mill?"

"Of course not. I just came to talk."

"Right. Search him, boys."

All at once Ben felt about ten hands pawing him in every place imaginable, and being none too gentle about it.

"Would you stop already!" Ben said. "I'm not looking for trouble."

"Neither was Dwayne Gardiner," Jerry replied somberly. "But he sure got it. And now there's a woman with no husband and a boy who'll grow up without a daddy. All because of people like you who care more about trees than human beings." His jaw clenched up with rage. "Grab him, boys."

All at once, Ben felt a dozen hands clamp down on him with viselike grips. He could barely wriggle, much less move.

"Someone got rope?"

"I know where some is," Caterpillar man answered. He ran down the dirt road, opened a storage bin, and pulled out a good length.

"Tie him up."

Ben tried to struggle, but it was useless. With all those hands on him, he couldn't budge.

"Take him down to the lot."

A moment later, all hands were jerking him down the way he came, toward the parking area. Clouds of dirt kicked up in his face, choking him, but there was nothing he could do about it. His arms were clamped tightly to his sides, and he had no control over his movements.

They kept moving till they got to the area where the vehicles were parked. Jerry nodded toward a huge eighteen-wheel flatbed truck. "Someone got the keys?"

One of the men in Caterpillar's group nodded.

"Good. Tie the rope to the hitching post."

The men tied one end of the rope around Ben's wrists, the

other end to the iron post at the back of the truck. He was beginning to have a very bad feeling about this . . .

"You're making a mistake," Ben said. He was trying to think of any words that might convince them, however pathetic they sounded. "I don't mean you any harm."

"Tell it to Dwayne's family." Jerry pulled Ben backward till the rope was extended and pulled taut, then he motioned for the man with the keys to jump in the cab.

"All right," Jerry said. A trace of a smile cracked his stony exterior. "Drag him."

* 20 *

"You can't be serious!" Ben said. Panic was setting in. Beads of sweat trickled down his temples.

Jerry didn't bother replying. He raised his arm and then, like an orchestra conductor marking the opening note, brought it down with a flourish.

All at once, the eighteen-wheeler lurched into Drive. Ben was jerked forward, hands and head first, onto the hard red dirt.

He hadn't expected that. He thought it would take the huge truck a while to warm up, that he would be able to jog behind it, at least for a while. Instead, it had taken off like a souped-up Camaro.

And it continued to barrel across the parking lot. Ben was dragged along the ground, his chin scraping the hard earth. Dirt flew up into his eyes, stinging them; he soon learned it was smartest to keep his eyes shut.

But all of that was minor compared to the pummeling his body was taking. He was battered by every bump, rise, and pothole. And there were lots of all of them. He was skinned and bruised and the truck seemed to be increasing in speed.

"Oof!" Ben's chin socked the ground hard. He could feel blood trickling down his neck, his cheeks. It stung so badly he almost didn't see the rock—

Until it was too late. It struck him square in the chest. Ben cried out in pain, but the truck kept moving and the rock rumbled under his body, cutting and bruising him all along the way. The hum of the engine told Ben the truck was accelerating. At the current speed, he was probably only looking at serious injuries. But if the truck moved any faster . . .

"Stop this!"

Ben heard the voice behind him, but he was in no position to check the source. The truck was still moving, and he'd spotted another rock with a sharp edge coming toward him. Fast.

"Stop this *immediately*! Stop or you're all out of work!"

The truck braked. Ben heard the hydraulic hissing before he actually felt any decrease in speed.

He stopped just inches short of the jagged rock. Up close, it looked positively lethal. If he'd been dragged over that, he'd be in seriously bad shape.

"I'm so sorry about this." A man he didn't know had crouched down and was untying the knots around Ben's wrists. "This is inexcusable. But don't worry. I'll take appropriate action. Listen, men, you're all—"

Both he and Ben looked all around. They were alone. The loggers had fled.

"Typical." The man made a clicking noise with his tongue, then finished untying Ben. He offered Ben a hand. "Are you all right?"

Ben slowly raised himself to a seated position. His whole body ached. His clothes were ruined, but he thought he could walk. "I'll live."

He pushed up to his feet, but his legs wobbled like jelly. The other man caught him and helped him back down to the ground. "Don't rush it, son. It'll be a spell before you get your strength back."

Ben decided to take his advice. He wiped a trickle of blood from his chin. "Thanks for intervening."

"No problem, son. They had no business doing this. The boys are just so riled up right now. Feel like they're under attack, like danger's coming at them from all sides."

Really? Ben thought. That's almost exactly how the Green Ragers say they feel.

Ben extended his hand. "Anyway, my name's Ben Kincaid."

"Jeremiah Adams," the man said. He was in his late fifties, with short-cropped hair and a spotty white beard on his chin. He was wearing jeans and a western shirt, complete with studs. "I'm the supervisor out here. I think you were coming to see me."

"You must be Granny's father. I mean Granville's. The prosecutor."

Adams laughed. "You know my little girl?"

"I do." Ben pushed himself to his feet again, and this time he was relieved to see that his legs held. "Could we go inside and talk?"

Ben followed the man as he led the way up the ramp and into the building. He tried his best not to wobble, but his left ankle felt twisted and kept dropping out from under him. Like it or not, he was going to limp; he decided the best he could do was to stare straight ahead and limp with dignity.

As soon as they passed through the front doors of the building, Ben was overwhelmed by the piercingly loud roar. Fierce, menacing, and metallic.

"Takes a mite to get used to that sawmill," Adams said as he shuffled down the main corridor. "Nowadays I barely even notice it."

Barely even *notice*? Ben thought, wincing. The man had to be kidding. Inside, the shrill roar was so insistent he could barely think, much less hear.

"I remember the first time I visited the mill, back before I worked here. 'Round '70, '71, I 'spect. Noise hurt my head so bad I started wearing earplugs. 'Course that didn't set too well with the regulars. They marked me down for some kind of sissy boy, if you know what I mean. So I took out the plugs and learned to deal with it. Haven't had any problems since. Oh, I get some ringing in my ears from time to time, but not enough to complain about."

I think I've got plenty to complain about already, Ben thought, but he decided to keep it to himself. He wasn't at all sure he could make himself heard over this din anyway.

They emerged in the main part of the building, the mill itself. Ben saw the long ramp where timber was loaded and the conveyor belt that brought it steadily closer to the big blade. And a big blade it was, too. Enormous—at least six feet in diameter, maybe more. Big enough to split a house, Ben thought, much less some puny five-hundred-year-old tree.

Ben watched as the men below used a large yellow crane to hoist a particularly large trunk onto the ramp. Another man in a hard hat standing a few feet from them pushed a button, and the conveyor belt lurched into action. A few seconds later, the huge rotating blade was slicing clean through the trunk like a knife through butter.

"Trunk like that, they'll have to split three or four times 'fore it's manageable enough to transport," Adams explained. "Be different if we were on a waterway, if we could float the timber to market the way they used to do. Even those big eighteen-wheelers like the one you got to see up close and personal have their limits."

The sawmill blade finished subdividing the trunk. A whistle blew somewhere outside. The workmen checked their watches. A few moments later, the blade began to slow. The insistent whine of the engine dropped in pitch until, to Ben's enormous relief, the noise faded.

"You're in luck, son," Adams said, chuckling. "Midmorning break. Engine'll be down for fifteen minutes. We can talk." He gestured for Ben to follow. They returned to the main corridor, then took a sharp left. Ben caught his reflection in a window as they passed; there was a streak of blood across his left cheek. He raised a sleeve and tried to make himself more presentable.

A few moments later, they were in a room that appeared to be Adams's office.

"Sorry about the clutter," he said. Clutter was an understatement. The office was packed with huge piles of paper, maps, and charts filling every available bit of floor space. There was a desk, but it was so buried under food wrappers and empty beer bottles that there wasn't a place to put a pencil. There did appear to be some framed photos hanging on the wall, but the trash and debris were so dense Ben couldn't tell what they were.

Check that, he told himself. There was one picture he could identify. It hung just behind the desk. A framed four-by-seven photo, slightly yellowed, of a teenage girl receiving her high school diploma. And if he wasn't mistaken, the girl was a considerably younger, though no less shapely, version of Granville Adams. Prosecutor Granny.

"That's my baby girl," Adams said as he wedged himself into the space between his desk and the wall. To Ben's surprise, once the litter was rearranged a bit, there turned out to be a chair back there. "So you know her?"

"I do," Ben said, not adding that he had a damned hard time thinking of her as anybody's baby girl. Most likely she ruled the roost from the day she came home from the hospital. "She's prosecuting the Gardiner case."

" 'Course she is," Adams said, beaming. "She's the D.A., ain't she?"

Ben nodded. "You must be very proud of her."

"That, son, is one whale of an understatement. Hell, I've always been proud of her." He gazed out his window, a large wall-length aperture affording a commanding view of the front parking area and the forest beyond. "Only had one time up at the plate—she's the only child I've got. But man, what a home run I hit. I never seen the like anywhere. Drop-dead gorgeous, ambitious, hard-working. And smart?" He made a long, low whistle.

"She is all those things," Ben agreed. And a few more he wasn't going to mention.

"I don't know where she got it all. Not from her daddy. That's for damn sure." His smile faded a bit. "My wife Jenny died before Granny turned five."

"I'm sorry, I didn't—"

"Don't worry about it, son. It's been a long time." He

pushed himself up in his chair. "No, I had to raise that girl all on my own. Though the truth of the matter is, she raised herself."

Ben could well imagine. He wondered if this might be a good time to lead the conversation to the more pressing matter at hand. "Do you mind if I ask you a few questions about Dwayne Gardiner? And his murder?"

"You're welcome to ask," Adams replied. "Like I told your little lady on the telephone, I don't know how much help I can be."

"Did you know Gardiner?"

" 'Course I did. He was one of my boys. Had been for some ten"—he shrugged—"I don't know, twelve years."

"Did you like him?"

"You bet. He was a good man. Hard worker. Even though he was only thirty and change, he was a logger from the old school. One that didn't mind pulling a long day and working up a good sweat. Knew the value of hard work. Knew the importance of what we're trying to do. The lifestyle we're trying to preserve."

"Did he have any friends? Family? Wife?"

"He had a wife all right. Lu Ann is one of the shapeliest, sexiest numbers in these parts. Not pretty in a classy way, like my little Granny. But she did have a certain appeal for a certain type of man, if you follow my drift. Like the type that likes to get drunk and do the hokey-pokey in the back of a pickup truck."

Ben nodded. He thought he got the general idea.

" 'Course Dwayne had plenty of friends, too. All his logging buddies, all the boys who spend every other night of their life out at Bunyan's slurpin' tall cool ones."

"Any enemies?"

Adams pressed his lips together, as if trying to think how exactly to put it. "I wouldn't say enemies, exactly. Dwayne never did anything that would cause a man to have enemies. But there was some . . . friction. Between him and some of the other boys."

"Over Lu Ann?"

"You're a quick one, ain't ya?" Adams winked. "Yes, sir,

when a man has a wife like Lu Ann, he's bound to be just a wee bit jealous. Almost has to be, really."

"And had reason to be?"

" 'Course I wouldn't know any of this from personal experience, you understand, but . . . I think it might be fair to say that some of the boys aren't always too good about honoring the sanctity of the marriage contract. If you know what I mean."

Ben did, and he was glad to hear it. This was the first glimmer he'd had of a possible motive for Gardiner's demise other than eco-terrorism. "Do you know of any specific cases?"

"Oh, no. Nothin' like that. I just know that with a gal like Lu Ann, the possibility is ever-present."

Well, it was a start, anyway. "Any other problems in Gardiner's life? Anything that might've caused some ill will or rancor?"

"I don't know if ill will is exactly the right word . . ."

"Don't worry about the words," Ben urged. "Just tell me what you're thinking."

After a few more moments, Adams spoke. "I mentioned before that Dwayne was a logger's logger. A true believer. Someone who was willing to take a stand to preserve our way of life."

"You said it, but I didn't really understand it."

"The logger is under attack right now, son. Least that's how we feel about it. There are folks out there threatenin' our way of life."

"You're talking about Green Rage."

"I am." He licked his lips. "I don't know where you stand, son. I don't know if you're really into this tree-hugging crap or if you're just a lawyer tryin' to make a few bucks. But there are people—criminals, is what they are—determined to make it impossible for a man to make a living in the logging business. Folks who want to see the lumberjack become an extinct species."

"And Dwayne was upset about this?"

"Dwayne came from three generations of loggers." He nodded his head grimly. "Yeah, I guess you could say he was upset about this."

"Upset enough to get himself killed?"

Adams leaned back against the wall. With his head so close to the photo of his daughter, Ben could easily see the resemblance. "I'm going to tell you something that's not altogether public knowledge, son, and I hope you'll respect the confidence in which it's given."

"If it doesn't relate to the case, I won't tell a soul. If it does, I can't make any promises."

"Fair enough." Adams eased forward. "We in the Magic Valley logging community have been aware for some time now that there is in our midst a . . . well, what's the word? Turncoat? Quisling? Someone reporting to the other side."

"A spy? But why?"

"Too many times, these Green Rage punks have known what we were doing, known what we were planning to do, almost as soon as we knew ourselves. The first few times, well, you just write it off to chance. But after a while it becomes apparent that somebody's doing some talkin'."

"What kind of talking?"

"Like tipping off Green Rage when we're planning to move into a new area."

"You mean, when you're trying to quietly go after the old-growth trees that are supposed to be protected?"

He held up his hands. "I don't want to quibble with you, son. I know that won't get us anywhere. Just suffice to say that we knew someone was talking."

"Did Gardiner know who it was?"

"No, he didn't." He set his lips firmly together. "But he was determined to find out."

"Did he have any leads?"

"It's possible, but if he did, he didn't share them with me. I do know this—he'd been asking some of the boys some pretty pointed questions, and some of them didn't take none too kindly to it."

"I don't understand that," Ben said.

"You got to understand what's goin' on here. Like I said, we loggers feel like we're under siege, like someone's tryin' to rob us of our way of life. What I never understood is why these eco-people, these high-minded out-of-towners, think they know more about the forest than we do. Or why it is they love trees more than they do people." He sighed. "I could never trust someone who puts trees first, because I know that deep down, that person doesn't love his fellow man. Probably doesn't love himself. Gives me the shivers to think about it, really. How can you appeal to a man's humanity if he doesn't have any?"

"Well, I don't think it's a sign of self-loathing to respect the natural forest."

"And why do you folks think you're the only ones who respect the forest? Let me tell you something, son. We loggers respect the forest—more than most. We have to; it's our lifeblood."

"How can you say you respect something you're tearing down?"

"We are not tearing down the forests. But we've got a job to do." Adams pressed his spread fingers against the desk. He was an amiable man, but Ben could see that his patience was being tried. "Do you know how many people the logging industry employs? How many families depend on logging for their livelihood?"

"But there are other ways to make a living. You don't have to kill trees."

"You don't have to defend murderers, either. But some folks still do it."

Ben decided to take that kick in the teeth with his mouth closed.

"For every tree we cut down," Adams insisted, "we plant two in its place."

"Which is admirable," Ben said. "But as a scientist was explaining to me just yesterday, the forest doesn't grow back the same."

"Why should it? Nature is about change. This planet has changed constantly since life began."

"But surely rows of evenly spaced saplings are no substitute for a vibrant, wild forest."

"If you were one of the men who depended on logging for a livelihood, you'd see it differently."

Probably true, Ben realized. Probably very true. "How

many of those men are there? I understand logging companies are employing fewer men every year."

Adams tilted his head to one side. "Well . . ."

"Profits are way up, but employment is way down. Why is that?"

"It's these eco-terrorists. Spiking trees and blowing equipment. We have to cut back."

"According to my client, you hire fewer men because you're replacing them with machines."

"There are advantages to mechanized labor," Adams admitted. "You don't have to worry about machines going on strike or complaining about unsafe working conditions. You don't have to pay Social Security on a machine, or for that matter, health insurance or disability benefits. Which is pretty important, since statistically the average logger will be disabled before he turns fifty-two."

"I read that logging is the most dangerous occupation in the country, bar none."

"It's true. Still, it's been our way of life, and we're not going to let you tree huggers—"

"Wait a minute. I'm not a tree hugger. I don't even like camping. I like air conditioning and wall-to-wall carpet." Ben squared himself opposite Adams's desk. "But I can't stand an entire industry claiming it's noble because it puts people first, when in fact it's simply using people to make profits. And if it's replacing men with machines, it should admit it, instead of using environmentalists as scapegoats."

Adams drummed his fingers on his desk. "Mr. Kincaid, I'm beginning to be sorry I pulled you away from those boys outside."

"You pulled me away when you wanted to. When you thought I'd learned a lesson and would feel indebted to my rescuer."

"What?"

"Don't try to con me. I've got eyes. And you've got a great view." Ben gestured toward the wide window behind the desk, with its spacious view of the front parking area. "You could've stopped that show outside before they'd dragged me an inch. But you didn't. You waited for the right moment."

"I don't know what—"

"I wouldn't be surprised if you stage-managed the whole thing. Had some of the boys get a bit rowdy so you could come in and rescue me. See if you could win me over to your side."

"You're just as sick and paranoid as those criminals you work for."

Maybe so, Ben thought as he stared down at Adams's angry face. But at this point, he wasn't entirely sure what to believe. Or who.

* 21 *

Ben was almost out of the sawmill when to his amazement he saw Amos Slade sitting in a comfortable chair in what looked like the mill kitchenette. He was flanked by a coffee-pot and vending machines; he had a half-eaten cruller in his left hand.

Ben knew it was like bearding the lion in his den, but for his client's sake, he plunged in. "I thought you had no official ties to the logging industry?"

"Mr. Kincaid." Slade smiled; bits of doughnut glaze crinkled along his lips. "I don't have any official ties. But they are kind enough to give me a place to rest my feet from time to time."

"Unofficially."

"But of course." Slade pointed toward a box on the table. "Care for a doughnut? We've got jelly-filled."

"Thanks, but no."

"You have a disagreement with Adams?"

"What makes you think that?"

Slade shrugged. "Would you believe I just had a hunch?"

"More likely you have his office bugged."

Slade laughed. "Well, anything is possible." He shoved the doughnut box down the table toward Ben. "Look, Kincaid, you've never done anything to me, and whether you believe it or not, I'm not your enemy. So do you mind if I give you a little advice?"

"Not unless you expect me to take it."

He laughed again. "I think I've got you pegged, Kincaid. You're Don Quixote."

"Excuse me?"

"You know what I mean. Tilting at windmills. Fighting for lost causes. That sort of thing."

"You're barking up the wrong—"

"Don't bother denying it, kid. I've had you checked out."

"What?"

"Don't act so astonished. You don't go into the courtroom unprepared, and neither do I. Did you think you were going to be able to waltz into this little melodrama and not get your hair mussed? That you could play with fire and not get singed? Well, wrongerino, kid. I've got your whole bleeding-heart background stored away in a file folder. As I'm sure those Green Ragers did before me."

"What's that supposed to mean?"

"You thought this was some sort of coincidence? That they just happened to stumble across exactly what they needed most? Sorry, kid, I don't believe in miracles. At least not at that level."

"Your problem is that you think everyone in the world uses the same underhanded tactics as you."

"You know, kid, I do think that. But it's not a problem. It's a reality." He raised his hand to his face and let his fingers dance a moment on his forehead. "Which is all getting me far afield from the tiny piece of advice I wished to convey. Here it is, kid: go home."

"You're wasting my time."

"No, I'm not, and I'm not joking, either. I'm vewwy vewwy serious. Go home. Catch a plane and fly back to sleepy little Tulsa. You'll be a lot safer back where Ma and Pa still rise with the chickens, everyone believes in God, and nobody's ever heard of nasty things like industrial sabotage or eco-terrorism. For your own sake, kid. You don't belong here. So go home."

"Well, thank you very much for your considerate advice. I promise to give it all the attention it merits."

Slade leaned forward. "You think I'm going to let you win this case? Let me disinform you. I won't."

Ben felt the hairs on the back of his neck rising. "I wasn't aware you had every juror in the county in the palm of your hand."

"Then you should be. I can get anything I want, Kincaid. It's just a question of time and money. And as far as this case goes, I've been given the green light."

"What does that mean?"

"You figure it out. I've been authorized to do whatever it takes to accomplish our objectives. And I will."

Ben tried to be brave, ignoring the fact that Slade was giving him the major-league creeps. "Look, it's this simple. I don't think George Zakin did it. And in any case, he's entitled to a defense. So I'm going to give it to him."

Slade let his hands flutter to his side. "I've got a surprise for you, chump."

Ben blinked. "What are you talking about?"

"Very soon your newfound employers will be racing back to the rabbit warrens they crawled out of, and you will be left here holding the bag. Very alone. And very vulnerable."

"If this is supposed to scare me, it isn't working," Ben lied.

"Like I said, I've got a surprise for you."

"A surprise?" Ben sputtered. "What is that, some—some kind of threat?"

Slade shook his head slowly back and forth. "I don't make threats." He lowered his eyes till they met Ben's. "I don't have to."

* 22 *

Tess crouched down behind the dense foliage at the edge of the clearing. As long as she stayed behind the greenery and didn't move, she should be safe from detection by the men congregated a few hundred yards away.

At least that was the theory.

"Tell me again why we're out here in broad daylight," Tess whispered to Al, who was crouched beside her.

"It's a reconnaissance mission," Al whispered back. He glanced at Rick, who was hovering just above them. "Although I wonder if we don't have an opportunity to do a little something more."

A trace of a smile played on Rick's lips. "Shhh. We don't want to be spotted."

"If we don't want to be spotted," Tess said, "why are we here?"

"Because we're predators, remember?" Al answered. "We have to go out when our prey is afoot."

Like that was a good answer or something, Tess thought. What on earth was she doing? Every mission she went on with these people seemed riskier and crazier than the one before. Sure, they had come to trust her. They were more comfortable talking to her, taking her into their confidence. But what a price . . .

"I know I'm the new kid on the block," Tess whispered, keeping her eyes fixed on the men in the clearing, "but this seems awfully risky."

Al looked unsympathetic. "Wah, wah, wah."

"I mean, think about it. Our last raid was in the dead of night, and we still almost got caught. We had to run almost two miles before we lost that team of loggers. That team that, I might add, was probably waiting for us all along, like a cat hovering by a mousetrap."

"We still got away with the cheese," Al noted.

"That time, yes. But coming out here in broad daylight is totally harebrained."

Al and Rick exchanged another wry glance. "We're monkey-wrenchers," Rick said, grinning. "We like harebrained schemes."

"And," Al added, "this one isn't even in the top ten."

"Oh yeah?" Tess said. She saw an opportune opening in the conversation. "What would be? Running around in a Sasquatch suit?"

Al drew his head back. He gave her a long look, then winked at Rick. "Little pitchers have big ears."

Rick nodded. "Loose lips sink ships."

"Exchange clichés some other time, okay?" Tess said. "You guys were behind the Sasquatch sightings, weren't you?"

Al looked away. "Whatever gave you that idea, my dear?"

"I just tried to imagine who might have a motive, my dear, and the only answer I came up with was Green Rage, several times over."

"We're tree huggers, remember? Not bear huggers."

"Bigfoot huggers," Rick corrected.

"Yeah, but if there was evidence of a rare, near-extinct life-form running around these woods, much less one as interesting and humanoid as Sasquatch, you'd be able to get an injunction to stop the clear-cutting."

Rick touched a finger to the side of his head. "Al, I believe she's a bit brighter than she first let on. Maybe we should put her in charge of operations."

Al shook his head. "A little too bright for me." He glanced at Tess. "Sorry to disappoint you, but the Bigfoot legend is not a grand eco-terrorist plot. Bigfoot sightings continue on their own momentum, like all myths, urban and rural. I don't know who started this current spate, but it wasn't us."

"Not that we didn't think about cashing in on it," Rick added. "We even sent Deirdre to Seattle for an appropriate costume. But we never used it."

"Sober second thoughts?" Tess asked.

Rick shrugged. "Turned out Al didn't look so hot in black fur. Angora goes better with his complexion."

Al rolled his eyes. "Let's return our attention to the matter at hand, team, shall we? They're moving."

There were two distinct groups of men in the clearing, both maybe three hundred feet from where Tess and Rick and Al were hiding. The first group of six men were loggers; Tess was sure of it. The other group was smaller, only three in number, and they were definitely not loggers. All three wore suits with thin ties; all three suits were some variety of black. Their white shirts gleamed in the bright noonday sun.

"Suits," Al had explained earlier. "Corporate execs."

"What would they be doing here?" Tess asked. "Out in the field?"

"Beats the hell out of me," he answered. "Probably trying to figure out how to get their systematic rape of these supposedly protected five-hundred-year-old trees back on line."

"Even after we blew their tree cutter?"

Al waved his hand. "A few hundred thousand bucks. In a forest like this, they could make it back in a week."

"That's probably why the execs are here," Rick added. "They're trying to figure out how to clear out this forest good and quick, before anyone knows what happened. 'Omigosh, Mr. Ranger. Did we do something wrong?' "

Al pounded his fist into the palm of his hand. "*Damn!* I just can't stand it anymore!"

Rick pressed down on his friend's shoulder. "Hey, man, chill. We're in hiding, remember?"

"How much longer can this go on? We fight and we fight and we fight, but these bastards just keep coming!" Al's jaw was tightly clenched. "They won't stop till every damn tree on the planet has been razed!"

Tess noted the tremor in his voice, the wild look in his eye. "Hey, Al. We need you to stay calm."

"I won't stay calm. I *won't*! I've had enough!" He pushed himself to his feet.

"Al, stay down. They'll see us!"

Al pulled away from her and turned toward Rick. "Do you still have the sugar?"

Rick hesitated before answering. "It's—it's broad daylight, man!"

Al snatched the backpack lying on the ground beside them. He opened the top flap and pulled out a half-filled bag of sugar.

"Al," Rick said edgily, "what are you thinking, man?"

"I'm thinking I've had enough."

Rick jumped between Al and the clearing. "Wait until the sun sets, okay? We can't do anything about it now."

"Just watch me."

There was nothing Rick could do to stop him. Another second and Al had left the safety of the foliage and entered the clearing.

"Al!" Rick hissed after him, but it was too late. Al was gone. Fortunately, they were still about three hundred feet to the rear of the huddle of men, and they were still engaged in a very animated conversation. Still, Tess knew all it would take was a stray look to the south and one of them would see Al, alone and exposed, creeping across the clearing.

She held her breath. Come on, Al, *move it*! The longer he was out in the open, the more vulnerable he was. And she didn't kid herself that she and Rick would be able to do anything to help him—alone, unarmed, outnumbered nine to three. If they saw Al, he was history.

She watched as Al continued his stealthy crawl across the yellow plain. Her palms were sweating and there was a tightness in her throat.

Al's objective was obvious—he was trying to get to the cars. The loggers had walked over from their base camp, but the suits had driven. Turned off the main transport road about two miles north, she guessed, and used the trail the men had already plowed—for use of eighteen-wheelers for hauling felled timber—to get into the clearing. A limo and two Ford GTOs, since each exec of course had to have his own transportation. These schmucks couldn't even conserve gas, much less trees. Al was planning to pour sugar down the crankcases or gas tanks. Or both. To put a monkey-wrench in those suits' plans they wouldn't soon forget.

Unless he got caught.

A few tense seconds later, Al reached the first car, the limo. Jesus God, she'd never been more nervous in her entire life. Not when she staked out Jackie O's private jet. Not when she hid in Michael Jackson's Dumpster. Not even when she ran for life itself two nights before with armed loggers dogging her heels. Actually, she would like to be doing some running right now. Being forced to stand still, being forced to wait—that was simply unbearable.

She watched, scarcely breathing, as Al flattened himself and crawled under the limo. Jesus, couldn't he make do with the gas line? Surely he didn't think he could get to the crank-cases, with those men scant yards away. Was there some other aperture under the car, something equally susceptible to the hydrating and hardening influence of sugar? She didn't know; she was still new to the monkey-wrenching game. But Al would know. He must have a plan. Even if she didn't have a clue what it was.

A few interminable seconds later, Al reemerged from the back of the car. He flashed them a quick thumbs-up, then crept over to the next car in line, the first of the Ford GTOs.

Tess's heart felt like it skipped a beat. *Come on!* she silently urged him, hoping that for once she might turn out to have the mental telepathy she had fantasized about as a child. One car is enough. They'll get the message. Get out of there!

But of course it wasn't enough. She watched as Al slid underneath the second car, still toting his bag of sugar. He didn't want the suits to be mildly inconvenienced. He wanted them positively crippled. He wanted them to spend the day out here, contemplating the environment they were trying to pil-lage, taking the measure of the fighting force they were up against.

She didn't swallow, didn't breathe, until she saw Al crawl out from under the GTO. Two down, one to go. Now if their luck could hold out just a short while longer . . .

But it didn't. Their luck ended the instant Al moved from

the safety of the second car toward the third. When his image flickered in the gap between the cars, someone spotted him.

"Hey, look!" one of the loggers shouted. She didn't know which, and it didn't matter, because a second later, all six of them were headed in Al's direction.

"Run!" she shouted. It was stupid, she knew. She'd blown their position, and she saw two of the loggers pause and glance in their direction. But she had to let Al know he'd been spotted; she had to give him a fighting chance to escape.

Al didn't need a second hint. He dropped the sugar and bolted back toward their hiding place, loggers close at his heels. He had maybe a fifty-foot lead and he was a good runner. But there were six of them, Tess realized, and they were probably no slouches in the physical fitness department themselves.

Six of them? She scanned the clearing. Two of the men had disappeared. She knew what that meant. They'd had the sense to split up—four in pursuit, while the other two tried to head them off at the pass.

"Come on!" Rick said, slapping her shoulder. He turned and bolted into the forest; she followed. She assumed he had seen the same thing she did and realized that they were all in jeopardy. It might be more collegial to wait until Al reached them, but they couldn't afford to take the risk.

At any rate, he was not far behind. She could hear him, even as she ran. He had left the clearing, had plunged into the forest, and he ran much faster than she did. If he wanted, he'd catch up in no time. But she knew that was probably not what he'd do. More likely he'd go a different way. He'd try to confuse the ranks even further. Lead them off in a different direction. Give her and Rick time to disappear.

"This way!" Rick commanded. She saw he was trying to steer her in a different direction. Stupid—she had to stop concentrating on Al and start trying to keep her own neck out of the noose. Rick knew the way back to their camp; she didn't. She had to stick with him or she would soon be lost.

She followed Rick as he plunged through the bramble and undergrowth. Plants and branches brushed past her, sometimes slashing her face. She didn't have the time to worry about it. She had to keep moving forward, keep plowing ahead.

She saw the fallen tree trunk just ahead of her. Rick had jumped it; surely she could do the same. Without breaking her speed, she leaped into the air.

She cleared the trunk with room to spare, but she landed with a thud. Her right foot touched down on something hard—a large rock, she thought—and her ankle twisted out from under her. Her body followed close behind, tumbling to the mud in an unceremonious heap.

Rick broke his pace. "Come on!" he growled.

Tess tried to push herself up, but she could tell her ankle wouldn't support her weight for a good long while. "Go on without me," she whispered.

Rick started to argue, then thought better of it. He turned and started to resume flight—

When they both heard the sound of twin cracking noises rippling through the still air.

Two shotguns. Just behind them.

"Lookee here, Sam," one of the men said. "I think I've caught myself an honest-to-God terrorist." The logger pointed his shotgun right at Rick and gave him a look that said he wouldn't hesitate a second before firing.

"I hate terrorists," the other logger said. "Goddamn criminals." He spat on the ground just beside Tess's face.

"You and me both." The man with the shotgun walked over to Rick, grabbed him by the scruff of the neck, and threw him down to the ground.

Suddenly Tess heard the sound of additional footsteps kicking through the forest.

"Well, look at this. Sam and Max done already finished the job for us. I guess we can have a little party."

Tess turned and, to her horror, saw two more loggers moving toward them, dragging Al's limp body behind them.

Dragging, because he could not walk. He didn't appear to be conscious. His eyes were closed and were already swollen and black. Blood trickled from his left ear.

"Looks like you started the party without us," the man with the gun said, glancing at the limp body dumped unceremoniously onto the ground beside Tess. "That wasn't very neighborly."

"Well, there's still a hell of a lot more to do." One of the men who had dumped Al snarled at Rick. "I guess you must be one of those Green Rage boys, right?"

Rick didn't answer.

"Well, I'm feeling a bit of rage right now myself," the man said. The two men with shotguns stepped forward, guns trained on Rick, while the first man primed his fist for action.

Tess turned away. She couldn't bear to watch. The sickening sound of it alone was almost more than she could bear. She tried to block it out, but no matter what she did, no matter what she tried, she heard each and every blow, each and every shrill cry of pain, and in time, each and every plea for mercy.

* 23 *

"What the hell did you think you were *doing*?"

Ben paced furiously outside the cell. He knew he was not doing a good job of controlling his emotions—wasn't really doing a good job of controlling anything. But sometimes it felt good just to let it rip.

"Do you understand that we're trying a murder case here? That it starts next week? That the death penalty is still very much a possibility?"

Inside the cell, Tess and Rick squirmed. Tess had managed to survive their capture by the loggers with only minor bruises and abrasions; apparently hitting a woman was still contrary to most loggers' code of ethics. But Rick had not been so fortunate; the pounding he'd taken had split open a cut above his right eye and dislocated his jaw. He'd been released from the hospital only shortly before Ben arrived. He had a bandage tied under his jaw and around his head, knotted at the top. He looked like a little boy with a toothache.

Even Rick's punishment, however, didn't compare with what Al had suffered. Al was still unconscious, still in the hospital. And likely to be there for a good while yet.

"You can't imagine what we've been through," Tess said. "Couldn't we have just a smidgen of sympathy?"

"No!" Ben fired back. "What you did was absolutely, positively stupid. In more ways than one."

"It shouldn't have been," Rick said, groaning. "It only became stupid when we got caught."

"Wrong. It was stupid the second you tried it. Because at that instant you put Zak's trial in jeopardy." He whirled around, swinging from one side of the cell to the other. "Who do you think is going to hear Zak's case, anyway? Does the phrase 'jury of his peers' ring any bells?"

Tess frowned.

"And what do you think those jurors are doing right now? Well let me tell you. They're reading news reports about the so-called eco-terrorists who were out playing high school pranks in the forest and got caught red-handed. Do you think that makes you look good? Do you think that makes Zak, the leader of the pranksters, look good? Do you think it's going to help me garner sympathy for him with the jury?"

"As you'll recall, we considered halting our activities pending the trial," Tess said. "We decided against it."

"Well, think again!" Ben spun around, furious. As if his job wasn't impossible enough already, he had to deal with these zealots running around whipping up community anxiety and antipathy.

Ben heard the clang of the metal door, then the clatter of footsteps coming down the corridor. Sheriff Allen was approaching; Maureen was close at his heels. She ran ahead, pressed herself against the cell door, and stretched her arms through the bars. "Oh, God! Rick! Tess! How are you?"

"I've been better," Rick mumbled, walking toward her. "But they say I'm going to live."

"Good. In that case—" She reared back her arm and slapped him sharply across the side of his face.

"Oww!" Rick screamed. He moved away, clutching his sore jaw.

"That's for being such an imbecile," Maureen said, teeth clenched. "And for putting the entire mission in jeopardy."

"It wasn't my idea!" Rick said, a pained expression on his face.

"I don't care. If you didn't start it, you should've stopped it." She paused, drawing in her breath. "I can forgive Tess. She's new—she could easily be led. Or misled. But you have no excuse, Rick. You're our acting leader. You're supposed to be responsible!"

"Al was the one—"

"You know Al well enough to know that he's always hot-headed. Always acts before thinking. That's why I never send him out unless you're with him. You're supposed to be the voice of wisdom." She pressed as far as possible through the bars. "Not an *asshole*!"

Sheriff Allen partly covered his face. "Should I step outside?"

Ben shook his head. "Don't. We may need you for riot control." Somehow, listening to Maureen's fury had helped calm his own. Ben eased Maureen away from the bars. "Look, I think we're all in agreement that this particular action was misguided—"

Maureen wrestled free of his hands. "You can say that again. In the future, all Green Rage activities will be discussed, analyzed, and voted upon by all members *before* they are executed. Understood?"

Rick looked at the floor sheepishly. "Understood."

Maureen threw up her hands. "I just can't get over how stupid this was. This must be the stupidest thing any Green Rager ever thought about doing!"

Sheriff Allen cocked an eyebrow. "Stupider than dressing up in a big hairy monster suit with a bright red nose?"

"There's something we're forgetting here," Tess said quietly, finding her voice now that the anger in the room was subsiding. "Something more important than any of this."

All heads turned in her direction.

She spoke but a single syllable. "Al."

All at once, their expressions turned somber. She was right. In the midst of the shouting and haranguing, they had almost completely forgotten Al, who was still in the hospital connected to an IV.

Better than any of them, he'd known the cost of taking on the Magic Valley logging community. And he'd paid the price.

After a long silence, Ben segued from his role as annoying moral conscience into his role as attorney-at-law. "Sheriff Allen, when do you think I'll be able to get these two released? I'm sure we can make bail."

"That won't be necessary." Allen unclipped the cell keys from his belt. "That's what I came to tell you. You're free to go."

Tess's eyes widened. "What? But the loggers who brought us in—the charges—"

"There aren't going to be any," the sheriff explained. "I gather the word came down from the central office. The logging company is dropping all charges."

"That doesn't make any sense."

"Actually, it makes perfect sense," Ben said. "Think about it. If they press the destruction of property charge, we're likely to raise the minor issue of assault and battery. They're better off letting it go and hoping we'll do the same. After all, Al is hurt pretty bad. The loggers are claiming they acted in self-defense, but if it ever came to trial . . ."

"Wow," Rick murmured. "The suits must be pissed at those loggers who trounced us."

"I doubt it," Ben said. "All in all, I suspect they'd rather have it known that some Green Ragers got their butts kicked than have the Pyrrhic thrill of lodging minor felony charges that might not even bring jail time. It will get across the message those suits most want heard: eco-terrorism is a dangerous business. And it will probably boost logger morale."

Rick became sullen and silent.

"Anyway," Ben continued, "if they're free to go . . ."

Sheriff Allen took the hint. He unlocked the cell door and escorted the prisoners out. "By the way," Allen said to Ben as they marched down the corridor, "I was thinking about dropping by your office later."

"Oh?"

"Do you . . ." He cleared his throat. "Do you by any chance know if that legal assistant of yours has dinner plans?"

"I'm her boss, not her social secretary."

"Right." He craned his neck awkwardly. "Well, I guess I'll just go by and ask her myself."

Ben frowned. "Excuse me, but didn't you have lunch with her today?"

Allen shrugged sheepishly. "I guess I did at that. But you know what my mama used to say. When you see something you want . . ."

Ben waved his hands. "I really don't want to hear this."

Allen opened the heavy metal door that led to the outer office. "You don't mind me seeing Christina, do you?"

"Of course not," Ben said sharply. "For that matter, I've got a two-hundred-pound investigator on my staff. Do you want to date him, too?"

* 24 *

After they left the sheriff's office, Rick and Tess and Ben and Maureen headed toward the hospital. Nothing had changed; Al still wasn't conscious. After a brief visit, Ben left for his office. Maureen walked with him. Ben wasn't sure if she appreciated his company or just didn't feel safe walking alone. Probably a bit of both.

As he and Maureen rounded a corner, Ben suddenly heard great peals of laughter emanating from the other end of the street. And he discerned two approaching figures, Christina and Sheriff Allen. Their arms were linked, and they were both sopping wet. Head to toe.

The four of them stood facing one another on the sidewalk. Christina opened her mouth as if she was about to speak, but another gale of laughter erupted before any words were spoken. She bent forward, convulsed with merriment.

Ben arched an eyebrow. "Sudden rain flurry?"

Christina looked up, her arms wrapped around her midsection for support. She tilted her head toward Allen. "He—he—" It was all she could manage. More hysterical laughter convulsed her.

Sheriff Allen stepped gamely into the breach. "We've been taking a walk," he said.

"Ah," Ben replied. "That explains it."

Christina leaned against the nearest brick wall for support, water dripping from her arms. "You wouldn't—" She stopped again, convulsed and overcome. "You wouldn't believe what this guy—" She could go no further. She glanced at Allen, then abruptly burst out laughing again.

Ben tried not to seem peeved. "How's the work on the prosecution exhibits coming?"

Christina bit her lower lip. "Oh, fine, fine. I'll be back in the office"—she drew in her breath, trying to regain control—"as soon as I put on some dry clothes!" More giggling ensued. Christina pounded on the brick wall, giddy and breathless.

"I'll see you there," Ben answered. He lightly tugged Maureen's arm, and the two of them moved on down the sidewalk. He knew he shouldn't be annoyed, but he was, just the same. Christina and the sheriff appeared to really be hitting it off. He supposed he was used to feeling as if he and Christina were a team, working together. In all the time he had known Christina, this was the first time he had felt like an outsider.

He and Maureen chatted most of the way back to his office, and Ben was relieved that the conversation didn't relate in any way to murder, eco-terrorism, or politics. Instead, she mostly talked about herself, which Ben greatly preferred. She had grown up in North Dakota, she told him, and had been twelve when her daddy, now deceased, took her to Benali State Park and taught her the rudiments of trekking and mountaineering.

She'd been hooked on the great outdoors ever since. Before he died, they'd traversed several peaks of varying difficulty, including Mount Rainier, her favorite.

"Do you do much hiking?" Maureen asked as they ambled down Main Street.

Ben squirmed a bit. He wanted to make a good impression, but he knew he was a pathetically unconvincing liar. "To tell the truth, the great outdoors and I have never really meshed."

She laughed. "How can you not like—outdoors?"

"Outdoors is always full of . . . things. Bugs and bees and bad weather. None of that ever happens in my apartment."

She laughed again. "Weren't you ever a Boy Scout? Haven't you been camping?"

"I have been camping," Ben admitted. "Once. In Arkansas. But someone else did all the work."

She glanced at him out the corner of her eye. "Would that be—your redheaded friend? Christina?"

"Yeah. How did you know?"

"Just a hunch. I saw from the start that the two of you were very close."

"We've worked together on many cases. We've become good friends."

"I had the idea that . . . maybe there was something more between the two of you."

"Between Christina and me? Nah."

"Are you sure she feels the same way?"

Ben slowed his step. "What? Of course . . . I mean, what do you—?"

"How long have the two of you worked together?"

Ben thought about it. It had been a good long while.

"And in that time, has she dated? Other than Sheriff Allen, that is."

Ben screwed his head around. "I don't really know."

Maureen nodded. "I just wondered if she's been waiting around for you all this time. Waiting for you to make a move."

"*Christina?* Nah."

"And I wonder how long it's fair to expect her to wait. Maybe she got tired of waiting, and that's why—"

"This is silly. I think you don't understand Christina and me."

"Maybe not." She glanced at him, and her eyes lingered. "But it's a subject that interested me."

Ben blinked. Interested her? What was she saying?

Maureen took a step closer to him. Her lips parted, and she stared at him with unblinking eyes. "I thought perhaps when the trial is over, you and I could spend some time together. Get to know each other better."

"I'd like that."

Ben approached the county building housing his office from the rear, the back alley. He'd learned a couple of days before that the other door just outside his office led to the fire escape, which had an old-style metal ladder that descended to the ground. He'd also learned that the ladder could be easily hooked and climbed from the back alley, which allowed him to get in directly without passing through the gauntlet of secretaries waving phone messages and asking questions.

It was twilight; the sun was setting and the street lamps were just beginning to flicker on. Magic Valley still had the old-style lamps—tall, wrought-iron posts on every street corner, like the ones in the small Oklahoma town where his maternal grandmother had lived. They had probably been gas lamps originally, in a previous generation. And someday they might be replaced with the high-powered fluorescent lighting one saw all over Tulsa—but he hoped not.

Ben had almost reached the bottom rung of the ladder when he heard a soft but insistent hissing from somewhere in the muddled darkness surrounding him. "Psst."

He whirled around in all directions. He didn't want to seem paranoid, but after the violence that had been visited on Green Rage earlier this day, almost anything seemed possible.

"Who is it?" he said, trying to pierce the darkness. "Where are you?"

He heard a scratching, a sound of movement, but no response.

"I know you're there," Ben said loudly. He was trying to make a show of being brave, but a show was all it was. Inside, he was petrified. If he ran up against a pack of rowdies from Bunyan's, he knew he wouldn't stand a chance.

"I'm dialing the sheriff on my cell phone," Ben shouted, hoping someone would believe it. "They can be here in seconds."

He heard the scratching noise again, and a second later, in the dim light he saw a petite young woman crawl out from behind the Dumpster at the end of the alley. "Don't call the police," she whispered, brushing off the sleeves of her tweed coat. "I just want to talk."

Ben didn't know what to do. She didn't appear very threatening. "Who are you?" he asked. "What's this all about?"

"My name is Peggy Carter," the woman answered. She stepped closer, till they were perhaps ten feet away from one another. "I work for Granny."

"In the D.A.'s office? What on earth do you want?"

"I can explain." She seemed extremely nervous. Ben was relieved to see he wasn't the only one. "I just want to talk to you."

"If this is some intimidation play, something Granny's cooked up to scare me off, you can quit before you start."

"No, that isn't it. That isn't it at all. I want to help you."

That took Ben by surprise. "You want to help . . . me?"

"Well, perhaps I'm putting this the wrong way. It isn't that I particularly want to help you. I just don't feel I have any choice. I won't let—" She shook her head. "Anyway, if Granny knew I was here . . ."

Ben was beginning to get the drift. This was an unauthorized visit.

He escorted Peggy up the rickety ladder and, after ensuring that the coast was clear, led her down the short corridor to his tiny office. He was glad to see it was unoccupied. Loving must be out investigating, he mused. And Christina is probably out with the sheriff getting an ice cream.

"What is it you want to talk about?" Ben asked after she was situated in the only chair.

She swallowed. "Alberto Vincenzo."

Ben shook his head. "Should I know that name?"

"Not unless you're big into the drug scene."

"Drugs?" He paused. "I remember Granny mentioned that Magic Valley was having a surge in drug use. Some kind of new designer drug."

"Right. We call it Venom. Twice as fast as crack, with twice the high. And twice as deadly."

"And this Vincenzo . . ."

"We believe is peddling the stuff. We've been alerted by the DEA and local law enforcement that he's in the area. And he's known to have some big-time connections to the drug scene."

"California?"

"And beyond. We're talking South America here. Mucho big time."

Ben nodded. "Does this relate to the Dwayne Gardiner murder?"

"Yes. Or no, but—" She frowned. "The truth is, I don't know. But we've had reports that Gardiner was behaving erratically shortly before his murder—hyper, disoriented, spaced-out."

"Like maybe he was sampling the new designer drug."

"Maybe, yeah. And if so, this Vincenzo character might've known him."

"Or even had a motive to murder him."

"I think that's pretty remote," Peggy said. "But I can't altogether eliminate the possibility. So I thought you should know."

"I'm appreciative, but why isn't this coming through official channels?"

Peggy glanced down at the floor. "Granny didn't, um, feel production to the defense was warranted."

"Why am I not surprised? I'm filing a complaint with the judge."

"I wouldn't do that if I were you."

"The prosecution has an obligation—"

"You don't have to lecture me about it. Why do you think I'm here?"

Ben bit his lip.

"But the fact is, Judge Pickens will take Granny's side. Believe me, I've seen it before. Those two are thick as thieves.

All you'll do is get me fired. And I really can't afford to be unemployed right now."

"I wouldn't say who my informant was."

"She'll know. It's not like Kip or Troy ever had a thought of their own."

"I can't believe the judge would ignore—"

"That judge used to dandle Granny on his knee, as he's fond of saying in open court. You're not going to convince him she's committed prosecutorial malpractice."

"Which is why she gets away with this kind of crap."

"True. But you have more important things to do than wasting time losing motions."

Ben didn't like it, but he realized she was probably right. First things first. "Do you have anything else you can give me?"

"I couldn't get the file. Granny grabbed it the instant I raised the issue, and I haven't seen it since. I have managed to liberate this photo."

She slid the standard Vincenzo mug shot across the table. Ben took one look, then winced. "Man, he is one seriously dangerous-looking man."

"Not someone you'd want to meet in a dark alley, huh?" Peggy said, grinning.

Ben shook his head. Huge pumped-up arms, strapping shoulder muscles, an evil-looking scar across the forehead—wait a minute. He'd seen this man before. In the dead of night, when he was breaking into the bookstore . . .

"I appreciate your coming forward," Ben said, setting the photo down. "I know it probably wasn't easy for you."

"I had to," Peggy said quietly. "I couldn't've lived with myself."

"What you've done makes a real difference. Every lead takes me another step forward. Who knows? This may be the piece that saves an innocent man."

"I don't believe he is innocent."

"But—"

"I've seen Granny's case. I don't see how it could possibly have been anyone else."

"Then why?"

"The only reason I'm helping you is because, stupid as it seems, I still believe in playing by the rules. My mother taught me to play fair, and I try to do it whether I'm on the playground or in a court of law. The law says a defendant gets a chance to use all exculpatory evidence to his benefit, and that everything the prosecution has that might help must be produced. I'm just making sure the rules are followed."

"If you came with me to the judge—"

Peggy cut him short with a wave of her hand. "No. That path would only lead me to the unemployment line. If not immediately, then in time. My little girl depends on me. I can't let her down."

"Thank you," Ben said. He pressed her hand. "If there's anything else you can tell me . . ."

She shook her head. "Well, this much I can tell you: I've seen the case, and I know Granny. I know what she's planning. I don't think you have any idea what you're up against." She passed hurriedly through the office door, shaking her head. "I don't think you have any idea."

* 25 *

Loving signaled the barmaid to bring him another Moosehead. The short round woman nodded, and a few seconds later a green stub-necked bottle with the cap popped appeared on the table before him.

He smiled, then tossed a fiver onto her tray. He'd been at Bunyan's for over an hour now, acting casual, looking for an opportunity to ingratiate himself with some of the local loggers. So far no one had taken the bait. Not that they hadn't noticed him; he saw the furtive looks, the quick sidelong glances. Manly men trying to decide whether he was neutral, one of them, or one of the tree huggers. Evidently they hadn't made up their minds; no one had come near him.

But it was almost eleven now and the place was filling up. He had deliberately sat at a table for four even though he was alone. The three empty chairs at his table were now the only empty seats in the bar. Surely something would have to break soon.

He hoped so, because in the meantime he was dying of boredom. Appearances to the contrary, this really wasn't his kind of place. He wasn't quite as black and white as everyone in the law office thought he was. Granted, his idea of a good time wasn't a night at the opera or listening to some of those endless folk songs the Skipper favored. But he also didn't much care for drinking his life away at some sleazy hole-in-the-wall. He liked to meet people, talk to them, swap ideas. And a good Arnold Schwarzenegger flick from time to time was okay, too.

He gazed up through the smoke at the neon shrine to Paul Bunyan. Obviously the patron saint of the bar, if not the whole community. A manly man if ever there was one. Except why, Loving wondered, if he was such a manly man, was there no Mrs. Bunyan? Or even a willing woman back at the logging camp? Paul was never seen with anyone except that big blue ox.

Loving shook his head. Now that was a sobering thought.

He was distracted from his reverie by the sound of the front door opening. Perfect—a group of three. And unless he misjudged, they were all loggers.

He tried not to watch them as the men scouted the bar and determined what he already knew—that there were no vacant seats except the ones at his table. He waited, absentmindedly admiring the cut of Paul Bunyan's jib, as he sensed one of the men coming closer.

"You using these chairs?"

Loving looked up abruptly, as if he had been deep in some profound thought. "What? Oh, no. Help yourselves."

The three men took the vacant seats and ordered drinks. One of them was older than the rest; flecks of gray were apparent in his hairline, particularly around the temples. The other two Loving guessed were in their early thirties, not much younger than Loving himself.

Loving didn't push it. He spent the first ten minutes or so gazing off into space, paying no attention as the three buddies chatted among themselves. They didn't introduce themselves, and he never caught their names, so he assigned names to them—Huey, Dewey, and Louie. Louie was the senior member of the troupe.

Only after a significant time had passed did Loving subtly turn his attention in their direction. He could tell their conversation (mostly about sports teams they wanted to win and women they'd like to boink) was running out of steam. These men probably came to this place every other night; they didn't have much to say to one another anymore.

Loving inclined his head toward the man closest to him—Louie. "Any of you boys have a dog?"

They glanced among themselves, as if not sure which should answer first. One of the younger ones—Huey—nodded noncommittally. "Sure. Bird dog."

"Irish setter," offered Dewey.

The senior member of the team jumped in. "Three Rottweilers. Why?"

Loving shrugged. "Oh, no reason. Got me a damned fine dog. Great Dane I call Rex. Good as any person I've ever known. Better'n most. I've been on the road for three weeks now and—well, hell. I miss my dog."

Huey smiled. "Oh, sure. That's rough. Three weeks. Hell of a long time to be apart."

"Got a wife?" Louie asked.

"Oh yeah," Loving answered. "But I miss my dog."

There were a few grins, and a few moments later, they were all laughing. Politics and women made for risky conversation starters, Loving thought. But dogs worked every time. "You boys from around here?"

Huey nodded. "Lived here all my life. You?"

Loving knew there was no point trying to bluff a man who'd lived in this tiny burg forever. "Nah. Just passing through."

Huey nodded. Loving could sense the prickles of suspicion

rising. "We don't get that many strangers through here. 'Cept the ones we don't want. What's your line of work?"

"Trucker," Loving grunted. He thought that would sound convincing; he'd done it for about five years, after all, before he met the Skipper. "Got a load of cranberries. Taking it to market in California."

"Oh," Huey said. Loving could sense him relaxing. Being a trucker was okay. Not as good as being a logger, but acceptable.

Huey glanced at his nearest buddy. "He's a trucker."

"I heard," Dewey said. "I'm excited. Gonna be here long?"

"Nah. Just putting up for the night. I was going to drive straight through, but—I dunno. I got curious."

"Curious?" Dewey said. "About Magic Valley?"

"Oh yeah. Been a lotta talk about this little town."

He detected a narrowing in Louie's eyes. "Talk? What kind of talk?"

" 'Bout that dude who got himself killed."

Huey nodded. "Dwayne."

Loving acted surprised. "You knew him?"

"Oh, yeah. We all knew him."

"Really? Damn." Loving adjusted his chair slightly. "What happened to him?"

"Goddamn tree huggers, that's what happened to him."

"Tree huggers?" He knew the men were watching him, measuring his reaction.

"*Eco-warriors,* they call themselves. People who love Mother Nature but will shoot their fellow man dead in his tracks."

"I hate that," Loving said, careful not to overplay his hand. "People should come first, you know?"

"Yeah, I know." Huey grimaced. "But the guy who plugged Dwayne, he didn't know."

"I heard the guy got burned up. Like, while he was still alive."

Dewey nodded his head grimly. "Poor Dwayne. Poor, poor Dwayne."

"Damn. That's rough. The guy have a wife? Kids?"

"Yeah. He had a little boy. And . . . Lu Ann." A look passed from Dewey to both of the other men.

"Lu Ann?" Loving tried not to seem too eager, even though he was finally moving the conversation to a topic the Skipper had particularly wanted him to investigate. "That his wife?"

Dewey nodded.

"Man, that's sad. She must be pretty torn up."

Another look passed among the three men. "You can check that out for yourself. She's sitting in the booth behind you."

Loving looked surprised, and the surprise was genuine. Subtly, trying not to attract attention, he turned till he faced the row of booths in the back.

He knew who they had to be talking about. She had long, wild auburn hair and was dressed in a tube top and tight white jeans. She wasn't crying, but the man she was with nonetheless appeared to be offering his comfort.

"Shouldn't she be, like . . . in mourning or something?" Loving asked.

"Lu Ann isn't the mourning type," Louie said—another curt pronouncement of wisdom from the senior team member. "As you can see, she has a busy social calendar."

Loving looked away. "Even before her hubby got charbroiled?"

"Long before. It was what you'd call a troubled marriage. Because she was what you'd call trouble."

She was what he'd call trailer trash, Loving thought. Or out here, maybe it should be treetop trash. "She have anyone special?"

Huey shrugged. "From time to time. Till the next one came along."

Loving watched surreptitiously as Lu Ann's escort's hands groped for the most accommodating parts of her anatomy. "Who's she with now?"

"Fella called Doug Curtis."

"He a logger?"

"Yeah. Well, not exactly." Huey corrected himself. "Used to log. Now I understand he works for a man called Slade."

Is that a fact? Loving thought.

"Why are you so interested in Lu Ann, anyway?" Dewey asked. A sharp line formed across his forehead.

"Oh, I'm not really." Loving turned quickly. Obviously, it was time to cool it. "Or maybe just a little. Like any other rubbernecker."

"Dwayne'd been actin' some kind of funny for several weeks, up until the burnin.' That woman had him on the ropes." Louie shook his head. "Well, less said about that the better."

"Agreed," Loving replied. He knew he couldn't push any harder without arousing suspicions. "You boys ready for another round?"

A quick glance, a shrug, a *why not?*, and another round was ordered. And Loving knew that once he paid the tab, their newfound friendship would be sealed.

An hour and a half later, Loving was buying his sixth round, and everyone at the table was beginning to act more than a little toasted—including himself. Truth was, he didn't drink that much anymore; he was getting too old for that nonsense, and besides, it was making him fat. He wasn't used to this level of consumption and it was making him woozy.

"Whad I don't unnerstand is how these tree huggers get away with it," Loving said. The word slurring was a nice touch, he thought, and at the moment it didn't require any acting. "I'd think you boys'd pound 'em into pulp."

"They hide," Huey said. He was leaning slant-wise on one elbow, commiserating. "They strike when no one's lookin', then run away and hide."

"Buddow do they know where you are?"

"There's a leak," Louie said, making another of the portentous pronouncements of which he was so fond. "Everybody knows it. We just don't know who it is."

"But when we find out," Dewey growled, *"pow!"* He brought his hand and fist together and almost missed.

"Who d'ya suspect?" Loving asked.

"We jus' don't know. Gotta be one of us, a logger, someone in town. Bud damned if we know who."

"I can't believe any one of us would be talkin' to those

damn tree freaks," Huey said, with ample revulsion plastered across his face. "I jus' can't believe it."

"Stranger things have happened," Loving said. "Even in a nice li'l town like thisss."

"Nice little town." Huey made a snorting, hiccuping sound. For a minute Loving was afraid he was going to barf. "Yeah, that's Magic Valley—Venom capital of the world."

"Venom? Whassat?"

"Hot new drug," said the sage Louie. "It's all over town. 'Specially in the schools. Some of the kids are hooked on it."

"It ain't just kids," Dewey corrected. "I think some of our cuttin' pals are samplin' the junk, too."

"Yer kiddin'!" Loving said. It was a gruesome thought—some chain saw–wielding logger high on drugs. "Why do you think so?"

"Cain't say," Dewey said, obviously taking great pleasure in his secrecy. "But I got my suspicions."

"But where's the stuff comin' from?" Loving asked.

Dewey lurched forward. At first Loving thought the man was going to head-butt him. Then he realized it was just his drunken way of directing Loving's attention.

Loving twisted around, staring in the direction indicated. He spotted a burly man slunk back in a dark corner. He had long black hair that draped down over his bulging shoulder muscles. Hard to see in the low lighting, but it looked like he had an ugly scar over his right eye.

"How d'ya know?"

"I don't know for sure. But every time he comes up to one of the boys, it's the same story. Within ten minutes he wants to talk about drugs. Gettin' high. Doin' junk." He shook his head. "Word's out on him."

Ben had contacted Loving before he'd gone out tonight and told him about his new lead involving a suspected drug pusher. Loving hadn't seen the picture yet, but judging from Ben's description, this thug could be the one.

As he watched, the big man slid out of his booth and started peeling bills off a fat wad of money. Loving decided to take the plunge. He knew he'd gotten about as much out of Huey, Dewey, and Louie as he was ever likely to, anyway.

"Pleasure talkin' to you boys." He slid out of the bar just a few seconds after his quarry.

The night air seemed cool and bracing—a delight after the smoky, dirty interior of the bar. Loving drank in several good deep swallows, purging his brain. He'd need a clear head if he was going to follow this goon without being spotted.

The man was heading east, back toward the heart of town. Fortunately, Loving had already learned the lay of the town, a task that took about ten minutes. He stayed on the opposite side of the street and held way back, staying as far away as possible without altogether losing the man.

Loving's quarry seemed to be heading somewhere in particular, somewhere in a hurry. Could be any of a million things, Loving realized. But if he could catch this clown making a drug sale, or better yet, making a drug sale to a logger, maybe someone Gardiner knew . . . well, he might be able to make the Skipper very happy indeed.

The burly man with the long black hair turned left, heading north. Loving waited until he was entirely out of sight, then crossed the street. He quickened his pace, not making a show of it, until his prey was back where he could see him. Once he had the man in sight, he slowed.

The man paused at a street corner, looking all ways at once, as if he expected to meet someone but didn't know which way he might be coming from.

That could be a problem. Loving started scanning the streets himself. If the man's rendezvous was coming from the same direction as Loving, or anywhere close, he'd be spotted. He'd have to pretend to be tying his shoe or waiting for a taxi—and hope they bought it.

Hard as he looked, though, Loving didn't see anyone. Even drug lords get stood up sometimes, Loving supposed. He turned back toward the street corner where his quarry was waiting.

The man was gone. Somehow, while Loving had been distracted, he'd disappeared.

Loving put his feet into first gear and began chugging across the street and down the sidewalk. Had the man spotted him? He didn't see how it was possible. Maybe he was just always careful. Maybe that was a smart way to be when your chief occupation in life was peddling illegal designer drugs.

Loving raced down the sidewalk, feeling the weight of every downed beer sloshing in his stomach. He was huffing more than he cared to admit, but he made it in less than thirty seconds.

Not that it mattered. There was no trace of the man. Not on this street corner, not on any street corner. Not that he could see, anyway.

He was about to turn away when he heard the sound. It was a tiny sound, an almost inaudible squeaking, like a door hinge turning, or a sneaker pivoting on pavement. Loving whirled, but he was way too late. Something long and hard came crashing down on his head.

Loving gritted his teeth together, wincing. He fell to his knees, trying to absorb the pain. He raised his hands, trying to stop the follow-up blow he knew would be coming.

But he was not successful. He cracked his eyes open just enough to see what looked very much like a baseball bat crashing down between his arms and cracking ominously against his shoulder at the base of his neck.

He cried out, then fell forward on all fours. He hated just sitting here like some lame animal, not trying to escape, but he couldn't muster the energy to move. He had to concentrate just to clear away the pain, just to think straight.

Which in the long run didn't matter at all. The bat came crashing down again, this time square on the back of his head, and after that everything, both inside his brain and out, turned to black.

* 26 *

When Ben climbed the fire escape and entered his office the next morning, he was surprised to find Christina—and Sheriff Allen—already there.

As soon as he passed through the door, the two of them jumped upright. Had they been holding hands? Ben wondered. Surely not. But they were both acting as if they'd been caught in the middle of something.

"Morning, Ben," Christina said, blowing her hair out of her eyes. "Didn't expect to see you this early."

Evidently not, Ben thought. "Did we get the rest of the paper discovery from the prosecutor's office?"

"Oh. We got it all right. But I don't think you're going to like it."

She pointed toward the opposite wall. Seven near-ceiling-high stacks of bound papers occupied almost a third of the tiny office.

"She's trying to bury us," Ben murmured. "Give us more than we can possibly sort through before the trial begins."

"Right. Probably fifty pages of good stuff, buried somewhere in a morass of garbage. But what can you do about it? Complain that the prosecution has given you too much?"

"I could complain that it came too late and ask for a continuance. But from what I hear, Judge Pickens would be unlikely to grant it." Ben scrutinized the tall stacks of paper. "Any rhyme or reason here?"

"None. Documents aren't organized or categorized in any useful fashion. Not even numbered. In fact, the pages of a particular document are often scattered through several piles."

Ben's lips pressed tightly together. "Granny really outdid herself here."

"You haven't seen the half of it yet."

Ben frowned; that sounded ominous. He took the top document off the stack closest to him. It took a moment for his eyes to adjust before he realized what Granny had done to him.

"Red," Ben said, throwing down the paper bitterly. "It's all been color-copied in red ink."

Sheriff Allen looked a bit perplexed. "You defense types got something against red?"

"It won't photocopy," Christina explained. "At least not on your garden-variety copier. Some of the newer color copiers can do it, but of course we don't have anything like that at our disposal."

"Which," Ben added, "since we'll need at least three copies of any exhibit we plan to use at trial, makes this tower of trash absolutely worthless to us."

Allen whistled appreciatively. "That Granny. She sure knows her business."

"That would be one way of putting it." Ben grabbed his windbreaker. "I'm going to talk to her. Right now."

"Is there any point?" Christina asked.

"Probably not. But I'll feel better if I've tried. I don't guess I need to tell you . . ."

Christina nodded. "Start wading through the paper."

"Roger."

Allen turned toward Christina, a stricken expression on his face. "You mean you're not going to be free at lunchtime?"

"Sorry, Doug. Work calls. Have a double helping of our usual for me, okay?"

Ben frowned. Doug? Our *usual*?

"I'm available for dinner, though," Christina added. "What do you say we go back to Mabel's? Try some more chutney."

Allen's face brightened. "That sounds great."

Ben tried to suppress his annoyance. "Look, Christina, I don't mean to interfere with your social calendar, but we've obviously got a ton of work—"

"Oh, of course." The sheriff straightened. "Anything I can do?"

"You? I meant—" Ben stopped himself. Now that the man mentioned it, there probably was. "Have you heard anything about a major-league thug called Alberto Vincenzo?"

Allen grunted. "Drug pusher. Yeah, I've read the reports. The DEA seems to think he's in our area. How did you know?"

Ben thought about telling him, but he knew it might get back to Granny, which would be fatal to Peggy. "Well, I've got a lot of sources. My question is whether he might have anything to do with the murder of Dwayne Gardiner."

"I don't even know for sure that he's here," Allen said. "That's just what I've heard. Although it makes sense. This new drug didn't come to Magic Valley by itself."

"Any reason to think Vincenzo is connected to the murder?" Christina asked.

"There are reports that Gardiner was behaving erratically shortly before he was killed," Ben replied. "Like maybe he was sampling a little Venom himself."

"I can do you one better than that," Allen offered. "I had reports from some of my deputies that Gardiner had been prowling the streets of the city late at night, something he'd never done before."

"Like maybe he was trying to score some drugs?" Christina asked.

"Or even maybe was helping push the junk. This new drug has really blitzed through this town. No one man could have done that alone."

There was a knock on the door. A moment later, Tess poked her head through. "Is this a private party?"

Ben grinned. "Yes. But you're invited."

She stepped inside. With four bodies inside, a desk, and seven skyscraper-like stacks of paper, there was barely enough room to move. "You guys like to keep things cozy, don't you?"

Ben saw Christina and Allen glance at one another. "Helps forge close working relations."

Tess laughed. "No doubt." She glanced up at the wall. "That must be the suit?"

Ben followed her gaze. The famed Sasquatch suit—black mask and all—was on a coat hanger dangling from a nail on the wall. "That it is. We probably need to get that back to Granny."

"I'd be happy to swap her for a few documents printed in conventional black ink," Christina said.

"You're right," Ben grunted. "Let her pick it up herself." He turned toward Tess. "Is there anything I can do for you?"

"I just wondered if anyone'd heard anything about Al," she answered. "I went by the hospital, but they wouldn't let me in to see him. Wouldn't tell me anything, either."

"That's my fault," Allen said. "I put a tight security net around him."

"Why?"

"Well, ma'am, it's pretty well known that your pal Al is one of the leading monkey-wrenchers. Responsible for a hell of a lot of property damage, from what I hear. It's best that he's kept well away from some of the folks in this town."

"Would that include you?" Ben asked pointedly.

Allen shook his head. "I think you've got the wrong idea about me. I don't bear any grudge against these Green Rage people—as long as they don't break the law. I think everyone's entitled to speak their mind. That's what this country is all about."

"You're saying you don't favor one side over the other."

"The only thing I favor is peace," Allen said with conviction. "All I want is for this unrest and unhappiness to go away." He fingered the brim of his hat. "Anyway, I just wanted to make sure your friend Al was safe while he recuperates."

"I appreciate that," Tess said. "Thank you." She turned and started for the door. The instant she opened it, a man stumbled through, collapsing into her arms.

Tess took a step back, trying to brace herself and to keep the man from slipping to the floor.

"Loving!" Ben raced forward, taking one arm and helping lead him over to the chair.

It was Loving all right, but he was not the stalwart tower of a man he usually seemed. His whole posture was hunched and bent. His T-shirt and jeans were smudged and grimy. Blood was caked around his mouth.

Christina threw her arm around him. “Are you all right? What happened?”

Loving opened his mouth several seconds before he actually spoke. Ben could tell he was having trouble making the words emerge. “I’m . . . not . . . sure.”

Christina ran her hands over his face, his head. “Someone hit you. Who was it?”

Loving slowly shook his head. “Don’t . . . know that, either.”

Eventually Loving pulled himself together enough to tell them the story of the night before. How he had followed the man with the scar out of Bunyan’s. How he had lost him, chased after him. How he had been clubbed from behind. Repeatedly.

“Guess they figured they couldn’t leave me on the street corner,” Loving said. His voice was a jagged whisper. “Woke up in an alley behind some trash cans. With the worst headache I ever had in my life. And that’s includin’ a few nights I shot tequila till the sun came up.”

“We need to get you to the hospital,” Christina said. “You might have been seriously hurt.”

“Aw, I don’t think—”

“Just the same, you’re going.” She helped Loving to his feet. “You’re in no condition to walk. I’ll call a cab.”

Transportation was arranged, and Christina took Loving away to be examined by an ER doc. Tess went with them, this time taking a note from the sheriff that would guarantee her entry to Al’s room. Which left Ben alone with Sheriff Allen.

“I think you can confirm those DEA reports,” Ben said. “Sounds like Loving found Alberto Vincenzo.”

“Or Vincenzo found him. I don’t know what’s happening to this town. People getting hurt, beat up.” He shook his head. “It’s not like it used to be. Do you think—”

“Think what?” Ben asked.

“Oh, I hate to meddle but—well, you do seem to be in the eye of the hurricane here. And it’s clear that we’ve got some bad eggs who are willing to do just about anything—including hurting other people. Do you think it’s safe?”

“You’re worried about me?”

"I'm worried about your legal assistant."

Ben rolled his eyes. Of course.

"She's tough, spunky, pushy. Mind you, I love all that. But it's exactly the kind of stuff that might get her hurt."

"Christina can take care of herself."

"Yeah. So could your investigator. And that Al fella. Except they're both in the hospital now. I sure wouldn't want—" He lowered his eyes, pressed his lips together. "Well, hell. I guess it's obvious by now. I'm pretty sweet on that little lady of yours."

Ben was beginning to feel distinctly uncomfortable.

"I think she's something special. But I guess you already know that." Allen paused. "Do you think she and I—I mean, is it possible we could—" He muttered something under his breath. "Oh, damnation!"

"If you have something to ask Christina," Ben said, "just ask her."

"Maybe I will at that." He gave Ben a quick nod. "Guess I'll be seeing you."

And then Ben was alone. Alone with two tons of red-inked paper, a Sasquatch suit, and his thoughts. Some of which were pretty unpleasant.

* 27 *

Ben knew he should probably check first with her receptionist, but he wasn't in the mood. He darted past the woman before she could stop him and zipped into Granny's office.

Granny was concentrating on the pile of papers on her desk. Apparently she sensed his presence; she looked up abruptly and cocked an eyebrow. "Don't folks back in Oklahoma know it's polite to knock?"

"We know," Ben answered, "but politeness is a courtesy that has to be earned."

"I see." She leaned back in her chair, a playful smile on her lips. The top two buttons on her blouse were unbuttoned, which, when she stretched back like that, became impossible to ignore. "What can I do for you, Mr. Kincaid?"

"I just came by to drop off my preliminary exhibit list." He opened his briefcase and withdrew a piece of paper.

Granny took it greedily. "Hope there are no big surprises here. I really hate surprises—" She stopped. "I think you've made a mistake, Kincaid. There's nothing written on this paper."

"Of course there is."

"I'm looking at it, Kincaid. It's blank."

"Nope. I wrote down my exhibit list right there."

"I telling you, there's nothing—"

"It's written in invisible ink."

Granny blinked. "Invisible ink?"

"Sure. You know, lemon juice. Didn't you have a childhood? Wait, don't answer that. I probably don't want to know."

A wry, not very amused smile played on her lips. "Is this your idea of a joke?"

"Nope. Just my way of fulfilling my legal obligations. In conformity with the customs and procedures of Magic Valley County. At least as they appear to me."

"Kincaid, everything I gave you was perfectly readable—"

"So is that. You have to hold it close to a lightbulb."

"A lightbulb?"

"Right. Let it get hot, but not hot enough to burn. The words will emerge. Of course you won't be able to photocopy it. But I gather that's not a problem here in beautiful downtown Magic Valley."

Granny pushed herself to her feet. "All right, Kincaid, let's stop pussyfooting around. What is it you want?"

"You know what I want. I want all the documents you're obliged to produce—you can keep the decoys—in normal photocopyable black ink. Not red, not green, not purple. Black."

"If you want black ink, you could have them retyped."

"I could if I had the time, which I don't, or the money, which I don't."

"Life's tough all around, Kincaid."

"Especially when your opponent doesn't play fair."

"Now wait just a minute. There's no obligation to produce photocopyable documents in the Rules of Criminal Procedure."

"I'm not talking so much about the rules of criminal procedure as the rules of common decency."

She wrinkled her forehead and moved toward him with a look that, if Ben hadn't known better, he would've thought was almost flirtatious. "That's an oxymoron, Mr. Kincaid. There's nothing common about decency."

Especially in this town, he thought, but managed to restrain himself from saying. "If you don't give me copies I can use, there will be consequences."

She pushed out her lower lip. "Aww. Are you gonna tell on me to the judge?"

"No, I think that would be a waste of time. I'm going to tell on you to the reporters."

"The—what?"

"I thought I'd start at the *Magic Valley Herald*. I've already made contact with a fellow there who's very interested in this case. I'll tell him what you've done and let him spread it to his readers—you know, all those people who elected you to office."

She snorted. "No one in this town will be remotely sympathetic to you or your client, Kincaid."

"Then I thought I'd tell the same story to the *Seattle Free-Press*. An ambitious woman like you—you can't be planning to stay in Magic Valley all your life."

Her face grew cold and stony.

"While I'm at it, I thought I might have a chat with the state attorney general."

"The attorney general!"

"Yeah, I've heard he's pretty interested in gross miscarriages of justice."

All traces of amusement bled out of her face. "What is it you want, Kincaid?"

"I've already told you. You've still got the originals. You can make copies a lot more easily than I can have them retyped. You should've done it in the first place; it would've been a lot simpler than this red-ink ploy."

"I'll take it under consideration."

"That's not good enough." He pushed out of his chair. "See you in the funny papers."

"All right, all right. I'll tell the copy squad to get on it. I don't know how long it'll take, though."

"The trial starts Monday. If we don't have the documents well in advance, I'll be petitioning for a continuance."

"Judge Pickens will never—"

"So we won't waste time with him. I'll go straight to the state supreme court. On an interlocutory appeal of right."

Her head lowered; her lips pressed together. "I'll get you the damn documents."

"Good. I'm glad we were able to work this out amicably."

Granny gave him a seriously unamicable glare. "Will there be anything else?"

"As a matter of fact, yes." Ben reminded himself to tread carefully. He had promised Peggy he wouldn't do anything that would expose her, and he wanted to keep his word. "I want all the information you've got on Alberto Vincenzo."

"Vincenzo?" Her head twitched ever so slightly. "Who's that?"

"The man who clobbered my investigator's head last night. Either him or someone working for him."

"Your investigator?" She seemed genuinely surprised. "Was he hurt?"

"He's got a nasty bump on his head, but he'll be okay. But I understand you have some DEA information on his assailant, or his assailant's boss, and I want it."

"And who told you that, may I ask?"

"Sheriff Allen, that's who."

"Sheriff Allen! But he's—"

"Yeah, I know. He's supposed to be on your side, and I'm sure he is. But it turns out he's also an honest man, and he has a conscience. So he told me the truth."

"I'm going to have to have a word with the sheriff."

"That's good, Granny. Chew the man out for having a conscience. You don't want that sort of thing catching on in your department."

"The issue is confidentiality."

"No, Granny, the issue is fairness. And now the issue is safety. I want to know that my staff is safe."

"So you're not suggesting this has anything to do with the Gardiner murder?"

Ben had tried to avoid this, tried to get at the file in a way that wouldn't throw any suspicion on Peggy. "Well, it's awfully suspicious that the man has taken such an interest in my investigator, isn't it? But bottom line, I don't know if it does or it doesn't. Either way, I want the file."

"If it doesn't relate, I have no obligation to produce it to you."

"My investigator has been assaulted—"

"And I'm sure Sheriff Allen is hard at work on the case. You, on the other hand, are a private citizen. You don't have any business butting into the investigation and you don't have any claim to the files."

"And if it does relate to the murder?"

"*If* isn't good enough."

Ben drew in his breath. "I have reason to believe Gardiner was using Magic Valley's hot new designer drug—Venom, right? If so, he probably had contact with Vincenzo."

"And you think that creates a motive for murder?"

"It's a better motive than you have for the man you're holding behind bars. I can see a major drug dealer committing murder before some myopic conservationist. And I think the jury might also."

"You're really stretching, Kincaid. I suppose you're just desperate."

"Maybe Gardiner and Vincenzo had a falling-out. Maybe Gardiner threatened to turn him in."

"You're speculating."

"Of course I'm speculating. And do you know why I have to speculate? Because you won't give me the file!"

She waved her hand dismissively. "You're assuming you'll find something wonderful in a file you've never seen."

"What is it with you?" Ben suddenly realized he was shouting. "Do you think this is all just a game? Do you think these cases are just convenient stepping-stones for career advancement? We're talking about people's lives!"

"This is all irrelevant anyway. I don't have any files."

"You're lying."

"How do you know?"

Ben bit his tongue. "Sheriff Allen said—"

"Sheriff Allen saw an alert come over the wire. So did I. So what? It's hardly the same as having a file."

Ben leaned across her desk. "I think you're lying, Granny. And when I prove it, you're going to be out of a job."

"Where do you get off, Kincaid?" Granny was shouting now, too. "You come off so goddamn high and mighty—when the truth is, you're just trying to get a murderer off the hook."

"Zak didn't—"

"Are you sure?"

Ben hesitated.

"Let's imagine for a moment that you're wrong, although I'm sure that's hard for you to imagine. Let's suppose for once that I'm right, and your client really did murder Dwayne Gardiner. That kind of changes everything, doesn't it? Because if that's true, then this murder is all *your* fault, you pompous twit."

"*My* fault?"

"You're the clown who got Zakin off the hook the first time he was up for murder. If you hadn't been so clever, he'd be serving time right now. And Dwayne Gardiner would still be alive. Got that, Kincaid? That's the bottom line. Gardiner would still be alive—if it weren't for you."

Ben fell silent.

Granny settled back into her chair. "I don't know how you sleep at night." She glanced up, contempt smeared all over her face. "You can go now. And close the door behind you."

* 28 *

Tess sat in the backseat of the Jeep, behind Rick and Maureen, as they discussed their plans. As far as she could determine, she was entirely within their confidence.

"Green Rage hasn't been at full strength since we lost Zak," Rick said, "and we've been in even worse shape since we lost Al."

"Agreed," Maureen said. "Each of us needs to focus on a particular goal and start driving toward it."

"Right." Tess knew Rick's jaw still hurt when he talked, but he wasn't letting it show. "Tess, have you heard anything more from your . . . source?"

Tess swallowed. This was the part she hated most—maintaining the lie that had gotten her into their good graces in the first place. But she had no choice. She knew if they ceased believing she had the inside track to the Cabal, they would lose interest in her quickly.

"Of course, I don't see John as often as I once did. Since I've been spending time with you."

"Maybe we need to curb that," Rick said. "The most important thing is that you maintain your contact with the Cabal. That information could be life or death for us."

Tess nodded. "I know. I'll make an extra effort to touch base with him. Don't worry, he'll come around." She laughed. "He can't resist me."

Maureen smiled. "Lucky for us."

They fell silent. Rick continued driving down the dark lonely country road.

"I'm glad Al is doing better," Tess said, breaking the silence. "I was really worried."

"We all were," Maureen said. "Till he came to. Sometimes when people have been unconscious for a long time, even when they come around . . ." She didn't finish the sentence. "But he seemed just like always. Same ol' Al. Docs say he'll be out of the hospital in another day or two."

"Damn those bastards!" Rick said suddenly, pounding the steering wheel. "I can't believe we're letting them get away with this. We should press charges."

"If we do, they do," Maureen reminded him. "The loggers will get fined, maybe probation for assault. Al will go to prison. It isn't a good trade. The best thing we can do is forget this happened and move on. Don't you agree, Tess?"

Tess didn't respond. She was lost in thought. Something they'd said—it didn't connect at first, but it was whittling away at the back of her brain. Slowly but surely the pieces were coming together . . . and something didn't add up.

"Tess?" Maureen repeated. "Did you hear—"

She never had a chance to finish the sentence. All at once Rick jerked the Jeep to the right, making a violent shift to the other side of the road.

"Rick!" Tess cried. "What are you doing?"

He didn't answer, but it wasn't necessary. By that time she'd seen the truck. A big red pickup, one with a backseat in the cab and an extra long flatbed. It was jacked up on oversize wheels. And it was trying to run them off the road.

"Who are they?" Maureen asked, rapidly buckling her seat belt.

"Can't you guess?" Rick said. He pressed down on the accelerator and tried to shoot past them, but he couldn't get free. The pickup matched their speed. Worse, it hung tightly in the left-hand lane, forcing them onto the shoulder and not letting them out. On the other side of the shoulder was a deep ravine; if Rick drove down into that, they'd never get out.

He tried varying his speed, but the result never differed. He slowed down, the pickup slowed down. He sped up, the pickup sped up. It didn't matter. The pickup matched him at every point.

"Try braking," Maureen commanded.

Rick complied. He pushed his speed up to about sixty and

then, without warning, he slammed down on the brake pedal, bringing the Jeep to an abrupt halt. The pickup shot ahead.

"Hallelujah," Rick muttered. "Now if I can just—"

He pulled the wheel hard to the left for a U-turn. Before he had even had a chance to turn the car sideways, though, he was blinded by a white glare from behind.

"Damn," Rick said, more in desperation than anger.

There was another pickup. Behind them.

Rick straightened out the Jeep and started barreling forward. At least he was off the shoulder now. But the first pickup had turned lengthwise across both lanes, blocking the road, lights out. Rick didn't see it till he was almost on top of it; by then he was going sixty, and his options were seriously limited.

"Look out!" Tess screamed.

Rick swerved hard to the right. He almost made it around; the corner of the Jeep grazed the side of the pickup, sending them hurtling even further off to the right.

Rick pumped the brake, but at that point, there was little he could do. The Jeep careened into the ravine, hitting the bottom hard.

Tess braced herself against the impact. Fortunately, there was little room in the back of a Jeep. It made the ride rather uncomfortable, but probably saved her life. There was almost nowhere she could go.

"Is everyone all right?" Tess asked. Rick nodded, although she saw a thin trickle of blood across his forehead. Apparently his head had hit the steering wheel on impact.

"Maureen?"

"I'm . . . here." Maureen seemed dazed, but not so dazed that she didn't understand the nature of their situation. "Let's get out of here," she whispered.

The three of them tumbled out of the derailed Jeep . . .

. . . and into the grasp of the loggers waiting for them.

"What's the problem, tree huggers?" the man in front asked. His face was masked but he was wearing a cowboy hat and seemed to be the leader. "Reckless driving is frowned on here in Magic Valley."

He had at least six friends—that was as many as Tess could

see. She knew there could be more in the background. They were all wearing masks, black cotton ski masks pulled down over their faces, with an opening for each eye. Two of the men grabbed each of them, pinning them in place.

"Let us go!" Rick shouted. "These women haven't done anything to hurt you."

As if in reply, the leader stepped forward and swung the point of his cowboy boot up between Rick's legs. Rick crumpled to his knees, crying in pain and gasping for air.

"I don't think I like his 'tude," the leader said. "He goes first."

Two of them shoved Rick in the general direction they wanted to travel, while the other four dragged Maureen and Tess.

Tess's brain was racing, trying to figure a way out of this predicament. She could tell them who she really was, but they wouldn't believe her. She could scream for help, but she knew she was too far away from anyone to be heard. She could try to escape but—seven to three? The idea was laughable. Even if she could get away, they could likely run faster than she. Plus they had trucks. It was hopeless.

The masked men dragged the three of them to a nearby grove of trees. "These folks are so damn fond of trees," the leader said. "Let's just let them hug on 'em. Permanently."

Two of the men shoved Rick up against the nearest tree. His arms wrapped around the trunk. Once he was in place, another man snapped a pair of handcuffs around his wrists.

"Very good," the leader said. "You can hug that little tree till the cows come home." He snapped his fingers. "Do the girls."

The other four men dragged Tess and Maureen to other trees of approximately the same size. They forced them to extend their arms, then snapped handcuffs over their wrists.

"What you're doing is wrong," Maureen said, her lips pressed against the trunk of an oak tree. "And illegal. We have a constitutional right to protest—"

"I'm sure you do," the leader said. "And we have a constitutional right to have a little fun on a Friday night. Don't we, boys?"

There was a general murmur of assent, coupled with grunts and dark laughter.

"Don't think you'll get away with this," Maureen said. "We haven't committed any crime today. We will prosecute."

The leader spat on the ground. "Will someone shut that bitch up?"

The man closest obliged. He raised his hand high and slapped her hard on the side of her face. Her head thudded against the tree trunk.

"Maureen!" Tess shouted. Her face was now pinned to another trunk; she could barely see her two companions. "Are you all right?"

"Shut up," the man hanging behind her said. "Or you'll get the same."

Tess bit her tongue. My God, what had she gotten into? And how could she possibly get out alive?

She was relieved to hear Maureen's voice, although it was much softer and less defiant than before. "What are you planning to do with us?"

"Well," said the leader, "I thought we'd administer a bit of behavioral modification. You see, we don't much cotton to outsiders coming into town and trying to tell us how to do things. Interferin' with our way of life."

He broke off, then turned toward his cohorts. When he spoke again, Tess's heart sank to the pit of her stomach.

"All right," he said, his voice booming with enthusiasm and malice, "who's got the whip?"

Loving parked himself on a bench at the corner of McKinley and Main and waited.

Times like these, he almost wished he hadn't quit smoking. At least he would have something to do other than just counting the seconds as they ticked by. Cigarettes were made for stakeouts. On the other hand, since he'd quit, he felt better, could run farther, and had a lot more energy. And, he reminded himself, his smoking habit was one of the things that drove his ex-wife into the arms of that speedboat salesman.

His eyes crinkled a bit around the edges. Upon reflection, maybe smoking wasn't a horrible thing after all.

He picked this corner because it allowed him to stay in the shadows while giving him the widest possible view of what he had learned was the low-rent district of Magic Valley. If any drug deals were going down in the middle of the night, this was surely where they would happen. At least that's what he was hoping.

Loving was desperate to catch up to Vincenzo again. He still couldn't believe he'd let that creep get the drop on him last night. Let him get away and got clubbed over the head in the process. That was just too humiliating. When he'd had to admit to the Skipper that he'd failed . . . well, that was just about the lowest moment in his life. He owed a lot to the Skipper. He didn't like to disappoint him.

They'd been together a while, hadn't they? Ever since Ben represented his ex-wife in their divorce case. He still thought of Donna from time to time. Mostly when he had a migraine or his wallet was empty. He still hoped someday he might find someone special, someone he wanted to spend some serious time with. But the thought of getting married again—man! It just made his blood run cold.

Speaking of which, it was pretty cold out here, for a hot summer night. Maybe if he sat on the west end of the block . . .

He turned to glance over his shoulder.

Someone was standing directly behind him. Someone big.

A strong pair of ham-sized hands soared over his shoulders and clamped down on his chest. "Don't move."

Loving froze. He felt the sweaty prickling of his skin, the sixth sense that told him he was in major trouble.

Slowly he brought his head around to look at the man who had the better of him.

Broad torso, huge muscled shoulders, and an ugly scar over his right eye. Long dirty black hair. And a baseball bat tucked under his arm.

Loving swallowed. There was no question about it. It was him. The man.

"I'm Alberto Vincenzo," the mountain behind him grunted. "And I'm pissed."

* 29 *

"Stop! *Please* stop!"

Tess didn't know how many times the man with the whip had struck Rick. She knew Rick's legs had collapsed out from under him; he was held in place by the handcuffs. She knew every crack of the whip was followed by a bloodcurdling scream. Out of the corner of her eye, she could see the tattered condition of Rick's shirt, could see the blood oozing up through the cloth. She knew it had been only a short while since Rick had his last violent encounter with loggers. How much more could he possibly take?

"Please stop! You're killing him!"

"Yeah," the leader said, "but we're not hurting the tree. And that's all you people care about, right?" His wrist flipped back and a second later, the whip cracked again. Rick cried out. His chin scraped down the bark of the tree that held him fast.

"Don't do this," Maureen said. "You won't gain anything by it."

"You're wrong about that, little lady," the leader answered. "I've already gained something by it. One hell of a lot of personal pleasure." The whip lurched forward again, slashing down on Rick's ravaged back.

Rick's cry pierced the darkness of the forest. It was like no sound Tess had ever heard before, like no sound she ever wanted to hear again. It made her flesh crawl, made tears stream out of her eyes.

"Stop it!" Tess shouted out. "You murdering bastard! *Stop it!*"

The leader's lips pressed against his ski mask. "I've had about as much of you as I'm going to take, little lady."

He marched over to Tess, still cuffed to the tree. She could feel him approaching; it made the hairs stand up on the back of her neck. He came up behind her and pressed his body against hers. "We don't much care for that dirty language around here," he whispered into her ear.

"Get away from me!" Tess barked.

He pressed all the harder, wiggling suggestively, invading all her private spaces. "Aw, come on now, honey. You're gonna hurt my feelings."

"Get away!" she screamed. She tried to push him back, but she was chained so tightly to the tree she could barely move.

"Be honest, lady. Don't you like it? Even a little bit?" She felt his head hovering over her shoulder, his lips pressing against her neck. A moment later he was nibbling her earlobe. "I think maybe you do."

"I don't!" Her voice was something between a scream and a growl. *"Get away from me!"*

The leader stepped back. Even though she could see very little of his face, it was evident he was not pleased. "I don't think I care much for your 'tude either, little lady," he said softly. She heard an amused rumble from the other masked men. "I think maybe your behavior needs some modification, too."

A cold chill gripped Tess's spine.

The leader reached for a leather sheath clipped to his belt. An instant later, he was holding a long sharp knife. Its shiny surface glinted in the moonlight.

He pressed the sharp tip of the knife against her side, just below her outstretched arm. He brought the knife slowly downward, tracing a line across her breast, her abdomen.

Tess was terrified. She wanted to scream, to cry out. She wanted to dissolve into tears, like a helpless child. But she knew that wouldn't help. She had to remain strong, had to try to keep her wits about her.

The leader moved the knife to the base of her neck, then began bringing it upward, fondling her with the cold steel blade. The knife pricked her in places; traces of blood rose to the surface of her skin, outlining the blade's path.

"What do you think now?" he said as the knife rested against her right cheek. "Do you suppose you could be a bit friendlier to me?"

Tess took a deep breath and tried to muster every ounce of strength left to her. "I want you to let me go," she said firmly. "I want you to let us all go. You have no right to do this."

His teeth clenched together with anger. "Don't say I didn't warn you."

He picked up the whip he had dropped by the side of the tree.

Oh my God, Tess thought. This can't be real. This can't be happening.

"I'll just get started," the leader said. His voice had recovered some of the buoyant good humor it had before. "And you let me know when you're feeling friendlier toward me. 'Cause that's when I'll stop."

"Please no," Tess whispered, tears streaming down her face. "Please. This can't be happening. This can't be real."

The leader's arm snapped back. She heard the crack behind her, and an instant later, she felt an intense pain, like nothing she had ever felt in her entire life, lacerating her back.

And then she knew that it was real.

It was Vincenzo. Loving was certain of it. He'd been knocking himself out trying to find the pusher man—and the pusher man had found him. Problem was, now that Loving had what he wanted, he was beginning to wish he didn't.

Loving braced himself, waiting for the first blow, the first swing of that baseball bat Vincenzo had tucked under his arm. He was pinned down on the bench, with Vincenzo's hands holding him firmly in place. If Vincenzo went after him now, in this position, there wasn't much Loving could do about it.

"What the hell is it you want?" Vincenzo barked.

Loving tried to choose his words carefully. "What makes you think I want anything?"

Loving felt a sharp blow against the side of his head. "Don't fuck with me, asshole. You think I'm a fool?"

"No," Loving said, trying to keep his voice level. "I don't think you're a fool."

"You think I haven't seen you? Skulkin' about? Tryin' to follow me? I got eyes everywhere, asshole." Loving felt another cuff on the side of the head. "Now stop screwin' with me and tell me what I want to know!"

"I work for Ben Kincaid," Loving explained. "He's the lawyer representing George Zakin, the man who's been accused of killing Dwayne Gardiner. Except Ben doesn't think he did it. And neither do I."

"So?" Vincenzo growled. "Why have you been watchin' me?"

"I wanted to ask you a few questions," Loving answered. He was trying to twist around subtly, to improve his defensive position, but Vincenzo had him pinned down like a fly.

"Like what, asshole?"

"Like whether you knew Gardiner."

"And what if I did?"

"Was he a customer of yours?"

"What the hell is it to you?"

"I think he was. I think he was hooked on your designer drug big-time."

"You're full of shit. You don't have nothin' on me."

"Maybe not now. But I've worked with Ben before, and I know that he won't stop looking. If you were involved in Gardiner's death, he'll find out. Doesn't matter what you do to me. He'll keep pounding away till he uncovers the truth."

"I can't allow that," Vincenzo growled, and all at once, Loving felt those viselike hands leave his chest.

Loving turned and saw Vincenzo had the baseball bat reared back, ready to swing. Loving lurched off the bench, but Vincenzo knocked him over. Loving tumbled down to the pavement.

Vincenzo sprang up like a jaguar; a second later, he was on the bench, hovering directly above Loving. He raised the bat over his head, then began the swift downward blow. Loving saw the bat coming, but there was nothing he could possibly do in time.

* 30 *

Tess felt utterly used, drained, and helpless. Three times the whip had cracked, and three times she had felt the searing pain on her back. She heard Maureen crying somewhere behind her, begging the man to stop. But her own voice was silent. She didn't have the strength. Not even enough to beg.

"How ya feeling there, sweetheart?" the leader asked. "Think you're ready to dance the hokey-pokey with me yet?" A brief pause. "No? Well, here we go again."

Tess heard the crack of the whip. Reflexively, her eyes clenched shut.

Wait a minute. That was something different. That wasn't a whip. That was a gunshot. Somewhere behind her.

"All right, *freeze*!" The voice sounded mechanical, like it was coming through an electric bullhorn. "This is the sheriff. Nobody move."

All at once, the seven masked men scrambled for cover. They moved in every which direction at once, diving into the nearest available brush.

"I said *freeze*!" The gun fired again, somewhere over their heads. An instant later, there was not a masked man in sight.

"Damn." She heard the sound of movement. A few seconds later, Sheriff Allen came into view.

"They're getting away," Tess murmured.

"I know that, damn it," he said. "But I think it's more important that I get you folks some medical attention." He glanced at her exposed back, then winced.

"Rick," Tess whispered. It was still hard to muster the energy to speak. "He's in bad shape."

"Worse than you? Hell." He jogged over to Rick, then saw

the damage. "Damn. *Damn!*" He jiggled the cuffs pinning Rick to the tree. "I don't suppose those boys gave you the keys?"

Rick didn't respond. He didn't appear to be conscious.

"Didn't think so. I'll be right back." Allen darted off into the darkness.

About a minute later he returned, this time carrying a small hand axe. "Good thing I had this in my truck. Brace yourself." He swung the axe around hard, severing the chain between the two handcuffs. Released, Rick tumbled to the ground.

"Thought that'd work," Allen mumbled. "Cheap plastic cuffs, anyway."

Out of the corner of her eye, Tess saw the sheriff heading in her direction. Thank God, she thought. Her arms ached with the thought of being released, of being free again. The nightmare had been real, but now, at last, it looked as if she was about to wake up.

Loving thought he was a goner; there was no way he could survive another blow from a baseball bat direct to his head. But just before the bat cracked his skull, Vincenzo hesitated.

Loving didn't know why, and he wasn't going to stop to ask, either. He rolled away, out from under Vincenzo, then pushed himself to his feet and ran. He felt embarrassed—like a damn chicken, but Vincenzo would've been a challenge for him even when circumstances were equal. When Vincenzo had a baseball bat and Loving was still recovering from a bad blow the night before, circumstances were hardly equal. The smartest thing he could do was run, so he did.

He raced down McKinley, hearing Vincenzo close behind him. He didn't dare look; even a momentary decrease in his speed might be fatal. He rounded the corner, spiraling out onto Main, where he saw a patrol car heading his way. Thank heaven—who said you can't find a policeman when you want one? Loving began flailing his arms, desperately trying to get the man's attention.

The deputy driving pulled the car over to the side of the road. "What's the trouble?"

"There's a man following me with a baseball bat, that's

what. Trying to kill me." Loving turned, but Vincenzo had disappeared. "He must've ducked down that alley. Don't let him get away!"

The deputy jumped out of the car and pulled his weapon out of the holster. Loving and the deputy both headed down the street, Loving leading, the deputy close behind. They rounded the corner and ducked into the alleyway, not breaking their speed. Loving tried to look every which way at once, checking all the side alleys, the doors, the windows. Finally they made it back to the bench where this disaster had begun.

Vincenzo was gone. In the blink of an eye he had vanished. Like he'd never been there at all.

Loving saw the deputy looking at him quizzically. "He was here," Loving said. "He was."

It was then that Loving spotted it, tucked just behind the bench.

The baseball bat. The thick length of pine that had almost shattered Loving's skull.

Vincenzo had left Loving something to remember him by.

Sheriff Allen took Tess, Maureen, and Rick to the Magic Valley Hospital. Tess's wounds were washed and dressed. They were serious, and they hurt every time she moved. But there was no reason for her to remain in the hospital.

Rick was a different story altogether.

"This is a hell of an avocation you folks have," Allen remarked. "Just when your one friend looks like he might get out of the hospital, your other friend is going in."

The lacerations on Rick's back were severe, traumatizing. He had regained consciousness, but he was unable to move, and the chance of infection was great. The doctors wanted him to remain under observation, at least for a few days.

Once Rick was deep in the throes of Seconal sleep, Sheriff Allen escorted Maureen and Tess out of the hospital. He made the two women fill out a complaint, although he admitted the chances of tracking down their assailants, when they hadn't seen any faces or recognized any voices, was remote.

Afterward, he took the two women back to their Jeep and helped pull it out of the ravine. Once it was back on the flat of the road, it seemed to work fine. It was banged up badly, but still operational.

Sheriff Allen bid them adieu. Maureen drove; Tess still had a hard time sitting up straight. About twenty minutes later, they pulled into the Green Rage camp.

Or what was left of it.

"Oh my God," Maureen said breathlessly. "Oh, God."

Tess couldn't think of anything to add.

Their camp had been destroyed. The tents had been leveled, smashed to the ground. All their equipment, including Deirdre's expensive scientific gear, had been smashed and destroyed. All their supplies had been dumped on the ground, ruined. Their clothes, books, and papers were strewn across the clearing. Some of their belongings had been burned. Tess saw all the pages of Deirdre's extensive dendrochronology notes crumpled and strewn about the clearing. Everything had been ripped, broken, or destroyed.

Worst of all, there was no sign of life. Not Doc, not Deirdre, not Molly, not any of the rest of the Green Rage staff. They were gone.

Tess's hand pressed against her mouth. After all they had been through—to come home to this. It was just too much, more than a person could bear.

Maureen's face was steely and her eyes were dry. Tess knew she was struggling, forcing herself to maintain control.

"Well," Maureen said evenly, "you warned us that the Cabal was planning some major retaliation. I guess tonight was the night." Her face began to crumble. A cheek twitched, a shoulder shuddered. And then all at once she fell apart. She bent over, pressing her head against Tess's shoulder. And she began to cry.

Tears streamed out of Maureen's eyes. Tess placed her hand on the woman's head, stroking her hair, trying to comfort her. But how could she possibly provide comfort, she wondered, when she felt so little herself? So much had happened tonight. So much had happened that—

Her eyes suddenly widened. In the midst of the excitement, she had almost forgotten. Forgotten what she had finally realized earlier that night.

She knew who had killed Dwayne Gardiner. And she thought she could prove it.

She knew.

It didn't seem fair, Sasquatch mused. One gaffe, one minor slipup, and the whole house of cards could come tumbling down. All the plans, all the goals, all crumbled into nothing. It just wasn't right.

But grousing wouldn't help anything. The fact was, there had been a mistake. Not a huge one; most people would've missed it altogether. But not her, not given who—or what—she really was. She may not have picked up on it immediately, but she would. If she hadn't already.

Whether it had worked its way to the forefront of her brain or was still lodged somewhere in her subconscious, the end result was the same.

She knew.

There was no question in Sasquatch's mind. No amount of hand-wringing and self-recrimination would help. There was only one choice now, only one possibility.

It was time for action.

Tess O'Connell could not be permitted to make use of what she knew. Most of all, she could not be permitted to tell what she knew, not in a newspaper article or anywhere else. She had to be silenced.

Blackmail? Bribery? All interesting possibilities, but Sasquatch knew ultimately they would not be successful. Even if she accepted, there would always be a partly opened door, the possibility that she would change her mind, that she would want more. That she would fall in love or get drunk or get greedy and say too much.

No. No halfway measures would be acceptable. She had to be silenced—and in the only ultimately reliable way.

The fatal way.

* 31 *

"What's the matter with you? Don't you have a clue what's going on out there?"

The sharp tone in Ben's voice would've seemed harsh if he were speaking to an axe murderer. The fact that he was speaking to his trial judge, Judge Tyrone J. Pickens, made it extraordinary.

"This town is in an uproar! Everyone's taking sides, hissing and cursing. You've got demonstrations in the street. Protests, blockades. Two fistfights in the city park. I got beaned by a rock on my way into the courtroom!"

Judge Pickens's face was twisted up in a knot. His pursed lips were like floodgates, doing everything possible to hold back his rising temper. "Listen here, Mr. Kincaid. I don't need to be lectured by some whippersnapper who just strolled into town."

"Evidently you do."

Pickens was livid. Steam rose from his judicial robes.

"Last night the Green Rage camp was destroyed. And I mean destroyed. Nothing was left. Thousands of dollars of equipment was ruined."

"Which doesn't even approach what your friends have cost the logging companies," Granny noted. She was staying at her table, remaining calm. Of course she could afford to, Ben realized. She didn't have to be an advocate when she had the judge doing it for her.

"Some members of the Green Rage team were seriously injured last night. Beaten. Even whipped. One of them is still in the hospital."

"Is this true?" Judge Pickens asked.

"A complaint has been made," Granny said. "We're investigating. As to whether it's true, well, with these people it's hard to tell."

"Hard to tell?" Ben's voice was approaching shrieking level; he tried to calm himself. "Sheriff Allen himself was a witness!"

Granny shrugged. "Like I said, we're investigating. But as of this time, we have no idea who was behind the alleged attack."

"Could we please stop playing games for just one minute? We all know perfectly well who was behind the attack. We may not know their names, but we know who it was."

"Even if that's true," Judge Pickens said, "I fail to see the relevance. This is not an environmental tribunal. We're trying a murder case."

"We're going to have jurors, aren't we?"

Pickens nodded.

"And the jurors are going to come from around here, aren't they?"

"Yes, of course, but—"

"How can we hope to pretend that the jury can be unbiased and unaffected by all the turmoil? This city is up in arms."

"It's not my fault your man is a terrorist. We all pay for the sins of our past."

"It's not a sin to want your grandchildren to know what a forest looks like," Ben said. "But it would be a sin to allow George Zakin to be railroaded just because the community is in a stir about eco-terrorists. Regardless of the evidence, the jury will associate him with the turmoil in the community. Even if only subconsciously, they'll vote guilty in the hope that it will put their anxiety to rest."

"You'll have the right to question the jurors during voir dire," Pickens said. "And I can promise you I won't allow any irrelevant matters to be brought up during trial."

"But eco-terrorism is not irrelevant," Granny said, rising to her feet. "To the contrary, the defendant's political and environmental beliefs form the basis for . . . one theory of motive."

"You see?" Ben said. "You know what she's saying? She's

saying she has no intention of avoiding those irrelevant matters. Just the opposite. She's going to fan the flames and milk the controversy for everything it's worth. She's going to try to whip the jury into a frenzy, to try to scare them into voting guilty."

Pickens shook his head. "I will say this only one more time, Mr. Kincaid. I will not permit *anyone* to make an improper argument in my courtroom. At the same time, I can't prevent the prosecution from pursuing their theory of motive."

In other words, Ben thought, you don't plan to do a damn thing. "Judge, please—this is not right. You've got to stop this from happening."

"What do you expect me to do? Cancel the trial? Set your man free?"

"No. Just move the trial somewhere else. Grant my motion for a change of venue."

"I've already ruled on that motion."

"I'm urging it again."

"Mr. Kincaid, once I've ruled—"

"Your honor, the circumstances have changed. This town has changed."

Pickens's voice rose sharply. "I will not revisit a matter that has already been resolved. I gave your motion my full and complete consideration at the appropriate time. I will not second-guess every decision throughout the course of the trial."

"Then at least grant me a continuance, your honor. Postpone the trial for a week, maybe two. Give the town some time to cool down."

"That's what this is all about, isn't it, Kincaid? A delay game. You delay the trial by changing the venue, by postponing the start date. Buying your man time."

"Your honor, that's not—"

"Well, I won't be a party to it. This murder trial will begin Monday morning, as scheduled. And that's the end of it."

"Your honor, please!"

Pickens pointed his gavel at Ben. "Kincaid, I've already ruled."

"But—"

"Kincaid, if I hear one more word out of you, I'll have you locked up!"

Ben bit down on his lip.

"I've put up with you as long as I have because I know you're from out of town. Maybe it's considered acceptable to treat the court in this contemptuous manner where you come from, but I will not tolerate it. Understand me?"

Ben slowly nodded, smoldering.

"Now I expect you to be in this courtroom ready to try your case Monday morning at nine sharp. And no more bellyaching, whining, or trying to get out of it. Got it?"

Ben wanted to say something, but thought better of it. He could see the sergeant at arms edging closer, just waiting for Judge Pickens to give him the nod. "Got it. Your honor."

"Good. I'm glad we understand each other. You need anything, Granny?"

"Not at all," she said, smiling. "The prosecution is ready to proceed."

"I'm glad to hear someone is." He banged his gavel. "This pretrial hearing is ended."

Everyone in the courtroom who wasn't already standing rose, and barely a second later, Pickens had disappeared into chambers.

Granny offered Ben a smile. "Smooth work with the judge," she said. "I think you're really starting to grow on him."

Ben gathered his things and left.

Ben hadn't been on the street for five minutes before he stumbled across trouble. There was a crowd gathering off Garfield, not far from Bunyan's. About forty people were huddled together in two distinct groups. He couldn't make out any of the many voices he heard, but he could tell the voices were loud. And angry.

As he approached, he saw Deirdre and Doc and Molly and two other Green Rage team members. He was glad to see they were all right. Apparently they had been at the camp when the strike team arrived to destroy it. They'd had to flee, before they became victims like the others.

Most of the onlookers, the ones in the larger group, were

loggers, or so Ben guessed. A few appeared to be mere spectators, locals probably, passersby attracted by the noise and conflict. But Ben noticed that all of them were standing behind the loggers. Green Rage stood alone.

"I want to know who did it!" Deirdre was screaming. "And I want to know now!"

The response was loud and confused. There was no designated speaker for the loggers; several spoke at once. Ben managed to pick up some pieces. "Don't know what you're talking about" and "Go back where you came from." Another voice rang out from the back: "Not like your people ain't destroyed our stuff!"

"That's different. This was scientific equipment. It couldn't have been used to hurt anyone or anything."

"Tell it to someone who cares!" the voice in the rear shouted.

"Three of my friends have been hurt," Deirdre said. "One of them is in the hospital. He's been whipped! Do you understand what I'm saying? *Whipped!*"

More scattered, simultaneous responses. "Don't know nothin' 'bout it" and "Probably deserved it." The crowd became louder and jeering. Several people shot unkind epithets in Deirdre's direction, most relating to her appearance or making sexual innuendos.

"And he wasn't the only one!" Molly added. "A *woman* was whipped last night. A bunch of tough lumberjacks against a defenseless woman! Now I want to know which one of you he-men had to prove your stud status by whipping a woman."

The crowd became more subdued. Apparently this bit of information was not yet common knowledge.

"We will not be frightened off!" Deirdre cried. "We will not let you destroy the forest!"

That brought the crowd back to life again. The shouting rose to a fever pitch. Fists were clenched. The two groups moved closer together.

Ben cut his way through the ranks, trying to intercede. "Deirdre, what are you doing? You're not a rabble-rouser."

"They destroyed my gear," Deirdre said, a catch in her throat. "They almost killed my—Rick. I have to do something."

"But this isn't accomplishing anything."

The corner of her lips turned slightly. "You might be surprised."

"All this is doing is stirring up more unrest. Now let's stop it."

Deirdre glanced over Ben's shoulder. "Well, perhaps you're right."

"I know I am." He turned to face the loggers. "That's it, folks. Show's over. Go home."

Grumbling and swearing, the crowd dispersed. A moment later, Deirdre said good-bye and started moving away with her Green Rage companions.

Three of the loggers had been driving pickups. Almost simultaneously, the pickups roared to life, shot into drive, lurched out of the parking lot . . .

And crashed. One after the other, the chassis dropped out from the bottoms of the trucks and crashed skidding onto the pavement, sparks flying.

The crowd, barely dispersed, began to regroup.

"Look!"

"What the—"

"What happened?"

What happened was immediately apparent. During the heated argument, chains had been tied to the rear axles of each of the three trucks. The other ends had been tied to a nearby lamppost. As soon as the trucks shot out of the lot and drove the length of the chain, the chain went taut and jerked the chassis out from under each truck.

Each of the three loggers jumped out of the cabs of their trucks, spewing anger and confusion.

"It was all a distraction!" someone in the crowd yelled. "The blond bitch held our attention while the others chained the pickups!"

"Where are they?" one of the loggers yelled.

"There they are!" a small boy shouted, pointing down Garfield. "They're getting away!"

"Get 'em!"

All at once, every logger in sight gave out a yell and started charging down the street. The Green Rage group heard the noise and started running. Ben only hoped they had the Jeep nearby, but he didn't see it. The loggers were moving much faster than the Ragers. At that rate, they'd catch up in minutes.

And then Magic Valley would have a full-fledged riot on its hands.

Ben swore silently. He didn't approve of this Green Rage stunt any more than he had the previous ones. But he didn't want to see Deirdre and the others massacred, and that's what would happen if this mob caught up with them. Ben's first instinct was to run after them, to try to help. But he knew he couldn't do much to even the odds. They needed some serious assistance. The law enforcement kind.

Much as it pained him, Ben turned the other direction and raced toward Sheriff Allen's office at the courthouse. He just hoped someone was in.

And he just hoped they could get back before it was too late.

* 32 *

"What the hell is that racket?"

Tess pushed the drapes to the side and peered outside. There was a major commotion on the street, but it wasn't close enough that she could see anything.

Every time Tess heard a noise from the street, she jumped three feet. And in the last few minutes, there had been a lot of noises.

Stay calm, girl, she told herself, as if that might actually do some good. You've been in tighter scrapes than this. Did you panic when the police caught you going through Madonna's luggage? Did you turn to jelly when Sean Penn took a shot at you? Of course not. You're a grown-up and a journalist—a journalist with a hell of a story to tell.

If she could only live long enough to tell it.

She had retraced all her steps, all her thoughts, all her conversations in her mind. Everything she had seen or heard since she first came to this backwater burg. And she had convinced herself she knew who killed Dwayne Gardiner. The killer had made a fatal error.

The only problem was that she was certain the killer would soon recognize the error, too. And as soon as that happened, the killer would be trying to remedy the mistake.

And the only way to remedy the mistake was to eliminate one Tess O'Connell.

She threw all her clothes and belongings haphazardly into her small suitcase. The clothes would be a mess when she arrived home—if she arrived home—but at the moment, fashion gaffes were the least of her concerns. She grabbed the bag, crossed the room in three giant steps, and flung open the door.

An instant after she opened it, she heard the sound of another door closing. It wasn't a loud sound. It almost wasn't there at all; it was more like a whisper, a soft whooshing of air. But she had heard it. At least she thought she had.

Why would someone close his door the instant she opened hers? Unless someone was watching her. Someone who didn't want to be seen.

She bit down on her knuckle. That was the problem with paranoia—it wasn't always unjustified. But when you were the paranoid one, it was impossible to know which concerns were ridiculous and which concerns might get your head blown off.

Well, she couldn't spend the rest of her life in her room—not if she wanted to get this story in print. She didn't even have a fax machine here. And she wasn't going to give up this Pulitzer sure-bet.

She took a deep breath and plunged into the hallway. So far, so good—no one jumped out of a hidey-hole with machine guns blazing. She walked rapidly down the corridor, dragging her suitcase behind her. She was glad she'd learned to pack light; she didn't need anything weighing her down.

She paced the full length of the corridor, then took a right turn and made a beeline for the elevator bank. When she reached the elevators, she slowed. Her footsteps stopped.

But someone else's didn't. Not right away, that is. She stopped, and then a heartbeat later, so did someone else. Almost perfectly in step with her. But not quite.

Tess felt an icy grip at the base of her spine. Someone was following her. And there was only one person who would have a motive to do that—

To hell with the elevators. She ducked into the adjoining stairwell and raced down the stairs, baggage bumping every step behind her. A few years before, when she had been determined to lose the unwanted and unneeded extra ten pounds she wore around her waist, she had started walking the stairs every day during lunch hour. Since the L.A. skyscraper she worked in had over forty floors, it was pretty strenuous exercise. Once up and down and she was usually bushed.

She just hoped she had retained some of those skills. Magic Valley wasn't L.A.; it was only five flights down. But at the moment, five flights seemed like an endless expanse.

She had almost made it to the fourth floor when she heard a pneumatic release of air. Someone else had opened the door. Someone else was in the stairwell.

She was not alone.

She tossed aside the suitcase. What did she need with a lot of clothes and underarm deodorant anyway? She had her money in her purse. What she needed was to make it to her rental car. Alive.

She was in a full-out run now, no holds barred. She raced down the stairs as fast as she could without falling, taking the steps two at a time whenever possible. She was making good time now—the third floor, the second . . .

But she could still hear the footsteps behind her, and they were moving just as fast. Whoever was chasing her seemed determined not to let her escape.

Tess hit the ground floor running. She thought about hailing the bell captain, trying to get help. But what if he wasn't at his station, what if she didn't make it in time? It all seemed too risky, in her panicked state. She didn't want to be trapped in this hotel a second longer. She wanted to be in her car, leaving the whole town in her dust.

She crossed the lobby quickly and headed for the parking garage. The hotel had valet parking, but the valet wasn't there. Just as well—she could do it faster herself. She snatched her keys from the pegboard at the valet station, then barreled into the parking garage scanning for space number twenty-two.

She ran up the nearest slope, checking the numbers painted on the asphalt outside each space. Twenty-two, twenty-two . . . the numbers she was seeing were in the thirties and getting bigger, not smaller. Where was it, damn it? She couldn't be sure how much space she'd put between herself and her pursuer, but she knew it wasn't nearly enough.

The numbers were still getting bigger. She must've gone the wrong way. She whirled around without breaking her speed, blazing down the slope heading the other way . . .

An arm reached out from nowhere and grabbed her.

Tess screamed.

She couldn't decide whether to scream at him or to scream for help, so she ended up doing both at once. *"Help! Let go of me!"*

"Hey, lady, relax, okay?"

Tess pulled herself together and stared at the man holding her arm. He wasn't the murderer. But she had seen that face before.

"I'm Johnny. The bellhop, remember? I've been working your floor. I showed you to your room."

A wave of relief flooded over her. He was the bellhop, for God's sake. The bellhop!

"I'm—sorry," she said breathlessly. "I thought someone was following me."

"You were right," Johnny said. He wiped the sweat from his brow. "I've been following you since you left your room. You dropped this."

It was her wallet. The boy was holding her wallet.

It was so pathetic she had to laugh. Here she was—scared

out of her skin, certain she was about to die—and all the man wanted was to return her wallet.

Tess tried to regain some tiny measure of her composure. "Thank you. It must've spilled out of my purse when . . ." When she sprinted down the hallway like a madwoman, she thought, but did not say. "I threw everything together in kind of a rush."

"It's all right, ma'am. I just didn't want you to leave without it."

"Of course." She opened the wallet. "Here, let me—"

"That's not necessary, ma'am. Just doing my job."

"Well, if you say so." She closed the wallet and tucked it back inside her purse. "Anyway, thanks again."

Waving, she started back in the direction where she now realized her car must be. What a fool I've been, she thought. What a fool I've made of myself. She started to laugh. It was so stupid now, in retrospect. A few noises in the street, a few creaks in the hallway, and she had totally lost it.

She found the Ford Taurus she had rented in Seattle and slipped inside. Jesus, it was just as well she was working this assignment alone. She'd never be able to live this one down back at the *National Whisper*.

She pulled up to the gate, waited for the crossbar to rise, then drove out onto Main Street. She hoped she didn't have to get into a big argument with the boss when she showed up. He had not been happy with her when last she spoke to him. And now she'd been out of contact for almost two weeks. He must be pissed royally. He's probably fired me a thousand times over.

But who was she kidding? When he got a whiff of what she had now, he'd be desperate to rehire her. For that matter, given what she now knew, almost any paper around would be happy to have her on the staff.

This was the chance she'd been waiting for, she told herself. Her ticket out of the tabloids. A whole new start. The beginning of something bigger. And better. And—

The hand emerging from the backseat clamped down on her right shoulder. "Time's up, Tess."

It was as if the whole world suddenly went silent. Time was

suspended; she felt frozen. The sound of the air rushing around her was deafening.

Someone was in the backseat of the car.

Tess screamed, but this time, no one heard. She tried to wrench herself away, but the arm came forward and wrapped itself around the base of her throat.

"Stop the car, Tess."

Like hell she would. She floored it, barreling down the street, blazing through an intersection. Maybe if she drove crazy enough, she could attract a little law enforcement attention.

The hand left her throat and clamped down on the steering wheel. The two of them grappled for control, Tess tugging one way, the arm from the backseat tugging the other. While the car continued to accelerate. Forty-five, fifty. Fifty-five, sixty . . .

All at once, the Taurus spun out of control. The car skidded sideways, trunk first, spiraling down the street. Tess pumped the brakes, but she was too late. The yellow brick wall—the north wall of Canfield's Grocery—came looming up in her windshield.

The car impacted the wall with a heart-stopping crash. Glass and metal splintered and flew, smoke streamed in all directions. The front end was so severely smashed that the hood was nearly invisible; the wall reached almost to the driver's seat.

The car stopped moving.

And so did Tess.

THREE

* *

The Real World, Muchachos

* 33 *

Ben watched as the sergeants-at-arms opened the back doors of the gallery and allowed the spectators to pour into the courtroom. He was impressed; it was a respectable showing, particularly for a small town like Magic Valley. Few seats were vacant. There was a tangible sense of excitement in the room, a feeling of anticipation. A realization that much was at stake.

Of course, Ben mused, when a capital murder case is being tried, there are always high stakes. A man could lose his life. But the sad fact was, that grim possibility was the least of the concerns of most of the people in the courtroom.

The largest and loudest contingency was from the logging establishment. They were easy to pick out; they were all huddled together on the left-hand side of the courtroom. Jeremiah Adams sat in the very front of the pack, where everyone could see him, and Ben had a hunch he wasn't here just as a proud papa who wanted to see his little girl in action. He was a representative, a symbol almost, for all the younger loggers huddled behind him. A senior statesman for the lumberjack crowd.

The exception to the rule was Slade. He was sitting on the opposite side of the gallery, in the back row, alone and apart. Ben wasn't surprised. After all, technically he had no connection to the logging industry. Not officially, anyway. Officially, he was just an independent contractor doing some consulting work. Probably most of the loggers didn't even know who he was or how much he had done for their noble cause.

Ben also spotted some representatives from the Green Rage camp—what was left of it. Al and Rick were still in much too bad shape to spend the day sitting on a hard bench in a muggy courtroom, but Maureen was there, and Deirdre and Molly and Doc and a few of the others. Ben had told them that they didn't have to attend, that it might even be best if they didn't, but they had insisted on being there to support Zak.

Whatever. Ben was just glad they were alive. After that stupid stunt with the chain and the trucks, the loggers were seeing blood. Luckily, Ben had managed to get to the sheriff's office before any major damage was done. Deputy Andrews, a young but enthusiastic member of Sheriff Allen's office, had immediately jumped into action, racing to the scene with sirens screaming. He showed up just about the time the loggers caught the Green Rage crew. They managed to land a few punches before scattering, but nothing more. The owners of the pickups filed complaints, of course, but they had no means of proving who had sabotaged their vehicles.

Just as Green Rage couldn't prove who had destroyed their camp the night before.

And so the circle of hate went on and on and on.

There were a few people in the gallery Ben didn't recognize. Townsfolk, he assumed. Locals with an abiding interest in law and order. Or maybe they just didn't have cable.

Ben saw another familiar face push through the back doors. It was Al! Ben hadn't seen him since his last visit to the hospital, but he seemed to be doing fine. His step was a little slow, but he was getting around just the same.

To Ben's surprise, Al stopped and exchanged a few whispered words with Jeremiah Adams. Talk about opposites attracting, Ben mused. What could those two possibly have to discuss?

There was a commotion in the back of the courtroom. Sheriff Allen and two of his deputies were bringing in the prisoner. As soon as they started down the nave, some of the loggers began to hiss. Epithets were hurled. A few of the men looked as if they might jump out and start a fight, but Sheriff Allen held them in check with a steely look.

Zak ignored it all. Ben was glad to see him maintaining his composure. He was looking good, all in all. He had gotten the suit Ben had sent over and had the sense to wear it. He'd also had an opportunity to groom himself; he'd cut his hair shorter, shaved, washed. Altered his general appearance from crazed eco-terrorist to Ricky Nelson.

Sheriff Allen escorted Zak to his chair at the defendant's table and removed his cuffs. "He's in your hands now, counselor."

"Thanks, Sheriff. And please pass on my thanks again to Deputy Andrews. If it hadn't been for him, that mob would've torn those Green Ragers apart."

"Will do." The sheriff tipped his hat. Ben saw him glancing in Christina's general direction. "By the way, do you suppose—"

"Sorry. We work during lunch when a trial is in progress. Probably dinner, too."

"Oh. Well. Too bad." He shuffled into the back of the gallery and found an empty seat.

Ben turned his attention to his client. "How're you doing, Zak?"

"I'm fine. What the hell's happening to Green Rage?" His forehead was creased with anger.

"What do you mean?"

"I mean, first Al, then Rick in the hospital! Rick and Maureen and Tess kidnapped and whipped. Deirdre's equipment smashed. The camp destroyed."

So he'd had a visitor. Someone who'd brought him up-to-date. Ben had intentionally not told him anything; he wanted his attention focused on the trial and the trial alone. "It's retaliation, of course," Ben said. "They're trying to get back at you. Trying to scare you off."

"Man, this is unacceptable! I've put too much time into this organization. I do not want to see it destroyed."

Ben laid a hand on his shoulder. "Zak, I know this is important to you, but it's not what this trial is about. Right now I need your energy focused on this courtroom. One hundred percent."

"I can't just overlook—"

"You can and you will," Ben said as forcefully as possible. "I'm not going to waste my time trying to get you cleared if you're not going to help. Understand? This trial is going to be plenty tough. I need you pulling with me. Got it?"

Zak frowned. "Got it."

"Good. Now face front and try to look like you just stepped off the set of *Leave It to Beaver*."

Zak smirked. "When do we get started?"

"Should be any minute now."

Christina appeared at his right and deposited a notebook and a tall stack of file folders on the table. "Here's your trial notebook," she said, pointing. "I think it's got everything you need. The list of jurors in the initial pool is up front."

"Thanks, Christina. You're the greatest."

She was looking a bit blurry-eyed, but Ben knew she was doing her best to mask it. Granny had finally delivered photocopyable documents on Saturday afternoon. Christina had spent the entire day and most of Sunday trying to catalogue the exhibits and get them into shape for use at trial. In addition to all her usual pretrial duties. He didn't know when she'd managed to do it all. But he was grateful that she had.

"Sorry you had to be up all night."

She shrugged. *"C'est la guerre."* She pointed toward the nearest stack. "These are copies of all the exhibits the prosecution anticipates they might get to on the first day of testimony. We probably won't get that far, but just in case."

"And tomorrow's exhibits?"

"Done."

Ben nodded. Christina was always thorough and prepared—and then some. She really was a treasure. One he probably didn't appreciate half as much as he should.

Not as much as Sheriff Allen, anyway.

"You're a lifesaver, Christina." Ben glanced up at her. "Christina, are you . . . all right?"

Her forehead crinkled. "All right? What do you mean?"

"Oh, I don't know. I just wondered if . . . you know. Everything's going all right."

The crinkles deepened. "What a strange question."

"It's not a strange question. You're a—a close friend and a coworker. Why is it strange to ask how you're feeling?"

"Because I've been working with you for years, and you've

never once inquired into my feelings. Are *you* feeling all right?"

Ben rolled his eyes. "I'm fine."

"Good." She punched him on the shoulder. "Concentrate on the trial, champ."

"Right." Ben glanced at his watch, then out in the gallery. "Excuse me for just a minute." Ben strolled down the nave till he arrived at the last row of the gallery, right-hand side. Slade was still sitting there, alone. "Come to watch the fruits of your labor?"

"I don't know what you mean." Slade gazed up with his usual placid, unruffled expression. "I hope you don't think I had anything to do with this murder."

"I wouldn't put anything past you, Slade. When is all this hate-mongering going to stop?"

"Again, I don't know what you mean."

"Oh, I think you do. You promised me something big was going to happen, and sure enough, it did. Now Green Rage has another man in the hospital and their camp has been destroyed. Thousands of dollars of equipment have been ruined."

"Green Rage has cost the logging industry millions of dollars."

"I'm not talking about lost profits, Slade. I'm talking about dispatching thugs to frighten and torture people."

"I have never condoned violence and I never will."

"Bull."

"It's true. Violence is inherently counterproductive, as this whole incident has proven. Not twenty-four hours after the Green Rage people were attacked, they struck back against the loggers."

"Who then struck back against Green Rage, right?"

Slade didn't answer.

"What's happened to Tess O'Connell, Slade? Where is she?"

No one had seen Tess since the day of the last pretrial hearing. Her car had been found on a side street just off Main, smashed into the side of a grocery store. Blood was found all over the steering wheel. But there was no trace of Tess.

"Where is she, Slade? What have your goons done to her?"

"Again, I must protest. I know nothing about this . . . Tess."

"Right. Just like you know nothing about the murder of Dwayne Gardiner. I think you're lying, Slade. And as soon as I have some time, I'm going to get to the truth about you and your nasty organization."

"What are you saying?"

"I'm saying that when I'm done with this trial, you're next."

"You're going to file some sort of action?"

"As a lawyer, as a writer—I don't know. I haven't decided yet. But I am coming after you. I'm going to expose your disgusting little Cabal for the corporate horror it is."

Slade leaned forward. His lips thinned, and his voice dropped to barely more than a whisper. "You're out of your league, Mr. Kincaid. Crawl back to your hole in the prairieland. You'll be nice and safe there. But don't mess with me."

"Because you're so strong and powerful?"

Slade did not break eye contact. "You have no idea."

The conversation was interrupted by a booming voice from the front of the courtroom. "Oyez, oyez, oyez. This court is now in session. The Honorable Tyrone J. Pickens presiding."

Despite himself, Ben felt a small clutching at his heart. This was it, then.

The trial was beginning. Ready or not.

* 34 *

The first order of the day was jury selection. This was the part of the trial many lawyers said was the most important, and the part Ben most hated. When it came to eliminating jurors, he had learned to trust Christina's instincts—because he had learned to distrust his own.

After all the work, all the investigation and preparation, witness interviews and evidence examination, document reviews and notetaking and everything else, it came down to this—choosing the twelve people who would sit in that box and decide whether George Zakin lived or died.

Ben listened attentively as the bailiff pulled names out of a hopper and announced them. Christina jotted the names down on his juror seating chart, then pulled whatever rudimentary information had been provided about each of them in advance.

"Charles Candy," the bailiff called out. "Jack Holstein. Nancy Cooper."

The names rushed in and out of Ben's brain. They didn't mean a thing to him. He focused on watching the people, trying to learn what he could with his eyes. Herbert Coburn was in his sixties, maybe seventies, but he approached the jury box with a slowness that was not related to his age. He didn't want to be here. Jack Holstein wore his hair longer than the Magic Valley norm, and he looked as if he might be part Native American. Would that make him more sympathetic to Zak's ecological fervor? It seemed a long shot, but that long shot might be the only one Ben got. Nancy Cooper couldn't pass through the center aisle of the courtroom without stealing a quick look at Zak. She knew who he was and she knew what case was about to be tried. And Ben got the definite impression she would love nothing more than to see a guilty verdict slapped across his forehead.

Or maybe he was being ridiculous. Was he trying to read too much into a quick glance? He leaned toward Christina and whispered in her ear. "What do you think about Cooper?"

"Definitely not," Christina whispered back, not looking up from her chart.

Ben beamed. Maybe his instincts weren't so bad after all.

He continued watching while the bailiff called thirty-two people up front. Folding chairs were added to the jury box so everyone would have a place to sit. The idea was to have enough people for a jury of twelve with two alternates—after each side had exercised its nine peremptory challenges. If any jurors were dismissed for cause, they would have to call more names.

Judge Pickens made a few preliminary remarks. Nothing Ben hadn't heard before. Thank you for serving as jurors. Important to listen attentively and answer the lawyers' questions to the best of your ability. Anyone who can't serve for medical reasons. The usual drill. Judge Pickens worked briskly through the essentials in an efficient, matter-of-fact manner. And he didn't appear to be trying to influence the outcome. Not yet, anyway.

Judge Pickens also walked the jurors through some of the preliminary questions the lawyers were certain to ask. He introduced every person in the front of the courtroom—lawyers, assistants, Zak—and asked if anyone knew them. He asked each juror to give his occupation, to tell whether he or she was married, and if so, what their spouse did. He asked if any of them had ever been a member of an organization called Green Rage (none) or if they had ever worked for a logging company (fifteen). Which, Ben couldn't help noting, was six more people than he had peremptory challenges.

Eventually it was time for the actual voir dire to begin. Being the prosecutor, Granny got first dibs. This was an advantage of incalculable value. She had the first chance to make a good impression, the first chance to try to convince them that everything she said was God's honest truth and everything Ben said was a crock of balderdash. For someone skillful enough to use it properly, it was a priceless opportunity.

And Granny turned out to be very skillful indeed.

Ben wasn't surprised. In a matter of minutes, he observed the combination of talent and style that built a rep that got her elected D.A. at such a young age. She came on strong and confident, but at the same time, she seemed to understand that there were lines she had best not cross. If she came on too strong, she would lose some of the jurors, particularly the older men, those most likely to mark her down as bitchy. If she came off too weak, of course, she wouldn't get what she wanted. She found a middle ground, a place likely to impress all while alienating no one.

Her dress reflected the same understanding of the necessary compromise. She was dressed in a light blue business suit—not quite cold, but not entirely warm either. A scarf around her neck provided a splash of color, a hint of femininity.

"Ladies and gentlemen of the jury," she said. She positioned herself just before the rail that separated the courtroom proper from the jury box. "We are asking you this day to serve on a jury that will consider a matter of grave importance, the gravest in our entire criminal code. Important issues are at stake—issues involving law and justice, the need for order in society, the importance of punishing wrongdoing. Obviously, with issues of this magnitude, it is critical that we have a jury that can adjudicate the evidence with a fair and open mind—a jury that won't shy away from the hard duties, that won't hesitate to do what has to be done when the time comes."

Ben could only marvel. She was an extremely effective speaker and advocate. She was already subtly pitching her case, already urging them toward conviction—and she hadn't even mentioned the case at hand. This common practice was, of course, entirely inappropriate. But she had given Ben nothing to object to.

Granny maintained an earnest but grave expression on her face. "I probably won't be revealing any secrets when I tell you that the case this jury will be asked to hear is a murder case, a capital murder case. The prosecution will be asking the jury to impose the maximum sentence. And that's why I have to ask the following questions."

Ben raised an eyebrow. Usually, prosecutors saved till last the unpleasant business of making sure the jury was *death-competent*—that is, able to deliver the death penalty if the evidence supports it. Apparently, Granny wanted no wimps on this jury. Given the fervor with which she went after it, Ben got the impression she wanted twelve venirepersons willing to push the plunger in the lethal syringe themselves.

"Is there anyone here who thinks they might not be able to vote for the death penalty? Even assuming the evidence proved guilt beyond a reasonable doubt? Anyone at all. Please, look deep into your hearts and try to be honest about this. Better that we find out now than that you find out later when you're in the deliberation room."

At first no one responded. Then, like bashful schoolchildren, three of the jurors raised their hands. A quick glance passed from Granny to Judge Pickens. Pickens thanked them for their time and excused them from the jury. Three replacement jurors were called.

Granny continued hammering on the death penalty for at least another forty minutes. Then she explored other possible grounds for jurors to be excused for cause—people who didn't believe in trials on religious grounds, people who had been previously convicted in criminal trials, and so on and so on. What she talked about almost not at all, Ben noted, was the enormous amount of local pretrial publicity and the possible bias it might cause. It wasn't hard to guess why Granny omitted this topic. Apparently she felt any pretrial publicity could only be to her benefit.

Ben also noticed that, regardless of what questions Granny asked, the jury seemed attentive, responsive, and quick to answer. Almost as if they wanted to help her. As if they liked her.

Granny was building a positive rapport with the jury. They were learning to trust her. When all was said and done, that was the most important thing a lawyer could do in voir dire. And Granny was doing it, effectively and effortlessly. Like a pro.

Which was bad news for Ben. And George Zakin.

Ben didn't get his chance at the jury until well into the afternoon. Granny worked them for over five hours, through the lunch break. More than a little excessive, by Ben's standards, but of course, in some jurisdictions, voir dire in a capital murder case went on for days. He decided to count his blessings.

Nonetheless, five hours was five hours, and by the time Ben got them, they were sick and tired of being questioned. That, too, Ben realized, might well be part of Granny's strategy. These people came to court to hear a murder case, and they wanted to get started, not monkey around with more lawyer questions. Ben would have to tread a treacherous tightrope—

doing his duty to his client by asking the questions that had to be asked without turning the jurors against him.

Granny had already covered most of the directly relevant questions. Which was just as well. Ben had learned from experience that he actually gained more from questions that didn't appear to have any obvious connection to the case at hand, questions that just allowed him to learn about the jurors themselves. So he tossed out a few softballs for starters, asking them about their hobbies, their children, their cars. The jurors were politely tolerant, but Ben knew that wouldn't last forever.

Ben quizzed an elderly man, one Conrad Sweeney. He was wearing suspenders with a bolo tie. His craggy face seemed set in a perpetual grimace.

"Mr. Sweeney," Ben asked, "what do you do now that you're retired?"

"Damn little," Sweeney grunted.

"You must do something to pass the time."

"Mostly I sit around and watch everyone else go to work."

"Is there anything else?"

"Nope. Nothing else."

"You're sure?"

Sweeney began to look annoyed. "Damn right I'm sure. I should know, shouldn't I?"

"There must be something you like to do in your spare time."

"Well," Sweeney said, "I like to smoke marijuana."

Ben blinked. *"What?"*

"Oh yeah. I like to smoke me a few reefers, then go out and ride my Harley. Mostly I cruise McKinley, check out the hookers, keep my eyes peeled for something sweet. You know how it is."

"You're kidding."

"Yeah," Sweeney said, "I am, actually. Had you going, though, didn't I?"

The courtroom exploded with laughter. Ben felt his face burning. This was just great. He was barely getting started, and he'd already been made an object of ridicule by a sixty-seven-year-old juror.

Ben turned toward the bench, hoping Judge Pickens would bring the courtroom back to order and admonish Sweeney to cut out the high jinks. Unfortunately, Pickens was too busy guffawing himself.

No matter what he did, Ben realized, he would be the outsider. Everyone else in the courtroom belonged in Magic Valley; he didn't. Ben had heard stories about lawyers being "hometowned" when they left the big city to try cases in rural districts. He just hoped he wasn't about to experience it firsthand.

Ben tried a different approach. "Mr. Sweeney, have you ever been called to a jury before?"

Sweeney shook his head. "Not once in sixty-seven years. Guess my luck finally ran out."

That one got an appreciative chuckle from some of the other jurors.

"Would you be pleased if you were chosen to serve on this jury?"

"Well, I'd be more pleased if it paid better."

"Is being on this jury something you want to do?"

"Oh, I suppose if I'm called, I'll do my duty and all that."

"But is it something you want to do?"

"I don't know. How much longer do you think you're going to be asking these fool questions?"

Another explosion of laughter, even louder than before. Ben tried to get a grip on himself. He was playing straight man for a would-be comedian—not an ideal situation. He decided it was best to move on.

He shifted his attention to Marjorie Preston, a middle-aged woman with big hair and a print dress, both of which looked as if they might have come from the June Cleaver style book. She worked part-time as a checkout clerk at Canfield's Grocery. "Mrs. Preston, can you tell me about your job?"

Her expression didn't seem to change as she spoke. "Oh, it's very boring."

Ben smiled. "As boring as this voir dire?"

"Oh, heavens no. Not that boring."

Well, he asked for that one, Ben thought, as once again he bathed in the laughter of the assemblage. "Mrs. Preston, do you understand that many witnesses will be called to the stand in the course of this trial?"

"I suppose it's inevitable," she sighed.

"Do you understand why witnesses are called before the jury?"

"So we can hear what they say and try to dope out whether they're telling the truth."

"Do you think you'll be able to do that, Mrs. Preston?"

Her chin rose. "I've seen a liar or two in my time, if that's what you mean."

"Do you think it's important to tell the truth?"

"I certainly do. You know where liars go." She extended her thumb and pointed downward.

Ben didn't even need to glance at Christina for this one. This lady was definitely off the jury.

He switched to the next man in line, Ken Whately, a farmer who lived about thirty miles outside Magic Valley. He was wearing scruffy blue jeans and cowboy boots. Ben assumed he checked his ten-gallon hat at the door.

Ben asked him a few preliminary questions about his farm. For once, the juror seemed not only cooperative, but garrulous. He took Ben through the whole planting season, crop by crop. He described all his machinery, down to the last tractor. He quoted the buy and sell prices for every harvest for the last five years.

"I can see you take your farming very seriously," Ben said, the first time the man came up for air. "Are you going to be able to concentrate on this trial or will your mind be out in the field?"

Whately frowned. "It's too hot for my mind to be out in the field."

"Right." Ben scanned the list Christina had given him of *must address* questions. Perhaps it was time he peeled one off the top. Whately might not be the ideal juror, but he was the best Ben had gotten so far.

The first was a delicate subject, one he preferred not to raise in voir dire. But since he wasn't sure yet whether he would put Zak on the stand, it needed to be covered. "Mr. Whately, you're familiar with the Fifth Amendment, aren't you?"

Whately appeared a bit uncertain. "That's . . . one of those amendments to the Constitution. Isn't it?"

"Right. You've probably heard about people taking the Fifth?"

"Oh." His face brightened a bit. "That's what crooks say when they don't want to talk."

Ben tilted his head to one side. "Not exactly. It's important that you as jurors realize that everyone has a right to avoid self-incrimination. No one can be forced to testify against himself. And no one can infer anything good or bad from a party's decision not to testify."

Whately nodded slowly. "I guess that's right."

"So let me ask you a question. What would you think if the trial was over and the defendant had not taken the stand?"

"I would assume his lawyer had a damn good reason for not letting him testify."

There was a sprinkling of chuckles. "Well, you see, sir, that's what we can't permit. As the judge will instruct you later in this trial, the jury is not permitted to draw any conclusion from the fact that the defendant has not testified. Not good or bad. Do you understand?"

"I . . . guess so."

"And do you think you can do it?"

"I'll give it my best."

"I'm sorry, Mr. Whately, but that isn't good enough. The judge will require you to answer that you can, or he will have you removed. We must have a jury that will honor the law. And that means that no inference can be drawn from a defendant's failure to testify. Can you go along with that?"

"I guess—I mean, yes. Sure."

"Thank you. Is there anyone else in the jury who thinks they might have a problem with this?"

No one raised his or her hand, but Ben knew that didn't mean much. He would have to ask each of them individually. No matter how long it took.

After he finished quizzing the jurors about the Fifth Amendment, Ben launched into the phase of his voir dire routine he knew by heart—because he got to deliver it every time. The discussion of the burden of proof.

This was a delicate subject. As a defense attorney, he wanted to impress upon the jurors what a stiff standard it was and how seriously it must be taken. At the same time, he wasn't allowed to define or explain what *beyond a reasonable doubt* actually meant. Any attempt to do so would be grounds for an immediate mistrial.

"In order to find the defendant guilty," Ben summed up, "you must find that, based upon the evidence presented at trial and nothing else, he is guilty beyond a reasonable doubt. Do you think you understand that, Ms. Taylor?"

Angel Taylor, a twenty-something blonde in the front row, nodded. "I think I've got the general idea."

"Will you be able to honor this standard?"

"I believe so."

"Do you understand everything this high standard of proof requires?"

"I believe so."

"What do you think about it?"

She sighed. "I think you've about exhausted this subject. Could we move on to something else?"

Ben had to smile.

* 35 *

Ben spent the remainder of the afternoon exploring the jurors' ties to the logging industry and the obvious tendency that might have to predispose them against Zak, and trying to assess the impact of pretrial publicity regarding the murder. As he soon learned, there wasn't a soul in the jury box who didn't know something about the murder. And it didn't take a mind reader to deduce that most of them assumed George Zakin had done it. All Ben could do was ask the jurors if they believed they were biased (none of them did, of course), and whether they thought they could be open-minded and fair (all of them did, of course). Unless someone admitted to bias, he couldn't get them removed for cause. He would have to use his precious peremptory challenges to root out the worst of them.

He tried to delicately address the subject of conservation, of ecology and efforts to protect the old-growth forest, but he almost immediately felt such an intense chill he backed off. This was not a sympathetic audience. The less he reminded them of Zak's environmental "extremism," the better off he'd be. He began considering ways to reshape Zak into something less controversial, like maybe a communist or a child molester.

By the end of the day, both sides were ready to pick a jury. Ben knew up front he couldn't eliminate everyone who ever worked for a logging company; that industry was far too pervasive in this part of the world. And it was even possible that people who had an up-close look at logging practices might be more sympathetic to Zak. So he took off the two that seemed most extreme and left the rest. He removed Mrs. Preston and Mrs. Cooper, then two other jurors he thought would be likely to convict even without evidence, much less evidence meeting any burden of proof. Granny peeled her six off as well—all, Ben judged, because they had seemed less than zealot-like in their determination to apply the death penalty. Which gave Ben a pretty good idea what she thought was most important.

Judge Pickens excused the dismissed jurors and told the lucky fourteen to be back in the courtroom at nine o'clock the next morning. And then court was in recess.

The preliminaries were over, Ben realized. Now the real work would begin.

"How do you think it went?" Ben asked Christina, after they returned to their office.

"Comme ci, comme ça," she replied. "Of course, the jury is going to be hugely pro-logging. But you knew that was in-

evitable when Judge Pickens declined to grant your motion for change of venue. Still, I think you got the worst of them off."

"We can only hope." Ben plopped down into the chair. "I thought voir dire was grueling. I wanted to ask a million questions. And I think they wanted me to stop before I started."

"Nonetheless, you plowed ahead and did what you needed to do." She smiled. "I can remember when you were too embarrassed to ask individual jurors questions. And today you did it for hours. You've come a long way, Ben."

"I was probably better off before. All I did was give them an opportunity to make me the butt of their jokes."

"Not necessarily a bad thing. Everyone likes to be the class clown on occasion. You gave them a chance to do it in court. Which may endear you to them. Just a bit."

"Sort of like . . . everyone loves the village idiot?"

She grinned. "Sort of. Any way you look at it, it's a good thing."

"Sounds great. They love Granny. They patronize me."

"I'm not sure they do love Granny. They respect Granny, just as they would respect a Doberman or anything else that might rip out their throats with its bare teeth. She's a *femme fatale* big-time, and they know it. But don't confuse that with love." She paused. "You're never going to make the jury forget you're an outsider, because you are. But you could possibly make them like you. More important, you could make them trust you." She leaned across the desk. "And that's the only way you're going to win this case."

There was a knock at the door. "Come in," Ben said.

After a moment's hesitation, Sheriff Allen poked his head through the doorway.

"Oh." Ben stood up and glanced at Christina. "I guess you two have a dinner date."

"Actually, no," Allen said. He tipped his hat and smiled in Christina's direction. "Although I wish I did. The little lady told me she was off-limits till the trial ended." He cleared his throat. "No, I came to see you, Ben."

"Me? Why?"

Allen cleared his throat again. There seemed to be something he needed to say—something he wasn't looking forward to saying. "Got a call on the radio from one of my deputies. Deputy Andrews."

"A fine fellow," Ben said. "He helped me break up a near riot."

"Right." A longer pause. More hesitation. "He's found something."

Something about Allen's expression sent a chill down Ben's spine. "Something? Or . . . someone?"

Allen nodded grimly. "Tess O'Connell. What's left of her."

Ben joined Sheriff Allen in his Jeep for a half-hour drive into the forest. On the way, Allen showed Ben where he'd broken up the whipping incident several nights before. Their destination, though, was a good fifteen minutes beyond that.

"This is pretty well off the beaten track," Allen explained. "It's pure coincidence that Andrews happened on it."

"What was he doing in the forest?"

"Oh, we try to patrol out here from time to time. Just as we do in the city."

"Patrol for what? Jaywalking grizzly bears? Spotted owls flying under the influence?"

"More like environmental radicals blowing up expensive equipment. Sabotaging machinery."

"You take your instructions from the logging companies?"

"Kincaid, try to get this through your head. I don't take my instructions from anyone. I'm not on anyone's payroll. Neither is my department. When we go out on patrol, we go looking for crime, regardless of the politics behind it."

"But you patrol in places where you'll catch environmentalists."

"Or loggers. If more of my men had been in the forest that night, your Green Rage buddies might not have lost their camp. And if I hadn't been driving around the night that whipping took place, three of your friends might well be dead now."

Ben bit his lip. Allen was right, of course. Ben was out of line. "I'm sorry. Trying this case has made me paranoid."

"Can't say as I blame you for that." They drove another fifteen minutes or so down a narrow dirt trail into the heart of the forest. Ben supposed that Allen probably had landmarks that he followed. For Ben, it was just trees and trees and more trees.

Eventually Allen pulled the Jeep over to the side of the road. "From here, we walk."

Allen checked his pocket compass and pointed. They headed off in that direction.

Not two minutes later, Ben saw Deputy Andrews in the distance. As they approached, Ben picked up on his distressed expression, the pasty white condition of his face.

"Where?" Sheriff Allen asked.

Andrews pointed, up high and to the left.

And there she was.

She had been nailed facefirst to the tree, with six sturdy iron spikes hammered through her arms, legs, and torso. She had been crucified, her arms stretched out and her legs splayed. Except on closer examination, Ben realized her arms weren't so much stretched out as . . . wrapped around the tree trunk.

She was a tree hugger, now. Literally. And finally.

* 36 *

"You gonna be all right?"

Ben nodded. He'd been sick—right after he'd gotten his first glimpse of the grotesque, blood-soaked corpse pinioned to the treetops. It was Tess all right, but nothing like the Tess he had met a few days before. This atrocity was more rag doll than human being.

He'd tried to contain himself, but to no avail. "Sorry. I don't normally react this way."

"Ben," Allen said, "there is no normal for something like this. It's not a normal situation."

Shortly thereafter, the rest of the crime team arrived. They began the deliberate process of collecting evidence, trying to find any trace of the monster who had done this.

The worst lot fell to the two men from the coroner's office. They were supposed to recover the body. But how? Could they pry her loose? The standard coroner's bag didn't include a claw hammer.

"We can't just leave her like this," Allen said bitterly. "Go back and find something that will do the job."

The coroner's men did as they were told. Ben noticed they didn't seem all that upset to be leaving the crime scene. But then, who would be?

Eventually, the coroner's team returned with ladders, heavy-duty prying equipment, and two more burly-looking associates. Ben didn't envy them in the least. The task they had before them was so gruesome he couldn't watch. He didn't even want to think about it.

The next two hours were spent photographing the crime scene and collecting trace evidence. Ben hung around, hoping the investigators might turn up something he could use at trial. One thing was certain: Tess was not killed by George Zakin, who had been behind bars when this murder occurred. Granny would no doubt claim that there were two different murderers at work. But if Ben could prove both killings were the work of the same killer, it would prove the killer wasn't Zak.

And—more disturbingly—it would prove that the true killer was still at large.

"I can't say that I see any connection between the two crimes at all," Sheriff Allen said, taking a short break from supervising the crime-scene detail. "The previous murder was of a logger. This victim was a Green Rager."

"You're assuming the motive is linked to the tree-cutting dispute," Ben said. "But what if it isn't? What if it's about something altogether different?"

"Like what?"

"If I knew that, this would be a very short trial. Unfortunately, I don't."

"You're just speculating, Ben."

"Maybe. But look at it this way. By all appearances, this crime was committed by someone in the logging camp. Someone free, on the loose, and capable of murder. Presumably, that person was around when Dwayne Gardiner was killed, too. So who's to say this sick bastard might not have committed the first murder?"

"I don't agree that it appears this crime was committed by a logger. I've grown up with loggers. Most of them are good, calm, decent men. This could just as easily have been done by one of your terrorist pals."

"Why?"

"How should I know? Maybe they had an internal dispute. Some fight for power or authority. I hear these terrorist groups spend half their time squabbling among themselves."

"Green Rage is not a terrorist group."

"Or maybe someone did it to throw suspicion on the loggers. Try to get your man Zakin off the hook."

Ben frowned. It was theoretically possible, he supposed. Disturbing, but possible.

"Thanks for inviting me out here," Ben said. "I probably won't sleep for weeks. But I needed to know what was happening."

"No thanks necessary. No matter what you think, the local law intends to give everyone a fair shake."

"I wish everyone in this town shared your intent. You think some of your men could give me a ride back to town?"

"Yep. You can ride in the coroner's truck."

Ben winced.

"Don't worry. They'll have room for you up front."

Well, that was a relief, anyway. "Thanks again, Sheriff. If there's ever anything I can do for you . . ."

A sheepish grin came over the man's face. "Well, you could put in a good word for me with that legal assistant of yours."

Ben nodded. Yes, he certainly could. And probably should.

But *would* he?

That was the question.

* 37 *

The second trial day in Judge Pickens's courtroom evidenced no diminution of local interest. If anything, there were even more spectators; Ben noted that the sergeants-at-arms had allowed more spectators in to fill the seats vacated by yesterday's jury pool. All the familiar faces Ben had noted the day before had returned.

Ben had barely slept. Even after he returned from the site where Tess's body was found, escorted by two coroner's attendants with distressingly lively senses of humor, he hadn't been able to sleep. The scene was too memorable, too horrific, and besides, he needed to practice his opening statement.

Of all the various components of a trial, this was perhaps the one Ben hated most. Although, come to think of it, he probably said that about every phase of the trial at one time or another. But in opening statement, it was possible to prepare in advance, to *can* it—and most lawyers did. Some of them were very polished speakers, adept at delivering rehearsed speeches.

Ben wasn't. He much preferred having another person to interact with, a witness or a juror. Standing in front of fourteen people and delivering a prepared monologue only served to remind him why public speaking was most people's greatest terror. And sleep deprivation wasn't making it any better, either. Judge Pickens had announced in advance that openings would be limited to a half hour for each side—a disappointment for Granny, a godsend for Ben.

When the sheriff's deputy brought Zak into the courtroom, he appeared even more furious than the day before. "What the hell is going on out there?"

Ben lowered his eyes. "You've heard about Tess."

"Damn straight." Zak reached up to brush back his hair, then realized he'd cut it short. "They say this woman was part of Green Rage? I never even met her."

"She was new," Ben said, repeating what Maureen had told him. "She was local."

"And they killed her? Man. This thing is out of control. Totally out of control."

Ben was inclined to agree. But unfortunately, nothing had happened yet that was likely to stop the pattern of strikes and strike-backs. At this rate, the spiral of hate would continue to expand until it finally culminated in something even more horrible than what happened to Tess.

"This group is falling apart!" Zak moaned. "They've got everyone so scared—even Deirdre won't go into the forest. How the hell is she going to find the world's largest cedar tree if she won't go into the forest?"

"I appreciate the dilemma," Ben said gently, "but at the moment, you have worse problems to worry about."

"Yeah, but—"

"And that's what I want you focused on. This trial. One hundred percent."

Zak folded his arms and gave Ben a grudging nod.

The bailiff made the usual announcement, and in walked the Honorable Judge Tyrone J. Pickens. The Time Machine was on time this morning, and Ben for one was relieved.

Pickens ran briskly through all the introductory instructions to the jury, admonishing them not to discuss the case till the presentation of evidence was completed, reminding them that their decision should be based upon the testimony and the evidence—and that what lawyers said was not testimony or evidence. On that happy note, he called for opening statements.

Granny took center stage with a solemn expression on her face. She signaled from the outset that there would be no fun and games during this opening. She wanted to impress them with the gravity of the crime—and the necessity of punishment.

"Dwayne Gardiner was only thirty-two years old," she said,

adopting the narrative tone of an evening newscaster. "He had a wife and a small boy." She paused, allowing the import of her words to sink in. "Dwayne had worked for WLE Logging all his adult life, since he was eighteen. He was a hard worker and a good one, often putting in as many as sixty hours a week. He was up for promotion, and had he lived another six months"—another ponderous pause—"he would probably have been given a position that would almost double his salary. He and his young wife would have been able to buy that three-room house on Lincoln they had their eye on. But now that will never happen."

Ben kept his hands planted firmly on the table. He could object on grounds of relevance—because none of this was—but he knew that would gain him little ground with the jury. He would wait for something more important.

"That will never happen because on July thirteenth, in the dead of night, his life was stolen by this man." Her arm shot back and pointed directly at Zak. "George Zakin killed Dwayne Gardiner—what's more, killed him in perhaps the most gruesome, agonizing way you could imagine. I will warn you in advance—this is not a crime for the weak-stomached. When you hear what happened, you will be disturbed by it—perhaps more disturbed than you have been by anything you've heard before in your life."

Ben shook his head. As if the crime wasn't bad enough already, Granny was determined to melodramatize it, to build suspense, to ensure that they would be horrified when they finally heard the details.

"Why did he do it? you may be wondering. Why would anyone commit such a heinous crime against an innocent, hard-working man? Well, George Zakin is a member of an organization called Green Rage. I'll bet you've heard of it. In fact, Mr. Zakin is the local leader of the group. Green Rage claims to be an environmental group, but its real purpose is to stir up controversy and turmoil by committing terroristic acts against loggers and logging companies.

"Green Rage came to town a few months ago, trying to stop the totally legal and federally approved logging of the Mount Crescent watershed. It seems the rule of law was of no importance to these Green Ragers; they were a law unto themselves. They began stealing equipment, sabotaging the mill. They even planted bombs on expensive logging equipment, blowing them up in dangerous high-octane explosions."

She pivoted, adopting a somewhat more contemplative tone. "Now, I don't know what you jurors think about people who use bombs. But in the wake of the World Trade Center and the hideous Oklahoma City tragedy, we in the law enforcement community are not very sympathetic to these tactics. But I'm not asking you to pass judgment on whether it's acceptable to use terroristic tactics to achieve political goals."

Like hell you're not, Ben thought.

"I'm simply telling you that the evidence will show that these tactics were used by Green Rage, that it was in fact a disturbingly common practice for this team of elitist radicals. So it is not altogether surprising, if nonetheless tragic, that the tree cutter Dwayne Gardiner tried to start on the night of July thirteenth had a bomb planted in it, a bomb that was rigged to explode when the ignition was turned. A bomb planted by George Zakin."

Granny kicked her head back, swishing her buoyant hair behind her shoulders, pressing her bosom forward ever so slightly. It seemed Granny was not opposed to using a hint of sex appeal to get her message across, either.

"You may be thinking—how do they know it was Zakin? Why not one of the other Green Ragers? Well, the truth is, some of the others may have been involved. In fact, some of them probably were, at least in the procurement of the bomb materials. We know these people have been stockpiling explosives for some time."

She took a deep breath. "But we also know the man who planted the bomb was Mr. Zakin. Mr. Zakin has both experience and expertise with bombs. We know Zakin was in the forest at the time of the murder—quite a coincidence, don't you think? Moreover, at the scene of the murder, we discovered actual physical evidence that proves Zakin is the culprit beyond a reasonable doubt. Zakin's fingerprints on shards of exploded metal. Footprints. Dental analysis. And more.

"I know what some of you may be thinking. You're wondering if perhaps the killing was an accident. Perhaps Zakin planted the bomb, but Gardiner only accidentally got in the way. You should be commended for these charitable thoughts, but unfortunately, the evidence will show otherwise. The evidence will show that Dwayne Gardiner was *shot* first—at near point-blank range—before the bomb went off. And may I also point out that this was not a passive bomb. This was a bomb rigged to explode when someone turned the ignition. And that's only part of the reason we are so confident this crime was not committed inadvertently."

She turned away from the jury as if lost in thought. In fact, Ben realized, she was drawing out the suspense, biding her time before she delivered her clincher. "You see, I've only told you part of the motive for Zakin's damnable act of homicide. There was the environmental aspect, yes, but there was also a . . . personal aspect. Witnesses will take the stand and tell you that Zakin knew the late Mr. Gardiner, that they had previously had a very public, very violent conflict. Zakin had a personal reason for wanting Dwayne Gardiner dead—a reason so abominable it will shock you when you learn the truth."

Ben had to hand it to her. Granny was like the Agatha Christie of trial lawyers. She intimated everything while telling nothing. She was saving all her best bits for maximum impact. The jury would be hanging breathlessly in anticipation every time she put a witness on the stand, waiting for the other shoe to drop. Waiting for the grisly truth, the untold secrets, the smoking guns, to be revealed.

"Ladies and gentlemen of the jury, when you have had an opportunity to consider all the evidence, all the testimony and all the exhibits, I am confident you will find what we at the D.A.'s office have known for some time—that George Zakin killed Dwayne Gardiner in cold blood. But when you deliver that verdict, your job will be only half done. At that time, you will be asked to determine the sentence to be rendered in judgment for this horrible crime. I warn you now, I will be asking for the most extreme sanction. But then isn't this a most extreme crime? Certainly the D.A.'s office thinks it is. Certainly

Dwayne Gardiner's wife and his now fatherless little boy think it is."

She paused, allowing the jury to conjure up the image of that grief-stricken family before proceeding. "But most important, by the conclusion of the evidence, I know you will believe it is. And therefore, I know you will do what is right. What is necessary. Each and every one of you."

She lowered her head, almost as if in prayer. "Thank you very much for your attention."

* 38 *

For Ben, the worst part of seeing Granny sit down was not simply that she had done such a spectacularly effective job. The worst part was knowing that this meant it was time for him to stand. And talk.

He heard Zak whispering in his ear. "Wow. That was pretty damn good. You think the jury bought all that?"

"Hard to say," Ben answered, expressing doubts he didn't really possess. "What did she mean about you having a personal motive?"

"Beats me," Zak said. "I think she's pulling rabbits out of her hat. Probably making it up as she goes along."

No, Ben mused, Granny was much too good a prosecutor for that. She knew that if she promised the jury something in opening, they'd be waiting for it during the trial. And if it didn't appear, they'd take it as a sign that either she was lying or her case was falling apart.

She wouldn't make that mistake. She wouldn't promise anything unless she was sure she could deliver. But what was it?

"Mr. Kincaid," Judge Pickens said, "would you like to make

your opening statement now, or reserve it until the start of your case?"

Like he would be crazy enough to let Granny's diatribe go unrefuted for ten seconds. "I'll open now, your honor."

Ben walked out from behind his table and faced the jury. He tried to move all the way to the rail, as Granny had done, but he just couldn't bring himself to do it. He felt as if he were invading their personal space. Instead, he found a comfortable spot a few feet from the rail and lodged himself there.

"Here's the straight skivvy," Ben said, trying to make eye contact with each of the jurors in turn. "George Zakin is a member of Green Rage. In fact, he's the team leader of the group that has been working in the forest just outside of town. It's also true that Green Rage—and George Zakin—oppose the continued clear-cutting of your old-growth forest. And it's true that Green Rage sometimes uses tactics commonly referred to as monkey-wrenching—tactics that probably wouldn't be approved of in your Sunday-school class. All of that is absolutely one hundred percent true."

He paused, making sure their eyes were still on him. "But this is also true. Green Rage has never, in the entire history of the organization, harmed any living creature in pursuit of its goals. Whatever rumors or gossip you may have heard to the contrary. They might spike trees or blow up machinery, but they do not hurt people. And neither does George Zakin." He made eye contact again, this time lingering a bit longer. "George Zakin—his friends call him Zak—did not kill Dwayne Gardiner. By the conclusion of the trial, I believe you will be convinced, as I am, that he is not the murderer. And what's more, you may have a pretty good idea who was."

Well, that got their attention, Ben was pleased to see. It was a strategy from Granny's playbook—give them something to look forward to. Ben only hoped Loving would scrape up enough information about Alberto Vincenzo to allow him to deliver on the promise.

"The evidence, when put before you and scrutinized carefully, will prove to be not nearly so damning as Madame Prosecutor would suggest. True—Zak was in the forest the night of the murder. Zak was in the forest every night, as was every other member of Green Rage. That's not a suspicious coincidence, that's just a fact. A fact the prosecutor hopes to take advantage of. The evidence will show that Zak was in fact with a Green Rage colleague—miles from the scene of the murder at the critical time—who will testify that he had nothing to do with it. And the evidence will show that the so-called physical evidence is either easily explained or altogether ambiguous. Either way, it doesn't prove Zak's guilt.

"And that's the most important detail," Ben continued, "because, as the judge will later instruct you, the defendant doesn't have to prove anything. In fact, we don't have to say a word if we don't want to, because we have no burden of proof. The burden of proof is entirely on the prosecution. Every element of their case has to be proved by them. And if they fail to prove any element, any at all—beyond a reasonable doubt—then the judge will instruct you that you have no choice in your verdict. You must find Zak not guilty." He leaned against the guardrail. "Let me say it again, just to make sure we're clear here. Regardless of what your personal feelings may be, regardless of your instincts, whether you like Zak, or what you think really happened, if his guilt is not thoroughly proved beyond a reasonable doubt, you must return a verdict of not guilty."

Ben couldn't lay it on any thicker than that. He'd made his point. Time to move on.

"Let me make one other point before I sit down. It may not be necessary; most of you probably already understand this. But I'm a lawyer, and I get paid by the hour, so let me go ahead and say it anyway."

A mild titter from the gallery; most of the jury remained stone-faced.

"This trial is not about politics. Don't let anyone try to suggest that it is. I'm aware that these environmental issues are complex, that there are two sides to every story. How many more forests can we afford to turn into pulp? How many jobs can we sacrifice to conservation? And I'm aware that many of you probably disagree with my client's position on these issues. That doesn't matter. Do you understand that?" He said it softly but insistently. "It doesn't matter. It's not what this trial is about. This trial is only about one thing: did George Zakin kill Dwayne Gardiner? Or more accurately, has the prosecution *proved* that George Zakin killed Dwayne Gardiner? I am convinced—I am absolutely certain—that you can make a full and fair determination of that question even if you disagree with my client's political beliefs. Even if you've worked for logging companies all your life. Even if you think Green Rage is just a bunch of troublemakers. You can still be fair. I know you can."

He glanced up at the bench. "Thank you, your honor. That's all I wanted to say."

* 39 *

After opening statements, Judge Pickens gave the jury a fifteen-minute recess to stretch their legs and powder their noses. Ben was grateful to have time to gear up for the prosecution's first witness.

"Nice job on opening," Christina whispered in his ear as he reviewed his notes. "I think you made your points very effectively."

"But do they like me?" Ben asked.

"It's early yet. At any rate, you played it straight with them, and I think they'll remember that."

After the break, the bailiff reassembled the jury, and Judge Pickens gave them a few more instructions. We are now entering the evidentiary phase of the trial, he told them, so pay close attention to everything you see and hear. You can't take notes. You can't ask questions. Just listen up. And so forth.

"The State calls Deputy Kyle Wagner to the stand," Granny announced.

From the back of the courtroom, an extremely young-looking peace officer made his way to the front. He did not appear particularly anxious to testify, not that anyone ever did. Wagner seemed especially pale and sickly, though. Ben wondered if the bailiff should distribute barf bags at the same time as he administered the oath.

Wagner was, predictably, wearing his uniform, sporting a fresh short haircut, and clean-shaven. Ben had the impression the man couldn't lie if his mother's life depended on it.

Granny introduced the young officer to the jury and led him through a few preliminary questions. "What do you do for a living?"

"I work for the sheriff."

"Would that be Sheriff Allen, here in Magic Valley?"

"Right." His voice was thin and wavering. If he was this distraught during the softball questions, Ben could only imagine what he might be like when they got to the crime scene. "I'm a deputy."

"I see." She asked a few more preliminary background questions, then moved to the night of the murder. "Would you tell the jury what you were doing on the night of July thirteenth?"

Like a well-trained dog, Wagner turned toward the jury box. "I was working the night shift."

"Were you the only one in the office?"

"Yes. Sheriff Allen and the other deputies were off duty."

"And could you tell us what night duty entails?"

"Usually, just sitting around staring at the phone. Sometimes I work the crossword." His lips turned up, making a goofy, lopsided grin. "Not much happens around here most nights."

"But this night was different, wasn't it?"

"Yes," he said, licking his lips, "it certainly was."

"What happened?"

Wagner straightened a bit. "Got a phone call. Told me there'd been some trouble out at a clearing on the south side of Mount Crescent. An explosion."

"An explosion? What did that make you think?"

"Objection," Ben said, rising to his feet. "What the officer thought is not relevant."

Judge Pickens sighed. "All right, Gra—er, Madame Prosecutor. Rephrase."

She nodded. "What did you do when you heard there had been an explosion?"

"I grabbed my hat and went out to investigate."

"Did you call for backup?"

"Not at that time, no."

"Why not?"

"Well, frankly, I didn't expect it to be any great big deal."

"An explosion?"

"Explosions have become all too common since those"—he stopped, glanced toward Zak—"since Green Rage came to Magic Valley."

"There had been prior incidents?"

"Like about two dozen," Wagner said. "More since. But before, they'd only blown up machinery and stuff. So I didn't have any reason to believe this would be any different."

"But it was different, wasn't it?"

"Oh, yeah." Wagner's eyes seemed wide and hollow.

"How long did it take you to get to the clearing?"

"Not long. Maybe twenty, thirty minutes. I knew where it was, and I knew"—another glance at Zak—"well, I knew the logging operation had moved in there. So I thought there might be trouble."

"Deputy Wagner, I know this won't be easy for you, but I have to ask anyway. Would you please tell the jury what you saw when you arrived at the clearing?"

Wagner nodded, although it was clear he was not anxious to do so. "Well, the first thing I saw of course was the tree cutter. Or what was left of it."

"Describe what a tree cutter is, please."

"It's a big piece of machinery. Like a tractor, with two big steel claws in front. They use it to—well, to cut trees, obviously."

"And what condition was this particular tree cutter in?"

"It had been blown to smithereens."

"Could you perhaps give us a more . . . detailed description?"

"The debris was everywhere. Big chunks of charred, blackened metal. Still hot to the touch. Some of the smaller pieces glowed red—they were that hot. I could tell it had once been a tree cutter, but to most folks, I think it would've just looked like a big hunk of junk."

"Was it salvageable?"

"Oh, no way. It was obvious that thing would never cut again."

"Did you notice anything else?"

Wagner's chin sank. "Yeah. I did."

"Please tell the jury what you saw."

Wagner swallowed. "Well . . . of course the whole area had been destroyed. Burnt grass. Couple of trees had caught fire—we're lucky we didn't have a full-out forest fire."

"Yes, yes," Granny said. "Tell them about the body."

"Objection," Ben said. "Leading."

Judge Pickens ran his tongue across the front of his teeth. " 'Fraid he's right, Madame Prosecutor. I think Mr. Kincaid is determined to make sure we play by the rules." His voice dropped, though not so much that the jury couldn't hear him. "Even if it does make everything take five times as long."

Granny returned her attention to the witness. "Deputy Wagner, please tell us what else you saw."

Now, having been properly cued, he went straight to what she wanted. "Well, I—I didn't see it at first." Ben noticed the trembling in his hands was becoming more pronounced. "Sad fact is, I almost tripped over the thing. Before I—I . . ." His voice drifted. " 'Fore I realized what it was."

"And what was it?"

"It was a person. Least it used to be." He swallowed. "I found the corpse. Burned to a crisp."

Granny paused a moment, allowing the jury to drink in that charming mental image. "Can you describe the state of the remains?"

"I'll try. I can't tell you what it was like seeing that—that nightmare right before my eyes, all alone, in the middle of the night." He clamped his hands down on the edge of the witness box. "It was all black, head to toe. There was barely any skin left, and what was left was black. I could see the skull, the exposed eye sockets. Some of his internal organs were visible, and they looked like—"

"Your honor, I object," Ben said. "This is not necessary."

"Overruled," Pickens said without even looking at him. "Please proceed, Deputy."

"The organs looked . . . charred. Cooked." Wagner had a pained expression on his face; Ben was afraid he might cry. "Some of the fingers and toes had been broken off. A spot on his chest looked as if it had been ripped open. There were even . . . animals . . ." He lowered his head. "Insects and birds and things. Eating what there was to eat. The whole body looked like someone'd stuck him on a rotisserie spit and turned up the heat. It was awful."

Well, Ben thought, Granny had promised the jury something gruesome—and she'd delivered on her promise. Emphasizing the horror of the crime would only make it all the more likely the jury would convict.

"You mentioned a . . . rip in the man's chest. Could you tell what caused it?"

"Looked like a gunshot wound to me."

Ben had to object. "Your honor, this witness has not been qualified as a gunshot wound expert or a coroner. Absent any evidence—"

"I could see the bullet inside the man's chest," Wagner said firmly. "How's that for evidence?"

Ben pressed his lips together. Not too shabby, as evidence goes. He sat down.

"Could you tell us where the gunshot wound was located, please?" Granny asked.

"Right here." He touched a spot on the right side of his chest, just below the collarbone.

"What did you do after you saw the corpse?"

"Well, 'course that changed everything. I got on my radio and called for assistance."

"And did they come?"

"Oh yeah. Sheriff Allen came personally, with several other deputies and crime scene specialists. They took control of the crime scene and relieved me."

"And what did you do then?"

Wagner looked up. His eyes were watery and he still looked

shaken. "Well, by then it was almost five in the morning. I went home. Tried to get some sleep."

"And did you?"

Wagner shook his head. "No, ma'am. Not a wink." He looked down at the floor. "I never even closed my eyes."

* 40 *

For a brief moment, Ben considered not cross-examining Deputy Wagner at all. There was no reason to believe he was lying; Ben didn't doubt a word he had said. And none of his testimony directly incriminated Zak, although Ben knew he had laid the groundwork for much evidence yet to come.

Still, Ben thought, it was always possible he might accomplish something. And he didn't like to give the jury the impression this was all the prosecutor's show, that he wasn't a player. He would remind them the defense existed, if nothing else. Best to give them their money's worth.

Ben walked to the podium. "Deputy Wagner, my name is Ben Kincaid. I'm a lawyer, and I represent the defendant George Zakin in this trial. I'd like to ask you a few questions."

"Okay," Wagner gamely replied.

"The whole time you were testifying, Deputy, I kept wondering—who called you?"

Wagner's head dipped. "Uh—what?"

"The call. In the middle of the night. Telling you about the explosion. Who called?"

"Oh. That was an anonymous tip."

"And you don't know who called?"

"No."

"Weren't you curious?"

"Anonymous tips aren't that uncommon."

"Deputy Wagner, how many people do you suppose were wandering around that forest at one in the morning?"

Wagner shrugged. "I don't know. Not many."

"But there are two people we know for certain were out there, right?"

Wagner shook his head. "Huh?"

"The victim. And the murderer."

"Oh, right. Right." His trembling intensified.

"So it's just possible your call came from the murderer."

"Well—"

"And that would give you a pretty good reason to find out who made the call, don't you think?"

"Well, by the next morning, we already knew that Zakin—"

"Excuse me. Did you see my client at the scene of the crime?"

"No."

"So all you know is that by the next morning the sheriff's office suspected George Zakin, right?"

"Yes."

"And since they already had an easy, convenient suspect, there was no reason to look for another one."

"Well, I hardly think—"

"Once you had your obvious suspect, the search for other suspects came to a halt."

"Objection, your honor." Granny jumped to her feet, looking extremely indignant. "He's not giving the witness a chance to answer. And he's not really asking questions anyway. He's making a speech."

"Sustained," Judge Pickens said. "The jury is instructed to disregard defense counsel's speechifying. And counsel"—he pointed his gavel—"if you don't behave yourself, I'll shut you down like a clam."

Yes, yes, Ben thought. Scold me all you want. The more the judge threatened, the more likely the jury was to remember what Ben had said. "Deputy Wagner, did you in fact make any effort to find out who made the anonymous phone call?"

"As a matter of fact, we did."

Ben drew back. Darn.

"We traced the call through phone company records.

Turned out the call came from a phone booth not far from Bunyan's—uh, that's a bar here in town. It would still be open that time of night. We asked around inside the bar, but no one knew anything. There was no way to determine who made the call."

"Do you remember anything distinctive about the call?"

"Distinctive?"

"Anything unusual about the voice? Anything that caught your attention?"

"Well . . . of course, I can't be sure, but"—he glanced quickly at Granny—"I thought it was a woman."

"A woman?"

"Right. I could tell whoever it was was trying to disguise her voice, but still and all, I thought it was female."

A woman, Ben thought. A woman who witnessed the explosion. Hmm . . .

"Deputy Wagner, what was your reaction when you saw the . . . remains of Dwayne Gardiner?"

"My reaction? I don't know what you mean."

"Well, if it had been me, I would've been pretty shaken up. Were you?"

His trembling hands almost answered for him. "I guess you could say that, yeah."

"Did you run?"

Wagner's brow creased. "What do you mean? I'm not a coward."

"I'm sure you're not. But we all have a flight reflex. If I'd seen that horrible corpse, I would have instinctively run away."

"Well . . . maybe I did. At first. But I came back."

"So you ran away, then came back a second time. Must've left a lot of footprints around the corpse."

Out the corner of his eye, Ben could see Granny rising to her feet, trying to think of an objection. As luck would have it, Wagner answered first. "Sure, I suppose."

"And what size shoe do you wear?"

"Size ten. Why?"

"Just curious. Thank you, Deputy." Ben exchanged a quick

glance with Christina. That bit of information would be filed away for later use. And while he was at it . . .

"One last thing, Deputy. After you called for backup, how long did it take for Sheriff Allen and the rest of the team to arrive?"

He shrugged. "Oh, I don't know exactly. Not long."

"How long. An hour? Maybe two?"

"I told you, it wasn't long."

"It takes half an hour just to get to the clearing from the sheriff's office. And most of these people were probably at home in bed."

Wagner ground his teeth together. "I'd guess it was an hour before the team arrived. Maybe an hour and fifteen minutes."

"And so, for that entire waiting period, you were alone at the crime scene. Is that correct?"

"That's correct."

"Did you stand still the whole time?"

Wagner's face crinkled up. "Did I stand still?"

"Right. Or did you move around periodically?"

Wagner's expression suggested that these were the dumbest questions he'd heard in his entire life. Which was fine with Ben. It was better if the witness didn't understand the significance of the question. Until it was too late.

"I suppose I must have moved around."

"I thought so, Deputy. Thank—"

"I don't think you understand. When I saw that—thing—that used to be a human being, it was just, it was—" He shook his head. "It was horrible. It was like nothing I'd ever seen before." He paused. "But I've seen it a lot since."

"What do you mean?"

His face fell, and his eyes began to well up. "I see it every morning when I go to work. Every time I hear the man's name. Every time I close my eyes. It . . . haunts me. Hard as I try to forget it, I can't. That image is always with me."

His head lowered, and his eyes turned watery. "And the worst of it is, I think it always will be."

* 41 *

After driving through the tangled trails and one-lane dirt byways of the Green River National Forest for more than an hour, it occurred to Loving that he was not at heart a country boy. Granted, he wasn't quite as bound to concrete and smog as the Skipper; he did enjoy the occasional hunting or fishing expedition. But when all was said and done, he was not really at home in these leafy green surroundings. He missed city conveniences, like, for instance, street signs. And if he saw one more squirrel dart out in front of his car, he was flooring it.

Not that he would ever share these thoughts with the Skipper. Ben needed to feel someone on the team was competent in the Great Outdoors. If it made him comfortable to believe it was Loving, well, so be it. Like his daddy used to say, it's not who you are that matters. It's who people think you are.

The directions Doc had given Loving were vague at best. But Loving couldn't complain—none of the other Green Ragers had helped him in the least. They all claimed they didn't have the slightest idea where Kelly might have gone. Which was odd. Because Loving had the distinct impression that they did; they just didn't want him to find her.

Now why would a bunch of do-gooders like Green Rage be keeping secrets? That was a question he found very interesting.

At long last, Loving spotted a low-lying wooden sign that directed him toward the SOPHIA CAMP. He turned his rental Jeep and drove another two miles or so in that direction. Finally, just around a sharp curve, he spotted a group of eight women at the top of a hill.

They were holding hands and, unless he was very mistaken, chanting.

Loving parked the Jeep, climbed out, and waited. He'd seen a picture earlier, so he knew which one he wanted. She was the one in the long blue sundress, short and heavyset, barefoot with long curly black hair.

Loving waited a good fifteen minutes until the ceremony was completed. He assumed it was a ceremony; for all he could tell it was an elaborate adult version of ring-around-the-rosy. But the closed eyes and solemn expressions suggested that something more serious was going on. Or at least that they thought something more serious was going on.

The group of eight began to disperse. A row of one-room log cabins lay a few hundred feet behind them, and Loving assumed that's where they were headed. He quickened his pace, ran around the hill, and cut off the woman in blue before she reached the main cabin.

"Excuse me," he said. "Are you Kelly Cartwright?"

The woman stopped, frowned. "It's possible. Who wants to know?"

"My name's Loving. I wanna talk to you about Green Rage."

Her face became red and livid. "Are you a Fed? Goddamn it. You are, aren't you? Don't you people ever give up?"

"Ma'am, I'm not—"

"Couldn't you go hassle a bank robber or serial killer or something? Why do you have to spend all your time bullying conservationists?"

"Ma'am, I'm not a Fed." He pointed at his T-shirt. "See? No white shirt, no black tie. I'm not a cop, either."

"Then what are you?"

Loving could think of about a million ways to answer that question, but figured it would be smarter to keep the conversation on track. "I'm a private investigator. I work for a lawyer in Magic Valley."

An eyebrow rose. "Not the one who's representing Zak."

"Yeah. Ben Kincaid. You know him?"

"Well, I've heard a lot about him." She frowned. "How's he doing?"

"The trial's just getting started. He's got a theory involving a local drug dealer, but so far he doesn't have much evidence to support it. Why?"

Her eyes darted away. "Oh . . . no reason. Just curious, I guess. So what do you want from me?"

"Information. You were still a member of Green Rage when the murder took place, weren't you?"

"Yeah. I was Zak's right-hand person."

"That's what I heard. Do you know anything about the murder? Anything that might help?"

"Well, I know Zak didn't do it."

"Were you with him? That night, I mean."

"No, nothing like that. I just know Zak. He talks tough, but he wouldn't hurt anyone." She glanced back at the cabin. "Look, if we're going to have this conversation, why don't we step inside?"

Loving followed her through the cabin door. He had to turn sideways and duck just to get through; whoever designed the portal wasn't thinking about people his size.

The furnishings were strictly utilitarian—a sofa, a bed, a dining table. The decorations were sparse; the place did not have a lived-in feel.

"We rent these cabins from the Forest Service on a weekly basis," she explained. "Sometimes we can stay another week, sometimes not. We get moved around a lot. So there's never much time to settle in."

Loving took a seat on the not-very-comfortable-looking sofa. "That sounds rough."

Kelly situated herself on the other end of the sofa, not far away at all. Their knees were practically touching. "We're just grateful to be in the forest," she said. "To be this close to the Goddess."

Loving opted to let that one pass. "Did you ever hear Zak talk about this Gardiner character? Or act like he might be plannin' to do something violent?"

"Oh, Zak talked all the time. He's been talking as long as I've known him. I don't take it seriously."

"How long have you known him?"

"Years. Since he moved out this way from Oklahoma.

We . . ." She hesitated a moment. "We were intimate once. At first. But that passed."

"Really. Were you angry about that?"

"Of course not. Love is meant to be free. I don't allow myself to get hung up by these patriarchal templates of right and wrong. I focus my energy on the here and now. Zak is free to act upon his natural urges . . . and he usually does. For that matter, so do I." She inched subtly closer to him. "If you know what I mean."

Loving hoped he didn't. "Did you ever hear anyone else act like they might wanna take a shot at Gardiner?"

She seemed slightly irritated to be dragged back to this mundane subject. "I'd never even heard of the man. Not till he turned up dead and the cops dragged Zak away. After rummaging through our camp."

"So you don't know why someone mighta killed him?"

"Sorry, I don't. And I wouldn't focus on it, even if I did. That is not the path to harmony. That is not the teaching of the Goddess."

Loving really didn't want to get into this at all, but he supposed he would be derelict in his duty if he didn't. "Mind tellin' me what you're talking about?"

"About the Goddess? It's Mother Nature. Gaia. Sophia. Whatever you care to call her."

"And she has . . . teachings?"

"Of course."

"Are they written in a book somewhere?"

Kelly laughed. "Mother Nature didn't publish a dissertation, if that's what you mean. Her teachings are everywhere. In the earth, in the air. All around us."

Oh, geez. Now Loving really wished the Skipper had made this visit himself. He was much more tolerant of wackos. "Is this . . . some kinda religion?"

"I wouldn't use that word. It's more like a belief system. Goddess worship is a female-centered focus for spiritual expression."

"Oh. Guess that's why I didn't learn about it in Sunday school class."

Kelly laughed. "You're a scream." She pressed her fingers

against his knee and held them there way longer than Loving thought was necessary.

"So, in this Goddess thing, God is a woman?"

"Oh, there's much more to it than that. The Goddess is not just a female God. She represents an entirely different concept. The Christian God is an all-powerful, transcendent deity. The Goddess is more tangible, more real. She's located in each individual and in all things in nature. She's everywhere. She connects with us because she's part of us. But she's also part of nature, which heightens our environmental awareness. That's the aspect that first drew me to Goddess worship."

Loving steadfastly maintained a straight face, even though this sounded to him like something the boys at Orpha's might spout after several six-packs. "I gotta admit, I never hearda this before. Who cooked this up?"

"No one cooked it up," Kelly said, but she didn't seem the least bit annoyed. "It's existed for centuries. Have you read Marija Gimbutas?"

Loving knew better than to bluff when he was out of his depth. "I don't think so. I've read Louis L'Amour."

She laughed again. "Gimbutas has proved that goddess worship was a prehistoric belief eradicated by patriarchal invaders about six thousand years ago. In fact, she says goddess worship goes back to 25,000 B.C. That's why farmers sometimes dig up those little female goddess statuettes."

"But don't you think those prehistoric beliefs probably died out . . . for a reason?"

"Yes, but it isn't a good reason. Most progress isn't, if you ask me. The prepatriarchal utopia was egalitarian, peace-loving, and entirely gynocentric."

Loving was blank-faced. "Entirely—"

"Centered around women."

"Oh. Oh." He tilted his head. "Well, that's okay. I like women."

"I'm glad to hear it." Somehow, without even appearing to move, Kelly had inched so close to him they were mere inches apart. "How would you like to get in touch with some of your . . . primitive urges?"

Loving was beginning to feel distinctly hot under the collar. "I don't think—"

"Don't think." She wrapped her hand around his thick neck. "Focus on the here and now."

"I don't—" Loving peeled himself off the sofa so abruptly Kelly tumbled over in his wake. "Not that it isn't tempting. But I'm on duty. So to speak." He rubbed a hand across his sweaty forehead. "Got work to do."

"I see. Pity."

"And I wouldn't wanna take advantage. What with the Goddess watching and everything."

Kelly smiled.

"Are you sure there's nothing more you can tell me about the murder?"

"Sorry. I know it must've taken you a while to find me. But I just don't know anything."

"Let me ask you one more question," Loving said. He kept one eye on the door, just in case he needed to beat a hasty retreat. "Why did you leave Green Rage?"

Her eyes drifted, just as they had when the group had been mentioned earlier. "What did they tell you?"

"They didn't want to talk about it."

She turned away. "Well, neither do I."

"Please. I'd really like to know."

"I'm sorry. No."

"Please." Loving knelt down and placed his hand on her knee. Boy, the Skipper was going to owe him big-time for this one. "I need to know."

Her head turned slowly back in his direction. "It's not that I wasn't committed to the cause. I was. I gave my heart and soul to Green Rage." Her voice dropped a notch. "And Zak. But there are some things I wasn't willing to do."

"Like what?"

"Like taking advantage of people. Manipulating them. Of course the Green Rage crowd would say, when you're wrestling with the devil, you have to get a little dirty. But honestly, if you get too dirty, how can you tell yourself and the devil apart?"

"What was it they wanted you to do?"

"It was something they were all planning to do. Something beyond the pale. So I left."

"And . . . do you know whether they did it?"

"I know they did. After I left. I'm certain of it." She placed her hand over the big strong hand on her knee and squeezed. "If they hadn't, you wouldn't be here now."

* 42 *

After the lunch break, Granny brought her next witness to the stand.

"The State calls Detective Arnold Cath."

Ben watched as Cath ambled up to the front of the courtroom. He was a middle-aged man with about thirty pounds he didn't need riding his midsection. He was wearing a suit jacket with complementary slacks, the standard issue plainclothes-cop-in-court regalia.

Granny quickly established the man's credentials, including the twelve years he'd spent covering homicides in the county. She touched on a few of his past cases. None of them meant anything to Ben, but they garnered appreciative nods from some of the jurors.

As before, Granny spent no more time on the preliminaries than was absolutely necessary. "What were you doing on July thirteenth? Say about two in the morning."

"Well, I was sound asleep in bed, like most everyone else, I expect." He seemed amiable and good-natured, an appealing witness. "Till the phone call came."

"And who was calling?"

"Sheriff Allen. He'd received a report of a homicide from one of his deputies. Poor kid had found the body—what was left of it—all by himself in the middle of the night.

Sheriff Allen asked if I'd come out and take charge of the investigation."

"Is that standard operating procedure?"

"Absolutely. Sheriff Allen's a fine officer, but he's not a homicide specialist. He always calls me when he has a murder on his hands. Not that that happens very often."

"And what did you do after you received the call?"

"Well, I told him I'd get out there as soon as I could. I live in Mount Collie, 'bout twenty-five minutes out of Magic Valley. Plus I had to get dressed, splash some water on my face. Then I had to find this crime scene out in the middle of the green leafy nowhere. I got lost about six times; had to get on my cell phone and have Sheriff Allen lead me in step by step."

"When did you arrive?"

"I think I got there about four-thirty, which I thought was pretty damn good, given the circumstances."

"And what did you do when you arrived?"

"I conferred with Sheriff Allen briefly, then took control of the crime scene."

Granny nodded appreciatively. "Detective Cath, for the sake of the jury, would you please explain what you mean by taking control of the crime scene?"

"Sure." He turned to face the jury box. "Everything I do can probably be boiled down into two categories: restricting access and preserving the evidence. Obviously, we don't want the crime scene contaminated. Something like seven out of ten homicides are solved in the first six hours based upon evidence found at the crime scene. We don't want to lose that window of opportunity. So I cordon off the area and post guards at the entrances, to make sure no one gets in unless they have my okay."

"And after that?"

"Then I start preserving the evidence on the site so it will still be there when the forensic teams arrive. I lay butcher paper down on the walkways so we can get in and out without damaging any evidence. In this case, out in the forest, there really weren't any walkways as such, so I just created some, around the perimeter of the area and through the middle, near the remains. That way our footprints wouldn't obliterate any evidence."

"And what else?"

"I make sure no one sheds on the crime scene or bleeds on it or moves things around. We want everything to be just as it was when the killer left. Once that's done, I admit the forensic teams."

"Such as?"

"The hair and fiber team. The photographers and videographers. Trace evidence teams. Fingerprint experts. And of course the coroner's team." He shuddered involuntarily. "Man, I wouldn't have wanted their job for all the tea in China."

"And did all these forensic teams you mentioned appear?"

"They certainly did. Took some of them a while to get out there, but they all made it."

"And did they find anything?"

"Objection." Ben had been taking it easy on the objections, trying not to alienate the jury. But this one he couldn't let go. "Hearsay. Detective Cath shouldn't be testifying about what someone else did."

Judge Pickens shrugged. "Well, I'll allow it."

"Your honor," Ben insisted, "it hasn't been established that the witness has any expertise in these various forensic fields."

"The prosecutor just asked if they found anything. He can answer that, if he knows, without going into any great detail about what was found. Will that make you happy, counselor?"

"Ecstatic," Ben murmured under his breath. Christina suppressed a giggle.

"So I'll ask you again," Granny said. "Did the forensic teams find anything? If you know."

"They did. They found footprints. And they also recovered a few fingerprints from a piece of the tree cutter that was thrown clear of the explosion."

"And were they able to identify the fingerprints?"

"Objection," Ben said. "Now the prosecutor is asking for analysis. Analysis that was not conducted by this witness and is not within his field of expertise."

"Very well," Judge Pickens said wearily, as if Ben were an

annoying insect that he couldn't quite swat. "We'll save that for the fingerprint expert."

Granny didn't seem particularly annoyed. And why should she be? They both knew she had the proper expert waiting in the wings. "Thank you very much. No more questions."

After the judge gave him the nod, Ben took his place behind the podium and launched into his cross-examination. He tried to adopt a tone somewhere in the middle ground—insistent, but not overbearing. He knew it was critical that he remain in control during cross or he wouldn't get anything. On the other hand, if he came on too strong with Mr. Friendly, the jury would resent it.

"Detective Cath, how reliable is the evidence found at the crime scene?"

Cath seemed a bit taken aback, but it didn't last long. His placid smile soon reasserted itself. "I'm not sure what you mean."

"Well, the jury has to know what they can believe, what they can trust. Can they trust the crime-scene evidence?"

"Of course they can."

"Isn't it true that evidence is only reliable if it hasn't been contaminated?"

He shrugged. "Sure."

"And if it has been contaminated, then all that evidence you mentioned is unreliable."

"Right. Garbage in, garbage out. That's why they have me on the scene."

Ben raised a finger. "Ah, but you didn't arrive at the crime scene till four-thirty, right?"

Cath chuckled. "Well, I can't deny it, since I just said so myself a few minutes ago."

Ben did not chuckle back. "No, you can't. Who was at the crime scene when you arrived?"

"No one, really."

"No one? Are you sure?"

"Well . . . except the obvious."

"And that would be?"

"The deputy who found the body."

"Deputy Wagner."

"Right, that's the one. And Sheriff Allen, of course."

"And who else?"

"I guess some of his deputies were there."

"Any of the forensic teams?"

"No. Well, the coroner's squad was there. They hadn't done anything yet."

"So, we've gone from 'no one, really' to—what? Eight or ten people?"

"But they were all members of the law enforcement team. It's not like they were tourists or anything."

"I understand that. But there were eight or ten people present."

"I suppose so."

"How many footprints did all those people leave?"

Cath paused. This was the question that tipped Ben's hand, that told one and all where he was going. Of course it was necessary to bring the jury on board sometime. But Ben knew that from here on out, the questioning would get a lot tougher.

Cath coughed into his hand. "I'm sure I don't know how many footprints they all left."

"But we can surmise it was quite a few, right?"

"Well . . ."

"They didn't all stand still like statues, did they?"

Cath made a sardonic smile. "No. They didn't all stand still. But they didn't walk around the corpse, either. They kept their distance."

"How do you know? You didn't get there until four-thirty."

"Because I asked them."

Ben gave the jury his best *aha!* expression. "Then you *were* worried about crime-scene contamination."

"I was not. It's standard procedure."

Ben looked at him incredulously. "It's standard procedure to ask the sheriff if he's mucked up the crime scene?"

"Just a matter of protocol. Nothing to be taken personally."

"But we know that Deputy Wagner walked near the body."

"Well—"

"He told us so himself. He examined the body when he arrived. In fact, he approached the body not once but twice."

Cath frowned. "I'm sure he was very careful."

"Me too, but nonetheless, that's a lot of footprints."

"Then he would be the only one. And one additional set of prints could be easily distinguished."

"What about Sheriff Allen?"

Cath looked dumbstruck. "Sheriff Allen is a trained professional. There's no way he'd stomp around a crime scene. He kept his distance."

Ben looked at him sternly. "Are you telling this jury that when Sheriff Allen arrived at the scene, having heard what happened, he didn't even go over to the corpse and take a look?"

"No. Absolutely not."

"What if the man was still alive? Wouldn't Sheriff Allen at least go over and see if he needed to call an ambulance?"

"Your honor, I must object." Granny was on her feet again. "Mr. Kincaid is asking the witness to speculate."

"No," Ben replied, "I'm examining the credibility of this witness's statement that no one walked on the crime scene before he arrived. That's the purpose of cross-examination."

Judge Pickens frowned. He glanced out at the many faces in the gallery, then looked back to Granny. "I'm afraid I'll have to overrule that objection."

Granny retook her seat, a sour expression on her face.

"So what about it, Detective Cath?" Ben reasked. "Don't you think Sheriff Allen at least checked to see if the victim was still alive? He'd be pretty incompetent if he didn't."

"I think it was obvious from the condition of the remains—"

"So he didn't even check?"

Cath pursed his lips. "I suppose he must've."

"Well, what do you know?" Ben said. "There's yet another set of footprints."

"Maybe. But that's all."

"What about the deputies? The coroner's team?"

"They had no reason to invade the crime scene."

"Are you telling me they weren't just the tiniest bit curious to see what had happened?"

"Perhaps they were. But they still wouldn't walk on the crime scene."

"How can you be sure?"

"Because they told me so!" Cath's amiability was slowly eroding away to nothingness.

"According to you, Sheriff Allen said he hadn't violated the scene, either. But you just admitted he probably did."

Cath's face was beet red. "I don't know what you're trying to do—"

"Oh, I think you do. I'm trying to establish that there were numerous footprints left at the crime scene before you arrived. The prints your forensic team lifted could've belonged to anyone."

"They have ways of screening footprints—"

"We'll see. For that matter, I wonder if all those men at the crime scene might not have left a few fingerprints behind. It would be hard to be there an hour and a half and not touch anything."

"Your honor, I object to this speechifying!" Granny said angrily. "Mr. Kincaid is not even asking the witness questions anymore."

"That one I'll sustain," Pickens said. "You have any more questions, counselor?"

"Not at this time, your honor." If Ben had learned nothing else during the past few years, he had learned to sit down when it was time to sit down. He'd created a wisp of reasonable doubt. If he let Cath talk any more, the witness would only try to undo the damage.

"Very well," Pickens said. He had a frown on his face, and his gaze was going straight out to Granny. Perhaps this case wasn't going quite as well as they'd expected? Ben could only hope. "We'll resume after a short break." He dismissed the jury, who filed out of the courtroom in a long line.

When Ben returned to counsel table, Zak gave him a swat on the arm. "Nice job, Ben. I knew I could count on you. You did it before and you'll do it again." He grinned. "You took that chump apart like a Tinkertoy."

"Don't get overconfident," Ben warned. "Cath was testifying out of his depth; that's how I was able to nail him. When Granny puts on her experts in each of those forensic fields, they will go to extreme lengths to prove to the jury that there was no contamination of the evidence."

"Just the same, you're doing a hell of a job." Zak leaned back in his chair and smiled. "I knew you were the right man for this job. I feel better already."

There was something disconcerting about his reaction, but Ben supposed that if the man wanted to see this as a good omen, that was his business. Given the stress he must be under, with a death sentence hanging over his head, he was probably entitled to any relief he could find.

Ben turned and was surprised to find Granny standing behind him.

"So, Kincaid, it seems you're not quite the sap you appear to be."

Ben arched an eyebrow. "Is that supposed to be a compliment?"

"But of course."

"Then thanks. But I'm just doing my job."

Ben would've given a great deal to know what thoughts were running through Granny's brain. Whatever they were, he suspected he wouldn't like them. "I will, too," she said softly. "Now more than ever."

* 43 *

When the jury returned from their mid-afternoon break, Granny called Dr. Lawrence Tobias, the county coroner, to the stand.

Probably a decision made based more on time and strategy than anything else, Ben reasoned. There was only about an hour and a half of court time left before Pickens would likely recess for the day. If Granny called a more important witness, one who would take longer, the testimony would be split over two days—which would give Ben all night to prepare for cross after having heard at least part of the testimony. Granny preferred to call a witness she could get on and off before closing time, so Ben wouldn't be able to think about what he'd heard at great length before crossing.

Dr. Tobias, Ben recalled, was almost the complete opposite of Dr. Koregai, the Tulsa County medical examiner to whom Ben was accustomed. Tobias lacked Koregai's implacable ease, his bearing. The sense that everything he said was unquestionably, inarguably true. At the same time, he had a common touch that Koregai never even approached. He seemed like one of the gang, not a demigod towering over their heads. And he knew how to talk to people, to communicate. Koregai might be a medical genius, but Ben wondered if Tobias might not be the better witness.

After about twenty minutes, Granny brought the witness to the case in question. "Did you perform an autopsy on Dwayne Gardiner?"

"Oh yes, yes," he said. He had a nervous twitch involving his upper lip somewhat reminiscent of a bunny rabbit.

"And when would that have taken place?"

"On the morning of July thirteenth. I wasn't present when the body was first brought to the morgue, earlier that morning. I came in about seven-thirty and started work."

A lovely way to start the day, Ben thought. Hope he hadn't had a big breakfast.

"Did you perform a standard autopsy?"

"Well . . ." Tobias appeared to be struggling for words, which struck Ben as unusual, since Granny had probably rehearsed this testimony a dozen times. ". . . *standard* would probably not be the correct word."

"And why is that?"

"That is because of the . . . uh"—he glanced at the jury, then looked away—"the condition of the remains."

"What was the condition of the remains, Dr. Tobias?"

"Severely burned. Third degree and then some, covering almost his entire body. There was little skin remaining, and what there was had hardened into eschar. Bones and skull were exposed, all blackened by fire. I don't think his best friends could have recognized him." Tobias paused, his expression serious but sad. "Using the Rule of Nines, which assigns a numerical value to each part of the body and rates the severity of body burns on a scale from one to one hundred—one hundred being the worst—I'd say Gardiner was a ninety-seven. At least."

"Did this create any complications for your autopsy?"

"Oh, yes. Yes indeed." He looked earnestly at the jury. "Everything becomes more complicated when a body has been burned that severely. You can throw the manual out the window. Most of the standard techniques don't work anymore. Most of the tests are invalid."

"Nonetheless, were you able to perform the autopsy?"

"Oh yes. Took me almost seven hours. But I did it."

"Dr. Tobias, we've heard testimony regarding a gunshot wound. Did you see any evidence of a gunshot wound?"

"I extracted a bullet from the upper right torso. Just below the clavicle."

"What did you do with the bullet?"

"I sent it to the ballistics office for testing."

Now why had Granny established that? Ben wondered. There was no ballistics expert on the prosecution witness list. Did she have an ace tucked up her sneaky little sleeve? Or was she laying a foundation, just in case the gun turned up?

"Did you notice anything else out of the ordinary, Dr. Tobias?"

"Well, as I said, the burns were extensive."

"Other than that."

"On the whole, there was very little to examine. As I said, most of the skin was gone, either as a result of fire, or the forest creatures that found the body before the sheriff did. Even his internal organs were burned, in whole or part." He paused. "I did manage to find faint traces of a bite mark on his left arm, however."

"A bite mark?" Granny's eyes widened, giving the jury a dramatic reaction Ben knew was more stagecraft than surprise.

"Yes. Indentations left by teeth were clearly visible."

"Do you know when this bite occurred?"

"In terms of what time of day, it's impossible for me to say with much accuracy. But I do know that the bite occurred before the burning."

Granny straightened. "Dr. Tobias, are there tests that can be run on bite marks? Say, to determine their origin?"

"That's outside my realm of expertise, but yes, there are such tests. And I understand they can be quite accurate."

Ben frowned. Granny was using one witness to prop up another—establishing an expert's credentials before he even took the stand. It was objectionable, but not worth annoying the jury.

"I must be losing my grip," Granny said abruptly. "Dr. Tobias, I haven't even asked you what the cause of death was. Were you able to make that determination?"

"I was," Tobias said. He turned somberly toward the jury. "The first instant I saw him. Mr. Gardiner burned to death."

"But," Granny said gently, "you mentioned a gunshot wound."

"It was not a fatal wound," Tobias said flatly. "Any gunshot wound is serious, but this one would not have been fatal, assuming he obtained medical attention within a reasonable time period. At any rate, it's not what killed him. It didn't have a chance."

"How do you mean?"

"Judging from the wound itself and the extent of deterioration in the surrounding tissue, I determined that the gunshot wound occurred very shortly before the body caught on fire. Probably no more than a few minutes before."

Granny paused, turning ever so slightly toward the jury. "You mean he caught on fire just after he was shot?"

"That's about the size of it, I'm afraid." Tobias seemed genuinely affected and regretful, expressing a sorrow that quickly infected the jury.

"Were you able to make any determinations regarding how the body might have been . . . ignited?"

"Not without resorting to external data."

"What do you mean?"

"Well, I've been told that a piece of heavy machinery was

exploded by a small bomb near where the body was found. That obviously could be a possible source of the fire."

Granny tried to clarify. "You're saying Gardiner may have been caught in the explosion."

"I'm not saying that he was exploded, no. If he had caught the full brunt of the explosion, the damage to his body would have been different. We would have found his remains in pieces. Mr. Gardiner's body was still intact, although horribly burned. All the evidence indicates that he moved under his own power, until of course the extent of the burning made that impossible."

"So what conclusion do you reach, doctor?"

"Objection," Ben said, rising. "She's asking him to speculate."

"I'm not asking him to speculate," Granny shot back. "I'm asking him to draw a conclusion based upon the available evidence. He's an expert; he's allowed."

"Overruled," Judge Pickens said briskly. "Sit down, Mr. Kincaid."

Ben did as he was told. He never expected the objection to succeed, anyway. What he wanted was to remind the jury that what they were about to hear was not a fact, but a guess. An expert's best guess, maybe, but still just a guess.

"What I concluded," Tobias answered, "was that at the time of the explosion, Gardiner, who had just been shot, was not so close to the bomb that he suffered the full brunt of the blast, but was close enough to catch fire once some part of the machinery, possibly the gas tank, ignited."

Ben pushed himself to his feet. "Again I have to object, your honor. This is pure speculation."

Pickens didn't wait for Granny to respond. He whirled in his chair and pointed his gavel toward Ben's head. "I've already ruled on your objection, Mr. Kincaid. Now sit down and shush." He paused, then added, "And if you can't keep that tongue still on your own, I can have you escorted to a tiny little room with barred windows where no one will be able to hear you. Savvy?"

Ben retook his seat. Pickens had probably been waiting all

day for Ben to give him an excuse to chew him out in front of the jury. Just as well he did it now and got it over with.

"Dr. Tobias, the prosecution will show that the defendant was wandering in the forest about one in the morning. Do you have any thoughts regarding the time of death?"

"Well, I received independent reports from some of the loggers at a camp not too far away that they heard an explosion a few minutes after one A.M. Given that the explosion, and the resulting fire, appear to have played a role, the death likely occurred at or just after one."

"How exactly would Gardiner catch on fire?"

"His clothes would probably ignite first. Cottons are somewhat more flame-retardant. Nylons and polyesters—which the victim was wearing—burn very quickly. Once the clothes caught fire, of course, unless the flames could be quenched, the body would soon begin to burn."

"And how would that feel?"

"Objection!" Ben shouted. "She's trying to inflame the jury."

Pickens's expression was grave. "I wasn't kidding about that room with the barred windows, counsel. You're overruled. Now sit down." He nodded toward the witness. "You may answer."

"Well," Tobias started hesitantly, "I don't think I have to tell anyone here that being burned is an . . . unpleasant experience. Most people who have been through it say it's the most intense feeling of pain anyone can experience. And in a situation like this, when the entire body was consumed, when death was certain, when there was no help or relief in sight . . ." He shook his head. "Well, I'm sure the pain was just . . . unimaginable."

"Would Mr. Gardiner have been likely to pass out?"

"We'd like to think so. But there's no medical basis for that assumption. To the contrary, given that he apparently moved some distance away from the exploded machinery, I'd have to say he was probably conscious very close to the time of his death."

Ben pressed his hand against his forehead. This testimony

was grossly objectionable and prejudicial, but Pickens had already ruled, and if Ben stood up again, Zak would probably be representing himself for the rest of the trial.

He glanced over his shoulder, wondering what effect this hideous testimony was having on the bereaved widow. To his surprise, he spotted no widow in the gallery. Everyone appeared affected by the testimony; several people had tears in their eyes. But he saw no trace of Lu Ann Gardiner.

"And how long would it be, Dr. Tobias? Until death occurred."

"I can't say with precision."

"Dr. Tobias, would it have been a quick death?"

Tobias's chin fell. "Not particularly, no. It could have been eight, ten minutes from when he first caught on fire until he was actually dead. And I expect every one of those minutes seemed like days. Agonizing, unbearable days."

"Thank you, Dr. Tobias." Granny turned away from the podium, her face grim and set. "No more questions."

* 44 *

Ben had hoped the judge would call for a break, to give the jury some breathing space and to break the grim mood Granny had established during her direct examination. Unfortunately, he didn't, and Ben knew why. He'd seen Pickens glance once too often at the clock on the wall. Pickens was hoping that if they blazed straight ahead, they might finish the witness before closing time.

There was no point in revisiting Tobias's testimony about Gardiner's hideous pain and suffering prior to death. Although the good doctor had engaged in considerable speculation and Ben could probably drive holes through his testimony in several places, it would serve no purpose. Best not to even remind the jury about that business. Instead, Ben would focus on the one aspect of Tobias's testimony that might actually incriminate his client.

Ben squared himself behind the podium. "Let's talk about the time of death."

Tobias seemed open and compliant. "Whatever you want."

"You gave an opinion about the time of Dwayne Gardiner's death, didn't you?"

"That's right. About one in the morning."

"It's standard procedure for coroners to give an opinion about the cause of death, isn't it?"

"I believe so, yes."

"But in most cases, that opinion is based upon medical evidence, isn't it?"

"I . . . would assume so, yes."

"But yours wasn't, was it?"

"I'm not sure what you—"

"Dr. Tobias, what are the standards by which a coroner establishes the time of death?"

Tobias seemed a bit unsure—the traditional wariness of the witness who hasn't quite figured out where the cross-ex attorney is trying to lead him. "Different doctors use different methods."

"Well, there's body temperature, for starters. That's one way, right?"

"Certainly. Of course."

"But that wasn't any help to you in the Gardiner case, because the corpse had been burned. Right?"

"That's true."

"And sometimes time of death can be determined from the contents of the corpse's stomach, true?"

"True. Absolutely true."

"But that didn't help you either, right? Due to the amount of damage the remains had suffered."

"That's correct."

"And so, not having any actual medical evidence at your disposal, you decided to guess."

Granny flew up. "Your honor, I object."

Pickens's teeth were grinding together. "Mr. Kincaid, I've had about enough of your misbehavior."

"Your honor," Ben said, "the jury has a right to know which of the witness's opinions are based on medical evidence, and which of his opinions are pure pie-in-the-sky guesswork."

"This man is the coroner for the entire county!" Pickens barked. "You will treat him with the respect he deserves. If you can't manage to do that, I'll have you replaced by someone who will."

"Yes, your honor." Ben sensed it was time to back down; Pickens was near the eruption point. "Dr. Tobias, your conclusions regarding the time of death were not based upon medical evidence, were they?"

"I disagree. Based upon my examination of the extent of the injuries, I determined that death would follow about eight or ten minutes after the body first caught fire."

"But that didn't give you a time of death. You only got the time of death by guessing."

"Well, I had reports of the explosion—"

"Exactly. You had hearsay accounts from people who aren't on the stand and can't be cross-examined. And hearsay accounts do not constitute medical evidence."

Granny was back on her feet. "Your honor, this man is an expert witness. He's allowed to consider hearsay when reaching his expert conclusion."

"I'm not saying he isn't," Ben shot back. "I just want the jury to understand that some of his opinions are based on medical fact and some of them aren't."

"But your honor," Granny insisted, "he's suggesting that—"

"Would you two stop bickering?" Judge Pickens snapped. "This isn't moving the trial along. Let's get back to the questions."

At least this time Granny got to share some of Pickens's wrath. "Of course, your honor." Just grin and bear it, he told himself. There had been a time when Ben took these sorts of attacks from the judge personally, when he worried and fretted about them. These days he realized they were just part and parcel of life as a defense lawyer—and even more so when you're the out-of-towner. Best to smile placidly and plow right ahead.

"Dr. Tobias, isn't it true that your only information regarding the time of the explosion came from third parties?"

"Yes," he said wearily. "That is true."

"So if those loggers had told you the explosion had occurred around two, you would now be telling the jury Mr. Gardiner died eight or ten minutes after two."

"I suppose so."

"And if they'd said the explosion was at three—"

"Yes, yes. I'd have said ten past three. What's your point?"

"The point is that if in fact the explosion was not at one in the morning but at two, then my client might not have been in the forest. Right?"

"I don't have any idea when your client was in the forest."

"Dr. Tobias, I think that's the absolute truth. All you know is that Mr. Gardiner died eight or ten minutes after the explosion. But you yourself have no idea when that actually was. Right?"

"Right, right. Fine." Tobias tossed his hands up in the air. "Whatever."

* 45 *

After Judge Pickens recessed trial for the day, Ben and Christina returned to the office, where they found a note tacked to the office door. It was from Sheriff Allen, and to Ben's surprise, it was for him, not her.

Ben hotfooted it over to a hotel on South Kennedy. Following the instructions on the note, he walked up to the fifth floor.

He stopped at the top of the stairs. A uniformed deputy was standing at attention, obviously planning to restrict further access.

"I'm Ben Kincaid. Sheriff Allen asked me to come."

The deputy nodded and waved him through. Ben marched down the short corridor till he located Room 52. He turned the corner and took a short step inside.

And gasped. The room was a wreck. The floors were so cluttered it was hard to walk. Pictures had been torn off the wall; drawers had been dumped. Lamps were overturned and destroyed. Even the television had been smashed.

Sheriff Allen appeared at Ben's side. "I see you got my message."

Ben nodded. "Boy, when you people search a room, you really search a room."

Allen shook his head. "We didn't do this. We found it this way."

"You—" Ben turned to face him. "But then—"

"You got it. The killer."

Ben took a few steps forward, tentative ingress into the maelstrom. "This is where Tess O'Connell was staying?"

"Right. Except get this—she wasn't a Green Rager, or at least that wasn't her principal mission in life. She was a reporter."

"A reporter? Like for a newspaper?"

"I guess you could call it that. She worked for one of those tabloids. The *National Whisper*. Offices in L.A."

"Then what was she doing out here?"

Sheriff Allen shrugged. "I have to assume she was working undercover on some story."

"About Green Rage? Hardly seems like the *National Whisper*'s cup of tea."

"It probably isn't. Actually, I've spoken to her editor, Murray Hamner, back in L.A. He says they sent her out here to do a story on Bigfoot."

"Bigfoot?"

"Hamner says she turned in a preliminary story, then disappeared. He lost contact with her. Said she didn't answer the phone, didn't return messages."

"She must have been working on something."

"My thinking exactly. But what?"

Ben crouched down and gazed at the debris covering the floor—clothing, books, papers—looking for anything that might give him some answers. She wouldn't have gone undercover in Green Rage just to get the straight scoop on Bigfoot. It had to be something else.

Could she have been trying to solve the murder of Dwayne Gardiner? Maybe she thought the Green Rage crew could tell her something about Zak that might provide a motive for murder. Or maybe she was acting on a lead of her own.

A sudden chill gripped his spine. It might explain why she had been killed. Maybe she knew something, something Ben hadn't figured out yet. Maybe she even knew who the killer was. And the killer wanted to make sure she didn't share that information with anyone else.

"How long have your men been sifting through all this stuff?"

"Since about two this afternoon. I got a call from Ossie Smith, the manager of this joint. He didn't know about the murder, but he knew no one had seen the occupant of Room 52 for several days. When no one answered his knock, he let himself in. And found . . . this." His hand swept across the room. "So he called me."

"Have you found anything that might give us a hint why Tess was killed?"

"Not so far. Nothing specific, anyway. I'm still hoping something will turn up. But at least one thing is obvious."

"What's that?"

"It must've been her murderer who came in here and tore the room apart. Probably took her room key off her body when he nailed her to that tree. I've checked—there was no room key in the purse we found in her rental car."

"That's a reasonable deduction."

"I can go further. The killer wouldn't risk coming up here and prowling around in her room unless he had a good reason."

"He was looking for something," Ben murmured.

"Bingo," Sheriff Allen echoed. "He or she."

It was more than just something Tess knew, Ben reasoned. She must've found something, or had something. Something tangible. Something the killer wanted back.

"How's the trial going, anyway?"

Ben shrugged. "This was only the first day of testimony. Granny made a few points on direct, and I managed to score a few on cross. But we're not into the critical testimony yet. Granny was just setting down the groundwork, laying the foundations. Most of the witnesses didn't directly incriminate my client. She'll be bringing out the heavy hitters soon."

"You can count on that." Allen shifted his hat from one hand to the other. "But I was wondering . . ."

Ben frowned. "Yes?"

"Since you aren't into the really tough stuff yet, I wondered if I could have your permission—"

"I'm not Christina's mother," Ben snapped.

"No, but—"

"She's a grown-up. She can do whatever she wants."

"Well, sure. I just—" Allen shuffled awkwardly from foot to foot. "You know, I never actually asked you about this business."

"What business?"

"Me and Christina. Going out and all."

"I told you before. We're just friends and coworkers."

"Well, yeah. I know that's what you said. But sometimes, what a man says, and what he feels . . ." He took a deep breath. "This is damned awkward. But look, if I'm stepping on your toes—"

"It's a free country. You do whatever you like. If you want to take her to dinner, take her to dinner."

"Well . . . good. That's fine. But I was hoping that maybe after dinner . . ."

Ben stopped short. "*After* dinner?"

Allen almost blushed. "Well, you know. We have been seeing each other for a good while now. I thought maybe she'd like to come back to my place and—"

"Christina has work to do."

"Oh. Well, sure . . . But I thought you said—"

"If you don't mind, I'm very busy."

Sheriff Allen frowned, then shuffled off toward the door to talk to one of his deputies.

Ben closed his eyes. What was with him, anyway? He was behaving like a fool and he knew it. It was Christina's life and Christina's business. The smartest thing he could do was just butt out.

But somehow he didn't want to butt out.

So what did he want? That was the $64,000 question, the question that so far he didn't seem able to answer.

But it was becoming abundantly clear that if he didn't answer it soon, it might be too late.

The television sparked to life. An eerie blue glow bathed the darkened room. And the VCR began to play.

After the tape was over, Sasquatch had to laugh. So much worry, so much concern. Desperation, even. And when it was all over, the tape didn't show a damn thing. It was too dark, too blurry. The image was herky-jerky and then it was gone altogether, when that damn reporter started running. After that, all you could see was dirt and grass.

It couldn't possibly be used to identify the person in the Sasquatch suit. Even Sasquatch's mother couldn't tell who was on that tape.

All that anguish had been for nothing.

Well, at least the worry had been eliminated. This tape couldn't be used by anyone. Sasquatch was safe again.

Too bad about the woman. But the error had been made, and that woman understood its significance. Now there was nothing left to worry about. Except . . .

The early word from the courthouse was that the defense lawyer was doing a damn sight better than anyone expected. Worse, that he was investigating, trying to figure out what *really* happened.

Sasquatch turned off the television set. That lawyer couldn't be permitted to ruin everything, just when it was starting to come together, just when it was beginning to look as though the worries had ended.

And if Sasquatch had to intervene to make sure that lawyer

didn't screw up the works, then so be it. Sledgehammers and spikes were in abundant supply, and there was a tree in the forest just his size.

* 46 *

It seemed as if Granny was in no hurry at all. Like a seasoned veteran, she had enough confidence in her case to wade methodically through the critical elements of a prima facie case, systematically including both the monumental and the minutiae, without worrying about losing the jury's interest. And Ben knew her confidence in the jury was not misplaced. She had baited them more than adequately during her opening statement. They would wait patiently until she had something exciting for them.

So she matter-of-factly dedicated the next morning of trial to forensic evidence. She called two more deputies from the sheriff's office, principally to talk about the procedures and cautions taken at the crime scene. Then she called two forensic technicians to discuss how the evidence at the crime scene was collected, how it was handled, how it was preserved. She was careful at all points to establish the chain of custody for each bit of evidence, trying to leave Ben no opening for questioning the purity of the evidence on cross.

The only remotely interesting bit of testimony came late in the morning, when Granny called Deputy Goldsmith to the stand. Goldsmith had first reported to the crime scene, then was instructed by Sheriff Allen to join him on an expedition to the Green Rage camp.

"First I went back to town and woke up the judge," Goldsmith said, glancing up at Pickens. "Then I got a search warrant. Then me and Sheriff Allen and two of the boys drove out to the Green Rage camp. Luckily, we'd had a report from some campers that gave us a good idea where the camp was that night. Even so, it took us a good half hour of driving around before we found it. When we finally did, we woke everybody up and started asking questions."

"Did you learn anything of interest?" Granny asked.

"Not from them. They didn't know anything about it. Or so they said."

"Did you conduct a search?"

"Definitely. We went through all their tents, all their papers and equipment."

"Did you find anything?"

"Yes, ma'am. The Bigfoot suit."

Granny brought out the costume, wrapped in clear polyethylene, and went through the rigmarole necessary to have it admitted into evidence.

"Deputy Goldsmith," Granny continued, "why was this Halloween costume of interest to you?"

"We'd been having a large number of Bigfoot sightings in the last few months prior to the murder. We always get some of that, but this was way above average. So we knew that either there really was a Bigfoot or someone was running around in a costume. And the latter seemed more likely."

"Does this have anything to do with the murder of Dwayne Gardiner?" Granny asked innocently.

Ben frowned. As if she didn't know.

"We thought so. See, the tough thing about that murder was trying to figure out who would be running around in the forest at that time of night. But we had three reports of Bigfoot sightings in the area that night, ranging from about a quarter after twelve until about one-thirty. Campers think they see things, then call us on their cellular phones. Anyway, those calls suggested that someone in the Bigfoot getup was awake and in the area—at exactly the time the murder took place."

"So you thought whoever was wearing the costume would be a murder suspect."

"Yeah. Particularly since the last report said that Bigfoot was running at full speed. Like maybe he was chasing someone."

Chasing someone? Ben thought. He couldn't chase Gardiner, not after the explosion. Was there a third person at the crime scene?

Come to think of it, Deputy Wagner had said the anonymous call about the murder had come from a woman.

Could it have been Tess? Could she have been there, at the crime scene? That would explain a great deal.

"I think we can all understand now why you were so interested in the suit, Deputy Goldsmith. Would you now please tell the jury where you found it?"

"Certainly. The suit was in the tent belonging to the defendant. George Zakin."

There was an audible gasp in the courtroom. Ben didn't know why—did they really think Granny would be bringing this up if the suit had been in someone else's tent? Nonetheless, the jurors' eyes all moved, if only briefly, toward Zak. And the expressions on their faces were not kind ones.

"Did he share the tent with anyone else?"

"Nope. It was his and his alone."

"Thank you, Deputy. No more questions."

Ben didn't even bother cross-examining. There was nothing to be gained. He didn't believe Goldsmith was lying, and like it or not, the suit had been in Zak's tent. That was just an unfortunate bit of evidence they were going to have to live with.

Next up, Granny called a fingerprint expert to the stand, a Michael Hightower. Hightower had found a latent thumbprint on a piece of metal plating, possibly part of the bomb casing. Evidently the metal had been thrown clear in the explosion and thus remained largely intact, preserving the print.

Which matched Zak's right thumbprint. Perfectly. Unquestionably.

Granny finished the morning by calling her next forensic expert to the stand. Mark Austin specialized in footprints, and as the jury soon learned, he had taken several from the crime scene, particularly from the area surrounding the corpse. Many, he explained, could be dismissed as having come from members of the sheriff's office or other investigators. But one set of prints could not. He had made plaster casts, which Granny had admitted into evidence and displayed to the jury.

Those prints were size elevens—the same size that George Zakin wore.

This time around, Ben definitely saw a reason to cross-examine.

"Mr. Austin, did you conduct an analysis of the tread left by these footprints?"

Austin, a short, prim man wearing a suit coat and bow tie, straightened. "Unfortunately, the ground was relatively dry the night of the murder. The print left did not have sufficient depth or distinction to identify the tread. So trying to trace the prints to a particular shoe was out of the question. What we could see was the broad outline of the print—that is, what size it was."

"Mr. Austin, before this thing gets too far out of control, let's be clear on just what exactly you're saying. You're not saying that George Zakin left those footprints, are you?"

"Well . . ."

"What you're saying is that someone—you don't know who—left those footprints."

"And whoever it was wore a size eleven. As does George Zakin."

"That's correct. And there are a whole heck of a lot of people who wear a size eleven, aren't there?"

"No doubt." Austin adjusted his bow tie. "But only one of them is on trial for murder."

"Mr. Austin, aren't the police supposed to use evidence to find the culprit, instead of picking a culprit and then finding evidence that fits?"

"Objection," Granny said. "Mr. Kincaid is way out of line. Again."

Judge Pickens made an unhappy grunting noise. "Kincaid, you almost got to spend last night in jail. Let's not go down that road again, all right?"

"Yes, your honor," Ben said placidly.

"And you may consider that your absolutely last warning."

Right, right. Bully. "Let me ask you a different question, Mr. Austin. How many people were at that crime scene?"

Austin shook his head. "Quite a few. Twenty or so, I would guess."

"And every one of them left footprints, right?"

"No doubt."

"Some of them, like Deputy Wagner, probably left a lot of footprints."

"Yes." Austin grinned. This was obviously a topic he had been prepared for. "But none of them wears a size eleven."

"Oh? And how do you know that?"

"Because I checked every single one of them."

Oh. Damn. "And none of them wore a size eleven?"

"None of them."

"You checked everyone who was at the crime scene?"

"Every single one."

His smug smile was almost more than Ben could bear. "And you're sure no one wore a size eleven."

"Right."

"Not a single person at the crime scene."

"Not a one."

"And you're sure of this?"

Austin drummed his fingers on the witness chair. "Absolutely sure."

All at once, Ben lurched forward, grabbed Austin's right shoe, and yanked it off his foot.

Austin rose. "What in the name of . . . !"

Judge Pickens pounded his gavel. "Kincaid! Have you totally taken leave of your senses?"

"Not totally," Ben answered. He turned the shoe around so Judge Pickens could see inside the opening. "Size eleven."

Austin froze.

"Permission to publish this shoe to the jury, your honor?"

Pickens responded with a grumpy wave of the hand.

Ben tossed the shoe to the female juror on the end of the first row and turned back to the witness. "Mr. Austin, it seems there was someone at the crime scene wearing size elevens after all."

Austin's mouth began to work, but not much sound was coming out. "I . . . never thought . . ."

"About yourself, right? You thought to check everyone but yourself."

"I guess."

"And of course you left footprints at the crime scene, didn't you? You didn't fly in?"

Austin frowned. "No. I walked from the car to the crime scene."

"So you must have left footprints."

His head fell. "So I must have left footprints."

"Thank you, sir. I appreciate your honesty." He started back to defendant's table.

"My pleasure," Austin said, as if acid were dripping from his tongue. "May I have my shoe back now?"

* 47 *

Ben stayed in the courtroom during the lunch hour and reviewed his notes. Maybe it was overkill, but he had never cross-exed anyone like this next witness before and he didn't know what to expect. Best to be as prepared as possible.

At one-thirty, the bailiff escorted the jury back into the courtroom and Judge Pickens reconvened the trial. Granny called her next witness.

"The State calls Dr. Richard A. Grayson to the stand."

The bailiff stepped out of the courtroom and called for Grayson, who was standing just outside the door. He was a middle-aged man, probably thirty or forty pounds overweight. He was bald, but compensated for it with an exceptionally bushy beard. He walked like a man altogether at ease with himself, one hundred percent confident, not a worry in the world.

Granny took him through the painstaking process of establishing his background and expertise. Dr. Grayson was a dentist who had an office in the suburbs of San Francisco, was a graduate of UCLA, and was a member of several medical and dental professional associations. But part of his office was devoted not to private practice but to research.

"What is the nature of your research?" Granny asked.

"I've spent the last eighteen years investigating ways to make trace injuries more apparent."

"Can you tell us what you mean by trace injuries?"

"Well, for instance, bite marks."

Several jurors' heads lifted. They had been all but dozing during the credentials, but now they began to see where this testimony was headed.

"Is there a reason why trace injuries would need to be made more apparent?"

"Dealing with trace evidence is always a problem for law enforcement," Grayson explained. He had an easy manner, informative, confident, but not too pretentious. "I think you've already gotten a taste of that in this trial. Footprints are found, but the imprint is not deep enough to identify the shoe tread. A bite mark is found on the victim's arm, but the impression is not sufficient to allow the coroner to make a conventional analysis via dental records. I've been working on ways to make what is not immediately apparent more so."

"You mentioned the process of identifying bite marks by conventional dental records. Could you explain that to the jury?"

"Certainly. It's really very simple. May I have my charts?"

Granny stepped back to her table and lifted a tall stack of enlarged exhibits mounted on poster board. She placed them on a lectern next to the witness stand. Ben winced when he saw the thickness of the stack. By the looks of it, they could all settle in for a long winter's nap.

Grayson stood next to the exhibits and pointed toward the first one, which appeared to be an enlarged bite mark on flesh. "This is an example of a good bite mark, that is, one that's absolutely clear. The indentations of most of the teeth are quite evident. Even so, there can be problems." He pivoted toward the jury. "The principal identification difficulties come from the fact that human tissue is soft. It can be stretched and compressed. Therefore, the record left by the bite can be distorted."

"Are there ways of dealing with that problem, Doctor?"

"Of course. We have a battery of tools for just that purpose. We use a measuring rule, scale or tape, moulages of the tissue and teeth indentation, and of course models of the suspect's teeth. Computers can also be used to create a probable range of orientations a bite mark could take. By comparing with the dental records of the suspect, we can determine whether the bite mark came from his teeth."

Grayson displayed the next poster board in the stack. What the jury saw was a long row of teeth, and beneath them, a series of numbers. "This is a standard tooth-numbering chart. It uses two of the most common tooth designation systems, Universal and Palmer, plus the new Fédération Dentaire International System." He pointed to the numbers beneath the first tooth on the left. "For instance, the lower right molar is designated number 30—on the Universal system, L.R. 6—on the Palmer, or 36—on the new FDI. Actually, the FDI recently changed its quadrant designations so that the first odd numbers consistently refer to the right side and the first even numbers consistently refer to the left side."

Absolutely fascinating, Ben thought. Probably had nothing to do with this case, but it made Grayson seem like one smart dental dude.

Grayson turned to his next chart. "On the right, beside the teeth, you can see the marking codes commonly used to identify teeth anomalies. Any unusual characteristics, rotations, tooth and bone color oddities—such as pink, yellow, or tetracycline discoloration—can be noted here. Antemortem dental records, those most commonly found in a dentist's office, will also typically contain notes regarding various treatments and services rendered. Postmortem records will not have that, but will typically provide far greater detail about the current condition of the teeth."

Grayson then took the jury through the remainder of his charts, explaining the role of X-rays and other dental tools, which he called *armamentaria*. All in all, Ben thought it was boring as hell, but it served Granny's purpose. After hearing the man rattle on in this manner for well over an hour, it was hard to doubt that he was in fact an expert in the science of forensic dentistry.

"And in this manner," Grayson concluded, "we are able to trace an injury back to the person who made it. After taking these extensive and detailed records, we simply compare the chart compiled on the injury with the chart compiled on the suspect. If they match, we know the suspect is guilty. Dental patterns are quite unique. They're like fingerprints; no two mouths are exactly alike."

Granny smiled. "Thank you, Dr. Grayson, for that exhaustive"—Ben would've said exhausting—"description of contemporary dental identification techniques. You indicated that you have been doing some research yourself. Why?"

"Well, these traditional methods work fine as long as the imprint of the wound is such that the teeth marks can be distinguished. But sometimes, even when there's been a good solid bite, the imprint is not immediately clear. As I said before, flesh tissue is soft. It's not the ideal medium for a bite mark. So I've been working on ways to make difficult bite marks more apparent."

"Have you had any success?"

"I have. It's taken years of research, but I've managed to develop a way of making visible imprints that would otherwise be invisible to the naked eye. Mind you, they're there. They just can't be seen without visual augmentation."

"How do you enhance the injury traces?"

"I use a long-wave ultraviolet light—what you would call a blue light. Then I wear a pair of yellow-lensed safety goggles that have been chemically treated in a solution I developed myself. The combination of the ultraviolet light and the chemically treated goggles enhances features on the surface of the skin."

"That seems amazing, Doctor. How does it work?"

"It's simple, really. For years, scientists have experimented with different light frequencies as a means of increasing visual acuity. We all know that light takes many forms, depending upon its frequency. Some of those forms are visible to the naked eye—what we call visible light—and some of them are not—such as infrared light and X-rays. But even though we can't see X-rays, we know that if they are used properly, they can enable us to see things that would not otherwise be apparent to the naked eye. My process is just the same. I use infrared light to make visible what is there, but can't be seen in the visible light spectrum."

"That's fascinating, Doctor. You should be congratulated for your pioneering research in this field." Ben wondered if she was going to offer him the Nobel Prize on the spot. "Have you done any work with regard to the current case, the murder of Dwayne Gardiner?"

"Yes I have."

"Please tell the jury what you've done."

Grayson retook his seat, then adjusted himself to face the jury. "I was asked to examine the bite mark found by the coroner on the victim's arm. The injury was clearly a bite mark, but the impression was not deep. To make matters worse, the burning of the skin in the area made any identification all the more difficult. Conventional identification techniques were of no avail."

"So what did you do?"

"I used the ultraviolet technique I described for you earlier. Frankly, I was not optimistic. The damage to the skin was so extensive I wondered if even my special techniques would work. Happily, they did."

"Were you able to make a dental identification?"

"I was. May I return to my charts?"

Judge Pickens nodded. Grayson retook his former position and pointed to the last remaining chart. "This is a record of the bite mark as it first appeared when the coroner discovered it. As you can see, the impression is vague in places and indistinct. It was not useful. But after being viewed through my special infrared process"—he overlaid a clear transparency that fit perfectly atop the principal chart—"it became this." Jurors' eyes widened, obviously impressed. What they now saw was an almost perfectly detailed row of teeth.

"Was this record sufficient to make a comparison?"

"It was. I obtained the dental records of the defendant, which the police had already subpoenaed. Watch what happens when I now lay his teeth on top of the enhanced bite mark." Grayson overlaid yet another transparency, bearing another row of teeth, precisely on top of the other. As was almost immediately apparent, it was virtually identical.

"Dr. Grayson," Granny asked, "in your opinion, does this constitute a match?"

"It most certainly does."

"Then let me ask you the most important question. Would you say, based upon your extensive medical knowledge and analysis, that this bite mark was made by the defendant George Zakin?"

"Indeed and without a doubt."

"Thank you, Doctor. I have no more questions."

* 48 *

Ben strode to the podium cautiously, planning his approach. He would have to be careful with Grayson. He would love nothing more than to take the good dentist down a peg or two. But he knew it wouldn't be easy; if nothing else, Grayson was a very smart man and a very experienced witness.

"Dr. Grayson, you mentioned that you have a private dental practice."

"That's correct." He seemed perfectly at ease, more than willing to answer Ben's little questions.

"But you don't actually spend much time filling cavities these days, do you?"

"I'm not sure what you mean."

"You spend most of your time now as a professional witness, don't you?"

"Objection to the phrase," Granny said. "It's offensive."

"I'll rephrase," Ben said, feeling gracious. "You spend most of your time testifying, right?"

"Well . . . I haven't really kept time records on myself."

"How many times have you testified in the last two years?"

"I don't know exactly."

"Well, I do." Ben glanced down at the research Jones had faxed him that morning. "Twenty-seven times in the last two years. Does that sound about right?"

"I suppose so."

"And every time for the prosecution."

Grayson appeared nonplussed. "In my experience, defendants rarely want their teeth traced."

That got him a brief titter from the jury box. Ben ignored it. "How much do you make when you're hired to work on a case?"

"It varies."

"You don't have a standard rate?" Ben glanced again at his notes. "Because I thought—"

"I get two hundred and fifty dollars an hour," Grayson said. Ben noticed a few jurors reacting to that bit of information. "Sometimes I work at a discount, when there's good cause involved."

How noble. "The fact is, you've become so popular in the last few years as a witness for the prosecution that you don't have to fill cavities anymore, right?"

"Yes."

"You've developed a reputation as the man who can see what no one else can see."

"I have been fortunate enough to participate in many successful prosecutions."

"And prosecutors are always on the lookout for someone willing to say anything—if the price is right. Aren't they?"

"Your honor!" Granny leaped to her feet. "That is grossly offensive."

Ben cut off Pickens with a ready apology. "I'm sorry, your honor. I withdraw the question." Might as well, he thought. The point is made. And he had a lot more ground to cover;

he couldn't afford to have Pickens go ballistic this early in the game.

"Dr. Grayson, would it be fair to say that your entire testimony hinges on the reliability of your blue-light special—that is, your infrared viewing technique?"

"I suppose."

"Without this special technique, you'll admit that it would be impossible to trace this bite mark back to my client—or to anyone else for that matter."

"That's true. That's why I was called in."

"Well then, since your entire testimony depends on the reliability of this procedure, let's talk about it. Is there any precedent for this at all?"

"Of course. Scientists have been experimenting for years with the use of blue light to enhance visual acuity."

"But no one else does what you're doing."

"It is a well-established scientific fact that skin fluoresces under a blue light."

"Excuse me, Doctor. Normal skin fluoresces under a blue light. Damaged skin doesn't. Right?"

Grayson tilted his head. "It seems you're better informed than I realized, Mr. Kincaid."

"Well, I try."

"It is true that damaged skin doesn't fluoresce."

"And the bite wound you examined was extremely damaged, wasn't it?"

"I was just mentioning that by way of example. My technique does not rely on skin fluorescence."

"What does it rely on?"

"Well . . . of course, that's very complicated."

"Is there a book I could read on the subject? Some kind of documentation? 'Cause I have to tell you, I've looked, and I didn't find any."

"I . . . I have not published my research."

"Because you want to keep this cash cow to yourself?"

Granny rocketed up. "Your honor!"

Pickens's teeth were tightly clenched. "Mr. Kincaid, I will not put up with this abusive conduct in my courtroom!"

"Sorry, sorry. I'm just trying to determine why this pioneering scientific research has not been published."

"I submitted it for publication," Grayson said. "Three different medical journals. They all declined to publish."

"Because they all thought it was a lot of hooey, right?" Ben looked up quickly. "That's a scientific technical term, your honor."

Pickens grunted his reply.

Grayson made a small coughing noise. "I attribute their hesitance more to professional jealousy."

"Professional jealousy?"

"You have to understand—there still tends to be a bit of the ivory tower in the scientific community. Research is supposed to be pure; if it becomes profitable, then it's tainted. Or so some believe. And as you pointed out yourself, my research has become quite profitable."

Ben nodded. "I see. Is that why you were drummed out of the American Academy of Forensic Sciences?"

Grayson squirmed slightly. "As a matter of fact, it is."

Ben glanced at his notes. "The stated reason for your expulsion was that you were, quote, 'failing to follow generally accepted scientific techniques' and 'affirming scientific opinions that could not be verified or reproduced.' "

"I'm sure they said something like that. Nonetheless, my technique works, and they just can't stand that."

"But it's true that you don't follow generally accepted scientific techniques."

"I disagree."

"Then show me your documentation. Prove to me that this blue-light business works."

"I don't know what you want."

"I want proof. Can you show me a picture of what you saw?"

"No. Photography doesn't work under infrared light."

"Did you ask an impartial third person to view the bite under the blue light?"

"No."

"In fact, no one else has been able to see any of the things that you claim to see under the light, right?"

"I can't speak for other people."

"In the world of science, a new technique cannot be accepted until the procedure can be documented. Until the results can be reproduced by other researchers. Correct?"

"I can't be blamed for the unwillingness of others to accept what is perfectly apparent to me. I know what I see."

"The world is full of people who know what they saw. Like ghosts. Or UFOs. But that doesn't prove they exist, does it?"

"Of course not."

"My legal assistant sees angels. My sister sees auras, though mostly only when she's had too much to drink."

"Objection!" Granny barked. "This is ridiculous."

"I agree," Ben said, "but you're the one who put the man on the stand. He might as well be using voodoo or alchemy to see those bite marks. Whatever it is he's doing, it has nothing to do with science."

"Mr. Kincaid," the judge said, "I will not permit this ranting—"

"I'm not ranting," Ben said, "I'm making a motion. I move that this witness's entire testimony be struck and that the jury be instructed to disregard."

Granny ran up to the bench. "On what grounds?"

"On grounds that this so-called scientific evidence doesn't hold water."

"All we have to do is show that it is based on generally accepted scientific principles," Granny argued. "I think we've done that."

"I agree," Judge Pickens said.

"You're both wrong," Ben said. "That isn't the test anymore. The Supreme Court ruled in *Daubert* v. *Merrill Dow Pharmaceuticals* that it wasn't enough. They held that forensic results must be validated scientifically. I've been spending the whole cross trying to find some scientific validity for what this voodoo doctor does, and I still haven't found it."

"That's just your opinion," Granny said. "He explained his scientific process."

"I agree," the judge said.

"If you'd read the case, you'd know that he's required to prove that this testimony is based upon good grounds, and that his technique can be and has been tested, meaning peer review and publication. He should document his error rates and control techniques."

Pickens looked down from the bench. "As a matter of fact, Kincaid, I have read the case, and I happen to know for a fact that the Court suggested those items as guidelines—not as a mandatory checklist. The ultimate decision is left to the discretion of the trial judge. And I find his testimony perfectly valid."

"He admits himself he can't show us any proof!"

"I've ruled," Pickens said. "Your motion is denied. Either ask some more questions or sit down. Personally, I'd prefer the latter."

Ben marched back to the podium. Pickens's ruling was, of course, no big surprise. But he hoped the jury was getting the picture. Regardless of what the judge said, they were always free to disregard any evidence they didn't find credible.

"Dr. Grayson, has anyone else endorsed or supported your findings?"

"Not as such. Although many scientists are experimenting with blue light."

"But you're the only one who runs around claiming to see things no one else can see with it?"

"I pioneered the technique, yes."

"You're a pioneer with no followers, right?"

Grayson sighed heavily. Was Ben finally managing to raise a few prickles on his tough hide? He hoped so. "I am confident that time and science will prove me right."

"Well, the *Woltz* case sure didn't, did it?"

Grayson looked up abruptly. His lips parted. "I—excuse me?"

"Three years ago, you testified in a prosecution for forcible rape against a man named Jackie Woltz, right?"

"That's . . . correct."

"That one didn't turn out so well, did it?"

Grayson frowned. He seemed to be having more trouble choosing his words than he had before. "The prosecution was unsuccessful. The defendant was released."

"There's a bit more to it than that, isn't there?" Ben peered down at the detailed court records Jones had sent him. "You identified Woltz as the rapist, based on yet another bite mark no one but you could see. Unfortunately for you, the hair and fingerprint evidence didn't match Mr. Woltz. And the DNA analysis positively eliminated him as a suspect."

Grayson drew up his chin. "I still stand by my findings."

"You're telling this jury that the fingerprints and DNA and hair—all the established forensic techniques—were wrong, but your totally undocumented technique was right?"

"I found that Mr. Woltz caused the bite wound. It's possible that someone else committed the rape."

"But that wasn't your testimony. You took the stand and said Woltz must have been the rapist. Indeed, and beyond a doubt, right? Weren't those your exact words?"

Grayson hesitated.

"Weren't they? If you're having memory problems, I've got a transcript right here."

"That's not necessary." His lips drew together like he'd been sucking a lemon. "That's what I said."

"And you were wrong."

"The jury disagreed with me."

"Everyone disagreed with you! Except maybe the desperate prosecutor who hired you!"

"I say again," Grayson repeated through clenched teeth. "I believe time and science will prove me right."

Ben folded his notebook. He should probably quit; he'd done about as much damage as he could. But he couldn't resist trying one more . . . possibility. "Dr. Grayson, did you ever give any consideration to insect bites?"

Grayson blinked. "Insect bites?"

"We know the corpse was found in the forest. We know there are animals and insects in the forest. I believe the coroner testified that the corpse was infested by insects before he arrived. Could this so-called bite mark have been made by insects?"

"I have found clear traces of molars, incisors—"

"But only under the blue light."

"There was a clear pattern—"

"What pattern?" Ben walked up to the last chart and removed the transparencies. "Look at this!" he said to Grayson, but really to the jury. "There's no pattern here. Just some random nibbling. It could be anything."

Grayson pointed toward the easel. "But look at the transparency!"

"The image on the transparency was drawn by you *after* you received my client's dental records. Correct?"

"It's true that I drew the chart. I had to. Photography doesn't work."

"So this isn't evidence of any sort, much less proof. You can't even prove this bite mark came from a human being."

"If you'll recall, even the coroner knew the victim had been bitten—"

"I've read the coroner's report, Doctor, and I listened to his testimony earlier. He said there was a bite mark. He never said it was a *human* bite mark. Because he couldn't prove it. And when all is said and done, you can't either." He turned away before Grayson had a chance to stammer out a response. "I have nothing more for this witness."

* 49 *

That evening, back at his office, Ben thumbed through his address book for the phone number for Tulsa Police Headquarters—Central Division. It seemed late for anyone to be at the office, but then again, he was. Ben punched in the number and waited. No one picked up the phone until the seventh ring.

"Homicide. Morelli here."

"Mike, is that you?"

"It's me, kemo sabe," said the voice on the other end of the phone.

"What are you doing at the office?"

"Working, natch. I don't have a life, remember? So how's everything in the Great Northwest?"

"Not so great." Ben leaned back in the rickety wooden chair behind the tiny desk in his office. "I'm in the middle of trying a murder case."

"So I hear. Let me guess. All the evidence points to your client, the odds are hopelessly stacked against you, but you think he's innocent and you're determined to prove it."

"How did you figure that out?"

There was a knowing chuckle on the other end of the phone. "Just a lucky guess."

"Look, Mike, I called for a reason."

"You need my help."

Ben stared at the receiver. "What are you, the psychic hot line?"

More chuckles. "I just know you're not one to call to ask about my health."

"Well, you're right. I'm having problems. I think there's a major drug dealer in this town, a big brick wall called Alberto Vincenzo. I think he's a very likely suspect for the murder my client has been charged with. And I think the prosecutor knows it, so she's suppressing all the evidence she has about him. Apparently the DEA has the goods on this character, too, but I've been calling the regional office in Seattle and I can't get them to send me anything or give me an appointment. I can't even get them to return my phone calls."

"So why are you calling me?"

Ben made a coughing noise. "Well, you are in the law enforcement community. I thought perhaps . . ."

"Ben, I'm just a cop. A lowly homicide detective in Tulsa, in the faraway state of Oklahoma. And you're thinking I might have connections in the federal DEA office in Seattle? You're delusional!"

"Well, I don't know. I thought maybe you might know someone who knew someone who knew someone else."

"This is really a stretch, Ben."

"That's what I said when you married my sister. But you did it anyway."

"Don't remind me." Ben listened patiently through several seconds of thoughtful silence. "Look. No promises. I'll do the best I can, okay?"

"That's all I can ask."

"And hey—take care of yourself out there. I get worried when you get into these messes and I'm not around to bail you out."

"Your concern is touching."

"Yeah, well, just try not to engage in hand-to-hand combat with any serial killers, okay?"

"I'll do my best."

After he finished talking with Mike, Ben pored over his notes for the next day of trial, not to mention an extremely interesting report he'd received from Loving, just back from Oregon. Around nine, Christina poked her head through the door. "Is this the cramped but classy office of Ben Kincaid, a.k.a. Ben the Giant-Slayer?"

Ben rolled his eyes. "Hello, Christina. Where ya been?"

"Procuring a little well-deserved liquid refreshment." As she stepped across the threshold, Ben saw she was cradling a large bottle of champagne and two flutes. She set down the glasses and began twisting off the wire cap.

"I think this is way premature," Ben said. "We don't have anything to celebrate yet."

"Baloney. You've been superb in the courtroom. Granny hasn't put a single witness of any importance on the stand that you haven't hurt on cross. And what you did to that sanctimonious dental quack—*wowzah!*"

"It's still too soon . . ."

"I bet Granny's not sleeping well tonight." Christina popped the cork and poured the champagne. "I had the pleasure of watching her today while you were crossing Grayson. She was definitely getting sweaty-palmed. You haven't given her an inch. If the jury voted today, it would be hands down for acquittal."

"But the jury isn't voting today. We still have several more witnesses—"

"But she hasn't done anything that truly tied Zak to the murder."

"The truth is, she hasn't tried. She's intentionally started with the least important witnesses. She's building slowly, letting the jury anticipate where she's going. And, I suspect, taking my measure."

"Well, right now, your measure is pretty damn good."

"Let's see what happens tomorrow." He gazed absently at the bottle of bubbly. It was a French sparkling wine—as if Christina would bring anything else. "So you've been out to dinner?"

"Yeah. I didn't think you'd mind."

" 'Course not. It's none of my business."

Christina's eyes crinkled a bit. "I meant I didn't think you'd mind if I did my trial prep after dinner."

Ben fidgeted with his pencil. "Oh. Right. That's what I thought you meant." His eyes averted. "So how many dinners with Sheriff Allen does this make?"

"Who said I was eating with Doug?"

"Doug?"

"That's his name."

"I figured as much."

"I never said I was eating with Doug."

Ben tugged at his collar. "I just assumed . . ."

"Well, you assumed correctly."

"And how many times have you gone out with him now?"

"I don't know. How long have you had me in this godforsaken backwater?"

Ben looked away. "Of course, it's none of my business."

"Of course." A mischievous smile played on Christina's lips. "Do you have a problem with this?"

"Of course not," Ben said, not looking up. "Like I said—"

"Doug is a wonderful talker. Not at all what you'd expect. Really very charming. Sophisticated."

"Sophisticated?"

"Oh, yes. You shouldn't be such a snob, Ben. Just because people live in a small town, it doesn't mean they're hicks."

"I never meant to suggest—"

"He is a bit homespun, to be sure. But that's just his way. Honestly, he's very well educated. Smart."

"Is that right."

"Oh yeah. And supremely self-confident."

"That's good, I guess. If you like that sort of thing."

"And very masculine."

"Do tell."

She mock-trembled, as if shivers were racing up and down her spine. "Something about him just makes me go all aquiver."

Ben gave her a long look. "You're putting me on, aren't you?"

"Of course I am, you dimwit!" She grinned from ear to ear.

"And may I ask why?"

"Because you're so easy!" She reached forward and ruffled his hair. "Although in a way, that takes all the fun out of it. It's like torturing a bunny rabbit."

Ben waited a moment, until her laughter faded and the room grew quiet. "But you do like him, don't you?"

She waited a long time before answering. "Anything wrong with that?"

" 'Course not. I was just curious. Since we're friends and all."

"Oh. Right." The tiny office fell silent and, for a protracted moment, strangely awkward.

Christina broke the silence. She turned toward the tall stack of exhibits waiting to be reviewed before the trial reconvened. "What say we start wading through those exhibits and figure out how we're going to whip Granny's butt in court tomorrow?"

Ben picked up his champagne flute. "I'll drink to that."

* 50 *

Granny Adams sashayed down the dark corridor listening to the rhythmic sound of her stiletto heels rat-a-tatting on the metal floor. She slowed her pace, preferring to let the man in the far room wait and wonder what lay in store for him.

Deputy Wagner had made all the arrangements as per her instructions. He may not have known what she was planning, but he was a dutiful soldier and he did as he was told. Just the sort of law enforcement officer Granny liked.

In her own good time, she reached the end of the gloomy corridor. There was one sentry posted outside the room, a uniform from the sheriff's office. She'd seen him before, but she couldn't possibly remember his name. Why should she? He was just an instrument, an extra ratchet wrench in her toolbox. And she couldn't be expected to remember every hammer and nail, could she?

"You can go now," she said to the sentry.

A worry line creased his forehead. "I'm not supposed to leave you alone with—"

"I can handle myself, Officer," she said briskly. "Scram."

The officer shifted his weight from one foot to the other. "No disrespect intended, ma'am, but Sheriff Allen told me—"

"I could eat Sheriff Allen for breakfast." Granny inched forward, pressing herself against him, practically nose to nose. "And spit him out again before lunch. Do you understand what I'm saying?"

"I—I—I—"

"Who's the boss around here, soldier?"

He mouthed a silent "You are."

"I'm glad we both understand that. If I need you, I'll call." She pointed toward the door. "Now get the hell out of here."

"Yes, ma'am." The officer turned quickly and scampered off down the corridor.

Granny smiled. There was nothing like a small but effective display of power to stimulate her juices. But now for the task at hand.

She was not looking forward to this. It was not something she particularly wanted to do. But the fact was, the trial was not going entirely the way she wanted. Granted, she still had many tricks up her sleeve, but she had to take precautions. She had to make sure this thing didn't slip away from her.

She opened the door and stepped into the small interrogation room. The prisoner was already seated and handcuffed to the table. "Good evening, Mr. Geppi."

Geppi lifted his head out of his arms. He had longish black hair that tumbled around his ears and shoulders. He appeared to be in his early thirties, maybe younger, and looked as if he hadn't shaved for several days. "Nice of you to show up. I been waitin' over an hour."

"I was delayed." She sat in the wooden chair at the opposite end of the table, pushed it back, and crossed her legs in a way she knew was bound to attract a little attention. "Want a cigarette?"

"No thanks. I don't do tobacco." His eyes flickered up and down. His lower lip twitched. "Mind tellin' me what this is all about?"

"Mr. Geppi, I thought it might be mutually beneficial if you and I had a little chat. Do you know who I am?"

He shrugged. "The deputy said somethin'. Like you work in the D.A.'s office."

She leaned forward, her full breasts just touching the table. "Mr. Geppi, I *am* the D.A.'s office." She paused, allowing the words to sink in. "I am the one who makes the decisions. I am the one who decides who goes free and who goes to prison for life. I am the one who holds your future in the palm of my hand."

"Is this a plea bargain? 'Cause if it's a plea bargain, I wanna lawyer."

"This is not a plea bargain." She smiled, an absolutely terrifying smile. "This is just a social chat."

He edged back as far as he could with the handcuffs fixing him to the table. "Look, this is makin' me nervous. I don't wanna do this, okay? I ain't done anything."

"I beg to differ, Mr. Geppi." She pulled a thin folder out of her soft leather briefcase. "You've been arrested for possession of an illegal narcotic, a dangerous designer drug that is creating tremendous concern and fear in this little community. Possession with intent to distribute."

"Distribute? No way, lady." He held up his hands. "I'm no pusher."

"That's not what my witnesses will say. They will identify you as a major supplier of this new drug, this scourge laying waste to the city's youth. They'll identify you as a major player, one with direct ties to the big boss man."

"Have you totally lost it? That's a crock."

"Nonetheless, it's what they'll say. And you know what that means? It means you could get ten years in prison. Ten long years. And given the current climate of the community, I think you'll serve every day of it."

"There's somethin' wrong here," Geppi insisted. Beads of sweat were popping out at his temples. "I didn't do none of that. I don't know any boss man. I was just looking for a good time. Bought myself a quick high. Someone's framin' me."

Granny did not reply, but the strong arch of her eyebrow told Geppi everything he needed to know.

"You," he whispered, his eyes widening. "You're the one settin' me up."

She did not reply.

"Why? What is it you want?"

She leaned back in her chair, uncrossing then recrossing her magnificent legs. "Have you been enjoying your stay in the county jail, Mr. Geppi?"

He frowned. "It ain't exactly the Holiday Inn."

"It'll seem like the Ritz compared to where you're going next." She paused, letting him think about the ramifications of that statement for a while. "How's your cellmate?"

"Huh? What?" He didn't follow.

"Haven't you been in the cell next to George Zakin?"

"Oh, right. The tree freak. What of it?"

"I just wondered." She laid her hands on the table and spread her long fingers. "Sometimes people talk in jail, you know. Not much else to do, I suppose."

Geppi's eyes narrowed. "What're you gettin' at?"

"Here's the situation, Mr. Geppi. Mr. Zakin is the leader of a group of people who have been stirring up a lot of trouble. They've decommissioned equipment and blown up cars and generally interfered with the townfolks' way of life. Lot of people don't care much for what those troublemakers are doing. And nobody cares for murder. A poor innocent logger got shot, then burned to death in the intentional explosion of some expensive logging equipment. He died slowly and painfully."

"And you think Zakin did it?"

"Oh, I know he did. It's proving it that's the trick. That's why I wondered if maybe you heard Zakin say something about the crime while he was in the cell."

"Sorry, lady. Ain't heard him mention it."

"Are you sure about that, Mr. Geppi? I want you to be absolutely sure about that. Because you see, ten years is an awful long time to be locked up in Collinsgate prison. It's a dirty, nasty place. Inmates are always gettin' hurt or killed. Slashed up bad. And a handsome young man like you—well, you would be very popular with some of the inmates that have . . . specialized tastes. If you know what I mean."

Geppi's teeth clenched up. "What are you gettin' at, lady?"

"I just want you to think very hard, Mr. Geppi. I want you to think very hard about whether maybe you've heard Mr. Zakin say anything about this crime he committed. Maybe even heard him confess to this crime he's committed." She drew her head up. "Because if you had heard him say something like that, it would make me very happy."

Geppi settled back in his chair. "How happy?"

"Very happy." She leaned forward, providing a generous display of cleavage. "Passionately happy."

"Are you offering me a deal?"

"No. Let me make that absolutely, unequivocably clear. I

am not offering you a deal. And there's a reason for that, Mr. Geppi. You see, if you were to remember that Zakin had confessed to you, and if you were to take the stand to testify to that effect, you would have to undergo cross-examination. And the first question the defense attorney would ask is whether you've made a deal with the prosecutors. Whether you've been offered immunity. And if you have to say yes, that's not going to look very good to the jury. That's going to give the defense lawyer a way to discredit you. The jury needs to think the only reason you're testifying is because of your profound sense of civic obligation."

Geppi snorted.

"Anyway, that's why I'm not offering you a deal. But I can tell you this." She leaned even further across the table. "I can tell that you will not be shipped off to Collinsgate tomorrow, because you'll be a material witness and we'll need to keep you close at hand. And I can also tell you that after the Zakin trial is over, after the man has been convicted, I would look very favorably toward any proposal you might make. I wouldn't even be surprised if the charges against you were dropped and it turned out we had just made a sad mistake."

"That ain't good enough," Geppi said. "I want a firm deal. I want it in writing."

"Listen to my words, you little pissant." She grabbed his arm and jerked him forward. "That isn't going to happen, understand? Not now, not ever. You have two choices. Either you get shipped out to Collinsgate and spend the next ten years as Cell Block Eight's gang-bang joy toy, or you'll testify about what George Zakin told you. And if you do a good job of it and Zakin is convicted, *then*—and only *then*—we'll talk about maybe doing some favors. Not before." She folded her arms across her chest. "That's the deal. Take it or leave it."

Geppi pressed his lips together bitterly.

"Speak up, asshole. Should I sign the transfer papers now? Or do we have an understanding?"

Slowly, hesitantly, Geppi began to nod.

Granny smiled. "Good. I'm glad we were able to come to terms. I'm looking forward to working with you." She leaned back luxuriantly in her chair. "I'm glad Zakin was foolish enough to spill the beans to you, Mr. Geppi. It's important that we law enforcement officers be able to put away trouble-makers and murderers. And it's important that the community have a sense of security, a sense of justice being done. And that means knowing that crimes are punished, that trouble-makers are taken off the streets. Hell, I wouldn't be surprised if Zakin told you he was behind the distribution of this new designer drug that's been plaguing our town. Maybe he pushes drugs to raise money for his terrorist activities, you know what I mean?"

"I'm beginning to get the general idea," Geppi said softly.

"I wouldn't be surprised to learn that there was more to the murder than just eco-politics, too. I wouldn't be surprised to learn that there was a more personal motive for the crime. That there was a connection between Zakin and the man who was murdered."

"Go on," Geppi said, nodding his head attentively. "I'm listening."

* 51 *

"The State calls Julie Cummings."

Ben watched as the prosecution's first witness of the day approached the bench. She was tall, lanky, about Zak's age. Her brown hair hung straight down, no frills. She was reasonably attractive, Ben thought, but she didn't look entirely comfortable in the elegant black dress she was wearing. Probably selected by Madame Prosecutor, unless Ben missed his guess.

While the witness was being sworn, Ben leaned toward Zak and whispered. "I'm worried about this. Nothing hurts worse than bad words from an . . . intimate acquaintance."

"Relax. Julie's a sweetheart. We understood each other."

"Then why is she testifying for the prosecution?"

Zak shrugged. "Who knows? Probably subpoenaed. Mark my word—she won't lay a finger on me."

Ms. Cummings took her seat in the witness box and Granny began her questioning. "Ms. Cummings, what do you do?"

"I'm the regional director for the Society for Prevention of Cruelty to Our Other-Than-Human Neighbors."

"And could you briefly tell the jury what that distinguished organization is?"

"It's an animal rights activist group. We're committed to using nonviolent means to prevent the mistreatment of animals."

"Were you with this organization six years ago?"

"Yes. I wasn't regional director yet, but I was there."

"And did you ever have an occasion to meet the defendant, George Zakin?"

"I did. He was also with the organization."

"And what was his role?"

"He was in the Operations section."

"And what did Operations do?"

"They were in charge of, well, operations."

"Such as . . ."

"Raids. We would raid animal testing laboratories, try to free the animals. Sometimes we would hold protest rallies outside a zoo or corporate headquarters. That sort of thing."

"Do you remember when Mr. Zakin joined the organization?"

"Yes, I remember it very well. I was against bringing him in."

Granny feigned surprise. "Really? Why?"

"Because he had a criminal record." Juror eyes widened with interest. Another of Granny's promises was being delivered on. "He'd been a member of an anti-Klan group in Montgomery and he'd been caught with a bunch of bomb ingredients. Plastique, if I remember correctly. He was charged with possessing illegal materials and conspiracy to use them. He did two years."

Granny pulled out the official records pertaining to Zak's conviction and went through the hoops necessary to have them admitted as exhibits so the jury would be able to examine them in the deliberation room. Ben didn't bother objecting. There was no point. Although mere arrests or accusations were not admissible, a felony conviction was.

"And why did that bother you, Ms. Cummings?"

"Well, I didn't think we needed a hothead in Operations. As I said, we're dedicated to the use of nonviolent means to achieve our ends. What did we want with some bomb expert? Even if he didn't make bombs for us, just having him around made us look bad."

"I gather you were overruled."

"I was. And Zak became a member of the organization."

Granny turned a page in her outline. "How did that work out?"

"At first, well. Much better than I expected, actually. He had a lot of energy—I have to give him credit for that. He got a lot of new programs rolling, and most of them were successful. I think his energy was contagious. He inspired others in the group to work harder, to become even more dedicated."

"Was there a downside to having Mr. Zakin in your group?"

"Not at first. But after the incident at Chesterson Laboratories, we all wished we'd never heard of George Zakin."

Ben whispered in Zak's ear. "Still think she's your understanding friend?"

Zak did not respond.

Granny continued questioning. "Could you tell the jury what happened at the Chesterson Laboratories, please?"

"Chesterson was one of the worst animal experimenters in the country, both in volume and degree. They went through hundreds of animals a year, most of them primates, and the experiments they performed on those poor animals were abominable. Pure torture. Killing them slowly to test a new mascara, that sort of thing. So we planned a raid. To set free the chimps imprisoned there."

"I take it the raid was unsuccessful."

"No, the raid was a huge success. We got in, got out, and the chimps were freed. But something happened we didn't plan on. One of the researchers was killed during or near the time of the raid. Needless to say, our group was blamed."

"Was any particular member blamed?"

Ben rose to his feet. "Objection, your honor. May I approach the bench?"

Judge Pickens nodded. Ben walked to the semi-privacy of the judge's station up front; Granny came scampering behind him.

"Your honor," Ben explained, "counsel is about to enter testimony relating to charges that were brought against my client after this Chesterson incident."

"How do you know?" Granny said. "Are you a mind reader?"

"No, but I'm not a fool, either. And I know that if I wait until after the cat is out of the bag, no ruling on earth will make the jury forget what they've heard. Judge, my client was charged with this murder, but he was completely exonerated. The jury voted unanimously for acquittal."

"Only because Kincaid did some fancy footwork during the trial."

Pickens's eyebrows lifted. "This Kincaid?"

"The very same," Granny said. "He's the genius who got Zakin off the hook—and back on the streets."

Judge Pickens looked as if he had an unpleasant taste in his mouth. "You must be very proud of yourself, Kincaid."

"Your honor, we all know that absent a conviction, evidence of prior arrest and charges is not admissible."

"That's not exactly true," Granny interjected. "It's not admissible to prove the truth of the matter asserted or to prove that he likely committed the present murder."

"What other reason could you possibly have?"

"We're using it simply to explain why Zak was booted out of the animal rights organization and to show that they considered him dangerous. This can come in as evidence of prior bad acts, pursuant to Rule 404b. I jumped through all the appropriate pretrial hoops."

"That's true," Pickens agreed.

"That's ridiculous," Ben snorted.

"What's the matter, Kincaid?" Pickens growled. "You think you're the only one who has any fancy footwork?"

"Your honor, it's perfectly obvious she just wants the jury to know that he was tried once before for murder. This will be grossly prejudicial."

"I'm sure it will be prejudicial to your client, Kincaid. But I believe the probative value outweighs the prejudice in this case. I'm going to let it in."

"Your honor!" Ben exclaimed. "This is absolutely—"

"I've ruled, Kincaid."

Ben's face tightened. "I move for leave of court to take an immediate interlocutory appeal on this issue."

"Denied."

"Your honor, this is simply wrong!"

Pickens brought out his gavel and pointed it so far forward it practically touched Ben's nose. "I've made my ruling, Kincaid. You can live with it or you can leave. Your choice."

Ben stomped back to defendant's table, fuming. That ruling was absolutely contrary to law, and he knew it. It could possibly be the basis for a later appeal, but he doubted that remote possibility would be of much comfort to Zak.

Granny repeated her question, and the witness answered, carefully choosing her words. "Many people believed George Zakin should be blamed."

Ben grimaced. Another unnecessary twist of the knife from Zak's "understanding friend."

"What was the reaction of your organization to all this?"

She pushed a few wisps of hair behind her ear. "Well, after that, the rest of the leadership finally came around to my way of seeing things. They realized he was dangerous, a loose cannon. Turned out he'd been agitating all along for the group to become more militant, to plant bombs, sabotage equipment. He was out of control."

"Out of control," Granny repeated, just in case someone missed it. "Dangerous. So what action did your group take?"

"We kicked him out, basically. We didn't want him."

"I can understand that," Granny said somberly. "It's just a shame that someone else did. No more questions."

Ben pressed his lips close to Zak's ear. "You were kicked out? You told me you left! You never said you were kicked out."

Zak didn't answer him.

"Well? Is it true?"

Zak shrugged. “I probably wouldn’t have used those words.”

Ben pressed his hand against his forehead. Great. Just great. As if he didn’t have enough to deal with. “When are you going to get a clue, Zak? You don’t keep secrets from your lawyer!”

Zak looked away sullenly, like a little boy scolded but not much chastened.

Ben took his place behind the podium. He had only one arrow in his quiver. He thought it best he fire it off before the jury dwelt too long on what they had just heard. “Ms. Cummings, I don’t want to be indelicate, but isn’t it true that you and the defendant were once . . . romantically involved?”

“We slept together, if that’s what you mean.” She answered matter-of-factly and without the least trace of embarrassment. “In the early days, before I knew him well. But it didn’t last long. I was never in love with him, and frankly, he was never very good in bed. It wasn’t any big deal.”

“Still,” Ben insisted, “you must have been somewhat . . . distressed when he left you.”

“Is that what he told you? That he dumped me?” She laughed loudly. “Let me tell you something, Mr. Lawyer. That’s not how it happened. I saw Zak come on to everything female that walked through the door. I didn’t need to be told he would be perpetually unfaithful, that he would always be looking for more women to conquer. And I didn’t care to be part of his harem. So I dumped him.”

Ben took a deep breath. This wasn’t exactly going the way he wanted. “Ms. Cummings, forgive me, but despite your protestations to the contrary, I’m detecting a very . . . bitter tone in your voice.”

“No, you’re confusing anger with bitterness. I am angry—I think he’s a dangerous, unreliable person, and I think he caused considerable damage to the animal rights cause. But I’m not bitter because he didn’t sleep with me anymore. I didn’t want him to sleep with me anymore.”

“Still, how can we be sure your testimony isn’t motivated by . . . well . . .”

“Look, if you’re trying to suggest I just made all this up to get back at him, forget it. I was asked by the prosecutor's office to tell what I know, so I have. But I've got no axe to grind. Frankly, until they called me, I hadn't thought about Zak for years."

Ben could see he was getting nowhere with her, and his cross-ex quiver was empty. He hated to end on such an unproductive note, but there was nothing else to ask her about. "No more questions."

As he took his seat, Ben tried to console himself. She had established that Zak knew how to make a bomb, that he had done it in the past. And that he was "dangerous." But she hadn't known anything about the present case. She certainly hadn't established that he made this bomb, the one that killed Dwayne Gardiner.

Which was true—Julie Cummings hadn't. But the next witness would.

* 52 *

"The State calls Leonard Cokey to the stand."

There were some witnesses, Ben mused, you could dress up and make presentable for court, and some witnesses you might as well not waste time trying. Leonard (Ben would be willing to bet he was normally called Lenny) fell into the latter category. Ben had rarely seen anyone who looked more miserable in a suit and tie. His face was nicked in half a dozen places; probably his first shave in weeks, Ben guessed. His sleeves and pant legs were too short; Granny probably found the suit for him in a secondhand store. Even as the bailiff administered the oath, Cokey tugged at his collar like it was strangling him.

"What do you do for a living, Mr. Cokey?" Granny asked.

He squirmed uncomfortably. "I'm a freelance wholesaler."

Uh-huh, Ben thought. Translation: thief.

"Could you tell us what you were doing on the night of July eleventh?"

"Uh, yeah. I was over at Georgie's. That's the pawnshop over on McKinley."

"And why were you there?"

"I've been a bit strapped this month so, uh . . . I was hocking my TVs."

Yeah, right, Ben thought. Translation: delivering stolen goods.

"Was there anyone else in the store?" Granny continued.

"Oh sure, sure." Cokey didn't seem able to sit still. He kept shifting positions, sitting on his hands. "Georgie was working the bar in the back."

"The bar in the back? What goes on there?"

"Well . . ." Cokey craned his neck awkwardly. "That's where he keeps the handguns but it's also my understanding that some illegal goods are sold there. From time to time. Of course I wouldn't know myself from personal experience."

Ben had had about as much of this shuffle-ball-change routine as he could take. Why didn't Granny just give the man immunity so he could tell what he knew without all this nonsense?

"Was there anyone else present in the pawnshop?"

"Yeah. Him." Cokey pointed across the courtroom. "The defendant."

The jury turned to check Zak, frowns plastered on many faces. What was an upright young conservationist doing in that den of iniquity?

"And where was he?"

"He was at the back bar, doing business with Georgie."

Granny nodded. "And do you have any idea what business was being transacted?"

"Well, it's not like I was eavesdroppin' or anythin'."

Of course not, Ben thought. Perish the thought.

"But I had to talk to Georgie, see? So I was waiting around. And I couldn't help hearing what they were talkin' about."

"And what were they talkin' about?"

"Bombs. Big bombs."

The people in the gallery held their collective breaths.

"What specifically were they discussing?"

Cokey leaned forward, his hands still pressed beneath his legs. "Georgie was supplying chemicals, see? I don't remember the names, but according to Georgie, if you mixed them together and ignited them—boom!" He threw his hands up in the air.

"And did the defendant receive these chemicals?"

"Oh, yeah. Paid big bucks for them."

"And you saw this with your own eyes?"

"I did. I swear. On my mother's grave."

"I'm sure that won't be necessary. Do you know what the defendant planned to do with the chemicals?"

Cokey nodded enthusiastically. "Oh, yeah. Heard enough to know the stuff was for a bomb."

"Did you hear any discussion of the intended target?"

"Yeah. I heard—"

"Objection," Ben said. "Calls for hearsay."

Granny was obviously expecting this one. "Your honor, the hearsay from this Georgie person is being admitted not to prove the truth of the matter asserted, but to put later statements by the defendant in context. And of course the statements from the defendant, being statements against interest by the accused, constitute a hearsay exception."

"The objection is overruled," Pickens declared. "Please proceed."

Cokey leaned toward the jury box. "What I heard was, Georgie asks him, 'You got plans for this?' And the other guy, the defendant, he just looks at Georgie real cold-like and says, 'Yeah. Big plans.' "

"Big plans?" Granny parroted. "And this was just two days before the explosion that took Dwayne Gardiner's life?"

"Yeah. And that ain't all. Georgie asks him what these big plans are, see?"

"And did Mr. Zakin reply?"

"Oh yeah. He gets all coy and sly-actin', and he says, 'I'm going to teach a logger a lesson he'll never forget.' "

The rumble through the courtroom was audible. People

turned and stared, eyes widened, across the courtroom. Every eye was focused on Zak. For the first time, they'd heard evidence that portrayed him as not only a bomber, but a bomber with malice. A bomber with a particular target in mind.

"That's not what I said," Zak whispered in Ben's ear. "That stupid weasel got it wrong. What I said was 'I'm going to teach some loggers a lesson they'll never forget.' "

"Oh, swell," Ben whispered back. "That's much better." He turned and looked at Zak coldly. "You planted that bomb, didn't you?"

"I was striking a blow for the cause, taking out some machinery. I didn't mean to hurt anyone. I specifically set the thing to detonate in the middle of the night, when there was no chance anyone would be on it."

"Except that someone was."

"But the bomb I planted wasn't in that clearing. It wasn't on that tree cutter. It was somewhere else, in the Crescent Basin old-growth region. And it was set to go off at three, not one."

"That's not going to make any difference to the jury," Ben shot back.

"Mr. Kincaid!"

Ben looked up abruptly. The Time Machine was trying to get his attention.

"Do you wish to cross-examine or not?"

Oops. He wondered how many calls he had missed while he and Zak were gabbing. "I'll cross."

Although, as he made his way to the podium, he wondered why. Cokey might be a total sleaze, but his testimony about seeing Zak buy bomb parts appeared to be essentially accurate. And Ben had a hard time getting his heart into a defense for a man who would set a bomb that—

He focused on the witness, clearing his head. He had an obligation to his client, and he had to fulfill it. Zak hadn't intended to kill anyone.

At least as far as Ben knew. But it was becoming abundantly clear that his client had not told him the whole truth.

"Mr. Cokey, are you sure that what Mr. Zakin said was 'I'm going to teach a logger a lesson he'll never forget'?"

"Well . . . yeah. That's what I heard."

"Is it possible that what the man actually said was, 'I'm going to teach some loggers a lesson they'll never forget'?"

"Well, geez. There ain't much difference."

"There's a world of difference, sir. It's the difference between a premeditated plan to strike against a particular person—which the prosecution has proved no motive for whatsoever—and a general plan to strike an economic blow against the logging industry."

Cokey fumbled a bit. "Well, I thought I heard what I heard."

"But are you sure?"

"I thought . . ."

"Mr. Cokey. Is it possible that what you heard Zak say was that he was going to teach a lesson to some loggers?"

Cokey shrugged, then frowned. "I guess it's possible."

"Thank you for that admission, sir. I appreciate your honesty." Not that it was really much of an admission. But Ben might as well build it up as much as possible. At this point, Zak needed all the help he could get.

* 53 *

Ben spent the rest of the cross picking away at Cokey's reputation, trying to establish that he was basically a low-life scuz who made a living swiping stuff and hocking it at Georgie's. By the time Ben was done, he doubted if any of the jurors thought of Cokey as a moral paragon. Unfortunately, he wasn't sure it would much matter in the long run. They didn't have to believe he was a saint to believe he overheard two people talking about bombs in the back room of a low-life pawnshop. In fact, this was one rare instance when the witness's sleazeball status might actually make his testimony seem *more* credible.

After that debacle, Ben would've been happy to call it a day, but unfortunately, Granny had another witness.

"The State calls Ralph Peabody to the stand."

Peabody was a young man, strong, well-built, and handsome. He had a thatch of curly blond hair that whipped over his forehead and hovered just above his eyes.

Granny established that he was thirty-two years of age, gainfully employed managing the Canfield Grocery, and a Magic Valley native. "Would you please tell the jury what you were doing on the night of July twelfth?"

July 12, Ben thought. Just before the murder. This could be bad news.

"I was at Bunyan's," Peabody answered, then added, "That's a bar here in town."

The expression on the jurors' faces told Ben no explanation was necessary.

"And why were you there?"

Peabody shrugged. "I was just hanging out. You know how it is. It was a Friday night, and there's not much to do on a Friday night here in Magic Valley."

That brought a few appreciative chuckles from the gallery.

"Were you alone?"

"Nah. I was with a couple of pals."

"But were there other people in the bar? Other than your group?"

"Oh, yeah. Of course."

"Anyone who might be in the courtroom today?"

"Him." Peabody pointed across the courtroom. "The defendant. Zakin."

Granny nodded. "Anyone else?"

"Gardiner. The guy who got killed. I didn't know who he was at the time, but when I saw his picture in the paper later, I recognized him."

"When did you first observe Mr. Gardiner?"

"I had to excuse myself at one point—'round about eleven thirty or so, I think. The bathroom is in the back; you walk down a kinda long corridor till you get there. When I was on my way out, I saw Mr. Gardiner in the corridor, facing me."

"And was he alone?"

"No. He was with the defendant. Zakin."

Granny nodded appreciatively. "So they did know each other after all. Were they talking?"

"Oh, yes, ma'am. I guess you could call it that. It was a pretty . . . heated conversation."

"And what do you mean by that?"

"Well, it didn't take much to see there was some serious bad blood between the two. They were shouting at each other, calling names. At one point Zakin shoved Gardiner backward, hard. That sort of thing."

"And did you hear what they were talking about?"

Peabody shifted his weight. "Now, you understand—I'm not one to butt in on something that's none of my beeswax—"

"Of course not," Granny reassured him. "But I'm sure in that narrow corridor it was impossible to avoid overhearing."

"Well, yeah. Exactly. Plus, they were blocking the way and kinda oblivious to everything else. I couldn't get past them."

"So what was it you heard?"

"Well, I never figured out what exactly it was they were so mad at each other about. But I heard Gardiner tell Zakin—"

"Objection," Ben said. "She's trying to drag hearsay into the courtroom again."

"Your honor," Granny said, "once again, this testimony is being offered only to put the defendant's statements in context and to show the defendant's state of mind, his obvious hostility toward the murder victim."

"That's a grossly prejudicial bit of speechifying," Ben said. "And I—"

"Plus," Granny continued, rolling right over his objections, "I would point out that Mr. Gardiner is deceased, which is the whole reason for this trial. The declarant is definitely unavailable; I can't call him to the stand. The only way I can get this critical piece of evidence before the jury is via Mr. Peabody."

Judge Pickens nodded. "The objection is overruled. Please proceed."

The witness continued. "So I heard Gardiner tell Zakin that he has to stop, has to stop immediately."

"And what was Mr. Zakin's response?"

"He just kinda laughs, real obnoxious-like, you know. Sort of a sneer, really. He says, 'Oh yeah? And what if I don't?' "

"Did Mr. Gardiner reply?"

"Oh, yeah. He got all quivery. He was shaking head to toe. His eyes were rolling around in their sockets—it was like he had the d.t.'s or something." Peabody gripped the rail before him. "And then he threatened Zakin."

"He did?" Granny leaned in close, subtly cueing the jury to do the same, to hang on every word. "How so?"

"Gardiner said he had connections to powerful people. He said he had the goods on someone who could hurt Zakin and his friends real bad—all he had to do was snap his fingers and make it happen."

"Indeed." Granny edged toward the jury box, holding their attention, drawing out the suspense. "And what was Mr. Zakin's response to this threat?"

"He gets real up close and personal to Gardiner, see? Grabs his collar and practically lifts him up in the air."

"Do you remember what he said?"

"Oh, yeah. Yeah. I don't think I'll forget that as long as I live. I've never seen such a mean, hateful look. He stares right into Gardiner's face and growls, 'Don't threaten me, chump. Or it'll be the last thing you ever do.' "

Granny paused, letting the words hang in the air, forcing the jurors to play the line over and over in their heads. "The last thing you ever do." She let several more seconds of silence elapse before finally returning to her table. "No more questions, your honor."

Ben was hoping for a recess, but his hopes were not fulfilled. "Do you have any questions for this witness, Mr. Kincaid?"

"Yes, your honor. May I have just a minute to confer with my client?"

Judge Pickens grudgingly nodded.

Ben leaned close to Zak and whispered so that no one else could hear. "What's going on here? You told me you never met Gardiner."

"Well, I didn't," Zak insisted. "I mean, not really. It was just that one time in the corridor."

Ben's eyes flared. "You lied to me. *Again!*"

"It's not like I planned to meet him!" Zak insisted. He seemed frenetic, grasping. "All I wanted to do was take a leak, and this moron stops me in the corridor. I didn't even know who he was till he told me."

"You lied to me," Ben said. "You lied to your own lawyer."

"Oh, what the hell's the big deal? The jury was going to find out anyway. It's not like you could've stopped it."

"If I'd known, I could've prepared the jury for it. I could've warned them that there was an angry meeting, but that it's no proof of murder. Instead, I told them you'd never met the man, which wasn't true. They think I lied to them." Ben glanced back over his shoulder at the jury box. "And they're not likely to forget it."

"Mr. Kincaid," Pickens said, drumming his fingers. "If you intend to cross-examine, now's the time."

Ben turned away from Zak. There was nothing he hated worse than crossing a witness who had basically just told the truth. People shouldn't be victimized for doing their civic duty. But he had to do something to undercut this testimony. If the jury believed Zak had threatened Gardiner just before he was killed, how could they help but convict him?

Well, at least there was one obvious cross-ex point he could score.

"Mr. Peabody," Ben began, "you're aware that my client was the leader of the local Green Rage team, aren't you?"

"Well, yes. Sure."

"And you're aware that they oppose many of the activities of the loggers in the area."

"Sure. I read the papers."

"So how can we know that your testimony isn't tainted by your pro-logger bias?"

"My what?"

"You said you've lived here all your life. You must have friends, family. Your customers at the grocery store."

"Not really. Actually, we Peabodys may be the only family in Magic Valley that've never had anything to do with the logging industry. Frankly, I tend to side with the environmentalists."

Ben felt his heart drop to the pit of his stomach. And the

only thing that could possibly make him feel any worse was seeing Granny fold her arms across her lap, a self-satisfied ear-to-ear grin plastered across her face.

"Mr. Kincaid?" Pickens said. "Will there be any more questions?"

Ben's brain was racing. One of the cardinal rules of cross-ex was: Never quit on a down note. But he had been scraping just to come up with one line of questioning, and it had exploded in his face. How could he poke holes in the testimony of a witness who was telling the truth?

"I guess not," Ben said. He left the podium and slithered back to defendant's table. This was, he thought, in all likelihood the worst cross-ex of his entire career. His client lied to him, the prosecutor blindsided him, and he couldn't do a thing about it.

The judge began his pre-lunch spiel to the jury. Zak leaned close to Ben and whispered, "Hey, this isn't going too well, is it?"

Ben just couldn't come up with the words.

* 54 *

After the disaster of the morning, Ben had hoped for a long lunch break, if not a recess for the day. He didn't get his wish. Judge Pickens called for a short lunch break, then asked everyone to be back in the courtroom by one. It seemed the prosecution was almost finished, and he wanted to get through them all by the end of the day.

"Well," Christina said, as she returned to the courthouse after lunch, "it wasn't a great morning. A few setbacks, a few big surprises. Things can only get better."

Ben tried to smile. "I hope you're right."

Unfortunately, she wasn't. As it turned out, the biggest surprises were yet to come. Starting with this one:

"The State calls Rick Collier to the stand."

Rick? Both Ben and Zak flew to their feet. *Rick?* The second in command at Green Rage? The man who'd just been discharged from the hospital? He couldn't be testifying for the prosecution!

But he was.

Ben ran to the judge's bench, Granny clicking her heels close behind him.

"What's going on here?" Ben demanded. "He's not on their witness list!"

"And I apologize for that, your honor. I really do." Granny was doing her best to seem contrite. "But this witness just came to our attention this morning."

"Baloney," Ben barked. "They must've subpoenaed him."

"We did not," Granny said emphatically. "He's a volunteer."

Ben stared at her, flabbergasted.

"You can check that with my staff if you wish. We had no idea he was coming; he just showed up—with important information that has a direct bearing on this case. I wasn't even there when he arrived; I didn't find out about it until the lunch break."

She rustled around in her leather satchel, then drew out a file folder. "We've prepared this motion to amend the witness list, your honor, and I filed it on my way back to the courtroom." She handed a copy to the judge, then to Ben. "I know this is irregular—"

"Irregular?" Ben barked. "It's outrageous!"

"But we simply had no choice," Granny urged. "And when you hear what he has to say, your honor, I think you'll agree that justice is best served by letting him speak."

"Your honor," Ben cut in, "I must object to this in the strongest possible way. This is trial by ambush! We've had no time to prepare."

Judge Pickens held up his hand, his signal that Solon was about to speak. "I'm going to let the man have his say."

"But your honor!"

Pickens looked at Ben sternly. "I've ruled, Kincaid, so

stop arguing. If you need extra time to prepare your cross-examination, I'll give it to you. If you need any other accommodation, I'll consider it. I'm sympathetic—this is an unusual situation. But Granny's right—we don't serve justice by silencing important witnesses. I'll let him speak, then let you do whatever you need to do to have a fair opportunity to cross."

"Your honor, this is reversible error!"

"I don't think so. I'm sure Granny has documented the fact that the witness arrived at the last minute"—Granny nodded—"and under those circumstances, there's precedent for allowing him to testify, so long as the defense is treated fairly. And that's exactly what I'm doing. Now stop arguing and let's get on with the show."

Ben returned to defendant's table, a grim expression set on his face. Critical information, Granny had said. Rick had critical information about this case. What could it be?

"What's going on?" Zak asked, yanking Ben's shoulder. "He's not going to testify against me, is he?"

Ben nodded curtly.

"Would you state your name, please?" Granny asked, after Rick was sworn.

"Rick Collier. That's short for Richard." Ben noted that Rick was pointedly not looking toward defendant's table.

"And what do you do for a living?"

Rick shrugged. "Well, it's not much of a living, but I'm currently working in the Green Rage organization."

"Really? So you worked with George Zakin?"

"Extensively. I was generally considered the next in the chain of leadership. After Zak."

"What's going on here?" Zak whispered in Ben's ear. "He can't testify against me. He's my friend!"

I wonder, Ben thought silently. I just wonder.

Granny continued her direct examination. "Would you say you spoke with Mr. Zakin on a regular basis?"

"Oh, yeah." He flipped his ponytail back. "Like every day."

"About Green Rage matters?"

"Sure. But not only that. We confided in each other, you know? We told secrets."

Secrets. The word carved out a hollow space in Ben's chest. He didn't like the sound of that at all.

"Would you say Mr. Zakin was a dedicated environmentalist?"

"Oh, yeah. Absolutely. And then some. He was always pushing. Always urging us to do a little more."

"A little more . . . what?"

Rick shifted his weight. He was still studiously not looking toward defendant's table. "Well, Zak's favorite line was 'It's not enough to talk the talk. You gotta walk the walk.' "

"Walk the walk," Granny echoed. "And what exactly did that mean?"

"It meant take action. It's true. People in the environmental world tend to gripe a lot about everything that's wrong, but they're hesitant to do anything about it. But not Zak. He was always ready to take action to promote the cause. He was willing to do anything. Absolutely anything."

"Like planting bombs?" Granny suggested.

"Objection," Ben said. "Leading."

Judge Pickens waved his hand in the air, as if he thought this objection was the most trivial annoyance in the world. "Sustained," he said wearily.

Granny amended her question. "What kind of action was he advocating?"

"Tree spiking. Sabotaging cars and equipment. And planting bombs."

"Mr. Zakin advocated bombs?"

"Oh hell, yeah. Man, he was the expert on the subject. He could tell you all about what kind of ingredients to get to make a certain kind of bomb. Where to get them. How to make a small, contained implosion or a large, widespread explosion. Apparently he'd done a lot of bomb work in the past. Green Rage had never been involved in that sort of thing before. But as soon as Zak was on board, he started pushing for it."

"Were the other members receptive to this idea?"

"A few were. Hotheads like Al Green. But most of us thought it was too dangerous. Sure, we want to save the forests, but despite what people say, we really aren't willing to put trees before people."

Granny adopted a level, earnest tone. "Mr. Collier, I need to ask you another question—a very important question, so please think carefully before answering. Do you know if George Zakin has ever planted a bomb?"

Rick didn't hesitate a moment. "Oh, yeah. I know he has."

"Do you know if he planted the bomb that killed Dwayne Gardiner?"

Again no hesitation. "I'm certain of it."

"And why is that?"

Rick turned to face the jury before answering. "Because he told me he was going to do it."

A gasp pealed out from the back of the gallery. More audible murmuring and whispering followed. Judge Pickens banged his gavel on the bench, but a good half a minute passed before he brought the courtroom back to silence.

Granny didn't hold back. "And why would he want to plant a bomb? To further the environmental cause?"

"Nah." Rick's lips turned down at the edges. "To get Dwayne Gardiner."

The air in the courtroom seemed to become thick, heavy, as if everyone and everything were suspended in time.

"Let me make sure I understand you, Mr. Collier. Are you saying Zakin planted the bomb with the express intention of harming Mr. Gardiner?"

"I think so, yeah."

"And why would he want to do that?"

Rick glanced up at the judge, the jury, out into the gallery—almost everywhere except at Zak. "Because he was sleeping with Gardiner's wife."

If the reaction in the courtroom had been audible before, it was near deafening now. Several people—reporters, probably—leaped to their feet and headed out the back doors to spread the word of this major new development. Whispering and gossiping went from a buzz to a roar. Judge Pickens pounded his gavel furiously, threatening to clear the courtroom, trying to restore order.

Ben took advantage of the momentary chaos to have a short, curt conversation with his client. He was so angry he could barely speak. "You told me you didn't know Gardiner," he said bitterly. "You said you had no connection to him."

"But I didn't!" Zak said, imploringly. "I never met him till that night in the bar. It was his *wife*—"

Ben placed his hand on his forehead. This was just hopeless.

As soon as the courtroom was quiet enough for her to proceed, Granny did so. "And how do you know Mr. Zakin was having an affair with Lu Ann Gardiner?"

"He told me," Rick replied. "Hell, he told me frequently. I gotta tell you, Zak may be a great environmentalist, but when it comes to women, he's kind of a pig. Of the chauvinist variety."

"How do you mean?"

"He was constantly trying to pick up women, in some of the sleaziest ways you can imagine. He'd lie, cheat, steal—whatever it took."

"And is this how he attracted the attention of Mrs. Gardiner?"

"More or less, yeah."

"How do you know?"

"I was there when it happened. I was in the bar when he first picked her up."

"And when was that?"

"Oh, about three weeks before the murder. Apparently they really hit it off, 'cause they were banging away"—he stopped, looked up at the judge— "oh—excuse me. They were, uh, engaging in, uh, carnal relations every chance they got. Zak was having a great time. Till the angry husband found out."

"And when was that?"

"Just before the murder. Zak found out when Gardiner met him outside the bathroom at Bunyan's."

"Were you there?"

"No. But Zak told me all about it. Told me Gardiner was acting real weird, almost crazy-like. Said he threatened Zak, so Zak threatened back."

"Was Mr. Zakin disturbed by this encounter?"

"Very. Zak has a short temper, and he was having too much fun with Lu Ann to give her up. So he started thinking of ways to put the husband—Gardiner—out of the picture."

"To put him out of the picture—permanently?"

"That's what I think happened, yeah."

"And why do you think that? Did you see him plant the bomb?"

"Unfortunately, no. But I did see him leave camp that night with a full backpack. In retrospect, I realize the bomb was probably stuffed in there. And he left with something else—the Sasquatch suit."

"That's a lie!" Zak hissed in Ben's ear.

Granny blinked. "The Sasquatch suit?"

Rick nodded. "Right."

"Did that belong to Green Rage or to George Zakin?"

"Well, actually, there were two of them. We had one when Zak came, but he didn't think it looked real enough, as if he was an expert on what Bigfoot really looks like. So he bought his own."

"And why would he leave with the suit in the middle of the night?"

"Zak loved running around in that costume, hovering around the periphery of campsites, trying to bait poor suckers into calling in Bigfoot sightings. He had this idea that if enough of those calls came in, the Forest Service would have to take them seriously. And if the forest was identified as the habitat of an endangered species, logging would have to stop."

"That's a lie!" Zak shouted, springing to his feet.

Pickens pounded his gavel furiously. Ben grabbed Zak's arm and pulled him back into his chair.

"Mr. Kincaid—" Pickens started.

"I'll take care of it, your honor." He gave Zak a look that spoke volumes. *Stay in your seat and shut up!*

Granny continued. "What time did Mr. Zakin leave the Green Rage campsite?"

"It was a little after midnight."

"And do you know when he returned?"

"Sure. I was still up. It was around two in the morning."

"Two in the morning," Granny repeated. "Shortly after the murder. Thank you, Mr. Collier. No more questions."

Ben looked up and saw every face in the courtroom, including those in the jury box, staring his way. But they weren't looking at him—they were looking past him, at Zak.

And Ben knew why. Before, there might have been some measure of doubt in the brains behind those eyes. But not any longer, not after this testimony. Now every one of them thought they were staring into the eyes of a cold-blooded killer.

* 55 *

Zak grabbed Ben's shoulder just as he was rising to cross. "He's jealous," Zak whispered.

Ben froze. At the moment he really didn't want a damn thing to do with this client of his. But he supposed he had to listen. "Jealous?"

"Sure. That's what this is all about. He's always been jealous. Jealous 'cause they made me the top man on the team—promoted me over him. Jealous 'cause I was always able to get the chicks—and he couldn't. You think he was in that bar just for a tall cool one? He was trying to get laid. But it never happened. I could do it; he couldn't. Plus, I had kind of a side thing with Molly, and he was pissed about that. Plus, he's sweet on Deirdre."

"Deirdre?"

"Right. He wants her bad. But she's not interested. And"—he fell silent for a moment—"he thinks, anyway, that she and I are . . . intimate. That's why he's turned on me."

Ben nodded, then walked to the podium. It was possible, of course. God knows Rick must have some motive for turning on his friend and colleague, and that could be it.

Or, Ben mused, it could just be that Rick thinks Zak is a

murderer and he has a moral obligation to tell what he knows. A disturbing possibility.

Ben cut to the chase. "Mr. Collier, it's a fact that you and Zak have been close friends, isn't it?"

"We've worked closely together. I never considered him a friend."

"Did he consider you a friend?"

"I don't know. Probably."

"Do you think he trusted you?"

"I don't know." Rick pulled himself up, almost defiantly. "If he trusted me not to tell that he murdered someone, then he made a mistake. I don't countenance murder, not for any cause. And I won't cover it up, either."

Ben frowned. This wasn't going to get him anywhere. "Isn't it true that you were jealous of your friend Zak's . . . success with women? A success you never had."

"Absolutely not. I thought he was a sexist slimeball. Sure, I like women, and I like to be with them. But not if it means treating women in that abusive, degrading way. Leading them on. Lying. Trying to make it with three different women at once. I just won't do it."

Swell, Ben thought. Strike two. What could he try next?

"What about Deirdre? The dendrochronologist on the Green Rage team?"

Rick's eye twitched. "What about her?"

"You're in love with her, aren't you? You wanted her. And Zak had her. Not you."

Rick took a deep breath, then released it. "It's true that I think Deirdre deserves something better than that . . . philandering pig who can't keep his zipper zipped. But then, I think every woman deserves better than that. And besides, I'm involved with someone else."

Ben sighed. Strike three—and you're outta there. He was going to have to try a different approach. Nothing he said was going to make the jury forget what they'd heard from this witness. The most he could hope for was to give them something else equally memorable. "Mr. Collier, you understand the difference between fact and supposition, don't you?"

"Sure."

"When you're testifying, you're supposed to give the jury facts. But I noticed that a lot of times, you were giving them supposition—which is a nice way of saying you were just guessing."

"Is this a question?" Granny asked.

"I'll get to it." Ben flipped hurriedly through the notes he had taken during Rick's direct examination. "For instance, you said that you were certain Zak built and planted the bomb that killed Gardiner. But you didn't actually see him make the bomb, did you?"

"Well, no."

"And you didn't see him plant the bomb."

"Of course not."

"You never actually saw him with a bomb in his hands."

"No. But his backpack—"

"His backpack was filled with something. But you don't know what it was. It might've been a bomb, or it might've been his dirty laundry. You don't actually know, right?"

"Well, I think we can assume—"

"So now you're assuming, is that right? And assuming, of course, is just another word for guessing."

"I thought it was logical—"

"You weren't put on the stand to play Sherlock Holmes, sir. You were called to tell what you knew. What you *knew*. And you don't know what Zak had in his backpack, right?"

"I suppose."

"And you don't know if he made or planted that bomb, right?"

Rick caught his breath, took a few moments to think. "He told me he was going to take Gardiner out of the picture."

"Did he? Were those his words? Or yours?"

Rick bit down on his lips. "Well, I don't remember his exact words."

"You'd better, because this is absolutely critical. We need to know if Zak really said this or if it's something that came out of your imagination. What did Zak actually say?"

Rick paused. Ben could almost see the wheels turning inside his brain. "I think what he actually said was 'I'm going to take care of Gardiner.' "

"Take care of him? Now that's quite a bit different, wouldn't you say?"

"Not really."

"Take care of him could mean anything. That could mean he's going to let the air out of Gardiner's tires or pour a beer down his pants. Or stop seeing his wife."

"Well, given what happened—"

"Aha!" Ben pointed across the podium. "Now we get to the truth of the matter. You're not testifying about what you know. You're filling in the blanks of what you don't know, based on what happened later."

"It's common sense—"

"It is not common sense. It's attitude. You could've filled in the gaps in such a way as to exonerate your friend. But instead you chose to do it in a way that would crucify him."

Granny rose to her feet. "Your honor, he's not questioning the witness."

Ben continued unabated. "That was a decision you made, Rick, not him. You decided to paint Zak in the worst way possible. And why, I wonder? Could it be because he was promoted over you and made head of this Green Rage team? Could it be that you thought with him executed, you'd have Deirdre all to yourself?"

"Your honor!" Granny shouted. "This witness is not on trial."

Judge Pickens pounded his gavel. "I've had enough of this, Kincaid. Sit down."

"What about it, Rick?" Ben continued, shouting over the din. "Tell us why you turned Judas on your best friend! Tell us why you're so desperate to get him out of the way!"

"Kincaid! Sit down!" Judge Pickens had risen to his full height. He was towering over the bench, his arms outstretched. He looked like he was about to throw the gavel across the room like a tomahawk. "This examination is *over*!"

Ben folded up his notebook and returned to his table. He just hoped his dramatic demonstration had some impact with the jury.

Ben's eyes met Christina's. They didn't have to speak; he knew what they were both thinking. The jury had it all now:

means, opportunity—and motive. It would've been a stretch to make the jury believe Gardiner was killed just because he was a logger cutting down trees. But a malicious adulterer taking out a jealous husband? That was altogether too easy. That had the ring of truth to it.

The very dangerous ring of truth.

* 56 *

After a much-needed fifteen-minute break, Judge Pickens reassembled the court for the last witness of the day. The last witness the prosecution was going to call.

And thank God for that, Ben thought. Could it possibly get any worse than this?

As it turned out, it could.

"The State calls Marco Geppi to the stand."

Ben watched as Geppi was escorted to the front of the courtroom. Ben knew he had been Zak's cellmate in the county jail for the last several days, but Zak had sworn that he hadn't known the man before and that he hadn't told him anything incriminating, so Ben hadn't worried about it. At this point, however, it was becoming increasingly clear to Ben that Zak's word wasn't worth a hell of a lot. And he also had learned that Granny didn't do anything for no reason. If she wanted to put this man on the stand—as the last witness in her case, no less—that was reason enough to worry.

Geppi wasn't wearing prison greens, but it wasn't hard to imagine him in them, either. His hair was unkempt and his chin was stubbled. Had Granny decided cleaning him up wasn't worth the trouble? Or had she perhaps decided he would be more convincing if he looked like exactly what he was?

"Would you state your name, please?" Ben noticed that Granny wasn't smiling; for once, she was not suggesting to the jury that this witness was her friend.

Geppi cleared his throat, slumped forward slightly. "Marco Geppi."

"And where do you live?"

"At the moment, here in Magic Valley."

"And where do you currently reside?"

Geppi cleared his throat. "Cell Five of the county jail."

That got the jurors' attention. "Why are you there?"

"I've been arrested. Possession of an illegal substance."

"Narcotics?" Granny was smart enough to get all the dirt out early, rather than to leave it for Ben to make hay about on cross.

"Yeah. That's the charge, anyway."

"And is anyone else currently residing in the county jail?"

"Yeah. Since I arrived, there's been a guy in the cell next to me. Him." He pointed across the courtroom. "George Zakin. He told me to call him Zak."

"Did you know Mr. Zakin beforehand?"

"No. Never met the guy."

"Had you heard of his organization—Green Rage?"

"Can't say as I had." He bowed apologetically toward the jury. "I don't read the papers much."

"Well then," Granny continued, "in the time that you've spent with Mr. Zakin, have you come to like him?"

"Oh, he's all right. Kind of a chatterbox. If I've got to be that close to someone for that long, I usually prefer it to be someone who ain't so fond of talking."

Some of the jurors smiled.

Granny crossed to the jury side of the podium. "What exactly does Mr. Zakin like to talk about?"

"He's probably gotten to 'bout everything at one time or another."

Granny allowed herself a grin. "Can you identify some of his favorite themes?"

"Oh, you know. Trees are dyin' all over the world and soon there won't be any left. Magic Valley may have the world's largest cedar. Loggers are all dimwits and scumbags. That sort of thing."

"I see. Did he by any chance mention the murder incident that caused him to be incarcerated?"

Ben felt a cold clutching at the base of his spine. He'd prepared enough witnesses for direct to know that nothing is left to chance. You don't ask a question unless you know the answer—and like it.

"Oh, yeah. In great detail."

Ben could see the jurors ever so slightly inching forward. They understood now why this witness had been called. And they were anxious to hear what he had to say.

"And why would he talk to you?"

"Well, in part, 'cause he was bored, and in part, I think, 'cause he likes to brag. He's pretty fond of talkin' about himself, or so it seemed to me. I don't know why. Maybe he thought if he made himself out to be the big man, I'd be less likely to hassle him."

"For instance, what did he say?"

"Well, he bragged about how good he was with bombs, how many bombs he's planted to blow up loggers' equipment and stuff. Man, that boy hates loggers—just hates 'em. His face gets all twisted up and weird every time he talks about them. He's kinda crazy on the subject."

Ben heard a whispering in his ear. "This isn't true," Zak said. "This conversation never happened."

Granny continued her examination. "Did he mention any specific crimes?"

"Well, he mentioned some logger named Gardiner."

"Gardiner?" Granny repeated. "Dwayne Gardiner?"

"Yeah, that's the one. Man, he really had it in for that poor chump."

"Do you know why?"

"Yeah. He told me all about it. Told me he'd been drill—er, um, you know . . . sleeping with the man's wife."

"He told you this?" Granny reiterated. "The defendant himself told you this?"

"Oh, yeah. In great detail. More than I wanted to hear. He told me about all the positions they tried and all the kinky stuff they did. I'm no prude, but even I was kinda grossed out by some of it."

"Did he tell you anything more about this . . . relationship?"

"Yeah. Told me that just before the murder, the chump husband—this Gardiner sap—found out about it. Said he was pretty damn angry, too. Threatened Zak within an inch of his life."

"And what did Zak say he did in response?"

Geppi squirmed a bit in his chair. He glanced up at Granny, then proceeded. "He said he figured he'd better go after Gardiner before Gardiner came after him."

"The defendant said that?" Granny said in a voice the jury couldn't possibly miss. "And you heard it?"

"Sure thing. With my own ears. Told me all about how he planted a bomb on this thing, this . . . um, tree cutter, that's what it was. Set the bomb, then lured the poor chump out there, shot him, got away to a safe distance—then blew the thing sky-high."

The reaction could not have been greater had another bomb gone off in the jury box. The jurors' eyes widened like balloons; they looked at one another with astonishment and horror.

Oh my God, Ben thought quietly, trying not to display any visible reaction. Oh my God. What now?

Granny adopted a quieter tone. "Did Mr. Zakin tell you anything else about this . . . fatal incident?"

"Yeah. Told me he watched from a safe distance. Told me he watched Gardiner catch on fire and burn. And he laughed. That's what he said. He said he laughed the whole time. And then he thought, You logging bastard. Your wife's ass is mine."

Zak pressed himself against Ben's shoulder. "This is complete fiction, Ben. You've gotta believe me. I never said these things." He pressed even closer. "You gotta believe me!"

Ben didn't respond, couldn't respond. He didn't know what to say. He didn't know what to believe anymore.

"Mr. Geppi," Granny asked quietly, trying not to break the aura of horror and disgust that had enveloped the jury box, "why did you come forward with this testimony?"

"Well, I thought someone ought to know. I mean, I've done

some bad things in my time. Things I'm ashamed of. But this dude was . . . *cold,* you know? To burn someone alive just so he could keep on screwin' his wife? To sit there laughin' while the poor schmuck burned to death? That just gave me the creeps all over. This dude needs to be put away permanently. That's why I came forward."

"Thank you, Mr. Geppi. No more questions."

No more questions indeed, Ben thought. No more questions needed. The stake had been driven through Zak's heart but good. He didn't know how Granny had gotten this man to testify, but he knew what the effect would be if Ben didn't destroy him on cross.

The effect would be to eliminate any doubt in the jurors' minds whatsoever that Zak was guilty of murder—murder so premeditated and horrible that it begged for the death penalty.

* 57 *

The man was lying, Ben told himself, as he marched up to the podium. Whatever else you may think about Zak right now, this witness is lying. Problem was, there is nothing more difficult than getting a self-aware, unrepentant liar to confess. He would have to come on strong, like he held all the cards and there was no way Geppi could possibly escape his grasp.

"What did the prosecutor promise you, Mr. Geppi?"

Geppi blinked rapidly, his face the picture of innocence. "Promise me? I don't get you."

"You made a deal. Your testimony for a quid pro quo. I want to know what it is."

Geppi shook his head earnestly. "There was no deal."

"Are you trying to tell this jury you were not offered anything in exchange for your testimony?"

"It's true."

"No promise of immunity? No suspended sentence?"

"Absolutely not."

"The man's telling the truth," Judge Pickens said, interjecting. "Any plea bargain or request for immunity would have to go through me, and I haven't seen it. There's no deal."

Ben clenched his teeth together. There had to be some arrangement. Geppi had nothing to gain by this personally; Ben couldn't believe he would come forward with this pack of lies on his own initiative. But how could he prove it?

"If you don't have anything yet, maybe a promise was made. A promise of some reward in the future."

"There is no deal," Geppi repeated.

"Maybe Granny told you that after this trial was over, the charges against you would be dropped."

"I have already instructed my attorney to plead guilty," Geppi answered. "I'm just waiting for sentencing."

Damn! Ben knew there had to be something. But whatever it was, Granny had built a wall around it so tall and strong he couldn't break through. "So you're telling me the only reason you're testifying today is because you have such a highly developed sense of civic duty?"

Geppi looked down at his hands. "That's not . . . the only reason."

At last! Ben thought. "And what's the other reason?"

Geppi spoke haltingly. "I . . . I have a sister. Had a sister. Angela. Just a scrawny thing—but pretty, in her way. She was killed at a gas station. No fault of her own—she was caught in the middle of a robbery. It didn't make any sense." His hand covered his face. "But when I heard this man talk—brag—about what he had done to this logger, I thought of my sister. She died for no reason, through no fault of her own, just as he did. I understand he had a family too, a wife and a little boy. A boy about the same age as Angela." His voice broke, then trailed off.

Ben stared at the witness stand. What was going on here? Was that man actually crying up there? Ben had marched in determined to bring out the truth, and now this slimy convict had taken total control of the examination.

He glanced over at the jury. As far as he could tell, they were entirely sympathetic. Two of them looked as if they were about to cry themselves. He had no way to impeach this melodramatic story about Angela, and he knew that battering the witness would not win Zak any points with the jury. But he couldn't sit down now, not on this note. There had to be something else he could try. Perhaps if he showed how unlikely it was that this conversation ever took place . . .

"Mr. Kincaid," Pickens said. "Are you done?"

"Not quite," Ben said. He looked squarely at Geppi's tear-streaked face. "My client denies your story. Every word of it."

Geppi looked away, dabbing his eyes. "I'm not surprised."

"Why would he tell you about this? He doesn't even know you. He's smart enough to realize you might testify."

Geppi shook his head, his face the mask of tragedy. "Don't you see? He was bragging. He's proud of it—he's proud of what he done. All the hurting and killing, all the fighting and turmoil—he thrives on it. He thinks he's some kind of hero. A freedom fighter for the revolution. But he's not." Geppi's voice became low and almost guttural. "He's not. He's just a murderer. A cold-blooded goddamned murderer."

Judge Pickens rapped his gavel, but Ben noticed his heart wasn't really in it.

Ben proceeded to bring out Geppi's priors, based on the criminal history the prosecution was required to provide. A conviction for petty theft, another for possession. Geppi didn't try to deny them. And none of it made the jury forget what he had said before.

"I'm done," Ben said bitterly. He grabbed his notebook and stepped down.

Pickens gazed across the courtroom. "Anything more, Madame Prosecutor?"

"Nothing, your honor. The State rests."

"We'll resume the trial Monday morning at nine with the defense." He gave his closing instructions to the jury, then rapped his gavel. "Court is in recess."

It seemed as if half the gallery rushed forward to defendant's table—reporters asking questions, locals hurling epithets. Ben nodded to Christina, implicitly asking her to become a human shield while he and Sheriff Allen got Zak out of the courtroom. They had much to do.

As he left, though, Ben couldn't help scanning the jurors, still transfixed in their fourteen chairs. Their faces were transparent; he felt as if he could see right through to their brains. He knew what they were thinking.

If they were voting today, here, now, they would find Zak guilty. Guilty of murder in the first degree. And they would recommend the ultimate sanction.

FOUR

* *

Thus Far and No Further

* 58 *

"First of all," Ben said, keeping his eyes on the road, "we have to keep our heads together. Things always look bleak when the prosecution closes its case. The jurors' minds will begin to change when we start putting on our witnesses. At the very least, they'll begin to doubt."

"I don't know," Christina replied. "I looked at those faces. And I didn't see much doubt."

Ben made a left onto the highway. "We still have Molly as an alibi witness. She can put Zak in an entirely different place at the time of the murder. And she has the most honest face I've ever seen in my life. How could anyone not believe her?"

"Maybe," Christina said noncommittally.

"And we have the drug-pusher angle—Alberto Vincenzo."

"You really think that'll fly?"

"I do. Granted, I could use some evidence. But at least we have a theory. A good faith theory. A reasonable theory. It has to make the jurors wonder if the prosecution is giving them the straight scoop."

They were taking advantage of the weekend break to drive their rental car to Seattle. Mike had finally gotten someone at the DEA to meet with them, although he pointedly made no guarantees about what would happen when they arrived.

It took Ben and Christina almost three hours to get to Seattle, but Ben didn't mind a bit. They could both use a break from the drudgery of trial. For that matter, Ben was glad to be out of town. The longer he stayed in Magic Valley, the more claustrophobic it seemed. The walls were closing in on him. All the secrets and plots and conspiracies were like tentacles from some great unseen behemoth, slowly but surely tightening around his throat.

It was time for a change of scenery.

They arrived in Seattle just before three in the afternoon. As it turned out, the regional DEA office was about three blocks from the Farmer's Market. They resisted the temptation to shop; they had work to do.

They found the office building and, with even more difficulty, managed to park. Then they found themselves killing time in the lobby, thumbing through *People* magazine articles.

It was almost four-thirty when a fortyish-looking woman stepped out the interior door. "Mr. Kincaid?"

"Right here," Ben said, jumping to his feet. Together, he and Christina followed the woman back to her office.

It was a nice-size office, and decently decorated, too, which Ben was glad to see—it meant they hadn't drawn someone at the absolute bottom of the DEA totem pole. In fact, as the woman—Madeline Chessway—explained, she was the regional administrator for narcotics-related investigations in the State of Washington.

"So," Ben said, "if there's a DEA investigation going on in the state, you're going to know about it."

"I think that's a fair assumption," she said, folding her hands on her desk. "Now what can I do for you?"

"I'm looking for information about Alberto Vincenzo," Ben said. "He's a drug dealer. And, I understand, the subject of a DEA investigation."

"What's your interest in Vincenzo?"

"I'm handling a legal matter for a client. A murder trial. And I think Vincenzo may be involved."

"Well, if you think Vincenzo is going to be your star witness," Chessway said, "you can forget about it."

"All I want at this time is information," Ben explained. "I'm trying to put a lot of puzzle pieces together. And I think knowing more about him might help me fill in the gaps."

"Is this a drug-related homicide you're trying?"

"That's what I don't know," Ben answered.

"It isn't so far," Christina explained. "But we're looking for alternative motives."

"I see." Chessway's head bobbed. "It's a fishing expedition."

"That's not so," Ben said firmly. "We've already received some information from . . . an informant suggesting a link between Vincenzo and the murder victim. We're just trying to learn more."

"Well, in any case, there's no way I can help you." Chessway was a sturdy woman; not fat, but substantial. Her body language suggested that she was not to be trifled with. "DEA files are confidential."

"I'm sure that's the standard procedure," Ben said, "and with good reason. But this is a special case."

"We can't make special cases."

"Surely when there's a murder trial—"

"Am I supposed to believe your trial is more important than our work? I don't know you, Mr. Kincaid. I don't know if you're trustworthy. If I give you confidential information, I could put an entire investigation at risk. Not to mention any number of DEA agents."

"Look, if you want me to swear some kind of oath—"

"What are we, children? You gonna cross your heart and hope to die?" She shook her head. "Sorry, Mr. Kincaid. No go."

Christina edged forward. Ben was happy to let her take the lead. She had much better people skills, and he knew he was flopping. "Ms. Chessway, I don't think you understand. If we don't get this information, an innocent man could be convicted. And executed."

Chessway matched her note for note. "No, ma'am, I don't think you understand. Thousands of innocent people die every year due to illegal narcotics. I will not comment on any ongoing investigations. That is the DEA's policy and I will honor it."

Ben was incensed. "You're willing to let a man die because of some . . . policy?"

"What makes you so sure there's an investigation involving this Vincenzo?"

Why was she playing coy? Ben wondered. Ben could tell

she recognized Vincenzo's name the instant he uttered it. "I've received some . . . information," Ben said guardedly. "I know the prosecutor has a file."

"Then ask the prosecutor to produce it."

"I did. She refused."

"Take it up with the court."

Ben shook his head. "The prosecutor denies knowing anything about any such file."

"Maybe she doesn't."

"No, she's lying. I'm certain there's a file. Or was. She may have destroyed it by now."

"If you believe the prosecutor has engaged in misconduct, you should complain to the judge."

"I've complained. The judge isn't sympathetic."

Chessway leaned back in her chair. "Then I really don't see what I can do."

"You're refusing to help?"

"I'm refusing to reveal confidential information."

Ben could feel his anger rising. It seemed like everywhere he went, everywhere he turned, there was some panjamdrum of officialdom standing in his way. All these so-called public servants were supposed to be acting for the public good. Instead, they were hiding behind their desks and playing games while an innocent man was being pushed closer to a lethal injection.

"I want to speak to someone else," Ben said.

"I'm sorry. I'm the only person with any supervisory authority in this area."

"Then I want to speak to your superior."

"I don't have a superior in this office. You can file a complaint with the D.C. office."

"I don't have time for that." Ben gave it one last try. "Let's make sure we understand one another. When this trial starts Monday, I intend to argue to everyone in earshot that Alberto Vincenzo was involved in this crime—maybe even that he was the true murderer. And when someone starts complaining that I don't have enough evidence, I'm going to explain that there's a reason for that. And the reason is that all the evidence is in the hands of the government—and they won't give it to me!"

"Mr. Kincaid—"

"The press will of course pick up on that and start asking questions. I'll have to tell them everything. I may even give them your name."

"Mr. Kincaid—"

"And this is what I'm going to tell them. If the prosecutor has information she's not providing, she's guilty of a gross violation of the discovery code. If she's destroyed the file, she's guilty of obstruction of justice, which is a felony. The only way I have of catching her is to get information from you. And you won't cooperate."

"Perhaps you should take this up with the attorney general."

"Believe me, I will. But that won't exonerate you. By your inaction, you may be condemning an innocent man to death."

"Are you suggesting your client really didn't do it?"

"I assume every client is innocent. I have to. That's what defense attorneys do. And I want that information!"

Chessway stiffened. Her chin rose. "Mr. Kincaid, I don't believe we have anything left to say to each other."

"I do." Ben stood up and leaned over the woman's desk. "If George Zakin is convicted because you wouldn't help, I'll make you wish you'd never been *born*!"

Chessway appeared stunned. Even Christina looked shocked. A tense silence permeated the room for untold seconds.

Chessway stuttered. "Is that some kind of threat?"

Ben grabbed his briefcase and headed toward the door. "I don't make threats."

* 59 *

Ben returned to his office just after dark. After he and Christina returned to Magic Valley, he'd caught a quick supper at a diner off Main Street. A quick supper and a boring one. He'd never liked dining out by himself. But Christina had informed him she already had plans for the evening. Probably off having a tutti-frutti soda with the sheriff, Ben mused. Or maybe he finally managed to get her back to his place.

Which left Ben alone.

Well, he had work to do. It would be nice to have Christina's company, but he knew she would get her work done before the trial resumed. He just needed to make sure he got his own work done.

Out of habit, he headed toward the alley in the back of the building. As he approached the fire escape, he recalled that the last time he'd been here, he'd found Peggy hiding behind the Dumpster.

A smile played on his lips. Very melodramatic, he thought on reflection, if unlikely. But he couldn't complain; her brave rendezvous had turned his case around.

He reached for the bottom rung of the ladder.

And heard a rustling noise behind the Dumpster.

He gripped the metal rung and froze. Could this be happening *again*?

"Peggy?" he whispered. At least before, it had not been pitch-black in the alley. Now it was. He couldn't see who or what was back here with him.

"Peggy?" he said again. The short hairs on the back of his neck were bristling. He couldn't make up his mind. Should he race up the ladder? It seemed safest. But if he'd done that before, he would never have heard what Peggy had to say.

"Peggy?" he repeated urgently. His knees were beginning to tremble.

"I ain't no Peggy."

The deep voice boomed out from the trash. Ben felt his entire body tense.

"Who is that?" Ben asked. His voice didn't sound nearly as strong as he wanted it to.

There was no answer—nothing verbal, anyway. But he began to detect movement, a dark silhouette moving toward him. A very large silhouette.

"Wh-Who is it?" Ben repeated. "Speak up."

The huge silhouette kept moving till it was barely a foot away from him. That close, Ben was able to perceive a few distinctive features. Huge, muscled shoulders. Long black hair. A scar over his right eye.

"Vincenzo," Ben said, almost under his breath. "You're Alberto Vincenzo."

Vincenzo's face was like a rock, solid and unsmiling. "I am."

"And what do you want?"

Vincenzo placed his fists on his hips. "I hear you're runnin' around tellin' people I committed some murder," he growled. "And that makes me very, very angry."

Maureen blinked, then blinked again. It was becoming difficult to see. A light rain had started falling, barely more than a mist, but it was fogging her wire-frame glasses. With every passing moment, she became a little blinder. It was a situation she hadn't anticipated. Without her glasses, she couldn't see. And she couldn't wipe off her glasses—since at the moment she didn't have the use of her hands.

There were four of them, she and Al, Deirdre and Doc, all lined up across the road, chained to three barrels. These were standard shipping barrels, except they had been filled with cement—all but a narrow passage at mid-height where a four-inch PVC pipe ran through the diameter. Once the barrels were in place, the Green Rage team positioned themselves between them, put their arms through the pipes, and linked up. They used chains to lock in their arms. Given time, they could remove themselves by releasing the chains, but it was impossible for a third person to force them out.

Al, just out of the hospital, was beside her. She had told Al to stay at their new base camp and rest, but he had insisted; he wanted to be a part of this. Given all he had been through, she didn't see how she could deny his wish.

It was a desperate action, but it was their last chance. A convoy of trucks and equipment was scheduled to move into the largest section of the old-growth forest this evening; once they were in place, the conflict would be over. The loggers would have won. The forest would be as good as dead.

They couldn't let that happen. At least not without a fight.

The loggers driving the trucks had been mad as hell when they saw the Green Rage team chained across the only road in, but short of out-and-out violence, there wasn't much they could do. After exchanging angry words and nasty names, the man driving the lead truck told them he was going after the sheriff.

Who, unless Maureen missed her guess, would be the man driving the car with the flashing red light, headed this way.

"Be strong," Maureen reminded her team. "We're doing this for the forest."

"And for Zak," Al added.

Maureen nodded. She hadn't meant to make this personal, but she knew that now, after so much treachery and violence, for many of them it was. "Don't let them get to you. Don't feel like you have to answer back. Don't even listen. Stay cool. And above all else, remember—no violence."

She watched as Sheriff Allen strolled toward the barricade of barrels and bodies. He passed through an angry mob of loggers, fourteen or fifteen of them, all killing time till they could continue the convoy.

Sheriff Allen glanced at Maureen. "You in charge?"

"For today," she answered.

"You know this is a public road. These people got as much right as anyone else to use it."

"They're bringing in the means of destroying this ancient forest," Maureen said calmly. "We can't allow that to happen."

"They've got permits," Allen said. "I've seen 'em. The Forest Service has given them the okay to log in here."

"The trees don't belong to the Forest Service. They belong to humanity."

"Well, ma'am, I'll tell you something. I tend to agree with you on that score. But like it or not, these men aren't breaking the law. You are." He ran his finger along the brim of his hat. "I'm going to have to ask you and your friends to move along."

"We're not leaving." She tried to keep her voice free from any ego or anger. It wasn't a statement of defiance. It was simply a statement of fact.

"Well, you're going to have to go sometime. You can't stay here forever."

Maureen didn't answer. She knew they didn't have to stay here forever. All they had to do was to stay long enough to screw up the logging company's plans and burn up their budget. Time was money, and if they could keep the loggers idle long enough, they would eventually abandon this project.

"Surely you don't think you're going to outwait the logging company, ma'am. Hell, you folks'll get hungry long before that happens."

Again Maureen did not respond, but she reminded herself quietly that they all had candy bars and other easy edibles tucked in their shirt pockets or jackets—someplace they could get to them, even without the use of their hands.

"I've had as much of this crap as I'm going to take!" It was the hothead driver of the lead truck. He had close-cropped hair and was wearing a red cap that matched his shirt. "I've got a schedule."

"I'm sure you do," Sheriff Allen replied. "But that doesn't change the situation any."

"They put me in charge here," the driver shouted. "If this job gets screwed, it's going to be on my head."

"Sir, please stay calm—"

"What the hell kind of cop are you, anyway?" The driver's teeth were clenched together with anger and rage. "Aren't you supposed to enforce the law?"

"What do you want me to do? Rip their arms out?"

"I expect you to do more than talk!"

Sheriff Allen somehow managed to maintain a calm, level voice. "The only way I see that we're going to get through this barricade is to get some sledgehammers and take out these barrels. And we can't do that now, after dark. It's going to have to wait for tomorrow, if I can get enough men together, or Monday, most likely."

"Goddamn it!" The driver yanked off his cap and threw it to the ground. "I'm so sick of these sanctimonious pricks screwing up our work. They think they can get away with anything!"

"Sir, please remain calm."

"I'm sick of it. Sick! Sick of the law looking the other way. They're not scared of anything. Because time and time again, they get away with it."

Sheriff Allen reached out. "Sir, why don't you come with me—"

The driver slapped his hand away. "Goddamn it, if you won't put some fear into these people, I will."

"Sir, please."

The driver didn't listen. He turned and went running back to his truck.

"Sir? I can't allow—"

Allen's voice was drowned out by the roar of the semi's engine. A moment later, his headlights came on, glaring into Maureen's eyes.

"Oh my God," Maureen whispered.

She could see the driver's face through the windshield, could see the crazed determined look in his eyes.

"No. Please no."

Sheriff Allen ran toward the truck, screaming and shouting, waving his gun in the air. It made no difference.

The driver wasn't listening. He was oblivious to outside interference. There was only one thing on his mind now—as he shifted into first gear and pressed down on the accelerator.

* 60 *

Ben felt his knees shaking, which in turn caused his body to begin trembling. He willed his body to stop, but unfortunately it wasn't listening.

"Pretty dumb," Vincenzo said. His lips were curled in an exceedingly unpleasant expression. "Coming out to a dark alley alone."

Ben took a deep breath. "I wasn't expecting trouble."

"You're running around town accusin' me of some murder, and you weren't expectin' trouble? You must be some kind of stupid."

"I'm just a lawyer." Ben was trying to keep his voice even, without much luck. Ben wondered how long it would take Vincenzo to cripple him. The time would be measured in seconds. "I'm trying to defend my client."

"I got no problem with that," Vincenzo said. The scar above his eye seemed to throb as he spoke. "But when you started trying to pin the rap on me, that's when you screwed up." He poked a finger in Ben's chest. "Big-time."

"I know you're behind the new designer drug here in Magic Valley," Ben said. Flapping his mouth could get him killed, he realized, but he had to try to get some information out of this man while he had the chance. "I know you had contact with Dwayne Gardiner."

"Is that so?"

"And I know you went after my investigator."

Vincenzo's head twitched. "How is he, anyway?"

"He's fine, no thanks to you." Ben checked both sides of the alley. If only someone would happen by—like a cop. If only Christina would come zooming up in a getaway car to rescue him. But none of that was likely to happen. He was on his own. "What is it you want from me?"

"I want you to keep your mouth shut!" he barked.

"And if I don't?"

Vincenzo stepped even closer. His head hovered just above Ben's. "There is no 'if you don't,' Kincaid. Either you stop talking about me, or you stop talking—period!"

"I have an obligation to my client," Ben said, breathing fast. "I won't back away from anything that might save his life." He raised his chin. "So if you're planning to kill me, go ahead and get it over with."

Vincenzo's neck and shoulders throbbed and pulsated. His face twisted up with rage. He looked as if at any moment he might boil over and explode.

Ben clenched his eyes shut, waiting for the first blow to land.

And then all at once, Vincenzo's rage seemed to dissipate. He stepped away from Ben.

By the time Ben had his eyes open again, he was startled to see Vincenzo was laughing.

"Damn, Kincaid, you really are a tough customer, aren't you?" He laughed again, then slapped Ben on the shoulder.

Ben was so surprised he didn't know what to do or say. "Does this—does this mean you're not going to kill me?"

Vincenzo shook his head and smiled. "Relax, Kincaid. I'm a cop."

"No," Maureen gasped, under her breath. "It isn't possible . . ."

But it was. As she watched, horror-stricken, chained to the cement barrel, the man driving the truck shifted into first gear and started toward them. And he was only a hundred feet away.

"Stop!" Sheriff Allen shouted. The rain had picked up, and he and the loggers were getting drenched. "Stop right now!"

But the driver didn't stop. Maureen doubted if he could hear over the roar of his own engine. And she doubted if it would have made any difference if he could.

Deirdre screamed. She was just to the right of Maureen, so the scream was piercing and startling. Maureen would've jumped a foot—if she hadn't been anchored in place. Trapped like a fly in amber.

"He'll stop short," Maureen said, trying to calm the rest. "He's just trying to scare us. He'll stop."

But he didn't stop. He kept inching forward. Fifty feet, then forty, then thirty, gaining speed all the way . . .

As the truck careened forward, Maureen could see the expression on the face of the driver. He was wild-eyed, excited. Enjoying himself. And going faster by the second . . .

"No!" Deirdre shouted.

"Brake now," Maureen yelled. "Now, or it'll be too late."

A moment later, they heard the sound of the driver hitting his air brakes. But the truck didn't stop.

The front left wheels hit a slick mud slide, a road hazard created by the fresh rain. Despite the hissing of the brakes, the truck continued to careen forward, gaining speed from its own momentum.

Time seemed to slow for Maureen. Even though she knew everything that followed occurred in the blink of an eye, it seemed like a long, protracted horror, like a nightmare that wouldn't end.

"No!" Deirdre shouted. "Please, God, no!"

Sheriff Allen, standing in front of the barricade, waved his hat and fired into the air. It did no good. The other loggers scrambled for cover, desperate to get out of the way. At the last possible moment Sheriff Allen dived to the side of the road.

Through the windshield, the driver appeared frantic. He jerked the steering wheel to the left, almost jackknifing the truck. But still the cab continued moving forward, coasting on the slick mud. It veered left, aiming toward the side of the road.

But it was too little, too late. The truck would miss the dead center, but was certain to clip the left side . . .

Where Doc was chained down between two cement barrels.

Maureen saw Doc's eyes fly open, his lips part. But he was too scared to scream.

Maureen clenched her eyes shut. She did not want to see, and she didn't. But hearing was almost as bad. She heard the squealing of tires, the hissing of air brakes, followed by the sound of a huge semi impacting on a man's body, the sickening popping sound as the body was ripped away from its arms, the crunching sound as the body was ground under the truck's huge wheels.

The horrible thud after what was left of the body was spit out the back and flung seven feet across on the dirt road.

"Doc!" Deirdre kept screaming, over and over again. *"Doc!"*

But there was no answer.

* 61 *

"A cop?" Ben said incredulously. "You?"

Vincenzo nodded. "DEA agent, actually."

"But . . . but . . . I thought—"

"You thought what you were supposed to think. What we wanted you to think."

"But Sheriff Allen said—"

"Unfortunately, Sheriff Allen isn't in on this. I'm sure you can understand the need for secrecy. We haven't told anyone who doesn't absolutely need to know."

Ben shook his head with amazement. "But if you're not the one who's spreading this new drug around town—"

"Who is? That's the question I'd like to have answered, too. That's the whole point of this undercover operation."

"But the sheriff said you had a record."

"I've been maintaining this undercover identity for over two years. It hasn't been easy, either. It takes a while before the big boys will trust you."

"But how—"

"This drug didn't debut in Magic Valley. I've been tracking it for almost three years. Started on the southern West Coast, near the border. When I wasn't able to trace it by conventional means, I went undercover—deep undercover. No one at the DEA or the Justice Department will acknowledge that I'm working with them, so don't bother trying. To grab the attention of the boys I wanted, I had to sever all contacts and leave no trails behind. It's been slow work, but I've finally managed to infiltrate some of the highest echelons of the mob drug racket. The boys who are making the junk, shipping it around the country."

"Why are you here?"

"Because hard as I've tried, I haven't been able to discover who's been distributing the junk throughout beautiful downtown Magic Valley. And that's important to know. Because even if I cut off one source, a resourceful distributor will just find another one. And Magic Valley will have the same problem all over again."

"You think it's someone local."

"Not necessarily. But it's someone here or someone who comes here frequently."

"Any leads?"

"Leads, yes. Answers, no."

"But—" Ben's face was the picture of confusion. "If you're really a DEA agent, why did you attack Loving?"

"I didn't. I knew he was following me after I left Bunyan's, and I tried to lose him. But someone else attacked him."

"Who?"

"I don't know. If I did, I might know who the real drug dealer is."

"But the next night, when you found him on the bench, you tried to kill him with a baseball bat."

"If I'd wanted to kill him, I'd've killed him. I had the chance; I let him get away. All I wanted was to scare him—and you—so you'd get off my case. Unfortunately, as Chessway and I have both now learned, you don't scare easily."

Ben leaned against the brick wall of the building. This was more than he could really take in all at once. It was as if the world was changing right before his eyes. "Then you had no connection to Dwayne Gardiner."

"I know he was using the drug. I don't know where he got it."

"Still, if you know he was using it, that sets up another potential motive for his murder. It just means the suspect is the real drug dealer, not you." Ben stepped forward. "I need you to testify."

"Sorry, Kincaid. Not a chance."

"I'm serious. This is important."

"I'm serious, too. No chance in hell I'll testify."

"A man's life is at stake!"

"I'm aware of that. I'm also aware that hundreds of kids are dying every month because they get suckered into using this unsafe drug. Is your man's life more important than all of those?"

Ben fell silent.

"I've been building up this undercover operation for more than two years, Kincaid. Two *years*. If I testify for you, my cover will be blown. Back to square one. And those kids will go on dying."

"I can subpoena you."

"Can you? Let me give you a clue—Alberto Vincenzo isn't my real name. And you won't be able to get service on me. Even if you could, my contacts at the DEA would quash it." He chuckled. "Believe me, they were pretty pissed after that scene you staged up in Seattle. Did you really tell Assistant Director Chessway you'd make her wish she'd never been born?"

Ben stared down at the pavement. "I . . . may have . . . um, said something along those lines."

"What balls. I love it." He grinned. "But seriously, if you start firing subpoenae and screwing up our investigation, they'll come down on you hard. Threats, injunctions. An IRS audit. Maybe you'll get picked up on parking tickets, or a reefer will mysteriously appear in your coat pocket. You don't want to screw with these people. Especially since, in the long run, it won't do you any good."

Ben's fists clenched. He wanted to find a way around all this, some way he could still help Zak. "If you're not planning to help me, why are you here?"

"Two reasons. For one, I want you to stop telling people I'm a murderer. That kind of attention I don't need. The big boys down south might not let me through the door if they think I'm too hot. I thought I could scare you into silence, but that didn't work. So now I'm taking you into my confidence and hoping you have the sense to keep the secret to yourself."

"And the other reason?"

"You may think I'm a coldhearted bastard who doesn't care if your client fries, but I'm not. If your man is innocent, he should be exonerated. So I didn't want to see you going into the courtroom telling everyone that the real murderer is Alberto Vincenzo—a man who doesn't even exist. You'd go down in flames. So as a personal courtesy, I'm giving you this tip—think of something else."

Easy to say, Ben thought. Not so easy to do.

"Anyway, I've gotta split." He started back down the alley.

Ben held up a hand. "Wait. If I need to talk to you again—"

Vincenzo shook his head. "You'll never see me again." An instant later, he had disappeared.

Ben fell back against the brick wall. What a night this had turned into. One moment he'd been certain he was about to die. The next moment he saw his entire defense theory crumble into dust.

He supposed it was best that he knew the truth, that he didn't try to convince a jury that Vincenzo was the murderer. But that left a gigantic hole in his trial notebook. He was a defense attorney with no defense.

What was he going to tell that jury Monday morning? How was he going to save Zak's life?

After Doc was crushed and the truck came to a halt, everything seemed to blur for Maureen. She was aware that in the midst of their panic and horror, the remaining members of Green Rage managed to extricate themselves from the barricade. It wasn't easy, but by relaxing their fists and twisting their arms, they were able to release themselves from the chains. Maureen was the first to get free, and the first to run back to see Doc.

Or what was left of Doc.

She hobbled off into the woods, where she spent at least ten minutes in dry heaves, sick as a dog. It had really happened, she kept telling herself. They had all known it was possible, had all talked about it. But no one had ever envisioned something so . . . horrible. No one foresaw this.

In the turmoil and confusion of the aftermath, in the rain that was now pounding down on them, only Sheriff Allen managed to keep his head together. He called for the coroner, then called for his homicide team members, who were getting more work in a week than they'd had the previous year. He tried to arrest the driver for reckless conduct homicide, but the man had disappeared.

Al finally freed himself from his chains. "They killed him!" he kept screaming, as if there was someone there who didn't already know. "They killed him!"

Sheriff Allen tried to subdue him. "Sir, please try to remain calm."

Al brushed the sheriff aside. "Doc is *dead*!"

"Please, sir. I think it would be best for everyone if you—"

"Get away from me!" Al rushed past him, making a beeline for the remaining group of loggers, now all huddled together on the side of the road. *"Murderers!"* he screamed. His face flushed red. Veins stood out in his neck.

Sheriff Allen ran up behind him. "Sir, I'll take care of this."

"You can't take care of anything!" Al screamed. "They destroyed our camp. They beat us up. They *whipped* Rick. They *killed* Tess. And now they've killed Doc. They ran him down like a dog. Like some cheap road kill!"

Maureen shuddered. She had never seen Al like this.

"Sir," Sheriff Allen insisted, "if you don't calm down, I'll have no choice—"

"This isn't over!" Al shrieked. He was inside the circle of loggers now, right in their faces. "You'll pay for what you've done here. You'll *pay*!"

"That's it," Allen said. He slipped a pair of cuffs over Al's right wrist, then whipped his arm behind his back. "I'm putting you under protective custody until you calm down."

"I will get back at you!" Al screeched, even as Allen hauled him away in the driving rain. His voice raised bumps on Maureen's flesh. "This isn't over. Doc will be avenged. You'll *pay* for what you've done!"

* 62 *

On Sunday, the town of Magic Valley was angry, confused, disoriented. By Monday morning, it was bedlam.

Ben spent the remainder of the weekend trying to make some sense of the tragedy, trying to figure out what had happened and why. Doc was dead—horribly so—and the logger who had mowed him down had somehow vanished. Ben managed to see a photo of the man the sheriff was circulating. Ben knew he had seen that logger before, but he couldn't place him at first. It was not until dinnertime that the light finally dawned.

He'd seen the man in the courtroom, the first day of trial. He'd seen him talking to Slade.

The man who killed Doc was a friend of Slade's—more than likely an employee. That put an entirely different perspective on everything.

Meanwhile, the overtaxed coroner's office collected Doc's remains and did their best to reassemble them. A funeral was scheduled. Ben thought it likely it would be a closed-casket ceremony.

Ben pleaded with the remaining Green Rage members to stay the hell out of sight. Al had gone into town for groceries and had almost been lynched. It seemed the town was taking the exact opposite of the reaction Ben would've expected; instead of being more sympathetic to the environmentalists, they were more hostile. Troublemakers, Ben heard passersby sniff. Only got what they asked for. Never would've happened if they hadn't barged in and started making trouble.

After the Al incident, the others agreed to remain either in the courthouse or at their new camp. But given the current climate, Ben wasn't sure even that was safe enough. He was only sure of this: this town was now a powder keg, a smoldering cauldron of hate and hostility.

And in the midst of all this turmoil, he was supposed to try a murder case. More accurately, he was supposed to put on a defense.

Except he didn't have one. Not anymore. Not after the meeting with Vincenzo. He had Molly, an alibi witness—but no theory. No way to make it stick. No way to make the jury believe it.

He spent most of Sunday preparing Molly to take the stand. To his relief, she was a fine witness—attractive, earnest, simple. Ben didn't see how even those with an axe to grind against Green Rage could find fault with her.

He tried not to let it show, but Ben knew perfectly well that if Zak had any hope at this point, it rested with her. He walked her through her testimony over and over again. He was pleased to see she was willing to put in the time.

"I don't care how long it takes," Molly said, brushing her long brown hair behind her ears. "I want to be there for Zak. I'll do whatever it takes to help him."

"I appreciate that," Ben said. "Very much." He had worried that if word got back to her about Zak's many affairs, as revealed in the courtroom, her ardor for him might diminish. Fortunately, that didn't seem to have happened.

"Zak has done so much for us," Molly said quietly. Her tone made him believe every word—just as he hoped the jury would. "This is my chance to pay him back a little."

By the end of the day, she was ready to take the stand. It wasn't much, perhaps, but she was all he had. Ben just hoped it was enough.

Monday morning, Ben met Christina outside the courtroom. "Ready to go?"

She nodded grimly. "So is Molly."

If Ben had a friend other than Christina in this courtroom, he didn't know who it was. Except for Molly, the Green Rage team had wisely decided to stay away. Nonetheless, the gallery and the hallways outside were packed, filled to the brim with angry, hostile spectators. Ben felt as if he were walking the gauntlet just trying to get to court.

By the time he arrived, Zak was already there, and Zak had already heard the latest news. There was no possible way Ben could console the man. He didn't even try.

All too soon Judge Pickens brought the court back into session. "Would the defense like to call its first witness?"

"We call Molly Griswold to the stand."

Molly made her way to the front of the courtroom. She was dressed in a simple but attractive dress, pastel blue and pink. Like something a teenager might wear to Sunday school. Which was exactly the image Ben wanted to convey to the jury.

After taking the oath, she took her seat in the witness box. Ben had her introduce herself, say where she was from, and establish that she was a member of the Green Rage team.

"Do you know a man called George Zakin?" Ben asked.

"Of course. I've known Zak as long as I've been in Green Rage. He's our team leader."

"Do you consider yourself his friend?"

"Sure. He's been very kind to me."

"Are you close?"

"I think so, yes." She bowed her head slightly. "We were . . . intimate. For a time."

"Molly, I'm going to ask you to turn your mind back to July thirteenth." Ben couldn't rid himself of an anxious pins-and-needles feeling. Too much rested on this witness. Every question intensified the nervous gnawing in the pit of his stomach. "Where were you around midnight?"

"I was at the Green Rage camp. In the forest."

"Asleep?"

"No. There had been a late strategy meeting. It went way overtime. It was just ending around midnight."

"Who else was at the meeting?"

"All the team leaders. Zak, Maureen, Al. Rick and Deirdre. Doc."

"So Zak was there—at midnight."

"That's right."

Ben drew himself up. "Molly, another Green Rage member, Rick, has testified that Zak left the camp about then, carrying a Sasquatch suit and a bomb. Do you recall anything like that?"

Molly looked directly at the jury. Her wide brown eyes seemed earnest and unblinking. "It's true that he left the camp. But he wasn't alone." She drew in her breath. "I was with him."

Several eyebrows rose in the jury box. Until then, they probably assumed Molly was on the stand as a character witness. Now they realized what she had to say was far more important.

"And the gear?"

"Didn't exist. I've seen the suit, but Zak didn't have it with him that night. And he certainly didn't have a bomb."

"Was he carrying a backpack?"

"No."

"You're sure about that?"

"Absolutely."

Ben nodded. Thank goodness. This was working like a charm. So why wasn't the gnawing in his stomach subsiding? "Where did the two of you go?"

"Not far from camp. About a mile down a trail—in the total opposite direction from where the tree cutter exploded."

"Why did the two of you leave camp?"

"Actually, it was my idea." She paused, then glanced at the jurors, just as Ben had told her to do. "I wanted to talk to him—alone. So we had to leave camp." She smiled. "Tents don't afford much privacy."

"What did you talk about?"

"Just us. Personal things. Our plans for the future. Probably boring to anyone else. But we had a lot to discuss."

"Did he mention any anger or hostility toward Dwayne Gardiner?"

"Never."

"Did he say anything about planting a bomb?"

"Absolutely not."

"How long were the two of you together?"

"A little over three hours."

Ben paused, letting the jury drink it all in. "Three hours? That would be from a little after midnight to a little after three?"

"That's correct."

"So you were with him at the supposed time of death. Around one A.M."

"That's true. We saw the flames and heard the explosion from a distance. We didn't know what it was at the time, but in retrospect, it's obvious that it was the bombed tree cutter."

"Did Zak ever leave you, Molly? Even just for a moment?"

"No. Not once."

"And you and Zak were never anywhere near the explosion?"

"That's right. Zak wasn't there." She looked directly at the jurors. "He didn't kill that man. I know it."

Internally, Ben treated himself to a huge sigh of relief. "Thank you, Molly. No more questions."

* 63 *

Ben sat down at defendant's table with a sense of calm like nothing he had experienced for days. Molly was so good up there, so sincere. The jury had to believe her. At the very least, her testimony must've planted the seeds of doubt—and that was all he needed to save Zak's life.

He watched as Granny strolled up to the podium. He knew perfectly well what Granny's first line of attack would be. And they were ready for it.

Granny didn't pull any punches. "Ms. Griswold, are you George Zakin's lover?"

"You mean now, or ever?"

"Ever."

She nodded. "There was a time . . . shortly after I came to Green Rage, when he and I were involved. But it's over now. Zak found someone else . . . and so have I. In fact, that's one of the main things we talked about that night. Just clearing the air." She paused. "So if you're planning to suggest that I would lie to save him because we're sleeping together, forget it. It won't wash. If anything, by your standards, I should be hostile to him, since he broke up with me. But none of this matters, because I wouldn't lie. Not for him or anyone else. I'm testifying today because what I have to say is the truth, and I don't want to see an innocent man convicted for a crime he didn't commit."

Yes! Ben squeezed his fists together. He wanted to jump up in the air and click his heels, but he suspected Judge Pickens wouldn't approve. Molly was brilliant, even better than in their practice sessions. He was on cloud nine.

After that humiliation, he expected Granny to give up and sit down. But she didn't. In fact, as he peered across the courtroom, he noticed that she didn't even appear particularly perturbed.

"Ms. Griswold," Granny said, "are you familiar with a clothes store on Lincoln called Emma's?"

"Sure. I know it well. I've been by there several times. They have some lovely dresses."

"Have you shopped there?"

Molly smiled. "Well, it's out of my price range. But I like to look."

A deep line furrowed Ben's brow. What was all this talk about dresses and shopping? What was Granny up to?

"Have you been inside?"

"Not often. I just like to window-shop."

The corners of Granny's lips turned up, in what was perhaps the most wicked smile Ben had ever seen in his life. "In fact, Ms. Griswold, isn't it true you were window-shopping in the early morning hours of July thirteenth?"

Molly looked horrified. "Of course not. Maybe later in the day—"

"No, in the early morning." She glanced down at her notes. "At one-fourteen A.M., to be precise."

"No. It isn't true!"

"Oh, but it is, Ms. Griswold. It is." She walked over to the bailiff, holding a large black-and-white photograph. "This photo was printed from a videotape. The videotape was inside the surveillance camera in Emma's—on the morning of July thirteenth. I have a copy of the original tape, which defense counsel is free to view at his leisure."

"How about now?" Ben said. He was getting a horrible, dreadful feeling that he knew what was on the tape.

"You can have it during the break," Judge Pickens said. "That'll be soon enough."

"It should've been produced before trial," Ben responded. "This isn't even on the exhibit list."

Granny held up her hands. "This is rebuttal evidence, your honor. We had no way of knowing defense counsel would put on this witness." She established the provenance and chain of custody of the tape and photo, then moved that they be admitted into evidence. The motion was granted.

Granny gave a copy of the photo to Ben, then passed another to the jury, so each of them could hold it in their hot little hands.

The photo was time- and date-stamped: 01:14 A.M., 07/13. The photo showed the front window of the store, and just beyond the window display, a face pressing up against the glass.

Even in the grainy black-and-white photograph, the face was unmistakable. It was Molly.

"Ms. Griswold, a passerby saw you in front of the window and, after she read about the murder the next day, thought it might be important, so she notified the store. They managed to save the tape before it was automatically erased." Granny passed another copy of the photo to Molly. "Care to explain?"

Molly stared at the photo with undisguised horror. "There must be some mistake."

"There's no mistake. I've checked and double-checked everything, just as I'm sure defense counsel will. There's no doubt about it, ma'am. You were there, in front of that store, just after one in the morning. Not in the forest. And not with George Zakin."

Molly's hand flew to her face. Tears began to stream out of her eyes. "Oh, God. I didn't mean to—" Her arm reached out toward defendant's table. "I just wanted to help you, Zak. I just—" More tears followed; her voice was choked with anguish. "I still love you, Zak. Even now. I still love you."

"Ms. Griswold," Granny said quietly, "you were not with George Zakin at the time of the murder, were you?"

At first she reacted only with tears. Then, after several painful moments, her head began to weave its way back and forth. "No."

Everything went silent, dead, as if Ben were traveling in an airplane but the engines had cut out and they were in free fall, spiraling downward toward an inevitable crash.

"Thank you," Granny said. "That's all."

Gradually the courtroom seemed to normalize. Molly returned to the gallery, glancing at Zak as she passed, then covering her tear-stained face with her hands. Ben felt himself reentering the stream of life as the judge called for a recess till the afternoon.

And with that, it was over. The cross-examination and, Ben knew, the absolute last vestige of hope for the defense.

* 64 *

"You knew she was lying!" Ben shouted, after they returned to Zak's cell. "You *knew* it!"

Zak was pacing back and forth across the tiny cell. "Hey, so I don't want to be fried. Sue me!"

"You let me put a liar on the stand! That's inexcusable!"

"Aw, clam up already."

"I have never in my life put on a witness I thought was lying—"

"And you still haven't."

"But everyone in that courtroom thinks I did! They don't know my idiot client doesn't have the sense to tell his lawyer the truth!"

Zak pressed himself into Ben's face. "Look, this isn't about you, okay? I'm the one who's on trial. It's about *me*!"

"That's the whole point, you blithering idiot. It *is* about you! And my defense of *you* has been systematically undermined because you don't have the sense to tell me the truth!"

Zak threw himself down on the cot. "It wouldn't have made any difference."

"It would! If I'd known Molly was lying, I would've told you we couldn't use her. In case you haven't noticed, the prosecutor isn't an idiot. She knows how to smoke out a liar. Putting perjured testimony on the stand could only hurt you. Which it did."

"Man!" Zak flung his head back on the pillow. "I still can't believe she cracked like that. Just because of a little picture. Stupid cow."

Ben's face burnt red, smoldering. "How dare you—" In frustration, he ripped the pillow out from under Zak's head and tossed it down in his face. "You should be calling that woman a saint! Do you know how hard it was for her to do that? To sit up there and perjure herself for you?"

"Uh, Ben." Christina was out of the firing line, at the side of the cell, next to the window. "About that."

"What?"

She motioned him over to the window. "Get a load of this."

Ben walked beside her, anxious to get away from his client. He craned his neck and peered through the paned and barred window.

The view wasn't very scenic—just an alley behind the jailhouse. But in this instance, that provided an eyeful.

There were two people in the alley leaning against a Jeep, and Ben knew both of them. One of them was Rick Collier, the turncoat Green Rager who had helped drive one of the biggest nails in Zak's coffin.

The other was Molly Griswold, who minutes before had stepped off the witness stand after Granny destroyed her.

And they were kissing.

Key words and phrases raced through Ben's brain. *He was a pig to women,* Rick had said. *Never treated them well.* And then Molly: *He was the one who broke up with me.*

She knew that store, Ben remembered. She'd been in there. She knew they had a video camera.

And then Ben recalled another phrase, one from last night's witness prep.

Zak has done so much, she said. *I just want to pay him back.*

The couple in the alley were still kissing. It was obvious that this was not a new relationship.

They had each managed to get back at Zak, Ben realized. Rick by exposing his true feelings. And Molly by hiding them.

Zak was alone in his cell lying on his cot when Granny appeared out of nowhere.

"Lawyer take a powder?" she asked.

Zak didn't even look up. He didn't know why she was here and he didn't care. "Hadn't he been here long enough? Man, if I go over that testimony one more time I'm gonna hurl."

Granny smiled. "I'm surprised he bothers."

"Well, he's an optimist. He still thinks there's hope."

"And you?"

"I don't pretend to know. What do you think, Madame Prosecutor?"

"I think you've got a date with the Big Needle," she said, approaching the bars. "But sometimes juries fool me. Not often, but sometimes. And I look at you and I think—well, he's handsome. Big baby-blue eyes. Used to handling himself in public. If he's really good on the stand, he might possibly sway one of the jurors. And unfortunately, one is all it takes."

"Is that why you're here?"

"As a matter of fact, yes. I've decided to take out a little insurance."

Zak sat upright. "What are you talking about?"

"When Kincaid puts you on the stand," she explained, "I want you to cave."

"What?"

"Refuse to testify. Take the fifth. Get mad. I don't care what you do. Just don't testify."

"You're out of your mind."

"I don't care if you answer the easy stuff, like your name and address. But when he takes you to the night of the murder, you freeze. You don't say a word."

Zak pushed himself off the cot. "Lady, I think trial stress has deadened your brain cells. You must be crazy if you think I'm going to take a dive on the witness stand."

"You know, I thought that would be your reaction. That's why I haven't been here before." She leaned forward, exposing a generous amount of prosecutorial cleavage. "I kept thinking—how can I get to him? He's basically self-centered, selfish, cares only about himself. I can't threaten him with anything worse than what I want—death. How do I get to him?"

Zak strolled slowly toward the bars. "And what did you come up with?"

"Well, I remembered how nice everyone says you are to one of those Green Rage clowns. Deirdre, to be specific. Rick Collier mentioned it. Even Kincaid mentioned it. At first, I figured she was one of your many female conquests, but my informants told me that wasn't so. So what the hell was she to you? I couldn't figure it out."

Zak's eyes grew dark and narrow. "And?"

"And so I sicced a team of investigators on it. And early this morning they finally brought me the answer I wanted." Granny smiled from ear to ear, like a crocodile with way too many teeth. "She's your sister."

"You bastard," Zak growled.

"Deirdre isn't even her real name. Her real name is Dana Zakin, but she changed it because—get this—she's hiding from the law. Seems there's a warrant out on her for possession of over ten kilos of cocaine, with intent to distribute."

"She didn't have anything to do with it!" Zak said. "She didn't even know about it. It was this asshole she was living with. But the apartment where the cops found the junk was in her name. And she was on the premises."

"You know, I figured there was probably some explanation like that. But it doesn't really matter, does it? Ten kilos—my goodness. That's worth at least eight years in the slammer. Even for a first offender. And you know, as I was telling someone else just the other day—life in prison is not fun. She'll be sent to the Collingsgate women's facility. It's a hellhole. Violence, cruelty, rape—it happens every day at Collingsgate. They'll love a pretty little thing like your sister." She shook her head. "Dana won't last a year."

Zak's teeth were clenched tightly together. "What is it you want?"

"I already told you. You go on the stand and zip your lips. If you do, I'll tear up my information and the cops back in Tulsa will probably never find her. But if you don't, I'm afraid your sister has a very bleak future. And a short one."

"But if I don't testify, they'll kill me!"

"Don't you get it yet, Zak? You're dead already. The only question is whether your sister goes down with you."

Zak's face twisted up in a bitter snarl. "You're a real bitch, you know it?"

"As a matter of fact, I do." She pushed forward on her tiptoes and kissed him on the lips. "And now you do, too."

* 65 *

Don't give up hope, Ben kept telling himself, as he approached the podium to begin Zak's questioning. The jury will know. You have to act as if you have all the cards. As if you have nothing to worry about. He'd had dark moments at trials before. He knew any trial could be turned around by one stellar witness.

He just hoped Zak was the one. Because he was the only one Ben had left.

"Would you state your name for the record, please?"

Zak cleared his throat. "George Zakin."

"And where do you live?"

"I've been staying here in or near Magic Valley for over four months now." He glanced at the jury. "I'm a member of Green Rage. In fact, I'm the team leader."

Ben spent several minutes having Zak talk about his activist background, first in the anti-Klan group, then in the animal rights organization, then in the environmental world. Ben hoped someone in the jury box would admire his dedication, his unselfish works—even if they didn't particularly admire the cause.

After that, they moved into more dangerous but necessary waters. He asked Zak about his prior bomb-related conviction. Zak handled the question with finesse. He didn't back away from the fact that he had occasionally built bombs to benefit a cause. But he emphasized that he always took extreme precautions to ensure that no living creatures would be caught in the explosion— only machinery. He had never hurt another human, he said.

"I know sometimes people have the wrong idea about environmentalists," Zak said. "That we love trees but hate people. But it isn't so. People always come first in my book. I just think people will be a lot better off if they still have an ozone layer, don't live in greenhouse temperatures, and can occasionally take their children for a walk through a verdant ancient forest."

Ben was modestly encouraged. He thought Zak was making a good impression—at least, as good as was possible, given the circumstances. At any rate, they were giving the jury something to think about when they retired.

"Thank you, Zak," Ben said when the background was completed. "Now I'm going to have to ask you a few questions about the crime with which you've been charged. I know some of this will be unpleasant for you. I just have to ask you to bear with me."

"Of course."

"Zak, did you know Dwayne Gardiner?"

Before answering, Zak glanced quickly at Granny, who was sitting at the prosecution table. That was odd, Ben thought. Why would Zak be checking her? "Not really," Zak answered. "The first and only time I ever met him was when he stopped me in the hallway in that bar, just before he died."

"What did he want?"

"The account you've already heard was essentially accurate," Zak said, turning toward the jury. "He had just found out his wife was having an affair, and he was angry about it. He threatened me. I tried to calm him down—without much luck."

"Did you threaten him?"

"Absolutely not. I am a firm believer in nonviolence. I would use force only in defense, and fortunately, it didn't come to that."

"Did you purchase bomb materials at Georgie's pawnshop?"

"I did."

"Did you say, 'I'm going to teach a logger a lesson he'll never forget'?"

"No, I did not. That's one part the witness got wrong. I was trying to explain the conservationist's viewpoint, how inflexible the logging industry is. I said, 'I'm going to teach some loggers a lesson they'll never forget.' "

"And what did you mean by that?"

"I meant that if they tried to harm us, or the forest, as of course they have repeatedly, Green Rage would take action to defend ourselves. In the same nonviolent manner that we always have."

"Now Zak," Ben said, "you say you're nonviolent, but you've also admitted using bombs. In most people's eyes, bombs are pretty violent."

"True. I guess what I should be saying is, we respect human life. We might hurt machinery in order to save a forest. But we would never harm a human being. Never."

"Zak, I'm going to have to ask you an unpleasant question

now. Were you having an affair with Dwayne Gardiner's wife?"

His lips made a little frown. "Yes. I'm not proud of that. It was a mistake. But I should point out that when I first met Lu Ann, over at Bunyan's, I didn't know she was married, and she didn't tell me, either. I didn't know till almost a week later—and even then I didn't hear it from her. By that time, well, things had already gone too far."

"Did you think about breaking up with her?"

"I did break up with her. Told her it was over. She wasn't happy about it, either. I gather relations between her and her husband were not too hot. Anyway, she was really mad—screamed and shouted, threatened me."

"And was this before or after Dwayne Gardiner confronted you?"

"Before. I figure it was only after she got ticked off at me that she told him. That's why the whole thing was so stupid—here he was yelling at me about an affair, and I'd already terminated the thing on my own."

Ben checked the jury out the corner of his eye. Having his client participate in adultery was never going to be a selling point, but Ben was convinced it was better to be up front about the negatives than to try to hide them. Juries were smarter than most people gave them credit for—and they were more likely to be forgiving to a confessed sinner than to a liar.

"Have you seen Lu Ann Gardiner? Since you terminated the relationship?"

"Not once. When it was over, it was over."

"Did you bear any ill will toward Dwayne Gardiner?"

"Of course not. If anyone had an axe to grind, it was him, not me."

"You didn't have any bad feelings toward him?"

"No. I was sorry he disagreed on the environmental issues—I wish we could get more loggers to see things from our long-term global perspective, rather than from their narrow economics-based viewpoint. But I had no grudge against him in particular."

"Thank you. Now I'm afraid I'm going to have to take you

back to the night of the murder. The early morning, actually. Okay?"

Zak shifted uncomfortably in his chair. He didn't say anything.

"Where were you at one A.M. on July thirteenth?"

Zak was still antsy, shifting. His eyes darted around the courtroom. "I . . . um . . ."

"Excuse me?"

Zak licked his lips. "I . . . uh . . . can't answer that."

Ben's head fell forward. "What?"

"I . . . I'm sorry. I can't answer the question."

"You *what*?" Ben stared across the courtroom, utterly befuddled. What the hell was going on here?

"I'm sorry, I just—ask me something else."

Ben was incredulous. Zak had systematically undermined his defense at almost every point. And now he was spoiling his own testimony.

"Zak, you didn't program the bomb to explode when the ignition was turned, did you?" It was a leading question, but Granny didn't seem interested in objecting.

"You mean . . . on the night of the murder, right?"

"Well, of course!" Ben tried to control himself. He couldn't believe this.

"I'm sorry, then." He folded his hands in his lap and looked down. "I can't answer that question, either."

"Zak?" Ben didn't know what to do, what to say. In all his years he had never encountered anything like this. "Zak, this is critical. You have to answer."

"I'm sorry. I can't and I won't."

The hell with subtlety. Ben cut to the highlight of his outline. "Zak, did you plant a bomb for the purpose of killing Dwayne Gardiner?"

He did not look up. "I'm sorry. I can't answer."

The buzz in the courtroom was growing audible and distracting. Everyone in the gallery seemed just as mystified as Ben.

"Well, look," Ben said, "you're on the stand, and you've sworn to tell the truth. So you don't have the option of silence. Answer the question."

Zak shook his head. "I won't."

"I insist."

"I'm sorry, no."

Ben looked up at the bench. "Your honor?"

Judge Pickens leaned forward. He was obviously just as confused as everyone else. "Son, you're on the witness stand. You have to answer the question."

"I'm sorry. No disrespect intended. But I won't answer."

Pickens's chest swelled. "Son, I don't think you understood me properly. I didn't ask you—I told you. Answer the question!"

"No. I won't."

"I will find you in contempt of court!"

"You can't make me answer," Zak said, looking away. "I'm taking the fifth."

Judge Pickens's lips parted. "Are you telling me," he said finally, "that you're taking the fifth—when your own lawyer is asking the questions?"

"That's right. I won't answer. Should I go?"

The buzz in the courtroom was building into a roar.

"Zak," Ben said urgently, "this is your last chance. You must answer."

"No." He rose to his feet. "Can I go now?"

Judge Pickens's mouth was still gaping. "I—I don't—" He turned. "Madame Prosecutor, you can still attempt to cross, if you wish."

"I don't see the point," Granny said. "I think it's clear to everyone what's happened here. Let's just wrap the trial up and let the jury do its work. Let justice be done."

Zak was excused from the bench. "Anything else from the defense?" Judge Pickens asked.

Ben couldn't believe it. His entire defense consisted of a theory that fell apart, an alibi witness who had lied, and a defendant who took the fifth.

His mind raced, grasping for something, anything, that he could possibly put before the jury. But nothing came. He had played every card in his hand.

There was no point in stalling. Whether he liked it or not, he had nothing else. "No, your honor, the defense rests."

"Very well. We'll resume in fifteen minutes for closing arguments." Pickens banged his gavel, and the courtroom went into an uproar.

Ben was still at the podium trying to make some sense of what had happened. Everyone in the courtroom seemed befuddled—judge, jury, spectators.

Everyone except the prosecutor. She didn't seem particularly confused, Ben noted. And she had rattled off that little speech about justice like a pro. Almost like it had been rehearsed.

Zak was off the bench and had returned to defendant's table. "Zak," Ben said, "I want to talk to you!"

Zak wouldn't look at him. "I don't want to talk to you. Deputy?" He motioned for his escort. "Take me back to my cell."

"Zak!"

He ignored Ben. The deputy hauled Zak toward the back door, leaving Ben in his wake.

Ben stood in the courtroom feeling utterly lost. What the hell was going on here?

He felt someone brush against his shoulder. It was Christina. "Do you understand what just happened?"

"No," Ben said grimly. "But I know what the result will be."

* 66 *

Granny spent almost an hour systematically reminding the jury of the enormous body of evidence pointing toward George Zakin. The fingerprints. The footprints. The eyewitness testimony. Zak's history with explosives. The personal grudge between victim and accused. The threat made just before the murder.

And she also pointed out that Zak had lied—that he had initially denied knowing Gardiner, denied planting the bomb. That he had bragged about the murder to a fellow prisoner. That he had put a former lover on the stand to lie for him. And even though she didn't specifically mention it, no juror could possibly forget Zak taking the fifth, refusing to talk to his own lawyer. "With all the evidence that's before you," Granny argued, "can you honestly say that there is any reasonable doubt about what happened? We all know what happened. Let justice be done. Find George Zakin guilty of murder in the first degree."

When it was his turn, Ben wasn't sure what to say. He did his best to conjure up some wisp of reasonable doubt, but he had the strong sense that no one was buying it. Molly's testimony had been a hard blow for the defense, but Zak's performance had created a barrier he just couldn't get around. How could he explain it? He didn't understand it himself. All he could do was avoid the subject. And there were few things more pathetic than a closing argument that avoids the subject weighing most heavily on the jurors' minds.

When arguments were completed, Judge Pickens reviewed the lengthy jury instructions. He dismissed the jurors, but instructed them to be back in the courtroom at nine to begin deliberations.

Nine A.M., Ben thought. We'll have the bad news before lunch.

Ben left the courtroom feeling more depressed than he ever recalled feeling in his life. Despite everything, his gut still told him Zak had not committed this murder. So why was he so determined to be convicted for it?

Ben parted with Christina. There was no more work to do; best that they both had some quiet time to brace themselves for the disaster that was surely coming.

Outside his hotel, on the street, Ben saw Maureen. She appeared to be waiting for him. "Hiya, Mo. How are you?"

"Stiff as a board," she answered. "I've spent the day with my arms stuffed in concrete barrels."

"What, still? After what happened to Doc?"

"We have no choice." Ben peered into her red, tired eyes.

"It's not like I wanted to. But those damn loggers are still trying to get into the forest. They weren't taking a holiday to mourn Doc's death. So we couldn't either." She turned slightly. "You can't believe the day I've had."

Ben almost smiled. "This hasn't exactly been a red-letter day for me, either."

"Trial didn't go well?"

Ben averted his eyes. "I'm afraid it . . . it doesn't look too good for Zak at this point."

"Oh," she said, barely audibly.

"I'm sorry I don't have better news for you."

"The whole group seems to be falling apart. Despite everything, our effort is failing. I can feel it. And I'm worried about Al."

"Al? What's wrong with him?"

"It's Doc. Al was right there when it happened, you know. Right beside him. Al's been uptight since the kidnapping, the whipping . . ." She shook her head. "But now he's over the brink. It's like something snapped inside him. I was chained to his barrel today, so I got to hear him rant for hours."

"What was he saying?"

"Crazy stuff. Didn't really make sense, most of it. Said he had something on the loggers, some secret. Said they were going to pay for what they'd done." She looked up abruptly. "He was consumed with hate. The same hatred I saw in the eyes of the loggers standing outside the barricade, calling us names, spitting on us." She drew in her breath. "I'm worried that Al is going to try something . . . dangerous. He's been staying out late at night, wandering in the forest, not telling anyone what he's doing. I'm just afraid." She peered up at Ben. "And I really couldn't stand to lose another member. I just—couldn't—" Her voice broke off.

Ben laid his hand gently on her shoulder. "Well, try not to worry about it."

"I have to worry about it. The only experienced members I've still got are Deirdre and Al, and Al is—" She couldn't complete her sentence. All at once she pressed herself into Ben's arms. "My God, Ben, we can't afford to lose anyone else."

Ben raised his hand and gently stroked her hair. "I know."

"You wouldn't think it would be so hard. All we want is to preserve what little is left. To keep some remnant of the natural world for our children."

"I know."

Her face turned up, and Ben saw tears trickling down her cheeks. They paused, the two of them, frozen for a moment, feeling the distance between them.

"You know, Ben," she said quietly, "the trial is all but over now, and we said that when the trial was over we might . . . spend some time together. You remember?"

"I remember," Ben said, gazing into her eyes. "Very well."

Their two faces moved closer together, lips parted, each inexorably inching toward the other . . .

"Now this is a cozy scene, ain't it?"

Ben and Maureen broke apart. On the side of the street, a large black sedan had pulled up next to them. Two men jumped out the side doors. Ben didn't recognize either of them, but they had a distinctly thuggish appearance.

Ben pushed himself in front of Maureen. "What do you want?"

"Want to have us a little powwow," the first man said. He grabbed Ben's arm and jerked him toward the car.

"Leave me alone!" Ben shouted. He tried to break away, but the man held him tight with a viselike grip. An instant later, the other man was behind him, shoving him forward. He fell headfirst into the backseat of the sedan.

"Stop!" Ben shouted, but before he could say another word, the first man brought his fist around and cuffed Ben on the side of the face. His head slammed backward against the car door.

"Let go of me!" Maureen screamed. Ben saw the other man grabbing her, forcing her into the front seat. *"Help!"*

Maureen gave the scream her best, but there was no one close enough to hear. Within moments she was strapped and belted into the front seat and the door was locked behind her.

"You can't do this," Ben said.

"Do you want another one?" the man beside him said, raising his fist in the air.

Ben saw he was in no position to argue. Pinned down, isolated from anyone who could help—more chatter would only serve to loosen his teeth.

The doors were closed and locked. The car began to creep forward.

"You bastards," Maureen spat out. "Haven't you done enough already?"

"Evidently not," said the voice behind the driver's wheel. That was when Ben noticed for the first time who was driving.

"It's *him*!" Maureen shrieked, white-faced. The tone of her voice made Ben's blood run cold. "It's the man who killed Doc!"

A thin smile curled on the driver's lips. "That was an accident, remember?"

"What are you planning to do with us?" Ben asked.

"You'll know soon enough," the man grunted. "What's your rush?"

Ben's jaw tightened. "I'd just like to know, you—"

"Sorry. We're not supposed to say."

"Can't you tell me anything?"

The man's face twitched. "I can tell you this. You ain't gonna like it."

Ben spent the next forty-five minutes or so with a paper bag over his head. It seemed they didn't want him to know where he was going. He could tell they had left town, had probably gone into the forest. But beyond that, he was clueless. All he could do was wait.

"Are you all right, Maureen?" he shouted at one point. His voice reverberated inside the paper bag.

"I'm fine. Given the circumstances."

The man beside Ben grunted. "Worried about your little lady, chump?"

"Don't hurt her. There's no reason to hurt her."

Ben felt a sharp jab in the ribs. "You ain't in a position to argue, chump."

They drove the rest of the distance in silence. Eventually Ben felt the car slow.

"We're here."

The man removed the bag over Ben's head. He was right—they were in the forest. Deep, deep in the thick of it.

Just behind the car, Ben saw a cabin. More of an outsized shack, really—wood planks forming most of the walls, faded from rain and sunlight.

"So this is it," he heard Maureen murmur. "The Holy Grail."

Ben frowned. "What?"

"Their headquarters," Maureen explained. "We knew the Cabal had a camp out in the woods somewhere. But we've never been able to find it."

Surveying the scenery, Ben could imagine why. They were at the peak of what appeared to be a small mountain, utterly isolated from everything below. There was only one road leading to the cabin, and nothing else in sight.

"Come on," the man beside Ben grunted. "Move your butt. You're wanted inside."

A few minutes later, Ben and Maureen were inside, both tied securely to upright chairs taken from an ancient dinner table. The chairs were old and not very sturdy. Ben suspected that, given half a chance, they could probably free themselves. Unfortunately, their captors didn't appear likely to give them half a chance.

Ben felt cold beads of sweat dripping down the side of his face. He didn't want to be a coward, but he was scared, and he knew it. They were alone, isolated—totally at the mercy of these men. Bad enough that he was in this situation—but Maureen was stuck here, too. He didn't like that a bit. The looks on those men's faces told him they were capable of anything. Anything at all.

"Now," the driver said, "let's talk. I'm Carl. You're Ben, right? And the lady with the sexy legs is Maureen."

"Go to hell," Maureen answered.

"Why have you brought us here?" Ben asked, straining against his bonds. They weren't tied that tightly. If he could just get rid of these jerks for a few minutes . . .

"Well, Ben," Carl answered, "to tell you the truth, we didn't want *you*. We weren't too happy when you set out to rescue Zakin from the hangman's noose, but from what I understand, your defense has been totally screwed, so who cares? We were after the lovely Maureen."

Ben felt an empty aching in his chest. He'd been afraid of this.

"What do you want with me?" Maureen asked.

"Well, I thought we ought to have a little talk. After all, you're in charge now, right?"

"Only because you loggers have killed everyone else!"

"Maureen, calm down. I think you have the wrong idea. Although maybe I shouldn't tell you. I think you're very sexy when you're angry." He smiled, a toothy smile Ben would've enjoyed rendering toothless. "We're not loggers. I've never cut a tree in my life."

Ben surveyed the four faces in the room. "These assholes don't care about eco-politics, Maureen. They're just hired thugs. They work for Slade. Where is he anyway?"

"Look, punk, I'm here to ask the questions, not you."

"Right." Ben forced himself to be brave, even though he was feeling anything but. "I bet he's here somewhere. Safely tucked away, but keeping a watchful eye on things." Ben looked around the cabin. "Hiding in a back room somewhere?"

"Listen to me!" In an instant, Carl was on his feet and brought the flat of his hand around to club Ben on the side of the face.

Ben winced. That smarted. The sharp sudden pain almost brought tears to his eyes, which he knew would not help him keep up his defiant façade.

"Now here's the story," Carl barked. "We've had it with your goddamn Green Rage. We've tolerated it as long as we're gonna. We've hit you again and again and again. But like stupid lemmings, you just keep coming. We're tired of it. We want you out!"

Maureen looked at him levelly. "We're not going."

Carl clenched his fist together. "Don't make this hard on yourself, lady."

"What are you going to do? Hurt me? Kill me?" Maureen leaned forward, pressing against the restraint of the ropes. "Are you going to kill all of us? Are you going to exterminate every person on earth who doesn't want to see the forests leveled?"

"Take it somewhere else, lady!" Ben could see Carl's anger was rising. "We just want you out of Magic Valley."

"Have you looked at this forest?" Maureen shouted back. "Have you *looked* at it? Some of those trees go back hundreds of years. We can't let you chop them down just to make more cardboard!"

"You can, lady. And you will." He drew his arm back, fist clenched.

"If you hit her," Ben said, cutting in, "you'd better be willing to kill me."

"Don't tempt me."

"Because you won't get away with it. So long as I'm alive, I'll make sure charges are brought against you." He paused. "I will hunt you down like a dog."

Carl smiled thinly. "You just don't get it, do you, Kincaid? There's a reason the Cabal exists. It's so we can do things the loggers can't do themselves. Because no one knows who we are. I could beat both of you to a pulp or worse, and never do a day in jail. Because, see, I don't exist. As soon as this is over, I'll disappear. You'll never see me again."

"There's always a way," Ben said.

"Not with us," Carl replied. "Others have tried. Others a lot better than you. No one's succeeded. And they never will." He turned back toward Maureen. "So let me ask you again. Are you going to cooperate? Agree to pull your team out of the forest? Or do I have to get rough?"

"You can do whatever you want, you bastard. I'll never agree."

"You say that now," Carl replied. "But you might change your mind later." He stepped closer to her, then straddled her tied legs and sat in her lap. He pressed his face to hers. "You might change your mind when you see the knife, see how sharp it is, how deep it cuts. You might change your mind when you feel your clothes being ripped off your body. You might change your mind when you're being hurt, abused, violated—"

"Shut up, you son of a bitch!" Ben shouted.

Carl didn't even blink. "You will change your mind, Maureen. The only question is whether you'll do it before I have my fun—or after."

"You're a disgusting pig," Maureen said, right in his face.

Carl drew in his breath, then slowly released it. "I'm sorry to hear you say that, Maureen. I really am. But I have a job to do." He reached into his pocket and removed a large switchblade. He pressed the trigger button and the blade popped out. "Where do you want it first?"

"Go to hell!" Maureen screamed, crying.

"All right then," Carl said, jaw clenched, "let's start with your face."

"No!" Ben shouted.

"Oh yes," Carl said, raising the knife. "We'll start with—"

His voice was cut off by a sudden booming noise. It was a huge, fluid noise; it made Ben imagine the word *whoosh!* drawn in a comic-book panel.

And an instant later, they began to feel the heat.

"See what's going on out there!" Carl shouted to one of his accomplices.

The man who had sat beside Ben in the car ran to one of the front windows and pulled away the tattered curtains. He turned back, his eyes wide with horror, a horror he was able to describe in a single word:

"Fire!"

* 67 *

All four men rushed out the front door.

"Don't leave us!" Ben shouted, but no one stopped.

"I can feel the fire from here," Maureen said, twisting her neck around, trying to see.

Ben didn't waste any time. As soon as they left, he started trying to get free. He pushed up with his feet, launching himself into the air. The chair clattered back down to the floor. He could feel the bonds loosening, but not enough to give him any slack. The chair didn't break.

He did it again, this time pushing even higher. He heard the chair creak a bit on impact, thought he felt a split—but that was all. He was still tied tightly to the chair.

Before Ben could make another attempt, a familiar, if dreadful figure appeared in the rear doorway.

"Slade!" Ben said, teeth clenched. "I know you were behind this. What's going on?"

"There's a ring of fire," Slade answered. He reached down and began untying their bonds. "All around us."

"You're letting us go?"

"I know you don't have a very high opinion of me," Slade said. "Maybe you shouldn't. But I'm not going to let you two burn alive." A few moments later, Ben and Maureen were free.

"Come on!" Slade shouted, pointing toward the door. The group raced outside. Almost instantly, Ben felt assaulted by the tremendous heat. Even though the fire was still a good fifty feet away, it felt as if he had stepped into the middle of it.

"But it hasn't been hot enough for a brush fire," Maureen said.

"This fire didn't just happen," Slade growled. "It was set." He waved a bread box–size metal can under her nose. Ben recognized the distinctive smell before he even saw it.

It was a gasoline can. And it was empty.

Maureen stared at the can. "Al," she murmured.

"What?" Slade said. "What are you talking about?"

Maureen wouldn't answer him, but Ben knew exactly what she was thinking. Al was over the brink, out of control, crazy with rage. Al had been staying out late at night in the forest. He had said he'd discovered something—something secret.

And he'd sworn to pay them back for what they did to Doc.

It was clear now what he'd uncovered. He'd found this secret hideaway. He'd probably waited from a distance till he saw people come back to it. And then he crept out of hiding and set the fire. Not realizing that his own colleague, Maureen, was inside. Not to mention Ben.

"If he wanted to kill us, why wouldn't he set the cabin on fire?" Slade asked.

"He doesn't just want to kill you. He wants you to suffer, like Doc did. He wants you to see it coming."

Slade ran a few feet around the shack, searching. "Looks like my associates got through the fire," Slade said. "But it's too late now. If we jump into the middle of that we'll be burned alive." He turned, scanning the horizon. "We might be able to get through in the car."

All together, the three of them started running toward the vehicle. Thick smoke clouds made breathing difficult. Coughing and tearing, they piled into the car.

Slade slid behind the wheel. "Here we go." He shoved the key into the ignition and turned it.

Nothing happened.

"What's wrong?" Maureen asked. A note of panic crept into her voice.

"I don't know." Slade turned the ignition again—with the same result.

"Come on!" Ben said. "We've got to go!"

"Talking won't get us anywhere." Slade pushed a button to pop the hood, then jumped out of the car. Ben followed him.

Slade stared down into the engine. In seconds he ascertained what had happened. He ran his finger through a white, granular smear, then touched it to his lips.

"Sugar," he said bitterly.

"Sugar?" Ben said. "What do you mean?"

Slade glared at Maureen. "It's a technique these bright young Green Ragers have for disabling automobiles. Put sugar in the crankcase. Or the gas tank. Or both. Stops the car dead."

"What are you saying?"

"I'm saying this car isn't going anywhere." He glanced at Maureen. "Good work."

She held up her hands. "I didn't have anything to do with this."

"One of your associates, then. A very thorough one." He

slammed the hood down. "And now we're all going to pay the price. All because of *you*!"

"Wait a minute," Maureen said. "This would never have happened if one of your men hadn't killed Doc."

"That would never have happened if you and your gang of trespassers hadn't illegally blocked the road."

"We wouldn't've had to, if your corporate masters weren't so determined to sacrifice our forests to make a buck!"

"We don't have time for this!" Ben shouted. "Like it or not, we're all in this together now."

"He's right," Slade said. His lips were pursed together; Ben knew he was thinking. He scanned the ring of flame encircling them, growing closer. "Let's spread out. See if we can find an opening anywhere in the flames."

They did as Slade bid. Ben ran the farthest, toward the opposite side of the cabin. No matter how far away he ran, though, he couldn't get away from the oppressive heat, the intense burning sensation. His face was flushed; sweat poured down his body. It was getting hotter; he was certain of it. Because the flames were coming closer.

He followed the fire around the back of the cabin. It was an almost perfect circle, with the cabin at the heart. He ran into Maureen, coming from the other direction. "I didn't find an opening. Did you?"

Maureen shook her head grimly. "No."

"I don't understand it."

"I'm afraid I do. Even in this crazed mental state, Al is very smart, very thorough. He probably saturated the ground with gasoline, forming the circle."

Ben gazed at the intense wall of flame. It made his eyes hurt; it was like peering into the sun—or more accurately, like peering into the pits of hell. "I can't tell how thick the wall is. Maybe if we made a run for it—"

"You'd be burned alive." Slade was coming toward them. "You'd be burning head to toe before you got through that wall."

"Then there's no way through," Maureen said breathlessly. "No way out."

"Now you understand the situation," Slade said. He stared

into the inferno. "There's no escape. We can't get out, and if we stay here much longer—" The flickering flames reflected in his eyes. "We'll all be dead."

* 68 *

Maureen pressed up against Ben. He cradled her in his arms. "I don't want to die," she said, her voice choking. "Especially not by—" Her voice broke off before she completed the sentence.

"We can't give up," Ben said. "We have to keep trying."

"Trying what?" Slade shook his head. "It's over, Kincaid. Might as well walk into the flames and get it over with."

"I won't accept that." He felt Maureen pressing into the crook of his neck, felt the tears spilling from her eyes. "We have to think about this logically."

"Logic!" Maureen laughed bitterly.

He pushed her away, holding her by the arms. "Look, what are our options?"

"We don't have any."

"Yes we do. If we can't go through the flames, then we either go under them or over them."

Slade stared at him incredulously. "Under them? Forget it, Kincaid. Even if we all worked together and had the proper tools—which we don't—we couldn't dig a tunnel under those flames in time. We'd be dead before we got anywhere."

"Agreed," Ben said. His brain was racing, barely one beat ahead of his mouth. "So we have to go over."

"Over?" Maureen said incredulously. "Unless you've got a red cape under that suit, I don't think it's going to happen."

"I can't fly, but a helicopter can. A copter could get in here and fly us out before the flames close in."

"You're dreaming, Kincaid," Slade said. "There probably aren't any copters within a hundred miles of this backwater."

"There are," Ben said firmly. "Two, in fact. Sheriff Allen told me. He flies one himself. They use them for mountain rescues."

Maureen looked up at Ben for the first time since he'd started talking. Despite the crushing heat all around them, Ben saw the tiniest glimmer of hope in her eyes. "But how do we call the helicopters here?"

"That's what I don't know," Ben said. "I'm sure eventually someone will report the fire. But by then it will be too late."

"A radio!" Slade slapped his hands together. "A radio!"

Ben rushed toward him. "Do you have one?"

"Yes. I mean, I think so. I've seen it in the closet. It isn't mine. One of the other men—"

"Never mind that," Ben said curtly. "Show us."

Slade led the way back into the cabin, running as fast as he could go. The circle of flame was growing detectably closer on all sides. Already Ben was beginning to feel singed, burned. Maureen's face was a bright red. And the smoke was so much thicker he could hardly breathe.

They would be dead even before the flames got to them, Ben realized. They'd be dead even sooner than they thought.

Slade led the way to a back room. He rooted around in the closet for several seconds, pushing aside dirty clothes and trash. Eventually he emerged with a large rectangular metal box.

"I think this is a radio," he said. "Isn't it?"

Maureen took it from him and set it on a nearby table. "It sure as hell is."

"But I don't know how to work it."

"Don't worry. I do." She glanced up at Ben. "Communications is my field, remember? This is a pretty simple shortwave setup. The owner is probably a ham radio hobbyist. We'll use the emergency channels; someone should be monitoring. The signal should be strong enough—"

She turned a knob on the front of the set and waited.

Nothing happened.

She clicked it back, then tried again. Nothing happened.

"Damn!" Muttering under her breath, she reached toward the back of the set till she found the catches that released the metal casing. She lifted the lid off and stared at the contents.

"What's wrong?" Slade asked. Ben could feel the edge in his voice. For an instant, it had seemed as if they actually had some chance of survival. And now—

"No power."

Slade stared at Maureen. "No power? But—"

Maureen pointed. "The battery's dead." She turned toward Ben, then took his hand and squeezed. "And so are we."

* 69 *

"No power," Slade said, to no one in particular. His eyes seemed dark and vacant. "No power."

"I'm afraid that's the size of it," Maureen said, batting back tears. "I like to think of myself as a miracle worker. But even I can't make a radio work without power."

"No power," Slade mumbled. He staggered, leaning against the wall. "No power."

Ben couldn't believe it. This horrible man who had once stood so tall and defiant—now he was babbling like an escaped mental patient. All of his toughness, all of his swagger and menace—it was all gone now. There was nothing left but a pathetic wretch who realized he was facing death.

"Isn't there some way to recharge the batteries?" Ben asked.

"They're not rechargeable," Maureen answered.

"Maybe there are some other batteries."

Maureen rummaged through the closet. "Sorry. Nothing."

"Damn." Ben bit down on a knuckle. There had to be something. Something he was missing, something he hadn't thought of. But what?

"It's over," Slade said. His face seemed to disintegrate; those strong chiseled features were melting away. "It's over."

"Get a grip," Ben said, disgusted.

Slade didn't hear him. He began to laugh, a bitter, eerie laugh. "After all I've done, all my plans . . ." He laughed even louder. "And now it comes down to this. Burning alive in some godforsaken shack in a goddamn forest!"

"Stop it, Slade," Ben said. "Stop it now."

Slade continued his maniacal laughter, even louder and creepier than before. "You just don't get it, do you? We're doomed. We're going to die in flames, in our own personal hell. Do you know what it is to burn to death? Do you have any idea how painful it is?"

"Stop it!" Ben shouted. Sweat flew off his face. He was feeling it, too—the heat, the sense of desperation. It would be much easier to be like Slade, to just relent. To give up. But if he did that, they were all finished.

"There must be some other way," Ben said. "There must be some other means of generating power."

"Power," Slade murmured, wiping his eyes.

"Right. Some other way to power the radio."

Slade's hand pressed against his chest. Ben could see he was having trouble breathing. The smoke was everywhere. "There's a—a—"

Ben squatted beside him. "What?"

"A—" He took a deep breath. "An emergency generator. In the other room. But that powers the lights, the fuses . . ."

"The radio has an AC plug!" Maureen shouted. "It could work. If you've got an extension cord and you could get some juice in the fuse . . . it just might work!"

Slade seemed stunned, dazed, as if he couldn't process the information quickly enough. "It can't . . ." he mumbled, barely rational. "Can't—"

Ben jerked him to his feet. "Come on, Slade. Show me where the generator is. *Now!*"

* * *

Ten minutes later, they had the generator going. Maureen found an extension cord, plugged the radio in, and began broadcasting. It wasn't easy. She had to try several frequencies, and broadcast conditions weren't ideal. For one thing, they were atop a mountain, deep in a forest. For another, they were surrounded by flames. Fortunately Maureen knew what she was doing.

During the tense minutes Maureen spent broadcasting her signal, Ben managed to bite every fingernail he had down to the nub. "Damn!" Her voice was cracking with desperation. "I'm not getting anything."

"But are they getting you?" Ben asked. "That's the important thing."

"I don't know. I can't tell. I'm not hearing anything."

"We're going to be cooked," Slade pronounced.

"I won't accept that," Ben said. "Even if the interference prevents us from hearing them, they might hear us. They could be on the way."

"Wouldn't matter if they were." Slade glanced toward the window, forcing Ben to follow his gaze.

The heat radiating through the closed window was so intense Ben had to take several steps back. His vision blurred; wavy lines of heat made the image before him seem to shimmer and float. But that didn't prevent him from seeing what was happening outside.

The fire had come closer—much, much closer. The perimeter of the flames was barely twenty feet from the shack. Maybe closer.

"We don't have time for a rescue," Slade said, his voice in his throat. "We don't have ten minutes."

* 70 *

"That's it, then," Maureen said. Her head fell into her arms, knocking aside the radio microphone. "It's really going to happen. We're going to burn to death."

"Trapped like flies," Slade said. "Pigs penned for the slaughter."

"Don't talk like that!" Ben shouted.

"Don't be a baby, Kincaid." Slade crumpled into a heap on the floor. "It's over. There's no way out."

"There's always a way. You can't just give up."

"Then you tell me, Kincaid. What should we do?"

Ben shielded his eyes and stared out into the raging inferno. There had to be a way—that's what Christina would say, if she were here. But Christina was always able to think of the solution, the way out. He wasn't coming up with anything.

"We can't go over the flames," Ben said, thinking aloud, "and we can't go under them."

"Then we're cooked," Slade said.

"No," Ben answered. "We have to go through them."

"Through them?" Slade said. "Are you kidding? I told you already, we'll be burned alive!"

"We'll be burned alive if we just sit here, that's for damn sure." Ben grabbed Slade's collar and yanked him up onto his feet. "I saw a well outside. Does it work?"

"I—suppose—"

"Good. We'll wet ourselves down before we go. Have you got a garden hose?"

"I—think so. In the back. But—"

"Good. Where does the well water come in?"

"There's a pump on the north side of the shack. Connects to the plumbing in the bathroom."

"Can you disconnect the pipe?"

"I suppose, but—"

"Good, do it. Then connect the hose to the water line."

Slade stared at him incredulously. "Surely you don't think you're going to put that fire out with a garden hose!"

"We don't have to put the whole fire out. We just have to make a path."

"That won't—"

"Just do it!"

For once, Slade took orders. Being shouted at and ordered about seemed to have rallied his brain cells, at least for the moment. He rummaged through a toolbox for a wrench, then headed toward the bathroom. While he was working, Ben gathered together some of the old clothes that had tumbled out of the closet.

"We'll wet these down and wear them when we go through," Ben explained.

Maureen seemed dazed and confused. "But we already have clothes—"

"We'll want to have something to wrap around our heads and arms. Socks over our hands. Plus, stop me if I'm wrong, but isn't your blouse some kind of nylon or polyester?"

Maureen glanced downward. "Yeah, I guess. Why?"

"Something I heard the coroner explain during the trial. Artificial fibers like nylon and polyester melt and burn more quickly. Cotton is more flame-retardant, especially when it's wet. Even if it eventually burns, it won't melt."

"Then by all means." Without a thought to modesty, Maureen ripped off her blouse and pulled on one of the red work-shirts lying on the floor.

Ben bundled together some of the other clothes and together they headed toward the front door. As they passed the kitchen, Ben stopped short. "Wait a minute."

"What is it?"

"I see something we can use." He walked to the sink and retrieved a jumbo box of dishwashing soap.

They ran outside and, all at once, the heat was so intense

Ben thought he would pass out on the spot. The smoke was blinding and choking, and the intense heat was so oppressive, so enervating, Ben felt as if he could barely move.

You have no choice, he told himself. You have to keep trying. You *have* to keep trying.

They found Slade on the north side of the shack. "The hose was the wrong size, of course," he explained. "So I'm using duct tape. And I found a spray gun and attached it to the end of the hose. That'll give us some more pressure."

"Very resourceful," Ben said. He was glad to see the man's brain was back in gear. He was probably the smartest of all of them.

Ben walked to the well, opened the cover, and poured in the entire contents of the box of soap.

"What's the point of that?" Maureen asked.

"Soapy water," Ben replied. "It's a great fire quencher. It's basically what professional firefighters use to put out fires. Since we don't have any fire extinguishers on tap, this is the best we can hope for." He distributed the extra cotton clothing to the others. "Now wrap this over every part of your body. Nothing should be exposed. Absolutely nothing."

"But how will we see?" Maureen asked.

"We don't have to see. We know where we're going. Hurry!" The flames were still a dozen feet away, but the heat was so intense Ben felt as if he was already on fire. Once the clothes were wrapped around them, he gave Slade the signal. "Okay, let her rip."

Slade lowered the pump handle and water began streaming out of the hose. After it ran for a few moments, they could see the consistency of the water changing. It was becoming cloudy, creamy—

Soapy water.

"It won't last long," Ben said. "We have to go now." He took the hose from Slade and turned it on all three of them, drenching them from head to toe. "Now link arms."

Slade did as he was instructed, but Maureen didn't move. Her head was turned the other way, staring at the wall of flame.

"Maureen!" Ben shouted. "Take my hand!"

"I can't," she said. Her voice was barely more than a whisper. Tears streamed out of her eyes. "Those flames—it's—it's too horrible. I can't!"

"You can," Ben said firmly. "And you will."

She shook her head sadly. She seemed spent, emptied, as if she had nothing left to give. "You go on without me."

"We're all going together." He grabbed her arm and jerked her forward. The three of them linked arms, as if they were playing some adult version of ring-around-the-rosy. Ben draped cotton shirts over their heads, took his bearings, then pulled a shirt down over his own face. He wetted them all down again, then turned the soapy water toward the flames.

"We're going to have to run," Ben said, "and run together. If we're in that for more than a few seconds, nothing will save us."

"I can't do it," Maureen sobbed, her voice buried beneath the damp cotton. "I can't."

"You can and you will," Ben said, tugging them toward the perimeter of the flames. "Here we go."

* 71 *

Ben fired the soapy water straight ahead of them and, with a sudden burst of speed, plunged into the flames. He forced the trio forward, racing at top speed, spraying everything that lay in his path.

Even though the flames were only a few feet thick, and they were only in the midst of the blaze for a heartbeat, it seemed like an eternity. The world went into slow motion, as suddenly Ben became aware of the all-consuming fire radiating all around him. He couldn't stop, couldn't even think about stopping because he knew if he did, it would be the end. They had to keep pressing through, not giving the fire a chance to catch.

Even if Ben couldn't see the flames, he could feel them, with every ounce of his being, on every inch of his skin. He was propelling himself forward on impulse power as one by one his bodily systems began to overheat.

The garden hose reached the end of its tether and jerked out of Ben's hands. He didn't stop—he couldn't—but he felt the immediate impact. It was as if the oven had been turned on High and suddenly there were flames shooting up from beneath him, broiling him, burning him alive—

And then they were out. They had cleared the flames. They tumbled into a heap, collapsing onto the dirt, just outside the wall of fire.

Ben ripped the shirt off his head. Even though the heat was still intense, they were out of the fire. They had made it through. It had seemed impossible, but together, they had done it.

"My arm!" Slade shouted.

Ben whipped his head around. Slade was on fire. The shirt over his head had slipped, and the man's sleeve had caught fire.

Ben jumped up and threw the shirt that had covered his own head around Slade's arm. He wrapped it tightly around till the flames were snuffed.

"My God, that hurts!" Slade said. He was gritting his teeth, fighting back tears. "But we made it. By God, Kincaid—we *made* it!"

Ben crouched beside Maureen. Her eyes were closed and her face was bright red. "Are you—are you all right?" he asked.

Maureen didn't answer, but she took Ben's arm and pulled him close to her. Their lips met, and they fell into a deep and urgent kiss. It seemed to Ben as if he had been waiting a lifetime for this, waiting forever.

He rolled over on his back and lay for a moment, gasping for air. They should move away from the flames, away from the crippling heat, but that could surely wait at least another second or two. He didn't realize until then how stressed, how dog-tired he was. Tired of thinking, tired of moving—tired of everything. All he wanted to do was rest. And wait.

Which is exactly what he did. Till he heard the familiar chopping sound of helicopter blades cutting through the superheated air outside. The wings of angels, Ben thought, as his smoke-baked eyelids closed. The wings of angels.

FIVE

* *

What You See

* 72 *

When Ben felt strong enough to walk, he hobbled down the infirmary corridor to the next room. He found Maureen lying on a bed in a hospital gown with an IV hooked up to her arm.

Ben entered the room. "How are you doing?"

Maureen saw him and beamed. "I've been better. But I'm alive."

Ben returned her smile. He was glad to see her so recovered. By the time the helicopters had landed, she was in such bad shape that he'd had to carry her on board while one of the deputies helped Slade, who had totally broken down. He was like a baby, babbling and crying. Maureen had kept her wits about her to the end, thank God, but she was gasping as if each breath was her last. She was asthmatic to begin with; protracted smoke inhalation could easily have killed her.

"How do you feel?" Ben asked.

"Well, my skin is pretty crispy, and my lungs feel like I've been swimming in dirt. But under the circumstances, I can't complain." She reached out for Ben's hand. "You look cute."

"I do?"

"Yeah. You should go outside more often. You look good with a little red in your face. Well, in this case, a lot of red in your face."

"Oh yeah?" Ben hadn't even thought to look in the mirror.

"Oh yeah. Your nose is bright red, like Rudolph. And Sasquatch, of course." She squeezed Ben's hand all the tighter. "Thank you," she whispered.

"Thank *you*. If you hadn't known how to work the radio, we'd still be up there."

"Nonsense. If you hadn't kept your wits about you and

made us think clearly, we'd have all died." She looked down for a moment. "Ben . . . I need to tell you something. I . . . have someone. Back home. In North Dakota."

Ben didn't say anything.

"More than just a someone, actually. We're married."

Ben nodded.

"You knew?"

"No. But I suspected there was . . . something."

"We haven't lived together for years. We were having some trouble, but . . . I don't know. After something like this happens to you, you get new priorities. Just a little while ago, I called him. I know this sounds ridiculous, but—I think we're going to give it another chance." She looked up at Ben, her eyes wide. "I'm—sorry."

"Don't be. I'm glad for you."

"I feel awful. You're not at all what I thought you were going to be, back—"

"When we first met?"

"Or even before." The smile faded from her face. "I have a confession to make. It's—horrible. I just hope you won't hate me." She swallowed. "God, I can't even make myself say it."

"Then let me say it for you. You set me up. Manipulated me so I'd take Zak's case."

Maureen looked stunned. "Ben!"

"Zak found out I was in town, read it in the paper or something. He knew I was a sucker for lost causes, but might not want to get involved with eco-terrorists. So you set up a little charade. When you found out I was in jail, you staged that stupid protest, knowing Sheriff Allen would let you spend the night behind bars. That gave you a chance to talk to me. You laid it on thick while we were locked up together, playing on my conscience. And then, to top it off, you hired some guys to stage that attack just after we were released, figuring I would fly to your rescue. Which I did. And that after we had fought side by side against a common enemy, we would bond and I would agree to take Zak's case. Which I did. I suspect you even played up to me a bit, acting like you liked me. Personally, that is. Just to keep me interested."

Maureen stared at him with amazement. "How did you find out?"

"My investigator, Loving, talked to Kelly, your former Green Rage colleague. She spilled the beans."

Maureen frowned. "Kelly resigned over it. She said we were being morally indefensible. I guess she was right." She glanced down at the floor. "You must hate me."

"Not in the least. You were fighting for a friend's life. I might quarrel with the way you did it, but . . . I can't argue with your goal."

"You're very generous." She gazed up at him. "You had it all right except on one point. I was playing up to you, but I didn't have to pretend." She pulled his arm, forcing him to bend closer. When he was near enough, she kissed him on the cheek. "You're a good human being, Ben."

He smiled back at her. "Well, I try."

* 73 *

When Ben returned to his office, he found Christina and Sheriff Allen standing close together, talking. He cleared his throat, then stepped into the office. "Any word yet?"

Christina shook her head. "Jury's still out."

"Blast."

"I thought you'd be pleased," Allen said. "Frankly, I didn't think it would take them half this long. Sounds like you must've given someone something to think about."

"Maybe," Ben answered. "Or maybe they've already voted to convict and are just debating whether to give Zak the death penalty. I know they're supposed to come out as soon as they reach a verdict, but juries are unpredictable. Sometimes they like to get it all over with at once."

"You gave it everything you possibly could," Christina said. "You have nothing to feel bad about. And speaking of feelings, how are you?"

Ben shrugged. "I'm fine. Throat's a little raspy and my face is tender. But nothing to complain about."

"That's good. When I heard what happened, I was—"

She was interrupted by a knock on the door. A moment later, a close-cropped, official-looking head poked through the door. "My name is Carlton Hodges. I'm looking for Christina McCall."

Christina stepped forward. "What's up?"

Hodges stepped into the office, followed by two other men, both of them dressed in near identical dark suits and white shirts. "You're under arrest."

Christina's eyes opened wide. "What?"

"I'm a federal agent, ma'am. DEA, working in association with the FBI." He grabbed Christina's wrists and snapped a pair of cuffs over them. "And you're under arrest."

Sheriff Allen pushed in between them. "What the hell is going on here?"

"Sir, please step aside. This doesn't involve you."

"I'm the sheriff in this county," Allen said, not backing down an inch. "And no one's going to make an arrest here unless I understand what's happening."

"It's a federal matter, sir."

"I don't care if it's a galactic matter. You're not taking her without my say-so."

Hodges glanced back at his two associates. Ben could imagine what might be going through their minds. They could do this by force. They had the authority. But it might be simpler if they got the sheriff's cooperation. "The DEA has been working on this for some time, Sheriff."

"Yeah. So?"

"We've been looking for the person or persons responsible for the distribution of the designer drug known as Venom." He glanced at Christina. "We believe we've found her."

"Christina? You must be joking."

"I assure you, sir, we're dead serious. We've been watching her for some time."

"You can't have any evidence."

"But we do." He turned toward Christina. "We found traces of methamphetamine on a table at Mabel's Diner last night—the table where numerous witnesses saw Ms. McCall have dinner."

Ben cut in. "Is that true, Christina?"

Christina seemed confused, unsure. "It's true that I ate there, but—"

"It was only trace residue—probably got some on her fingers and brushed it on the table. Still, no one would have it on their fingers unless they'd been in contact with the drug."

"But I wasn't," Christina said. Her eyes were wide and frightened. "I don't know what you're talking about."

Hodges was unimpressed. "You'll have plenty of time to tell your story to your lawyer. Come along, ma'am."

Sheriff Allen grabbed the man by the arm, stopping him. "Where are you taking her?"

"To a holding cell at the county deportation center, first. Then off to Collingsgate."

"Collingsgate!" Ben said. "I've heard that's the worst hell-hole in the whole prison system."

"These are very serious charges," Hodges answered, "and her chances of getting bail are virtually nonexistent."

"Collingsgate!" Allen barked. "That's a festering pit of violence and rape. Even murder."

Hodges sighed. "We've been trying to get additional funds for our penitentiary system for years, sir. But somehow, making life better for prisoners never seems to rank very high on the taxpayers' priority list." He tugged more forcefully on Christina's arm. "Come along, ma'am."

"Ben! *Do* something!" Her eyes were wide and pleading. "Don't let them take me away like this!"

Ben hesitated. "There must be some mistake—"

"There's no mistake. Please, let us do our job."

"Ben!" Tears were welling up in Christina's eyes, and Ben knew why. Her pathological fear of imprisonment, the remnant of her previous nightmarish stay in jail. The prospect of a revisit was horrifying to her. "Please help me!"

"How long do you think she'll be in Collingsgate?" Ben asked.

"Hard to say exactly," Hodges answered. "But the federal courts are pretty backed up right now, as you probably know. It'll be at least six months before her case comes to trial. Probably more like a year. Maybe two."

"Two! *Two years!*" Christina's voice became shrill and desperate. "Don't let them take me! *Please!* Don't let them!"

Ben held out his hands. "I—don't know what I can do."

"Ben, please! *Please!*" Tears streamed from her eyes. She was pleading, begging. "Don't let them take me away. I can't stand it, Ben. I know I can't. I'll die."

"You'll die?" Sheriff Allen said. "But, honey—"

"She means it," Ben said. "She was imprisoned once before and it almost killed her. If they lock her up again—" He shook his head ruefully.

"Ben, please help me!"

"I'm sorry, Christina—"

"I mean it, Ben. I'll *die*!" Her face was red and blotchy; her nose was running and she didn't even notice. Her own private demon, her darkest fear, was becoming a horrific reality.

Ben held out his hands helplessly. "I'm sorry, Christina. I don't know what I can do."

"Well, I do." Sheriff Allen stepped forward, his jaw firm and set. "Hodges, you can't take this little lady away."

"I don't think you understand," Hodges shot back. His two associates moved perceptibly closer, ready to go into action if necessary. "We've got her dead to rights."

"No, I don't think you understand," Allen shot back. "Your drug dealer isn't her. It's me."

For a protracted moment, no one spoke.

"What?" Hodges said at last.

"You heard me. I'm your man. I don't know how the stuff got on her dinner table. I was there—maybe I brushed the tablecloth. Maybe it rubbed off when we held hands. But I'm your man."

Hodges did not release Christina. "Sheriff, if this is your idea of being noble—"

"I'm not trying to be noble. I'm just stating the facts. You don't believe me, go search the shed behind my house. You'll find tons of the stuff. I can tell you who's supplying me with the dope. I'll tell you anything you want." He gazed over at Christina. "Just let the lady go."

Christina's eyes were wide and blurry. "Doug, don't do this."

Allen shook his head. He took off his sheriff's hat, removed his badge, then collapsed on the desk. "No. It's long overdue. I've had it. I've hated myself every second since I started this nasty business. Time to bring down the curtain."

Ben stared at him. "But why?"

"I think I told you about the situation in my family, Ben. My mom—desperately ill, can't get medical insurance. Her bills run a hundred thousand a year, and don't think for a moment that hospital in Seattle would keep her if I stopped paying. They wouldn't. Got a mentally retarded sister in an institution—that ain't so cheap, either. They all depend on me. And I couldn't cut it. Not on what a sheriff makes. I had to find some more money."

"But why drugs?"

"It's hard to explain. Looking back, it all seems so crazy. I made a bust, caught this scumbag I'd been chasing for weeks. Caught him red-handed with tons of junk, stuff he got from some mob outfit down in L.A. He started talking about how easy it was to make a fortune, how grateful his mob bosses could be, how they'd like to be tied into someone who really knew the town and could get the junk circulated. I shouldn't have listened—but I did. I kept thinking—if I just did it for a year, maybe two, I could make a couple million bucks. Invest it wisely, and it could take care of my mom and my sister for the rest of their lives. It made sense. In a crazy sort of way." He drew in his breath, then slowly released it. "So I sold out. And I've been miserable ever since."

He removed his gun belt and dropped it on the floor. "But enough already. It's time I took back responsibility for my life." He gazed at Christina's stunned, flustered face. "I'm not going to let them drag you to some hellhole for a crime I committed."

Christina reached out with a trembling arm and took his

hand. "But, Doug, surely you knew that if you peddled drugs—"

"I didn't know then how much damage this damn Venom could do, how many lives it could ruin." His eye twitched. "But I sure as hell found out."

Ben nodded. "From Dwayne Gardiner. Right?"

Sheriff Allen's eyes darted up. "You know?"

Ben's eyes met Allen's. "I do."

Allen looked away, his face filled with disgust. "Dwayne was one of the first to get hooked on the stuff. No big surprise there—the man hated his job, hated his wife, and hated himself. He knew Lu Ann was a tramp, but there wasn't anything he could do about it. He was a mess—an easy target for Venom." Allen gazed down at the carpet. "It was a habit he couldn't afford. So I gave him a night job. I made him my main distributor. That way I could get the stuff around town without anyone but him knowing I was the one behind it. Up till then, I'd been using disguises, but this was much better. Much safer. And Dwayne liked it. Made him feel important, strong. You heard that fellow from Bunyan's testify that Dwayne said he knew someone powerful in town. Well, I guess that was me. All in all, it worked for everyone." His lips pressed together bitterly. "Till Dwayne got out of control. Till he got greedy."

"What happened?"

"He wanted more money—lots more. So much I couldn't even have paid my mother's medical bills. Can you imagine? After making a criminal of myself, I still wouldn't be able to pay her bills. He threatened that if I didn't cough up the cash, he'd expose me."

Ben stepped behind Allen and spoke in a quiet voice. "That's why you killed him, isn't it?"

Allen looked up suddenly. He stared at Ben, sizing him up. "This whole thing—the DEA, arresting Christina—it was a setup, wasn't it?"

Ben nodded.

Christina's jaw dropped. "Ben! Is that true?"

"I'm afraid so." Ben turned back toward Allen. "I knew you killed Gardiner, but I didn't have any way to prove it. I needed you to confess. And I couldn't think of any way to make that happen." He paused. "Except to make you think it was necessary to save someone you . . . cared about."

Christina stared at Ben in disbelief. "You tricked him? *Used* him? And me!"

Ben didn't disagree. "I didn't know why you killed Gardiner, but I knew you weren't an evil person. Not in your heart. I knew it had to be eating away at you. So I thought that if I just created the right scenario—"

"I'd talk." Allen's head bobbed. "I'd spill out everything I've been wanting to say for months, but couldn't." He laughed bitterly. "You're a smart man, Kincaid."

Ben frowned. "I don't feel like one."

Allen jerked his thumb toward Hodges. "Is he in on it?"

"Of course. I had a . . . contact in the DEA. She helped me set up this sting."

"But how did you know? How did you figure it out?"

"It was something you said, something that didn't mean anything at the time, till Maureen reminded me of it earlier today in the infirmary. When I was at the jailhouse visiting Tess and Maureen, you made a joking reference to the Sasquatch suit and described it as having a bright red nose. Problem is, I've seen the suit that your deputy recovered—I had it in my office. The face is entirely black. Zak helped explain the problem; he told me there were two suits—the first one Green Rage had, and the second one which Zak bought himself but never wore. Except the one that was never used—as far as Zak knew—was the one with the red nose. So how did you know about it? I asked the Green Ragers if they'd lost it or shown it or even mentioned it to you or anyone else, but they all said they hadn't. That's when I realized you must've been there when Gardiner was killed. You must have stolen the suit and worn it yourself."

Allen nodded his head sadly. He was beyond lying now; he didn't have the strength—or the desire. "I swiped the suit from Zak's tent, then put it back when I was done. As one of my deputies mentioned at trial, some campers had tipped us off to the location of the Green Rage camp. I knew your man Zak planted a bomb on a tree cutter. Got a tip from Georgie—the man at the pawnshop who sold him the ingredients—and started following him around. Saw him do it. But instead of arresting him, I removed the bomb and took it to another location, another tree cutter. Zak put a timing mechanism on the thing, but I knew enough about bombs—I got sent to that bomb school in L.A., remember—to alter it, to rig it to explode when the ignition was turned. I lured Gardiner out there, telling him I was going to give him the money he wanted. I didn't plan to kill him—I just wanted to put on a big show, to scare him off, that was all. But he started arguing with me, yelling. Demanding money. Then he started fighting. Had a crowbar over my head ready to bash my brains in. That's when I had to shoot him. I didn't shoot to kill; I just wanted to stop him. And after that, I flipped out. Just ran for it. And you know the rest. Dwayne tried to follow me on the tree cutter and—"

"Boom," Ben said. "No more Dwayne Gardiner." He looked up. "And Tess?"

The two men exchanged a long look. Ben could see in Allen's eyes that he was tired of lying, tired of hiding. He wanted to be clean again.

"Tess was there that night, watching us from a distance. She videotaped the whole thing. The tape wasn't clear enough to make out my face, but I didn't know that till after she was gone and I rummaged through her hotel room and found it. Even without the tape, though, she figured out I was the killer—probably the same way you did."

"So you killed her, too."

"That's why I wasn't around when you needed someone to break up the riot downtown, why you had to get Deputy Andrews. I was . . . with Tess." He cradled his face in his hands. "I didn't mean to kill her, either. Didn't plan to, anyway. I was chasing her. I needed to talk with her, to find out what she knew, see if we could make a deal. But she panicked, and her car swerved into a wall. She died in the crash. I took her body to the forest and nailed it up to throw suspicion off myself. Make it look like it was just part of the local war."

His voice broke. "I don't know what happened to me. I really don't. I tried to do the right thing. It's just—one mistake led to another, and before I knew what was happening—" He was crying like a baby now, without guard, without control. "Even after Dwayne and Tess were gone, I had another problem—a bigger one. Guilt. I've been killing myself every day of the week. I can barely sleep. I hated seeing another man accused of my crime, but what could I do? I didn't have the guts to come forward, to do the right thing." He held out his hand and lightly touched Christina's hair. "But when I saw you in trouble, saw them about to take you away—I knew it was over. I knew it all had to end."

Without speaking, Hodges removed the cuffs from Christina's wrists. Even without being asked, Allen held out his hands. Hodges slipped the cuffs over the man's wrists, then quietly led him out of the office.

Leaving Ben and Christina alone together.

Ben wanted desperately to say something to her, but he couldn't think of anything that wouldn't sound contrived or fake or insincere.

"You used me," Christina said. Her face was wet and blotchy, but her eyes were fixed and furious. "You used me to get to him."

"I'm sorry," Ben said. "It was the only way."

"You could have told me."

"And asked you to be an accomplice in this plan to trap the man you—you were—friendly with? I couldn't do that to you."

"You should've trusted me," she said bitterly. She spun around and, without saying another word, left the office, slamming the door behind her.

* 74 *

Zak stared through the cell bars at Ben with wide-eyed wonder. "You're kidding!"

"Would I kid about a thing like this?"

"The charges are dismissed?"

"All of them. As soon as they finish processing the paperwork, you'll be free to go."

"Yes!" Zak jumped up into the air and whooped. "I knew it. I *knew* it!"

"Knew what?"

"I knew you'd pull through for me. You did it before and you did it again." He reached through the bars and slapped Ben on the shoulder.

Ben pressed his lips together silently.

"How did you ever get Granny to agree to dismiss?"

Ben shrugged. "She didn't have much choice. We brought her a detailed confession from the real murderer—a confession witnessed by multiple persons, including three federal agents."

"Man, this is great. This is so great." Zak jumped up again and swatted the overhead light. "You're a miracle worker, Ben."

"Hardly."

"If there's anything I can ever do for you—anything at all—all you have to do is ask."

Ben looked up. "You mean that?"

"Oh, yeah, man. 'Course I do. Anything you want, it's yours."

"Okay. Stop with the bombs."

Zak floated down to earth. "What?"

"You heard me. No more bombs. You may think you're striking great blows for freedom and liberty, but you're not. Every time you resort to violence, you set your cause back. Violence never solves anything in the long run. It might bury problems, but it doesn't solve them."

"You're wrong, man. We have to be strong."

"Then *be* strong. You don't need a big macho bomb to be strong."

"Those bastards out there don't listen to reason."

"Zak, if you keep setting bombs, eventually you're going to kill someone. Even if Allen tampered with the bomb that killed Gardiner, the fact remains that you created the instrumentality of murder. If you keep at this, someone else will die. Maybe it'll be an accident, but the poor schmuck caught in the explosion will be just as dead."

Zak grimaced. "Anything else, Mom?"

"Well, yeah, since you asked. You could stop being such a pig with women."

"What are you, some kind of feminist?"

"I don't have to be a feminist to see that you've been a total jerk, taking advantage of others, thinking only of yourself. That's no way to treat anyone, man or woman."

"Jeez. My lawyer, Jiminy Cricket."

"Yeah, well, you asked." Ben folded his arms. "Anyway, the work's done. You'll be free soon. So do me a favor and don't get arrested for murder again, okay?"

Zak smiled. "Deal." He laughed. "So how did the jury take it? They were probably pissed."

Ben shook his head. "I don't think so. If anything, they were relieved. No one enjoys deliberating on a capital charge. And particularly given the circumstances—I expect they felt they had been prevented by a hairbreadth from making a horrible mistake."

"So you think they were going to convict?"

Ben looked at him levelly. "After that stunt you pulled up on the stand? How could they not?"

"Hmm. Guess you're right."

"Speaking of which," Ben said, pressing against the cell door. "Care to explain that little travesty to me?"

Zak turned his head. "I . . . don't think I can."

"Zak, look at me. *Look. At. Me!*" Zak grudgingly turned his head. "Have you learned nothing from this whole experience?"

"Like . . . don't get thrown in jail in small towns?"

"No, you idiot. Like, it's always best to tell your lawyer the truth. Think about it. You lied about the Sasquatch suit, and that was the first major strike against us. You lied about the bomb, and that was the second major blow. And you lied about Gardiner's wife, and that nearly crucified us! So for once, just once in your stupid life, would you tell me the truth?"

"I don't know . . . I'm gonna have to think about it."

"Zak, let me do the thinking, okay? Frankly, it isn't exactly your specialty." Ben reached through the bars, grabbed Zak's shirt, and yanked him against the door. "Tell me what happened. Now."

* 75 *

Granny's office hadn't changed much, Ben observed, and neither had she. The office was still a mess; if anything, there were even more stacks of files and even more crumpled fast-food wrappers than before. She was on the phone, apparently giving an interview. No, she didn't consider the new revelations about the Gardiner murder a personal setback. She believed the whole town, including hard-working civic servants like herself, had been manipulated by a self-serving cadre of drug pushers, environmental fanatics, and lawyers, all working in concert to thwart justice. To the contrary, it was a testament to the zealous and unflagging efforts of her office that they were finally able to uncover the truth.

Ben had to smile. As if she had had anything to do with it.

When she was finally finished, she hung up the phone. "Why are you here, Kincaid? Just come to gloat?"

"No, I wanted to talk with you."

"Yeah? Well, the feeling isn't mutual."

"It's very important."

Granny glanced at the clock on the wall. "I can give you five minutes. Assuming I don't get bored first."

"I don't think that'll be a problem." Ben reached into his briefcase. "Your first ethical violation, in my opinion, was when you produced important documents buried in a sea of extraneous paper—all printed in red ink."

She waved him away. "I later corrected that . . . inadvertent error."

"On the eve of trial, yes. But it unquestionably compromised my defense."

Granny made a great show of yawning. "Sorry, Kincaid, but you're not beating the boredom test."

"Your second ethical violation was the suppression—even destruction—of exculpatory evidence. That's more than just an ethical violation—that's a criminal offense. Obstruction of justice. You had a whole file on Alberto Vincenzo, and you knew—or thought, anyway—it was relevant to the Gardiner case. But you didn't produce it."

"What file? I don't know what you're talking about."

"I know you had it."

"Oh yeah? Prove it."

"I can't."

Granny settled back in her chair. "Anything else, Kincaid?"

"Your third ethical violation was bribing Marco Geppi to fabricate a false jail-cell conversation to hang Zak. That's more than just an ethical violation, too. That's suborning perjury."

She fluttered her eyes. "And you can't prove that either, right?"

"We're looking for Geppi. But he blew town and crawled back into the woodwork as soon as you released him. As I'm sure you anticipated he would."

"Time's almost up, Kincaid."

"And your fourth and most heinous ethical violation was

when you blackmailed Zak into tanking on the witness stand. You've done some pretty evil things, Granny, but screwing with the testimony of a man on trial for his life—that's just beyond the pale."

"Again, I don't know what you're talking about."

"You will. Zak told me all about it."

"The embittered defendant and his attorney try to strike back against the prosecutor. It's all too trite. No one will believe it."

"I think you're wrong."

"Who knows this town, Kincaid? You or me?"

"I still think that when—"

"It's hopeless. You have no proof."

"I will." Ben leaned forward. "You see, now that Zak doesn't have a murder charge hanging over his head, he's going to talk about how you tried to blackmail him into silence. In detail. He'll tell everyone—locals, Feds. He'll go on television if he has to. And eventually we'll find someone who knows something. Maybe the deputy who admitted you to the jailhouse. Maybe another prisoner who overheard something. Maybe Geppi will reappear. If Zak makes a big enough fuss, something will shake out."

"He'd better not." Granny sprang forward like a panther. "You tell that little prick that if he opens his mouth, his sister's ass is grass. I wasn't kidding around with him. She won't see the sun for ten years!"

"Thank you very much." Ben pulled his hand out of his coat pocket to reveal a tiny Sony tape recorder. "I agree that I would've had a hard time making the charges stick just based on Zak's word. But your confession might do the trick."

Granny's eyes went wide. Her face was a vivid red. "Confession? I didn't confess—"

Ben smiled, then rose to his feet. "We'll let the U.S. Attorney decide about that, okay?"

Granny ran around her desk. "Give me that tape, Kincaid."

"No chance."

Her face twisted up in a knot. "You'll give me that tape if I have to beat you to a bloody fucking pulp." She looked like she could do it, too.

It was Ben's turn to feign a yawn. "A threat of violence. It's just too trite."

She clenched up her fist. "I'll show you trite—"

"Loving?"

From just outside, Ben's enormous investigator poked his head through the door. "Need somethin', Skipper?"

"I don't know." He smiled at Granny. "Do I?"

Granny's face was livid. She looked as if she might explode at any moment. But she kept her mouth shut.

Ben gathered his briefcase and headed toward the door. "See you in court, Granny."

* 76 *

Ben stood at the crest of the hill and gazed out at the forest all around him. This was the same location to which he had been brought by force only a few days before, but now everything was different. The landscape was so changed that an unknowing observer gazing at Before and After photos would never have guessed they were of the same site. Probably wouldn't have guessed they were of the same planet.

The shack was entirely gone, burned. All that was left was blackened rubble—and not much of that. A thick gray ash powdered the hillside.

The verdant view that once crested the hill was now black. Black and black and black. Burned beyond recognition. Plants, ground cover, trees. The fire had spread hundreds of feet in all directions before the team from the Forest Service had managed to extinguish it. What once had been a thriving example of nature's wonder in all its bounty was now nothing but charred desolation.

As Ben had said before, he was no nature lover. But gazing

out at this waste, this ruin, this spoilage—it just made him want to cry.

But he held it back. He didn't have time for such indulgences. He had work to do.

He saw Maureen drive up the blackened road, park, climb out of her Jeep. He hadn't visited her since he left the infirmary. He was glad to see her again; she looked much better now.

And a few minutes after that, Ben saw a bright red pickup driven by Jeremiah Adams—head foreman of the Magic Valley sawmill, lifelong logger, supervisor, and father of the former Magic Valley district attorney.

"What the hell's she doing here?" Adams said as soon as he spotted Maureen. "You didn't tell me there were gonna be any of them here."

Maureen wasn't any happier to see him than he was to see her. "It seems Ben neglected to give either of us many details. What's up, Ben?"

Ben braced himself. He knew this was not going to be easy. "I just wanted to get the two of you together. You're both the respective local heads of your factions now, and—well, I just wanted you to talk. Explore possibilities. Consider one another's needs and wants. See if you can't maybe put an end to all the hate and violence and turmoil and just—work things out."

Adams ripped off his cap and swore. "Jesus H. Christ."

Maureen rolled her eyes. "Where do you live anyway, Ben? Disneyland?"

"I'm serious. You're both adults. There's no reason why you can't sit down and talk."

"To what end?" Maureen said bitterly. "He's never going to agree with me."

"She's right," Adams added. "I ain't never gonna agree with her."

"You don't have to agree with each other," Ben said. "Just try to understand each other."

"I understand her," Adams said. "She cares more about trees than she does about people."

"And he cares more about making a buck than he does

about our natural resources." She looked at Ben sharply. "See? We understand each other perfectly."

"Would you listen to one another? You sound like children. Turning important issues into a playground squabble."

They both folded their arms. Neither spoke.

"You have to think of something," Ben continued. "Some solution. You've got to stop labeling each other villains and treating each other accordingly. Don't you see?" He stepped forward, arms outstretched. "It's all a matter of perspective. No one thinks of themselves as a bad guy. No one intends to be evil—they do what they do for a reason. Green Rage destroys equipment—to save the trees. The loggers harass the environmentalists—to save their jobs. They both believe in what they're doing. Granny subverts trial procedure—to keep criminals off the streets. Even Sheriff Allen had a reason for his horrible actions. None of us are all good or all evil. Labeling your opponent as evil doesn't help. The only solution is to work together and try to come to an understanding."

"We'll come to an understanding," Adams said, "when we've driven these meddlers out of the forest."

"Or maybe we'll drive you out of the forest," Maureen said emphatically. "We've done it before."

"No," Ben said. "You have to stop the fighting."

Adams pursed his thin lips. "Bull."

"Ditto," Maureen said. "We'll keep fighting. We have to."

"You *can't* keep fighting!" Ben shouted.

"We have to," Maureen insisted. "If we keep fighting, we'll win."

"Wrong. If you keep fighting, you'll destroy each other."

"That's a load of—"

"You don't know what—"

"*Look* at this!" Ben shouted. He windmilled his hands. "Just look!"

The two antagonists fell silent for a moment and gazed out at their surroundings. The shack was destroyed. The landscape was destroyed. Trees were charred. All that remained as far as the eye could see was black and dead.

"This is what you'll end up with," Ben continued. "You've been fighting for months, and what has it gotten you? Three people are dead. Millions of dollars worth of equipment on both sides has been ruined. Wasted. And four hundred old-growth trees burned, right here on this hilltop. And to accomplish what? *Nothing,* that's what. Nothing at all."

He saw Maureen and Adams look at one another, tentative glances out the corners of their eyes. Finally Adams spoke. "We're not the ones who set that fire."

"No," Ben answered, "but if the people you employed hadn't assaulted Green Rage, hadn't run poor Doc down, it never would've happened. You're both responsible."

The two fell silent again. Ben felt a strong breeze whistling through his hair. He remembered that he was high up on a mountain—and that the trees that had once sheltered the summit were now gone.

"Think, Maureen," Ben said quietly. "You were trapped in that shack, trapped with your enemy, flames all around us. It was hopeless. The only reason we survived is that the two warring factions worked *together*. Slade knew about the radio. You knew how to work it. Slade knew about the generator. You knew how to use it. Slade knew about the well and you both helped pull each other through the fire. If you hadn't worked together, we'd all be dead now."

Ben took a deep breath. "People—it's the same thing here. You've got to stop fighting and learn to work together. Before you destroy each other. And everything and everyone caught in the middle."

Adams was the first to speak, after a long, heavy silence. His voice was much quieter than before. "Won't make any difference about the Magic Valley forest. It's all scheduled and prepped. I can't stop it."

"I can't countenance the destruction of any old-growth trees," Maureen said.

"Talk to each other," Ben urged. "See if you can't work out a solution."

"Why did you haul *me* out here, anyway?" Adams asked. "What makes you think I'd be remotely interested in making peace with these tree huggers?"

"Because you're the leak," Ben said flatly.

"What?" Adams's face twisted up. "What do you mean?"

"You're the inside man who's been feeding information to Green Rage about logging activities. You've been doing it for months."

A wide range of expressions fluttered across Adams's face, till finally it settled into a simple look of resignation. "How did you know?"

"I didn't—for sure. But I was told repeatedly that Slade and the loggers were looking for a leak, and I knew it had to be someone relatively high in the local logging hierarchy. I saw you whispering with Al in the courtroom the day the trial began, and I couldn't imagine what you would have to talk about. Unless . . ."

"I didn't do anything that would set back the logging," Adams said firmly. "Or put any of our boys out of work. I just didn't want anyone to get hurt."

Maureen's lips parted. "You did more than that. If you're Al's informant—you fed us information that enabled us to blockade the road and stop the illegal harvesting of old-growth trees in the Crescent mountain basin."

"You see," Ben said, gently pushing them together. "You two have more in common than you know."

Maureen raised her eyes to meet Adams's. Their eyes locked, and for a long moment, neither looked away.

"Well," Adams said at long last, "I guess I'm willing to try. Can't hurt to try, I s'pose." He tentatively held out his hand.

Maureen hesitated only a moment before taking it. "No," she said quietly. "It can't hurt to try."

Ben closed his eyes. Maybe there was some hope for this planet after all.

* 77 *

Ben had been having such a splendid day he almost hated to do anything more. Better to split a bottle of champagne with Loving and savor the moment. His last three meetings were get-togethers he'd been looking forward to for a good long while. The next meeting was one he'd give a great deal to be able to skip altogether. But there was no avoiding it.

He found her in a park not far from the hotel where they'd both been staying. She was sitting on one end of a seesaw, her chin in her hands, her feet in the dirt.

She did not look up as he approached. "Mind if I join you?" He straddled the opposite end of the seesaw, bouncing Christina a foot or two into the air. "How are you?"

She shrugged, just barely.

"Nice weather, don't you think? It was a little smoky in town after the fire, but that seems to have passed."

He leaned back on the seesaw, propelling her even higher into the air, thinking that might compel a response. It didn't.

"Al's been caught," Ben said. "He'll stand trial for arson, maybe attempted murder. I was thinking I might represent him. I mean, we know he did it, but given the circumstances—" He started again. "They've also got Slade's hoods, including the one who ran down Doc, but Slade himself disappeared shortly after he was airlifted out of the forest. Half the state and federal law enforcement community is looking for him, but so far, no luck. I hope they'll catch him—but I have my doubts. He's a pretty slippery creep, used to taking care of himself."

He sighed. Her silence was cutting, rending the air between them like the swath of a scythe.

"I'm just so relieved," Ben said, continuing his babbling soliloquy. "I was so worried—so afraid that maybe, just maybe Zak was the murderer. Maybe he'd been a killer all along and it was my fault he was released the first time so he could kill again. I can't tell you what a weight this lifts off my shoulders."

Christina still didn't look up, didn't answer.

"Christina, I'm so sorry about what happened. I couldn't think of any other way to compel Sheriff Allen to talk. I knew he liked you. And I knew he had a conscience. I just had to figure out a way to tap into it, to give him the excuse I thought he wanted, deep inside, to confess."

He drummed his fingers on the iron handle. God, he wished she would talk. Yell or scream or shout or something.

"I thought about telling you beforehand, but if I did, that would make you an accomplice to the trick. It didn't have anything to do with trusting you. I just didn't think I could put you in the position of having to manipulate a man about whom you cared."

"I know that," Christina whispered. "I knew it then. I was just—stunned, I guess. The thought of going to jail again—"

"I know," Ben said. "I promise I'll never do anything like that again."

Christina shook her head. "Preventing Zak from being convicted of a murder he didn't commit is a lot more important than my temporary discomfort."

"Yes, but it was more than just playing on your terror of jail. It was taking advantage of your personal relationship. Using you to expose the man you'd—you'd become close to."

Christina let out a soft, empty laugh. "Ben, you are so utterly . . . clueless." She smiled, but it was not a happy smile. "I liked Doug fine, but I was never serious. I was just—" She bit down on her lower lip. "Never mind. Just never mind. Let's leave."

"No," Ben said, "I want to say something. A few days ago, Maureen told me I was being selfish—about you. I didn't understand what she was saying, but I think now maybe I do. I expect so much of you. I expect you to drop everything and come running every time I get the impulse to take some case. I become immersed in the case, so you have to, too. I don't have a social life, so you can't either. Who knows—if I hadn't gotten in the way, you might've remarried, had some children. A life of your own."

"Ben—"

"Let me finish. I've sucked up your whole life for years now. And it isn't fair to you. I don't want to hold you back, Christina. You've got to live your own life, and I don't want to get in the way."

"Ben, will you just shut up for a minute and listen?" She kicked back with her legs and lowered herself to the ground. "I don't know what that woman has been telling you, but let me give you the straight scoop. I'm in charge of my own life. I had to learn at an early age to take care of myself, and I've been doing it ever since. Not to disillusion you, but you haven't forced me to do anything. I'm the one who's been making all the choices, all along. I decided to become a legal assistant, then later to go to law school, because it's what *I* wanted to do. I decided I didn't want to be another corporate law firm zombie, so I hitched my wagon to you, because I thought the work you were doing was more important than helping corporations screw one another back at the law firm. But make no mistake about it, Ben—you didn't make me do anything. It was my decision the whole way."

"Oh." Ben felt breathless just from listening to that illuminating spiel.

"And I'll tell you something else." She jumped off the seesaw, flinging Ben downward. She walked to the other side of the seesaw. "I don't regret a minute of the time we've spent together. Not one minute."

She headed back toward her end of the seesaw, then stopped. "Except maybe that business with the creep who kept cutting off women's heads and hands. I could've lived without that. But the rest of it—"

She turned and, smiling, gave him a firm thumbs-up.

* 78 *

"I found it! I really did! *I found it!*"

Deirdre burst into Ben's hotel room just as he was packing. She was breathless with excitement, barely able to communicate.

"Found what?"

"The tree! The one I've been looking for all this time!"

Ben's lips parted. "You mean—the world's largest cedar tree?"

"Yes! I'm almost certain of it. It's huge—over a hundred and seventy feet tall and twenty feet in circumference. And over seven hundred years old. Older than the Declaration of Independence. Hell, older than Columbus. This tree was huge when Henry the Eighth took his first wife. It was old by the time Lincoln was writing the Emancipation Proclamation!"

"Can you show me?"

"Can I? Come on!"

Ben rushed downstairs, following in Deirdre's wake. He wondered if all dendrochronologists were this excitable. Certainly at the moment, she was not the traditional image of the cool, logical scientist. More like a high school senior who'd just been asked to the prom.

Ben climbed into the back of the Jeep, squeezing in next to Maureen. "So," he said, "is she excited?"

Maureen winked. "I think you could say she's excited."

Deirdre slid into the driver's seat and pushed the Jeep into first gear. "You have to understand," she said as she zoomed down Main Street, taking the quickest route out of town and into the forest, "these trees have individuality. They're like people—friends—and each one of them is different."

"So this one is like your great-great-grandfather?" Ben asked.

Deirdre laughed. "More like my great great great great great great great great great grandfather. But he's magnificent. I've never found anything like this before. Not in my entire career."

"How did you locate it?"

"I've been searching systematically since I arrived. Several campers had made reports of huge old-growth trees, but their directions were never very precise. I had to do a lot of wandering around, following hunches, analyzing the growth patterns. It's taken months." Her grin spread from ear to ear. "But I *found* it! Last night, long past midnight, I found it. I could barely sleep! It's huge—bigger than the recordholder in Forks."

They continued driving, taking the northbound path into the forest, then moving onto a northwest trail, plunging deep into the dense foliage, past the site of the murder, even past the site of the recent fire. Deirdre was taking them all the way, deep inside the forest.

Ben had to wonder once more at the marvelous and beautiful diversity of the ancient forest. There was so much life here, he thought. So much variety. Even a city boy like himself could share in Deirdre's excitement.

Finally, when they were considerably deeper in than Ben had been before, Deirdre stopped the Jeep. "This is as far as we can go on wheels," she explained. "From here on out, we walk."

Except with Deirdre in the lead, it was more like a run. Ben did his best to keep up, tripping over bramble, letting branches sweep across his face. They yelled for Deirdre to stop, slow down, but she wasn't listening. She was unrestrained, uncontrollable. She was going to meet a new old friend and there was no holding her back.

Until at last they arrived.

"No," Deirdre said, almost under her breath.

Ben was well behind her. He kept running, huffing and puffing, holding the stitch in his side, till he finally arrived at the point where Deirdre had frozen in her tracks.

"No," he echoed, when he saw what she saw.

"Oh, God," Maureen said, pulling up behind them. "Oh, please God, no."

The tree was gone. That tree and all its companion trees—gone.

The clear-cutters had moved in, just that morning, from all appearances. But they had been busy. As usual, they started work with the largest and therefore most profitable trees, then moved outward in concentric circles, taking all the rest. There were four tree cutters working the area, systematically using their huge mechanical arms to grip and slice one enormous trunk after another.

In the space of a few hours, more than two hundred trees had been leveled.

"No!" Deirdre screamed. She ran forward, weaving between the cutting machines and fallen branches. Like a pigeon homing in on an old companion, she led them directly to the spot.

The tree was now nothing but a stump, flattened, less than a foot off the ground.

"My God!" Deirdre cried. Her face was wet with tears. "He's been here since before Columbus." There was a catch in her throat, like something was being ripped out of her insides. "Before *Columbus*!"

Ben didn't know what to say. There were no words to express what he was feeling, much less anything that would be of any comfort to Deirdre. Instead, he simply stared at the flattened remains of that once-great cedar, and the remains of all the other immense cedars surrounding it, on and on, around and around, as far as he could see—the remnants of hundreds of lives that had survived for hundreds upon hundreds of years, only to be destroyed in a single morning.

* Acknowledgments *

I would like to express my appreciation to the dozens of forest rangers, loggers, scientists, and environmentalists who were willing to talk to me or my wife as I researched and wrote this book. I'd particularly like to thank Brita Cantrell, state director of The Nature Conservancy, for her assistance regarding the environmental issues discussed, as well as insightful suggestions stemming from her lifetime experience with the outdoors; and Daman Cantrell, of the Tulsa Public Defender's office, for his assistance with various issues of criminal law.

As always, I must thank my friend and editor Joe Blades, surely one of the finest editors and human beings in all of publishing, for his support and guidance. I also want to thank Arlene Joplin, of the Oklahoma City U.S. Attorney's office, for reading the manuscript before publication and giving me her always invaluable comments. And I must thank my wife, not only for her usual work as collaborator and editor, but also for her considerable research efforts that made this book possible.

My e-mail address is: willbern@mindspring.com—and I welcome mail from readers. Continued thanks to Michelle Salazar, who has established the William Bernhardt Web Page at: www.mindspring.com/~willbern/ (no period—but don't forget the tilde).

The environmental facts, statistics, and information presented in this book are true, all taken from unbiased sources. All the actions depicted in the conflict between loggers and environmentalists are based on true events occurring during the last fifteen years. I'm sure there are and will continue to be a variety of opinions about how we should deal with our exponentially growing ecological crisis, but about these facts there is no question:

Before Europeans arrived, almost fifty percent of this country was covered by virgin forests. As recently as 1850, more than forty percent still was. Today, less than one percent is. And the trees are still being cut—even in our national forests.

—William Bernhardt

If you enjoyed William Bernhardt's DARK JUSTICE, don't miss Ben Kincaid's next thrilling case:

SILENT JUSTICE

by

WILLIAM BERNHARDT